Mystery and Detection
with the
Thinking Machine

2

Mystery and Detection
with the
Thinking Machine

Volume 2

Jacques Futrelle

Coachwhip Publications
Landisville, Pennsylvania

Mystery and Detection with The Thinking Machine, Volume 2
Copyright © 2009 Coachwhip Publications

ISBN 1-930585-71-3
ISBN-13 978-1-930585-71-3

Cover: Fingerprint © MarFot; Pistol © Chris Harvey

Coachwhipbooks.com

CONTENTS

Kidnapped Baby Blake, Millionaire

I

Douglas Blake, millionaire, sat flat on the floor and gazed with delighted eyes at the unutterable beauties of a highly colored picture book. He was only fourteen months old, and the picture book was quite the most beautiful thing he had ever beheld. Evelyn Barton, a lovely girl of twenty-two or three years, sat on the floor opposite and listened with a slightly amused smile as Baby Blake in his infinite wisdom discoursed learnedly on the astonishing things he found in the book.

The floor whereon Baby Blake sat was that of the library of the Blake home, in the outskirts of Lynn. This home, handsomely but modestly furnished, had been built by Baby Blake's father, Langdon Blake, who had died four months previously, leaving Baby Blake's beautiful mother, Elizabeth Blake, heart-broken and crushed by the blow, and removing her from the social world of which she had been leader.

Here, quietly, with but three servants and Miss Barton, the nurse, who could hardly be classed as a servant—rather a companion—Mrs. Blake had lived on for the present.

The great house was gloomy, but it had been the scene of all her happiness, and she had clung to it. The building occupied relatively a central position in a plot of land facing the street for 200 feet or so, and stretching back about 300 feet. A stone wall inclosed it.

In Summer this plot was a great velvety lawn; now the first snow of the Winter had left an inch deep blanket over all, unbroken save the cement-paved walk which extended windingly from the gate in the street wall to the main entrance of the home. This path had been cleaned of snow and was now a black streak through the whiteness.

Near the front stoop this path branched off and led on around the building toward the back. This, too, had been cleared of snow, but beyond the back door entrance the white blanket covered everything back to the rear wall of the property. There against the rear wall, to the right as one stood behind the house, was a roomy barn and stable; in the extreme left hand corner of the property was a cluster of tall trees, with limbs outstretched fantastically.

The driveway from the front was covered with snow. It had been several weeks since Mrs. Blake had had occasion to use either of her vehicles or horses, so she had closed the barn and stabled the horses outside. Now the barn was wholly deserted. From one of the great trees a swing, which had been placed there for the delight of Baby Blake, swung idly.

In the Summer Baby Blake had been wont to toddle the hundred or more feet from the house to the swing; but now that pleasure was forbidden. He was confined to the house by the extreme cold.

When the snow began to fall that day about two o'clock Baby Blake had shown enthusiasm. It was the first snow he remembered. He stood at a window of the warm library and, pointing out with a chubby finger, told Miss Barton:

"Me want doe."

Miss Barton interpreted this as a request to be taken out or permitted to go out in the snow.

"No, no," she said, firmly. "Cold. Baby must not go. Cold. Cold."

Baby Blake raised his voice in lusty protestation at this unkindness of his nurse, and finally Mrs. Blake had to pacify him. Since then a hundred things had been used to divert Baby Blake's mind from the outside.

This snow had fallen for an hour, then stopped, and the clouds passed. Now, at fifteen minutes of six o'clock in the evening, the moon glittered coldly and clearly over the unbroken surface of the snow. Star points spangled the sky; the wind had gone, and extreme quiet lay over the place. Even the sound from the street, where an occasional vehicle passed, was muffled by the snow. Baby Blake heard a jingling sleigh bell somewhere in the distance and raised his head inquiringly.

"Pretty horse," said Miss Balton, quickly indicating a splash of color in the open book.

"Pitty horsie," said Baby Blake.

"Horse," said Miss Barton. "Four legs. One, two, three, four," she counted.

"Pitty horsie," said Baby Blake again.

He turned another page with a ruthless disregard of what might happen to it.

"Pitty kitty," he went on, wisely.

"Yes, pretty kitty," the nurse agreed.

"Pitty doggie, 'n' pitty ev'fing, ooo-o-oh," Baby Blake was gravely enthusiastic. "Ef'nit," he added, as his eye caught a full page picture.

"Elephant, yes," said Miss Barton. "Almost bedtime," she added.

"No, no," insisted Baby Blake, vigorously. "Pity ef'nit."

Then Baby Blake arose from his seat on the floor and toddled over to where Miss Barton sat, plumping down heavily, directly in front of her. Here, with the picture book in his hands he lay back with his head resting against her knee. Mrs. Blake appeared at the door.

"Miss Barton, a moment please," she said. Her face was white and there was a strange note in her voice.

A little anxiously, the girl arose and went into the adjoining room with Mrs. Blake, leaving Baby Blake with the picture book outspread on the floor. Mrs. Blake handed her an open letter, written on a piece of wrapping paper in a scrawly, almost indecipherable hand.

"This came in the late afternoon mail," said the mother. "Read it."

"'We hav maid plans to kiddnap your baby,'" Miss Barton read slowly. "'Nothig cann bee dun to keep us from it so it wont do no good to tel the polece. If you will git me ten thousan dolers we will not, and will go away. Advertis YES or NOA ann sin your name in a Boston Amurikan. Then we will tell you wat to do. (sined) Three. (3)'"

Miss Barton was silent a moment as she realized what she had read and there was a quick-caught breath.

"A threat to kidnap," said the mother. "Evelyn, Evelyn, can you believe it?"

"Oh, Mrs. Blake," and tears leaped to the girl's eyes quickly. "Oh, the monsters."

"I don't know what to do," said the mother, uncertainly.

"The police, I would suggest," replied the girl, quickly. "I should turn it over to the police immediately."

"Then the newspaper notoriety," said the mother, "and after all it may mean nothing. I think perhaps it would be better for us to leave here to-morrow, and go into Boston for the Winter. I could never live here with this horrible fear hanging over me—if I should lose my baby, too, it would kill me."

"As you say, but I would suggest the police, nevertheless," the girl insisted gently.

"Of course the money is nothing," she went on. "I would give every penny for the boy if I had to, but there's the fear and uncertainty of it. I think perhaps it would be better for you to pack up Douglas's little clothes to-night and to-morrow we will go to Boston to a hotel until we can make other arrangements for the Winter. You need not mention the matter to the others in the house."

"I think perhaps that would be best," said Miss Barton, "but I still think the police should be notified."

The two women left the room together and returned to the library after about ten minutes, where Baby Blake had been looking at the picture book. The baby was not there, and Miss Barton turned and glanced quickly at Mrs. Blake. The mother apparently paid no attention, and the nurse passed into another room, thinking Douglas had gone there.

Within ten minutes the household was in an uproar—Baby Blake had disappeared. Miss Barton, the servants and the distracted mother raced through the roomy building, searching every nook and corner, calling for Douglas. No answer. At last Miss Barton and Mrs. Blake met face to face in the library over the picture book the baby had been admiring.

"I'm afraid it's happened," said the nurse.

"Kidnapped!" exclaimed the mother. "Oh," and with waxen white face she sank back on a couch in a dead faint.

Regardless of the mother, Evelyn ran to the telephone and notified the police. They responded promptly, three detectives and two uniformed officers. The threatening letter was placed in their hands, and one of them laid its contents before his chief by 'phone, a general alarm was sent out.

While the uniformed men searched the house again from attic to cellar the two other plain clothes men searched outside. Together they went over the ground, but the surface of the snow was unbroken save for their own footprints and the paved path. From the front wall, which faced the street, the detectives walked slowly back, one on each side of the house, searching in the snow for some trace of a footprint.

There was nothing to reward this vigilance, and they met behind the house. Each shook his head. Then one stopped suddenly and pointed to the snow which lay at their feet and spreading away over the immense back yard. The other detective looked intently then stopped and stared.

What he saw was the footprint of a child—a baby. The tracks led straight away through the snow toward the back wall, and without a word the two men followed them, one by one; the regular toddling steps of a baby who is only fairly certain of his feet. Ten, twenty, thirty feet they went on in a straight line and already the detectives saw a possible solution. It was that Baby Blake had wandered away of his own free will.

Then, as they were following the tracks, they stopped suddenly astounded. Each dropped on his knees in the snow and sought vainly for something sought over a space of many feet, then turned back to the tracks again.

"Well, if that—" one began.

The footprints, going steadily forward across the yard, had stopped. There was the last, made as if Baby Blake had intended to go forward, but there were no more tracks—no more traces of tracks—nothing. Baby Blake had walked to this point, and then—

"Why he must have gone straight up in the air," gasped one of the detectives. He sank down on a small wooden box three or four feet from where the tracks ended, and wiped the perspiration from his face.

II

"All problems may be reduced to an arithmetical basis by a simple mental process," declared Professor Augustus S. F. X. Van Dusen, emphatically. "Once a problem is so reduced, no matter what it is, it may be solved. If you play chess, Mr. Hatch, you will readily grasp what I mean. Our great chess masters are really our greatest logicians and mathematicians, yet their efforts are directed in a way which can be of no use save to demonstrate, theatrically, I may say, the unlimited possibilities of the human mind."

Hutchinson Hatch, reporter, leaned back in his chair and watched the great scientist and logician as he pottered around the long workbench beside the big window of his tiny laboratory. It was here that Professor Van Dusen had achieved some of those marvels which had attracted the attention of the world at large and had won for him a long list of honorary initials.

Hatch doubted if the Professor himself could recall these—that is beyond the more common ones of Ph. D., LL. D., M. D., and M. A. There were strange combinations of letters bestowed by French, Italian, German and English educational and scientific institutions, which were delighted to honor so eminent a scientist as Professor Van Dusen, so-called The Thinking Machine.

The slender body of the scientist, bowed from close study and minute microscopic observation, gave the impression of physical weakness—an impression which was wholly correct—and made the enormous head which topped the figure seem abnormal.

Added to this was the long yellow hair of the scientist, which sometimes as he worked fell over his face and almost obscured the keen blue eyes perpetually squinting through unusually thick glasses.

"By the reduction of a problem to an arithmetical basis," The Thinking Machine went on, "I mean the finding of the cause of an effect. For instance, a man is dead. We know only that. Reason tells us that he died naturally or was killed.

"If killed, it may have been an accident, design or suicide. There are no alternatives. The average mind grasps those possibilities instantly as facts because the average mind has to do with death and understands. We may call this primary reasoning instinct.

"In the higher reasoning which can only come from long study and experiment, imagination is necessary to supply temporarily gaps caused by absence of facts. Imagination is the backbone of the scientific mind. Marconi had to imagine wireless telegraphy before he accomplished it. It is the same with the telephone, the telegraph, the steam engine and those scores of commonplace marvels which are a part of our everyday life.

"The higher scientific mind is, perforce, the mind of a logician. It must possess imagination to a remarkable extent. For instance, science proved that all matter is composed of atoms—the molecular theory. Having proven this, scientific imagination saw that it was possible that atoms were themselves composed of more minute atoms, and sought to prove this. It did so.

"Therefore we know atoms make atoms, and that more minute atoms make those atoms, and so on down to the point of absolute indivisibility. This is logic.

"Applied in the other direction this imagination—really logic—leads to amazing possibilities. It would grade upward something like this: Man is made of atoms; man and his works as other atoms make cities; cities and nature as atoms make countries; countries and oceans as atoms make worlds.

"Then comes the supreme imaginative leap which would make worlds merely atoms, pin point parts of a vast solar system; the vast solar system itself merely an atom in some greater scheme of creation which the imagination refuses to grasp, which staggers the mind. It is all logic, logic, logic."

The irritated voice stopped as the scientist lifted a graded measuring glass to the light and squinted for an instant at its contents, which, under the amazed eyes of Hutchinson Hatch, swiftly changed from a brilliant scarlet to a pure white.

"You have heard me say frequently, Mr. Hatch," The Thinking Machine resumed, "that two and two make four, not sometimes, but all the time—atoms make atoms, therefore atoms make creations." He paused. "That change of color in this chemical is merely a change of atoms; it has in no way affected the consistency or weight of the liquid. Yet the red atoms have disappeared, eliminated by the white."

"The logic being that the white atoms are the stronger?" asked Hatch, almost timidly.

"Precisely," said The Thinking Machine, "and also constant and victorious enemies of the red atoms. In other words that was a war between red and white atoms you just witnessed. Who shall say that a war on this earth is not as puny to the observer of this earth as an atom in the greater creation, as was that little war to us?"

Hatch blinked a little at the question. It opened up something bigger than his mind had ever struggled with before, and he was a newspaper reporter, too. Professor Van Dusen turned away and stirred up more chemicals in another glass, then poured the contents of one glass into another.

Hatch heard the telephone bell ring in the next room, and after a moment Martha, the aged woman who was the household staff of the scientist's modest home, appeared at the door.

"Some one to speak to Mr. Hatch at the 'phone," she said.

Hatch went to the 'phone. At the other end was his city editor bursting with impatience.

"A big kidnapping story," the city editor said. "A wonder. I've been looking for you everywhere. Happened tonight about 6 o'clock—It's now 8:30. Jump up to Lynn quick and get it."

Then the city editor went on to detail the known points of the mystery, as the police of Lynn had learned them; the child left alone for only two or three minutes, the letter threatening kidnapping, the demand for $10,000 and the footsteps in the snow which led to—nothing.

Thoroughly alive with the instinct of the reporter Hatch returned to the laboratory where The Thinking Machine was at work.

"Another mystery," he said, persuasively.

"What is it?" asked The Thinking Machine, without turning.

Hatch repeated what information he had and The Thinking Machine listened without comment, down to the discovery of the tracks in the snow, and the abrupt ending of these.

"Babies don't have wings, Mr. Hatch," said The Thinking Machine, severely.

"I know," said Hatch. "Would—would you like to go out with me and look it over?"

"It's silly to say the tracks end there," declared The Thinking Machine aggressively. "They must go somewhere. If they don't, they are not the boy's tracks."

"If you'd like to go," said Hatch, coaxingly, "we could get there by half-past nine. It's half-past eight now."

"I'll go," said the other suddenly.

An hour later, they were at the front gate of the Blake home in Lynn. The Thinking Machine saw the kidnappers' letter. He looked at it closely and dismissed it apparently with a wave of his hand. He talked for a long time to the mother, to the nurse, Evelyn Barton, to the servants, then went out into the back yard where the tiny tracks were found.

Here, seeing perfectly by the brilliant light of the moon, The Thinking Machine remained for an hour. He saw the last of the tiny footprints which led nowhere, and he sat on the box where the detective had sat. Then he arose suddenly and examined the box. It was, he found, of wood, approximately two feet square, raised only four or five inches above the ground. It was built to cover and protect the main water connection with the house. The Thinking Machine satisfied himself on this point by looking inside.

From this box he sought in every direction for footprints—tracks which were not obviously those of the detectives or his own or Hatch's. No one else had been permitted to go over the ground, the detectives objecting to this until they had completed their investigations.

No other tracks or footprints appeared; there was nothing to indicate that there had been tracks which had been skillfully covered up by whoever made them.

Again The Thinking Machine sat down on the box and studied his surroundings. Hatch watched him curiously. First he looked away toward the stone wall, nearly a hundred feet in front of him. There was positively no indentation in the snow of any kind so far as Hatch could see. Then the scientist looked back toward the house—one of the detectives had told him it was just forty-eight feet from the box—but there were no tracks there save those the detectives and Hatch and himself had made.

Then The Thinking Machine looked toward the back of the lot. Here in the bright moonlight he could see the barn and the clump of trees, several inside the enclosure made by the stone wall and others outside, extending away indefinitely, snow laden and grotesque in the moonlight. From the view in this direction The Thinking Machine turned to the other stone wall, a hundred feet or so. Here, too, he vainly sought footprints in the snow.

Finally he arose and walked in this direction with an expression of as near bewilderment on his face as Hatch had ever seen. A small dark spot in the snow had attracted his attention. It was eight or ten feet from the box. He stopped and looked at it; it was a stone of flat surface, perhaps a foot square and devoid of snow.

"Why hasn't this any snow on it?" he asked Hatch.

Hatch started and shook his head. The Thinking Machine, bowed almost to the ground, continued to stare at the stone for a moment, then straightened up and continued walking toward the wall. A few feet further on a rope, evidently a clothes line, barred his way. Without stopping, he ducked his head beneath it and walked on toward the wall, still staring at the ground.

From the wall he retraced his steps to the clothes line, then walked along under that, still staring at the snow, to its end, sixty or seventy feet toward the back of the enclosure. Two or three supports placed at regular intervals beneath the line were closely examined.

"Find anything?" asked Hatch, finally.

The Thinking Machine shook his head impatiently.

"It's amazing," he exclaimed petulantly, like a disappointed child.

"It is," Hatch agreed, cheerfully.

The Thinking Machine turned and walked back toward the house as he had come, Hatch following.

"I think we'd better go back to Boston," he said tartly.

Hatch silently acquiesced. Neither spoke until they were in the train, and The Thinking Machine turned suddenly to the wondering reporter.

"Did it seem possible to you that those are not the footprints of Baby Blake at all, only the prints of his shoes?" he demanded suddenly.

"How did they get there?" asked Hatch, in turn.

The Thinking Machine shook his head.

On the afternoon of the next day, when the newspapers were full of the mystery, Mrs. Blake received this letter, signed "Three" as before:

"We hav the baby and will bring him bak for twenny fiv thousan dolers. Will you give it. Advertis as befour dereckted, YES or NOA."

III

When Hutchinson Hatch went to inform The Thinking Machine of the appearance of this second letter late in the afternoon, he found the scientist sitting in his little laboratory, finger tips pressed together, squinting steadily at the ceiling. There was a little puzzled line on the high brow, a line Hatch never saw there before, and frank perplexity was in the blue eyes.

The Thinking Machine listened without changing his position as Hatch told him of the letter and its contents.

"What do you make of it all, professor?" asked the reporter.

"I don't know," was the reply—one which was a little startling to Hatch. "It's most perplexing."

"The only known facts seem to be that Baby Blake was kidnapped, and is now in the possession of the kidnappers," said Hatch.

"Those tracks—the footprints in the snow, I mean—furnish the real problem in this case," said the other after a moment. "Presumably they were made by the baby—yet they might not have been. They might have been put there merely to mislead anyone who began a search. If the baby made them—how and why do they stop as they do? If they were made merely with the baby's shoes, to mislead investigation, the same question remains—how?

"Let's see a moment. We will dismiss the seeming fact that the baby walked on off into the air and disappeared, granting that those tracks were made by the baby. We will also dismiss the possibility that the baby was with anyone when it made the tracks, if it did make them. There were certainly no other footprints but those. There were no footprints leading from or to that point where the baby tracks stopped.

"What are the possibilities? What remains? A balloon? If we accept the balloon as a possibility we must at the same time relinquish the theory of a preconceived plan of abduction. Why? Because no successful plan could have been arranged so that that baby, of its own will, would have been in that particular spot at that particular moment. Therefore a balloon might have been floated over the place a thousand times without success, and balloons are large—they attract attention, therefore are to be avoided.

"There is a possibility—a bare one—that a balloon with a trailing anchor or hook did pass over the place, and that this hook caught up the baby by its clothing, lifting it clear of the ground. But in that event it was not kidnapping—it was accident. But here against the theory of accident we have the kidnappers' letters.

"If not a balloon, then an eagle? Hardly possible. It would take a bird of exceptional strength to have lifted a fourteen-month child, and besides there are a thousand things against such a possibility. Certainly the winged man is not known to science, yet there is every evidence of his handiwork here. Briefly, the problem is—granting that the baby itself made the tracks—how was a baby lifted out of the relative centre of a large yard?

"Consider for a moment that the baby did not make the tracks—that they were placed there by some one else. Then we are confronted by the same question—how? A person might have fastened shoes to a long pole and rigged up some arrangement of the sort, and made the tracks for a distance say of twenty feet out into the snow, but remember the tracks run out forty-eight feet to the box you say.

"If it would have been possible for a person to stand on that box without leaving a track to it or from it, he might have finished the tracks with the shoes on a pole, but nobody went to that box."

The Thinking Machine was silent for several minutes. Hatch had nothing to say. The Thinking Machine seemed to have covered the possibilities thoroughly.

"Of course, it might have been possible for a person in a balloon to have put the tracks there, but it would have been a senseless proceeding," the scientist went on. "Certainly there could have been no motive for it strong enough to make a person invite discovery by sailing about the house in a balloon even at night. We face a stone wall, Mr. Hatch—a stone wall. It is possible for the mind to follow it only to a certain point as it now stands."

He arose and disappeared into an adjoining room, returning in a few minutes with his hat and overcoat.

"Of course," he said to Hatch, "if the baby is alive and in the possession of the kidnappers, it is possible to recover it, and we'll do that, but the real problem remains."

"If it is alive?" Hatch repeated.

"Yes, if," said the other shortly. "There are in my mind grave doubts on that point."

"But the kidnappers' letters?" said Hatch

"Let's go find out who wrote them," said the other, enigmatically.

Together the two men went to Lynn, and there for half an hour The Thinking Machine talked to Mrs. Blake. He came out finally with a package in his hand.

Miss Barton, with eyes red, apparently from weeping, and evident sorrow imprinted on her pretty face, entered the room almost at the same moment.

"Miss Barton," the scientist asked, "could you tell me how much the baby Douglas weighed—relatively, I mean?"

The girl gazed at him a moment as if startled. "About thirty pounds, I should say," she answered.

"Thanks," said The Thinking Machine, and turned to Hatch. "I have twenty-five thousand dollars in this package," he said.

Miss Barton turned and glanced quickly toward him, then passed out of the room.

"What are you going to do with it?" asked Hatch.

"It's for the kidnappers," was the reply. "The police advised Mrs. Blake not to try to make terms—I advised her the other way and she gave me this."

"What's the next step?" Hatch asked.

"To put the advertisement 'Yes' signed by Mrs. Blake in the newspaper," said The Thinking Machine. "That's in accordance with the stipulations of the letters."

An hour later the two men were in Boston. The advertisement was inserted in the *Boston American* as directed. The next day Mrs. Blake received a third letter.

"Rapp the munny in a ole nuspaipr ann thow it onn the trash-heape at the addge of the vakant lott one blok down the street frum wear you liv," it directed. "Putt it on topp. We wil gett it ann yore baby wil be in yore armms two ours latter. Three (3)."

This letter was immediately placed in the hands of The Thinking Machine. Mrs. Blake's face flushed with hope, and believing that the child would be restored to her, she waited in a fever of impatience.

"Now, Mr. Hatch," instructed The Thinking Machine. "Do with this package as directed. A man will come for it some time. I shall leave the task of finding out who he is, where he goes and all about him to you. He is probably a man of low mentality, though not so low as the misspelled words of his letter would have you believe. He should be easily trapped. Don't interfere with him—merely report to me when you find out these things."

Alone The Thinking Machine returned to Boston. Thirty-six hours later, in the early morning, a telegram came for him. It was as follows:

"Have man located in Lynn and trace of baby. Come quick, if possible, to — Hotel. Hatch."

IV

The Thinking Machine answered the telegraphic summons immediately, but instead of elation on his face there was another expression—possibly surprise. On the train he read and re-read the telegram.

"Have trace of baby," he mused. "Why, it's perfectly astonishing."

White-faced from exhaustion, and with eyes drooping from lack of sleep, Hutchinson Hatch met The Thinking Machine in the hotel lobby and they immediately went to a room, which the reporter had engaged on the third floor.

The Thinking Machine listened without comment as Hatch told the story of what he had done. He had placed the bundle, then hired a room overlooking the vacant lot and had remained there at the window for hours. At last night came, but there were clouds which effectively hid the moon. Then Hatch had gone out and secreted himself near the trash pile.

Here from six o'clock in the evening until four in the morning he had remained, numbed with cold and not daring to move. At last his long vigil was rewarded. A man suddenly appeared near the trash heap, glanced around furtively, and then picked up the newspaper package, felt of it to assure himself that it contained something, and then started away quickly.

The work of following him Hatch had not found difficult. He had gone straight to a tenement in the eastern end of Lynn and disappeared inside. Later in the morning, after the occupants of the house were about, Hatch made inquiries which established the identity of the man without question.

His name was Charles Gates and he lived with his wife on the fourth floor of the tenement. His reputation was not wholly savory, and he drank a great deal. He was a man of some education, but not of such ignorance as the letters he had written would indicate.

"After learning all these facts," Hatch went on, "my idea was to see the man and talk to him or to his wife. I went there this morning about nine o'clock, as a book agent." The reporter smiled a little. "His wife, Mrs. Gates, didn't want any books, but I nearly sold her a sewing machine.

"Anyway, I got into the apartments and remained there for fifteen or twenty minutes. There was only one room which I didn't enter, of the four there. In that room, the woman explained, her husband was asleep. He had been out late the night before, she said. Of course I knew that.

"I asked if she had any babies and received a negative. From other people in the house I learned that this was true so far as they knew. There was not and has not been a baby in the apartments so far as anyone could tell me. And in spite of that fact I found this."

Hatch drew something from his pocket and spread it on his open hand. It was a baby stocking of fine texture. The Thinking Machine took it and looked at it closely.

"Baby Blake's?" he asked.

"Yes," replied the reporter. "Both Mrs. Blake and the nurse, Miss Barton, identify it."

"Dear me! Dear me!" exclaimed the scientist, thoughtfully. Again the puzzled expression came into his face.

"Of course, the baby hasn't been returned?" went on the scientist.

"Of course not!" said Hatch.

"Did Mrs. Gates behave like a woman who had suddenly received a share of twenty-five thousand dollars?" asked The Thinking Machine.

"No," Hatch replied. "She looked as if she had attended a mixed ale party. Her lip was cut and bruised and one eye was black."

"That's what her husband did when he found out what was in the newspaper," commented The Thinking Machine, grimly.

"It wasn't money, at all, then?" asked Hatch.

"Certainly not."

Neither said anything for several minutes. The Thinking Machine sat idly twisting the tiny stocking between his long, slender fingers with the little puzzled line in his brow.

"How do you account for that stocking in Gates's possession?" asked the reporter at last.

"Let's go talk to Mrs. Blake," was the reply. "You didn't tell her anything about this man Gates getting the package?"

"No," said the reporter.

"It would only worry her," explained the scientist. "Better let her hope, because—"

Hatch looked at The Thinking Machine quickly, startled.

"Because, what?" he asked.

"There seems to be a very strong probability that Baby Blake is dead," the other responded.

Pondering that, yet conceiving no motive which would cause the baby's death, Hatch was silent as he and the scientist together went to the house of Mrs. Blake. Miss Barton, the nurse, answered the door.

"Miss Barton," said The Thinking Machine, testily as they entered, "just when did you give this stocking,"—and he produced it— "to Charles Gates?"

The girl flushed quickly, and she stammered a little.

"I—I don't know what you mean," she said. "Who is Charles Gates?"

"May we see Mrs. Blake?" asked the scientist. He squinted steadily into the girl's eyes.

"Yes—of course—that is, I suppose so," she stammered.

She disappeared, and in a few minutes Mrs. Blake appeared. There was an eager, expectant look in her face. It was hope. It faded when she saw the solemn face of The Thinking Machine.

"What recommendations did Miss Barton have when you engaged her?" he began pointedly.

"The best I could ask," was the reply. "She was formerly a governess in the family of the Governor-General of Canada. She is well educated, and came to me from that position."

"Is she well acquainted in Lynn?" asked the scientist.

"That I couldn't say," replied Mrs. Blake. "If you are thinking that she might have some connection with this affair—"

"Ever go out much?" interrupted her questioner.

"Rarely, and then usually with me. She is more of a companion than servant."

"How long have you had her?"

"Since a week or so after my baby"—and the mother's lips trembled a little— "was born. She has been devoted to me since the death of my husband. I would trust her with my life."

"This is your baby's stocking?"

"Beyond any doubt," she replied as she again examined it.

"I suppose he had several pairs like this?"

"I really don't know. I should think so."

"Will you please have Miss Barton, or someone else, find those stockings and see if all the pairs like this are complete," instructed The Thinking Machine.

Wonderingly, Mrs. Blake gave the order to Miss Barton, who as wonderingly received it and went out of the room with a quick, resentful look at the bowed figure of the scientist.

"Did you ever happen to notice, Mrs. Blake, whether or not your baby could open a door? For instance, the front door?"

"I believe he could," she replied. "He could reach them because the handles are low, as you see," and she indicated the knob on the front door, which was visible through the reception hall room where they stood.

The Thinking Machine turned suddenly and strode to the window of the library, looking out on the back yard. He was debating something in his own mind. It was whether or not he should tell this mother his fear of her son's death, or should hide it from her until such time as it would appear itself. For some reason known only to himself he considered the child's death not only a possibility, but a probability.

Whatever might have resulted from this mental debate was not to be known then, for suddenly, as he stood staring out the rear window overlooking the spot where the baby's tracks had been seen in the snow—now melted—he started a little and peered eagerly out. It was the first sight he had had of the yard since the night he had examined it by moonlight.

"Dear me, dear me," he exclaimed suddenly.

Turning abruptly he left the room, and a moment later Hatch saw him in the back yard. Mrs. Blake at the window watched curiously. Outside The Thinking Machine walked straight out to the spot where the baby's tracks had been, and from there Hatch saw him stop and stare at the slightly raised box which covered the water connections.

From this box the scientist took five steps toward a flat-topped stone—the one he had noticed previously—and Hatch saw that it was about ten feet. Then from this he saw The Thinking Machine take four steps to where the sagging clothes-line hung. It was probably eight feet. Then the bowed figure of The Thinking Machine walked on out toward the rear wall of the enclosure, under the clothes-line.

When he stopped at the end of the line he was within fifteen feet of the dangling swing which had been Baby Blake's. This swing was attached to a limb twenty feet above—a stout limb which jutted straight out from the tree trunk for fifteen feet. The Thinking Machine studied this for a moment, then passed on beyond the tree, still looking up, until he disappeared.

Fifteen minutes later he returned to the library where Mrs. Blake awaited him. There was a question in Hatch's eyes.

"I've got it," snapped The Thinking Machine, much as if there had been a denial. "I've got it."

V

On the following day, by direction of The Thinking Machine, Mrs. Blake ordered the following advertisement inserted in all Boston and Lynn newspapers, to occupy one-quarter of a page.

To The Persons Who Now
Hold Douglas Blake:

"Your names, residence and place of concealment of Douglas Blake, fourteen months old, and the manner in which he came into your possession are now known.

"Mrs. Blake, the mother, does not desire to prosecute for reasons you know, and will give you twenty-four hours in which to return the baby safely to its home in Lynn.

"Any attempt to escape of either person concerned will be followed instantly by arrest. Meanwhile you are closely watched, and will be for twenty-four hours, at which time arrest and prosecution will follow.

"No questions will he asked when the child is returned and your names will be fully protected. There will also be a reward of $1,000 for the person who returns the baby."

Hutchinson Hatch read this when The Thinking Machine had completed it and had stared at the scientist in wonderment.

"Is it true?" he asked.

"I am afraid the child is dead," repeated The Thinking Machine evasively. "I am very much afraid of it."

"What gives you that impression?" Hatch asked.

"I know now how the child was taken from that back yard, if we grant that the child itself made the tracks," was the rejoinder. "And knowing how it was taken away makes me more fearful than I have been that it is not alive; in fact, that it may never be seen again."

"How did the child leave the yard?"

"If the child does not appear within twenty-four hours," was the reply, "I shall tell you. It is a hideous story."

Hatch had to be content with that statement of the case for the moment. None knew better than he how useless it would be to question The Thinking Machine.

"Did you happen to know, Mr. Hatch," The Thinking Machine asked, "that in the event of the death of Douglas Blake, his fortune of nearly three million dollars left in trust by his father would be divided among four relatives of Mrs. Blake?"

"What?" asked Hatch, a little startled.

"Suppose for instance, Baby Blake was never found, as seems possible," went on the other. "After a certain number of years, I believe, in a case of that kind there is an assumption of death and property passes to heirs. You see then, there was a motive, and a strong one, underlying this entire affair."

"But, surely there wouldn't be murder?"

"Not murder," responded The Thinking Machine tartly. "I haven't even suggested murder. I said I believe the child is dead. If it is not dead who would benefit by his disappearance? The four whom I named."

"Well, suppose Baby Blake fell into the hands of those people. It would be comparatively an easy matter for them to lose it in some way—not necessarily kill it—have it adopted in some orphan asylum, place it anywhere to hide its identity. That's the main thing."

Hatch began to see light faintly, he thought.

"Then this advertisement is to the people who may be holding the child now?" he asked.

"It is so addressed," was the other's reply.

"But, but—" Hatch began.

"Once upon a time a noted wit, who was of necessity a student of human nature," The Thinking Machine began, "declared there was one thing carefully hidden in every man's life which would ruin him should it be known, or land him in prison. He volunteered to prove this, taking any man whose name was suggested. An eminent minister of the gospel was named as the victim. The wit sent a telegram to the minister, who was attending a banquet: 'All is discovered. Flee while there is opportunity,' signed 'Friend.' The minister read it, arose and left the room, and from that day to this he has never been seen again."

Hatch laughed, and The Thinking Machine glanced at him with an annoyed expression on his face.

"I had no intention of arousing your laughter," he said sharply. "I merely intended to illustrate the possible effect of a guilty conscience."

When the flaming advertisement in the newspapers was called to the attention of the police, they were first surprised, then amused. Then they grew serious. After a while an officer went to Mrs. Blake and asked what it meant. She informed him that she had acted at the suggestion of Professor Van Dusen. Then the police were amused again; they are wont to feign an amusement which they never feel in the presence of a superior mind.

That afternoon, Hatch, who by direction of The Thinking Machine, was on watch again near the Blake home, received a strange request from the scientist by telephone. It was:

"Go to the Blake home immediately, see the picture book which Baby Blake was looking at just before his disappearance, and report to me by 'phone just what's in it."

"The picture book?" Hatch repeated.

"Certainly, the picture book," said the scientist, irritably. "Also find out for me from the nurse and Mrs. Blake if the baby cried easily, that is from a slight hurt or anything of that kind."

With these things in his mind Hatch went to the Blake house, had a look at the picture book, asked the questions as to Baby Blake's propensity to weep on slight provocation, and returned to the 'phone. Feeling singularly foolish, he enumerated to The Thinking Machine the things he had seen in the picture book.

"There's a horse, and a cat with three kittens," he explained. "Also a pale purple rhinoceros, and a dog, an elephant, a deer, an alligator, a monkey, three chicks, and a whole lot of birds."

"Any eagle?" queried the other.

"Yes, an eagle among them, with a rabbit in its claws."

"And the monkey. What is it doing?"

"Hanging by its tail to a blue tree with a coconut in its hands," replied the reporter. The humor of the situation was beginning to appeal to him.

"And about the baby crying?" the scientist asked.

"He does not cry easily, both the mother and nurse say," replied Hatch. "They both describe him as a brave little chap, who cries sometimes when he can't have his own way, but never from fright or a minor hurt."

"Good," he heard The Thinking Machine say. "Watch in front of the Blake house tonight until half past eight. If the child returns it will probably be earlier than that. Speak to the person who brings him, as he leaves the house, and he will tell you his story I think, if you can make him understand that he is in no danger. Immediately after that come to my home in Boston."

Hatch was treading on air; when The Thinking Machine gave positive directions of that sort it usually meant that the final curtain was to be drawn aside. He so construed this.

Thus it came to pass that Hutchinson Hatch planted himself, carefully hidden so he might command a view of the front of the Blake home, and waited there for many hours.

Mrs. Blake, the mother of the millionaire baby, had just finished her dinner and had retired to a small parlor off the library, where she reclined on a couch. It was ten minutes of seven o'clock in the evening. After a moment Miss Barton entered the room.

The girl heard a sob from the couch and impulsively ran to Mrs. Blake, who was weeping softly—she was always weeping now. A few comforting words, a little consolation such as one woman is able to give to another, and the girl arose from her knees and started into the library, where a dim light burned.

As she was entering that room again, she paused, screamed and without a word sank down on the floor, fainting. Mrs. Blake rose from the couch and rushed toward the door. She screamed too, but that scream was of a different tone from that of the girl—it was a fierce scream of mother-love satisfied.

For there on the floor of the library sat Baby Blake, millionaire, gazing with enraptured eyes at his brilliantly colored picture book.

"Pitty hossie," he said to his mother. "See! See!"

VI

It was an affecting scene Hutchinson Hatch witnessed in the Blake home about half-past seven o'clock. It was that of a mother clasping a baby to her breast while tears of joy and hysteria streamed from her eyes. Baby Blake struggled manfully to free himself, but the mother clung to him.

"My boy, my boy," she sobbed again and again.

Miss Barton sat on the floor beside the mother and wept too. Hatch saw it, and received some thanks, heartfelt, but broken with a little sobbing laughter. Then he had to dry his eyes, too, and Hutchinson Hatch was not a sentimental man.

"There will be no prosecution, Mrs. Blake, I suppose?" he asked.

"No, no, no," was the half laughing, half tearful reply. "I am content."

"I would like to ask a favor, if you don't mind?" he suggested.

"Anything—anything for you and Professor Van Dusen," was the reply.

"Will you lend me the baby's picture book until to-morrow?" he asked.

"Certainly," and in her happiness the mother forgot to note the strangeness of the request.

Hatch's purpose in borrowing the book was not clear even to himself; in his mind had grown the idea that in some way The Thinking Machine connected this book with the disappearance of the child, and he was burning with curiosity to get the book and return to Boston, where The Thinking Machine might throw some light on the mystery. For it was still a mystery—a perplexing, baffling mystery that he could in no way grasp, even now that the baby was safe at home again. In Boston the reporter went straight to the home of The Thinking Machine. The scientist was pottering about the little laboratory and only turned to look at Hatch when he entered.

"Baby back home?" he asked, shortly.

"Yes," said the reporter.

"Good," said the other, and he rubbed his slender hands together briskly. "Sit down, Mr. Hatch. It was a little better after all than I hoped for. Now your story first. What happened when the baby was brought back home?"

"I waited as you directed from afternoon until a few minutes to seven," Hatch explained. "I could plainly see anyone who approached the front gate of the Blake place, although I could not be seen well, remaining in the shadow of the building opposite.

"I saw two or three people go up to the gate and enter the yard, but they were tradespeople. I spoke to them as they came out and ascertained this for myself. At last I saw a man approaching carrying something closely wrapped in his arms. He stopped at the gate, stared up the path a moment, glanced around several times and entered the yard. He was carrying Baby Blake. I knew it instinctively.

"He went to the front door of the house and there I lost him in the shadow for a moment. Subsequent developments showed that he opened this front door, which was not locked, put the baby down and closed the door softly. Then he came rapidly down the path toward the gate. An instant later I heard two screams from the house. I knew then that the baby was there, dead or alive—probably alive.

"The man who had brought it also heard the screams and accelerated his pace somewhat, so that I had to run. He heard me coming and he ran, too. It was a two-block chase before I caught him, and when I did he turned on me. I thought it was to fight.

"'There was a promise of no arrest or prosecution,' he said.

"I assured him hurriedly, and then walked on down the street beside him. He told me a queer story—it might be true or it might not, but I believe it. This was that the baby had been in his and his wife's care from about half-past six o'clock of the evening it disappeared until a few minutes before when he had returned it to its home.

"The man's name is Sheldon—Michael Sheldon—and he is an ex-convict. He served four years for burglary, and at one time had a pretty nasty record. He told me of it in explanation of his reasons for not turning the baby over to the police. Now he has reformed and is leading a new life. He is a clerk in a store here in Lynn, and despite his previous record is, I ascertained, a trusted and reliable man.

"Now here comes the queer part of the story. It seems that Sheldon and his wife live on the third floor of a tenement in northern Lynn. Their dining room has one window, which leads to a fire escape. He and his wife were at supper about half-past six—in other words, a little more than half an hour from the time the baby disappeared from the Blake home.

"After awhile they heard a noise—they didn't know what—on the fire escape. They paid no attention. Finally they heard another noise from the fire escape—that of a baby crying. Then Sheldon went to the window and opened it. There on the fire escape was Baby Blake. How he got there no human being knows."

"I know now," said The Thinking Machine. "Go on."

"Puzzled and bewildered they took the child off the iron structure, where only the barest chance had prevented it from falling and being killed on the pavement below. The baby was apparently uninjured save for a few bruises, but his clothing was soiled and rumpled, and he was terribly cold. The wife, mother-like, set out to warm the little fellow and make him comfortable with hot milk and a steaming bath. The husband, Sheldon, says he went out to find how it was possible for the baby to have reached the fire escape. He knew no baby lived in the building.

"He looked long and carefully. There was no possible way by which a man could have climbed the fire escape to the third floor, and therefore certainly no way by which a fourteen-month-old baby could climb there. There is a fence there which is pretty tall, say six feet, but even standing on this a man would have had to leap straight up in the air for five feet, and nobody I know could do it with a baby in his arms, particularly when the snow was there and everything was so slippery a person could hardly hold on.

"It seems that then Sheldon made inquiries of some of his neighbors, occupants of the house, but no one could throw any light on the subject. He did not tell them then of the baby, indeed, never told them. First, from the fine quality of the clothing, there had been an idea in his mind that the baby was one of a well-to-do family, and he remained quiet that night hoping that next day he might be able to learn something and possibly get a reward for the return of the child. He had given up the problem of how it got where he found it."

Hatch paused a moment and lighted a cigar.

"Well, next day," he went on, "Sheldon and his wife both saw the newspaper account of the mysterious disappearance of Baby Blake. The photographs of the missing child convinced them that Baby Blake was the child they had—the child they had really saved from death. Then came the question of returning the child to its home or turning it over to the police.

"Instantly the fact that a threat had been made to kidnap the child and a demand for ten thousand dollars made was borne in on Sheldon he became frightened. Remember he had a bad record. He was afraid of the police. He did not believe that he—however innocent he might be—could go to the police, turn over the baby and make them believe the strange story. I readily see how some wooden-headed department officials would have made his life a burden. I know the police. It is ninety-nine dollars to a cent they would have made him a prisoner and perhaps railroaded him for the kidnapping."

"Yes, I see," interrupted The Thinking Machine.

"So then he and his wife tried to devise a method of getting the baby back home. They thought of all sorts of things, but none satisfied them entirely. And they were still debating this point and considering it when your advertisement promised immunity. As a matter of fact it scared Sheldon. He imagined that you knew, and knew if he were even remotely connected with the matter it would get him in trouble. Then he resolved to take the baby back home on the promise of immunity."

There was a little pause. The Thinking Machine sat staring steadily at the ceiling.

"Is that all?" he asked at last.

"I think so," replied Hatch. "And now how—how in the name of all that's good or evil did that baby disappear from the middle of its own back yard and then suddenly appear on a fire escape three blocks away, to be taken in by strangers?"

"It's quite the most remarkable thing I have ever come across," The Thinking Machine said. "A balloon anchor, which picked up the child by its clothing, through accident, and then dropped it safely on the fire escape might answer the question in a way. But it does not fully answer it. The baby was carried there.

"Frankly I will say that I could see no possible explanation of the affair until the day you and I were talking to Mrs. Blake and I stood looking out of the library window. Then it all flashed on me instantly. I went out and satisfied myself. When I returned to the library I was satisfied in all reason that Baby Blake was dead; I had had such an idea before. I was firmly convinced the child was dead when I put those advertisements in the newspapers. But there was still a chance that he was not.

"Several seemingly unanswerable questions faced me when I found the end of the baby's footprints in the snow. I instantly saw that if the baby had made those tracks it had been lifted suddenly from the ground, but by what? From where? How had it been taken away? The balloon I could not consider seriously, although as I say it offered a possible solution. An eagle? I could not consider that seriously. Eagles are rare; eagles powerful enough to lift a baby weighing thirty pounds are extremely rare, practically unknown save in the far West; certainly I never heard of one doing such a thing as this. Therefore I passed the eagle by as an improbability.

"I satisfied myself that there were no other footsteps save the baby's in the yard. Then—what? It occurred to me that someone standing on the little box might have reached over and lifted the child out of its tracks. But it was too far away, I thought, and if someone did stand there and lift the child that someone could not have leaped from that box over the stone wall, which was approximately a hundred feet away in all directions.

"I saw the stone ten feet away. Could a man stand on the box and leap to the stone? Generally, no. And from the stone, where could he have gone? Obviously nowhere. I considered this matter not minutes, but hours and days, and no light came to me. I was convinced, though, that the box was the starting point if the baby had made the tracks. I was now fairly certain that the baby did make the tracks. He wanted to get out in the snow, was left alone, opened the front door and wandered out.

"Then it all occurred to me in a new light. What living animal could have stood on the box and lifted the child clear four feet away, then leaped from there to the stone, and from the stone where? The clothes line is eight feet or so from the stone. It is a pretty sturdy rope and capable of bearing a considerable weight, supported as it is."

He stopped and turned his eyes toward Hatch, who listened eagerly.

"Do you see it now?" he asked.

The reporter shook his head, bewildered.

"The thing that lifted Baby Blake from the snow stood on the box, leaped from there to the stone, from there to the clothes line, along which it climbed to the end. From the wooden support at the end it is a clear distance of fifteen feet to the nearest thing—the swing. This thing made that leap, climbed the swing rope, disappeared into the trees, moving through the branches freely from one tree to another, and dropped to the ground nearly a block away."

"A monkey?" suggested Hatch.

"An orang-outang," nodded The Thinking Machine.

"An orang-outang?" gasped Hatch, and he shuddered a little. "I see now why you were positive the child was dead."

"An orang-outang is the only living thing within the knowledge of man which could have done all these things—therefore an orang-outang did them," said the other emphatically. "Remember a full-sized orang-outang is nearly as tall as a man, has a reach relatively a third longer than a very tall man would have, and a strength which is enormous. It could have made the leaps and probably would have made them rather than step in the snow. They despise snow, being from the tropics themselves, and will not step in it unless they are compelled to. The leap of fifteen feet to the swing rope from the clothes line would have been comparatively easy, even with a child in its arms.

"Where could it have come from? I don't know. Possibly escaped from a ship, because sailors have strange pets; might have gotten away from a menagerie somewhere, or a circus. I only knew that an orang-outang was the actual abductor. The difficulties of a man climbing the fire escape where the baby was found were nothing to an orang-outang. There it would have merely been a leap up of five feet."

The Thinking Machine stopped as if he had finished. Hatch respected this silence for a moment, but he had questions yet to be answered.

"Who wrote the kidnapping letters demanding money?" was the first.

"You found him—Charles Gates," was the reply.

"And the letter written after the abduction demanding twenty-five thousand dollars?"

"Was written by him, of course—but this was a bluff. This poor deluded fool imagined that someone would actually go out and toss $25,000 on a trash-heap where he could find it, and then he could escape. That was his purpose. He knew nothing of the whereabouts of the baby. He beat his wife when he found, instead of money, I had put some good advice in the newspaper bundle for him."

"But the stocking in his room, and your question to Miss Barton?"

"This man did write a letter threatening kidnapping before the baby disappeared. It was perfectly possible that after the kidnapping he stole the little stocking and two or three other things from the laundry, for Miss Barton noticed they were missing, or got someone to do so for him. And, the baby being gone, he was intending to send these to the mother, one at a time, I imagine, to make her believe he had the child. That is transparent. I asked Miss Barton the question about giving them to Gates to see if she did— her manner would have told me. I instantly saw she did not—had never even heard of him, as a matter of fact. I also dropped that remark about there being $25,000 in the package to see what effect it would have on her."

"And the facts you had about the baby's fortune going to relatives of Mrs. Blake in the event of the baby's death?"

"I got from her, by a casual question as to the succession of the estate. There was still a possibility that the baby was in their hands despite the manner of its disappearance. As it transpired they had nothing whatever to do with it. The advertisement I put in the paper was a palpable trick—but it had the desired effect. It touched a guilty conscience. The guilty conscience feared it was trapped and acted accordingly."

"It seems perfectly incomprehensible that the baby should have come out of it alive," mused Hatch. "I had always imagined orang-outangs to be extremely ferocious."

"Read up on them a bit, Mr. Hatch," said The Thinking Machine. "You will find they are of strangely contradictory and mischievous natures. Where this child was permitted to escape safely others might have been torn limb from limb."

There was silence for a time. Hatch considered the matter all explained, until suddenly the picture book occurred to him.

"You 'phoned to me to see the picture book and tell you what's in it," he said. "Why?"

"Suppose there was a picture of a monkey in it," rejoined the other. "I merely wanted to know if the baby would know a monkey, in other words an orang-outang, if it saw one. Why? Because if the baby knew one it would not necessarily be afraid of one in the flesh, and would not of necessity cry out when the orang-outang picked it up. As a matter of fact no one heard it scream when taken away."

"Oh, I see," said Hatch. "There was a picture of a monkey in the book. I told you." He took out the book and looked at it. "Here," and he extended it to the scientist who glanced at it casually, and nodded.

"If you want to prove this just as I have told it," said The Thinking Machine, "go to the Blake home to-morrow, put your finger on that picture and show it to Baby Blake. He will prove it."

It came to pass that Hatch did this very thing.

"Pitty monkey," said Baby Blake. "Doe, doe."

"He means he wants to go," Miss Barton exclaimed to Hatch.

Hatch was satisfied.

Two days later the *Boston American* carried a dispatch from a village near Lynn stating that a semi-tame orang-outang had been killed by a policeman. It had belonged to a sailor, from whose vessel it had escaped more than two weeks before.

Five Millions by Wireless

Within the great room, dim, shadowy, mysterious as the laboratory of some alchemist of old, and foul with the pungent odors of strange chemical messes, there blazed a single light, a powerful electrical contrivance fitted with reflector, and so shaded that its concentrated rays beat down fiercely upon a table littered with scientific apparatus; and bending over the table was a man, an odd, almost pathetic little figure, slight to childishness, small of stature, attenuated. His hair was a straw-colored thatch thrown back impatiently from a domelike brow, increasing in effect the abnormal size of his head. His eyes were narrow slits of pale blue, squinting petulantly through thick spectacles; his wizened, clean-shaven face was white with the pallor of the student; his mouth was a straight, bloodless line. His hands, busy now at some microscopic labor, were slender and almost transparent under the blinding glare from above; his fingers long, sensitive, delicate.

The door opened, and an elderly woman appeared with a tray.

"Some coffee and rolls, sir," she explained. "Really you ought to have something, sir."

"Put them down." The little man didn't lift his eyes from his work; he spoke curtly.

"And if you should ask me, sir," the woman continued, "I'd say you ought to stop whatever you're a-doing of, and take some rest, sir."

"Tut, tut, Martha!" the little man objected. "I've only just begun."

"You've been a-standing right there, sir," Martha denied, in righteous indignation, "ever since Sunday afternoon at four o'clock."

"What time is it now?"

"It's ten o'clock Tuesday morning, sir."

"Dear me, dear me!"

"You haven't slept a wink, sir," Martha complained, "and you haven't eat enough—"

"Martha, you annoy me," the little man interrupted peevishly. "Run along and attend to your duties."

"But, sir, you can't keep a-going like—"

"Very well, then," and there was a childish tone of resignation in the master's voice. "It's Tuesday, you say? Tell me when it's noon Wednesday."

Martha went out with a helpless shrug of her shoulders, leaving him alone.

Hours passed. The coffee, untasted, grew cold. Motionless, the little man continued at his labors with tense eagerness in his narrow eyes, oblivious alike of the things about him, and of exhausted nature. The will beneath the straw-colored thatch knew not weariness.

And this was "The Thinking Machine"—Professor Augustus S. F. X. Van Dusen, Ph. D., F. R. S., M. D., LL. D., et cetera, et cetera—logician, analyst, worker of miracles in the exact sciences, intellectual wizard of his time; this the master mind, exalted by the cumulative genius of generations gone before, which had isolated itself on a pinnacle of achievement through sheer force of applied reason. Once he had been the controversial center of his profession, riding down pet theories and tentative surmises and cherished opinions, and setting up instead precise facts, a few rescued from the chaos he had himself created, more of his own uncovering. Now he was the court of last appeal in the sciences.

The Thinking Machine! No one of the honorary degrees thrust upon him willy-nilly by the universities of the world described him half so accurately as did this title—a chance paradox applied by a newspaper man. Seemingly tireless, calm, unemotional—unless one counted as an emotion the constant note of irritation in his voice—terse of speech, crabbed of manner, and possessed of an uncanny faculty of separating all things into their primal units, he lived in a circumscribed sphere which he had stripped of all illusion. The mental precision which distinguished his laboratory work characterized all else he did. If any man ever reduced human frailties, human virtues, and human motives to mathematics that man was The Thinking Machine.

It has been my pleasure to set down at another time and place some results of The Thinking Machine's investigations along lines disassociated with abstruse problems of his profession, these being chiefly instances in which he had turned the light of cold logic upon perplexing criminal mysteries with well-nigh mathematical precision.

Also, it has been my pleasure to relate at length some of those curious adventures which led to The Thinking Machine's incongruous friendship for Hutchinson Hatch.

Hatch was a newspaper reporter, a young man of vitality and enthusiasm and keen wordliness; he was a breath of the outside to this odd little man, who never read papers, who rarely came into contact with things as they are, who had not even the small vices which bring individuals together. It had been Hatch who first applied the title of The Thinking Machine to the eminent scientist, and the phrase had stuck.

Perhaps not the least interesting of the adventures of these two together was that which culminated in the bestowal upon The Thinking Machine of the Order of the Iron Eagle, second class, by Emperor Gustavus, of Germania-Austria. It so happened in that case that the fate of an empire and the future of its royal house lay for a time in The Thinking Machine's slender hands. Failure on his part certainly would have changed the history of Europe, and probably the map. This problem was purely intellectual, and came to his attention at a time when physical vitality was at its lowest, after forty-eight hours' unceasing work in his laboratory.

The door opened, and Martha entered.

"Martha," the eminent scientist stormed, "if you've brought me more coffee I shall discharge you!"

"It isn't coffee, sir," she replied. "It's a—"

"And don't tell me it's already twelve o'clock Wednesday."

"It's a card, sir. Two gentlemen who—"

"Can't see them."

Not for an instant had the squinting eyes been raised from the work which engrossed The Thinking Machine. Martha laid the card on the table; he glanced at it impatiently. Herr Von Hartzfeldt!

"He says, sir, it's a matter of the utmost importance," Martha explained.

"Ask him who he is and what he wants."

The unexpectedness of the answer Martha brought back straightened The Thinking Machine where he stood.

"He says, sir," she reported, "that he's the ambassador to the United States from Germania-Austria."

"Show him in at once."

Two gentlemen entered, one Baron Von Hartzfeldt, polished, courtly, distinguished in appearance, a famous figure in the diplomatic world; the other of a more rugged type, shorter, heavier, with bristly hair and beard, and deeply bronzed face. For an instant they stared into the wizened countenance of the little scientist with something like astonishment.

"We have come to you, Mr. Van Dusen, in an extremity the gravity of which cannot be exaggerated," Baron Von Hartzfeldt began suavely. "We know, as all the world knows, your splendid achievements in science. We know, too, that you have occasionally consented to investigate more material problems—that is, mysteries of crimes, and—"

"Please come to the point," The Thinking Machine interrupted tartly. "If you hadn't known who I was, and hadn't needed me, you wouldn't have come. Now, what is it? This gentleman—"

"Pardon me," the ambassador begged, in polite confusion at the curt directness of his host. "Admiral Hausen-Aubier, of the royal navy, commanding the Mediterranean Fleet, now visiting your city on his flagship, the *Friedrich der Grosse*, which lies in the outer harbor."

The admiral bowed ceremoniously, and, accepting a slight movement of The Thinking Machine's hand as an invitation to seats, the two gentlemen sat down. Not until that moment had the scientist realized his own weariness. The big chair offered grateful relaxation to tired limbs, and, with his enormous head tilted back, narrowed eyes turned upward, and slender fingers precisely tip to tip, he waited.

"One of my officers has disappeared from the flagship—rather, has utterly vanished," said Admiral Hausen-Aubier. He spoke excellent English, but there was a guttural undercurrent of excitement in his tone. "He went to his stateroom at midnight; next morning at seven o'clock he was gone. The guard at his door had been drugged with chloroform, and can tell nothing."

"Guard at the door?" questioned The Thinking Machine. "Why?"

Admiral Hausen-Aubier seemed oddly disturbed by the question. He shot a hasty glance at Baron Von Hartzfeldt.

"Ship discipline," explained the diplomat vaguely.

"Was he under arrest?"

"Oh, no!" This from the admiral.

"Do you sleep with a guard at your door?"

"No."

"Any of the other officers?"

"No."

"Go on, please."

"There isn't much to tell." There was bewilderment, deep concern, grief even, in the bronzed face. "The officer's bed had been occupied, but there was no sign of a struggle. It was as if he had arisen, dressed, and gone out. There was no note, no shred or fragment of a clew—nothing. No one saw him from the moment he entered his stateroom and closed his door—not even the guard. There were half a dozen sentries, watchmen, on deck; neither saw nor heard anything out of the ordinary. He isn't aboard ship; we have searched from keel to signal yard; and he didn't go overside in a ship's boat; they are all accounted for. He is not a particularly strong swimmer, and could not have reached shore in that way."

"You say the guard had been chloroformed," The Thinking Machine went back. "Just what happened to him? How do you know he was chloroformed?"

"By the odor," replied the admiral, answering the last question first. "In order to enter the officer's suite it was necessary—"

"Suite, did you say?"

"Yes; that is, he occupied more than one stateroom—"

"I understand. Go on."

"It was necessary to pass through an antechamber. The guard slept there. He says it must have been after one o'clock when he went to sleep. Next morning he was found unconscious, and the officer was gone." He paused. "There can be no question whatever of the guard's integrity. He has been attached to the—the officer for many years."

With eyes all but closed, The Thinking Machine sat motionless for minute after minute, the while thin, spidery lines of though ruffled the domelike brow. At last:

"The matter hasn't been reported to the police?"

"No." Admiral Hausen-Aubier looked startled.

"Why not?"

"Because," Baron Von Hartzfeldt answered, "when it was brought to my attention in Washington by wire, we decided against that. The affair is extremely delicate. It is inadvisable that the police even should so much as suspect—"

The Thinking Machine nodded.

"How about the secret service?"

"That bureau has been at work on the case from the first," the diplomatist replied; "also half a dozen secret agents attached to the embassy. You must understand, Mr. Van Dusen, that it is absolutely essential that no word of the disappearance—not even a hint of it—be allowed to become public. The result would be a—a disaster. I can't say more."

"Perhaps," suggested The Thinking Machine irrelevantly, "perhaps the officer deserted?"

"I would vouch for his loyalty with my life," declared the admiral, with deep feeling.

"Or perhaps it was suicide?"

Again there was a swift interchange of glances between the admiral and the ambassador. Obviously that was a possibility that had occurred to each of them, and yet one that neither dared admit.

"Impossible!" the diplomat shook his head.

"Nothing is impossible," snapped The Thinking Machine curtly. "Don't say that. It annoys me exceedingly." Fell a short silence. Finally: "Just when did your officer disappear?"

"Last Tuesday—almost a week ago," Admiral Hausen-Aubier told him.

"And nothing—nothing—has been heard of him? Or from him? Or from any one else concerning him?"

"Nothing—not a word," Admiral Hausen-Aubier said. "If we could only hear! If we could only know whether he is living or dead!"

"What's his name?"

"Lieutenant Leopold Von Zinckl."

For the first time, The Thinking Machine lowered his eyes and swept the countenances of the two men before him—both grave, troubled, lined with worry. Under his curious scrutiny, the diplomatist retained his self-possession by sheer force of will; but a vital, consuming nervousness seemed to seize upon the man of the sea.

"I mean," and again the scientist was squinting into the gloom above, "I mean his real name."

Admiral Hausen-Aubier's broad face flushed suddenly as if from a blow, and he started to his feet. Some subtle warning form the ambassador caused him to drop back into his seat.

"That is his real name," he said distinctly; "Lieutenant Leopold Von Zinckl."

"May I ask," The Thinking Machine was speaking very slowly, "if his majesty the emperor has been informed of Lieutenant Von Zinckl's disappearance?"

Perhaps The Thinking Machine anticipated the effect of the question; perhaps he did not. Anyway, he didn't look around when Admiral Hausen-Aubier came to his feet with a mighty Teutonic exclamation, and strode the length of the big room, his face dead white beneath the coat of bronze. Baron Von Hartzfeldt remained seated, apparently fascinated by some strange, newly discovered quality in the scientist.

"We have not informed the emperor of the affair as yet," he said, at last, steadily. "We thought it inadvisable to go so far until every effort had been made to—"

The Thinking Machine interrupted him with an impatient gesture of one slender hand.

"As a matter of fact, the situation is like this, isn't it?" he queried abruptly. "Prince Otto Ludwig, heir apparent to the throne of Germania-Austria, has been abducted from the royal suite of the battleship Friedrich der Grosse, in the harbor of a friendly nation?"

There was an instant's amazed silence. Suddenly Admiral Hausen-Aubier covered his face with his hands, and stood, his great shoulders shaking. Straining nerves had broken at last. Baron Von Hartzfeldt, ripe in diplomatic experience, seemed merely astonished, if one might judge by the face of him.

"How do you know that?" he inquired quietly, after a moment. "Outside of the secret service and my own agents, there are not six persons in the world who are aware—"

"How do I know it?" interrupted The Thinking Machine. "You have just told me. Logic, logic, logic!"

"I have told you?" There was blank bewilderment on the diplomatist's face.

"You and Admiral Hausen-Aubier together," The Thinking Machine declared petulantly.

"But how, man, how?" demanded Baron Von Hartzfeldt. "Of course, you knew from the newspapers that his highness, Crown Prince Otto Ludwig, was visiting America; but—"

"I never read newspapers," snapped The Thinking Machine. "I didn't know he was here any more than I knew the battleship *Friedrich der Grosse* was in the harbor. It's logic, logic—the adding together of the separate units—a simple demonstration of the fact that two and two make four, not sometimes, but *all* the time."

Admiral Hausen-Aubier, having mastered the emotion which had shaken him, resumed his seat, staring curiously into the wizened face before him.

"Still I don't understand," Baron Von Hartzfeldt insisted. "Logic, you say. How?"

"I'll see if I can make it clear." And there was that in the manner of the eminent man of science which was no compliment to their perspicacity. "You tell me an officer has disappeared, that his guard was chloroformed. The officer was not under arrest, and no other officer aboard ship had a guard. I assume, therefore, for the moment that the officer was a man of consequence, else he was mentally irresponsible. An instant later you tell me how to enter the officer's suite—not stateroom, but suite. Ergo, a man of so much consequence that he occupies a suite; a man of so much consequence that you didn't dare report his disappearance to the police; a man of so much consequence that public knowledge of the affair would precipitate disaster. Do you follow the thread?"

Fascinated, the two listeners nodded.

"Very well," The Thinking Machine resumed, in that odd little tone of irritation. "There are only a few persons in the world of so much consequence as all that—that is, of so much consequence aboard a ship of war. Those are members of the royal household. I am of German descent; hence I am well acquainted with the histories of the German countries. I know that Emperor Gustavus has only one son, Otto Ludwig, the crown prince. I know that no reigning king has ever visited America; therefore logic, inexorable, indisputable logic, tells me that Prince Otto Ludwig is the officer who occupied the royal suite aboard your ship."

He paused, and readjusted himself in the great chair. When he spoke again, it was in the tone of one who is thoughtfully checking off and verifying the units of a problem he has solved. His two visitors were staring at him breathlessly.

"Of course, no royal person save a son of the house of Germania-Austria would be occupying the royal suite on a Germania-Austrian battleship," he said slowly. "Proper adjustment of the actual facts leading straight to the crown prince removed instantly as a possibility a vague suggestion that the officer with the guard at his door, while not a prisoner, was mentally irresponsible. I've made myself clear, I hope?"

"It's marvelous!" ejaculated the diplomatist. "If any man can lead us to the end of this mystery, you are that man!"

"Thanks," returned The Thinking Machine dryly.

"You said," Admiral Hausen-Aubier questioned tensely, "that his highness had been abducted?"

"Certainly."

"Why abducted instead of—of—murdered—" He shuddered a little. "Instead of suicide?"

"That man who is clever enough and bold enough to board your ship and chloroform a guard is not fool enough to murder a man and then drag him out over the guard and throw him into the sea," was the reply, "or to drag him out and then murder him. In either event, such an act would have been useless; and as a rule murderers don't do useless things. As for suicide, it would not have been necessary for the prince to chloroform his guard, or even to leave his stateroom. Remains, therefore, only abduction."

"But who abducted him?" the admiral insisted. "Why? How was he taken away from the ship?"

The Thinking Machine shrugged his narrow shoulders.

"I don't know," he said. "Either one of a dozen ways—aeroplane, rowboat, submarine—" He stopped.

"But—but no one heard anything," the admiral pointed out.

"That doesn't signify."

There seemed nothing to cling to, no tangible fact upon which to base even understanding. Aeroplane—submarine— 'twas fantasy, preposterous, unheard of. Hopelessly enough, Admiral Hausen-Aubier turned back to the one vital question:

"At any rate, the prince is alive?"

"I don't know. He was abducted a week ago. You've heard nothing since. He may have been murdered after he was taken away. He may have been. I doubt it."

Admiral Hausen-Aubier arose tragically, with haggard face, a light of desperation in his eyes, his powerful, sun-dyed hands pressed to his temples.

"If he is dead, do you know what it means?" he demanded vehemently. "It means the fall of the royal house of Germania-Austria with the passing of our emperor, who is now nearly eighty; it means the end of our country as a monarchy; it means war, revolution, a—a republic!"

"That wouldn't be so bad," commented The Thinking Machine oddly. "There'll be nothing but republics in a few years; witness France, Portugal, China—"

"You can't realize the acute political situation in my country," Admiral Hausen-Aubier rushed on, heedless of the other's remark. "Already there are dissensions; the emperor holds his kingdom together with a rod of iron, and his people only submit because they expect so much of Prince Otto Ludwig when he ascends the throne.

"He is popular with his subjects—the crown prince, I mean— and they would welcome him as emperor—welcome him, but no one else. It is absolutely necessary that he be found! The future of my country—our country," and he turned to Baron Von Hartzfeldt, "depends upon finding him."

Seemingly some new thought was born in The Thinking Machine's mind. His eyes opened slightly, and he turned upon Baron Von Hartzfeldt inquiringly. Apparently the ambassador understood, for he nodded.

"He is revealing diplomatic secrets," he said, with a slight movement of his shoulders; "but what he says is true."

"In that case—" The Thinking Machine began; and then he lapsed into silence. For minute after minute he sat, heedless of the nervous pacing of Admiral Hausen-Aubier, heedless of the constant interrogation of the ambassador's eyes.

"In that case—" the ambassador prompted.

"Is Crown Prince Otto Ludwig here incognito, or is it generally known that he is in this country?" the scientist questioned suddenly.

"He is here officially," was the response; "that is, publicly. The government of the United States has received him and entertained him, and you know all that that means."

"Then how do you—have you—accounted for his disappearance?"

"Lies!" Admiral Hausen-Aubier broke in bitterly. "He is supposed to be dangerously ill, confined to his stateroom aboard the *Friedrich der Grosse*; and no one except the ship's surgeon is permitted to see him. We have lied even to our emperor! He believes the prince is ill; if he understood that his son, the heir apparent, was missing, dead, perhaps—ach, Gott! Every moment I am expecting sailing orders—orders to return home. I can't go back to my king and tell him that the son he intrusted to my care, the hope and salvation of my country, is—is—I can't even say dead—I could only say that I don't know."

There was something magnificent in the bronzed old sailorman—something at once rugged and tender and fierce in his loyalty. The Thinking Machine studied the grief-stricken face curiously. Unashamed, Admiral Hausen-Aubier permitted the tears to gather in his eyes and roll down his furrowed cheeks.

"I don't care for myself," he explained huskily. "I do care for my country, for my prince. In any event, there remains for me only dishonor and death."

"Suicide?" questioned the scientist coldly.

"What else is there?"

"That," The Thinking Machine murmured acridly, "would improve the situation a lot! If I had committed suicide every time I had a problem to solve I should have been very dead by this time." His manner changed. "We know the prince was abducted; he is probably not dead, but we have no word of him or from him; therefore, there remains only—"

"Only what?" The question came from his two visitors simultaneously.

"Only a question of the most effective way of establishing communication with him."

"If we knew how to communicate with him, we'd go get him instead!" declared Admiral Hausen-Aubier grimly. "There are eight hundred men on the battleship who—"

The Thinking Machine arose, stood staring blankly at the two, much as if he had never seen them before; then walked over to his worktable, and shut off the great electric light.

"It's easy enough to communicate with Prince Otto Ludwig," he said, as he returned to them. "There are half a dozen ways."

"Then why, if it is so easy," demanded the diplomatist, "why hasn't he communicated with his ship?"

"There's always a chance that he doesn't want to, you know," was the enigmatic response. "How many persons know of his disappearance?"

"Only five outside of the secret service and the embassy agents," Admiral Hausen-Aubier answered. "They are Baron Von Hartzfeldt here, the guard, the ship's commander, the ship's surgeon, and myself."

"Too many!" The Thinking Machine shook his head slowly. "However, let's go aboard the *Friedrich der Grosse*. I don't recall that I've ever been on a modern battleship."

Night had fallen as the three men, each eminent in his own profession, boarded a small power boat off Atlantic Avenue, and were hurried away through slashing waters to the giant battleship in the outer harbor. There for an hour or more the little scientist pottered about the magnificent suite which had been occupied by Prince Otto Ludwig. He asked one or two casual questions of the guard; that was all, after which he retired to the admiral's cabin to write a short note.

"If," he remarked, as he addressed an envelope to Hutchinson Hatch, "if the prince is alive we shall hear from him. If he is dead we will not." His eye chanced upon a glaring headline in a newspaper on the desk:

PRINCE OTTO LUDWIG DANGEROUSLY ILL.
HEIR TO THRONE OF GERMANIA-AUSTRIA
CONFINED TO SUITE ABOARD THE BATTLE-
SHIP "FRIEDRICH DER GROSSE."
NO ONE PERMITTED TO SEE HIM.

The Thinking Machine glanced at Admiral Hausen-Aubier.

"Lies!" declared the rugged old sailor. "Every day for a week it has been the same. We are compelled to issue bulletins. Ach, Gott! He must be found!"

"Please have this note sent ashore and delivered immediately," the scientist requested. "Meanwhile, I haven't been in bed for three nights. If you'll give me a berth, I'll get some sleep. Wake me if necessary."

"You expect something to happen, then?"

"Certainly. I expect a wireless, but not for several hours—probably not until to-morrow afternoon."

"A wireless?" There was a flicker of hope in the admiral's eyes. "May—may I ask from whom?"

"From Crown Prince Otto Ludwig," said The Thinking Machine placidly. "I'm going to sleep. Good night."

Three hours later Admiral Hausen-Aubier in person aroused The Thinking Machine from the lethargy of oblivion which followed upon utter physical and mental exhaustion, and thrust a wireless message under his nose. It said simply: *O.K. Hatch.*

The Thinking Machine blinked at it, grunted, then turned over as if to go back to sleep. Struck with some new idea, however, he opened his eyes for an instant.

"Issue a special bulletin to the press," he directed drowsily, "to the effect that Prince Otto Ludwig's condition has taken a sudden turn for the better. He is expected to be up and around again in a few days."

The sentence ended in a light snore.

All that night Admiral Hausen-Aubier, haggard, vigilant, sat beside the wireless operator in his cabinet on the upper deck, waiting, waiting, he knew not for what. Darkness passed, the stars died, and pallid dawn found him there.

At nine o'clock he ordered coffee; at noon more coffee.

At four in the afternoon the thing he had been waiting for came—only three words: *Followed suggestion. Communicate.*

"Very indistinct, sir," the operator reported. "An amateur sending."

The Thinking Machine, wide awake now, and below deck discussing high explosives with a gunner's mate, was summoned. Into the wireless cabinet with him came Baron Von Hartzfeldt. For an instant the three men studied in silence this portentous message from the void.

"Keep in touch with him," The Thinking Machine instructed the operator. "What's his range?"

"Hundred miles, sir."

"Strong or weak?"

"Weak, sir."

"Reduce the range."

"I did, sir, and lost him."

"Increase it."

With the receiver clamped to his ears, the operator thrust his range key forward, and listened.

"I lose him, sir," he reported.

"Very well. Set at one hundred." The scientist turned to Baron Von Hartzfeldt and Admiral Hausen-Aubier. "He is alive, and less than a hundred miles away," he explained hurriedly. Then to the operator: "Send as I dictate:

"*Is—O—L—there?*"

The instrument hissed as the message spanned the abyss of space; in the glass drum above, great crackling electric sparks leaped and roared fitfully, lighting the tense faces of the men in the cabinet. Came dead silence—painful silence—then the operator read the answer aloud:

"Yes."

"Mein Gott ich lobe!" One great exclamation of thanks, and Admiral Hausen-Aubier buried his face in his hands.

To Baron Von Hartzfeldt the whole thing was wizardry pure and simple. The Thinking Machine had summoned the lost out of the void. While a hundred trained men, keen-eyes, indefatigable, wary as ferrets, were searching for the crown prince, along comes this withered, white-faced little man of science, with his monstrous head and his feeble hands, and works a miracle under his very eyes! He listened, fascinated, as The Thinking Machine continued:

"Must—prove—identity—Hausen—Aubier—here—ask—O—L— give—word—or phrase—identify—him."

Suddenly The Thinking Machine whirled about to face the admiral. The answer should prove once for all whether the prince was alive or dead. Minutes passed. Finally—

"It's coming, sir, in German," the operator explained:

"Neujarstag—eine—cigarre."

"New Year's Day—a cigar!" Admiral Hausen-Aubier translated, in obvious bewilderment. Swiftly his face cleared. "I understand. He refers to an incident that he and I alone know. When a lad of twelve he tried to smoke a cigar, and it made him deathly ill. I saved him from—"

"Send," interrupted The Thinking Machine:

"Satisfied—give—terms."

And the operator read:

"Five—million—dollars!"

"Five million dollars!" exclaimed the admiral and the diplomatist, in a breath. "Does he mean ransom?" Baron Von Hartzfeldt asked, aghast. "Five million dollars!"

"Five million dollars, yes," the scientist replied irritably. "We're not dealing with children. We're dealing with shrewd, daring, intelligent men who have played a big game for a big stake; and if you love your country and your king you'd better thank God it's only money they want. Suppose they had demanded a constitution, or even the abdication of your emperor? That might have meant revolution, war—anything." He stared at them an instant, then swung around to the operator. "Send," he commanded:

"We—accept—terms—"

"Why, man, you are mad!" interposed the diplomatist sharply. "It's preposterous!"

But The Thinking Machine said again evenly:

"We—accept—terms—specify—by—mail—place—time—manner—of—settlement."

The crashing of the mighty current in the glass drum ceased as the message was finished, and with strained attention the three men waited. Again a tense pause. At last the operator read:

"Also—assurance—no—prosecution."

And The Thinking Machine dictated: *"Accept."*

"Wait a minute!" commanded Admiral Hausen-Aubier hotly. "Do you mean we are promising immunity to the men who abducted—"

"Certainly," replied the scientist. "They're not fools. If we don't promise it, all they have to do is break off communication and wait until such time as you will promise it." He shrugged his shoulders. "Or else stick a knife into your prince, and end the affair. Besides, prosecution means publicity."

With clenched hands, the admiral turned away; no answer seemed possible. Heedless of the things about him, Baron Von Hartzfeldt sat dumbly meditating upon the staggering ransom. It would take days to raise so vast a sum, if he could do it at all; and his private resources, together with those of Admiral Hausen-Aubier, would be drained to the last dollar. Even then it might be necessary to call upon the royal treasury. That would be a confession; out of it would come only dishonor and—death.

The Thinking Machine dictated:

"Accept—we—pledge—Hausen—Aubier's—word—of honor."

And the answer came:

"Satisfied—mailing—details—to-night—will—communicate—to-morrow—noon."

The attenuated thread which had linked them with the unknown was broken. Somewhere off through space they had talked with a man whom human ingenuity had failed to find— 'twas another of the many miracles of modern science.

The morrow brought a typewritten letter incapable of misconstruction. It was the usual thing—an open field, some thirty miles out of the city, a lone tree in the center of the field, a suit case containing the money to be left there. The letter concluded with a paragraph after this fashion:

YOUR PRINCE'S LIFE DEPENDS UPON RIGID ADHERENCE TO THESE INSTRUCTIONS. IF THERE IS ANY ATTEMPT TO WATCH, OR TO IDENTIFY US, OR MOLEST US, A PISTOL SHOT WILL END THE AFFAIR; IF THE BAG IS THERE, AND THE MONEY IS IN THE BAG, HE WILL BE ABOARD SHIP WITHIN FIVE HOURS. REMEMBER, WE HOLD YOUR PLEDGE!

"Crude," commented The Thinking Machine. "I was led to expect better things of them."

"But the money, man, the money?" exclaimed Baron Von Hartzfeldt. "It will be absolutely impossible to get it unless—unless we call upon the royal treasury."

His face was haggard, his eyes inflamed by lack of sleep, and deep furrows lined his usually placid brow. He leaned forward, and stared tensely into the pallid, wizened face of the scientist, who sat with head tilted back, his gaze turned steadily upward, his slender fingers precisely tip to tip.

"Five million dollars in gold," The Thinking Machine observed ambiguously, "would weigh tons. It would take five hundred ten-thousand-dollar notes to make five million dollars, and I doubt if there are that many in existence. It would take five thousand thousand-dollar notes. Absurd! There will have to be two, perhaps three, of the bags."

"But don't you understand," Baron Von Hartzfeldt burst out violently, "that it's impossible to raise that sum? That there will be none of the bags? That some other scheme—"

"Oh, yes, there will be three of the bags," The Thinking Machine asserted mildly. "But, of course, there will be no money in them!"

Admiral Hasuen-Aubier and the diplomatist digested the statement in silence.

"But you have pledged my word of honor—" the old sailorman objected.

"Not to prosecute," the scientist pointed out.

"Absurd!" The ambassador came to his feet. "You have said we are not dealing with children. Why put the empty bags there? If they find they are empty, the prince's life will pay forfeit; if we attempt to surround them and capture them, the result will be the same; and, besides, we will have broken our pledge."

"I've never seen any one so fussy about their pledges as you gentlemen are," observed The Thinking Machine acridly. "Don't worry. I shall not break a pledge; I shall not attempt to surround them and capture them; I shall not, nor shall any one representing me, or any of us, for that matter, be within miles of that particular field after the bags are placed. They shall reach the field unmolested and unwatched."

"You are talking in riddles," declared the diplomatist impatiently. "What do you mean?"

"I mean merely that the men who go to get the bags of money will wait right there until I come, even if it should happen to take two weeks," was the enigmatic response. "Also, I'll say they'll be glad to see me when I get there, and glad to restore Prince Otto Ludwig to his ship without one penny being paid. There will be no prosecution."

"But—but I don't understand," stammered the ambassador.

"I don't expect you to," said The Thinking Machine ungraciously. "Nor do I expect you to understand this."

Impatiently he spread a newspaper before the two men, and indicated an advertisement in black-faced type. It was on the first page, directly beneath a bulletin announcing a sudden change for the better in Prince Otto Ludwig's condition. The admiral read it aloud blankly:

"WIRELESS IS ONLY MEANS COMMUNICATION CAN NOT BE TRACED. USE IT. SAFE FOR ALL. COMMUNICATE WITH SHIP IMMEDIATELY. WOULD ADVISE YOU ERECT PRIVATE STATION."

That was all of it. It was addressed to no one, and signed by no one; if it had any meaning at all, it was merely as a curious method of advertising wireless telegraphy. Inquiringly at last the baron and the admiral raised their eyes to those of The Thinking Machine.

"The abductors of Prince Otto Ludwig had not communicated with the ship," he explained tersely, "because they could devise no way they considered absolutely safe. They knew the secret service would be at work. They didn't dare to telegraph in the usual way, nor send a messenger, nor even a letter. Our secret service is an able organization; they understood it was not to be trifled with. All these things considered, I didn't believe the abductors could hit upon a plan of communication which they considered safe. I inserted that advertisement in all the newspapers. It was a suggestion. They understood, and followed it. You will remember their first communication."

Baron Von Hartzfeldt came to his feet suddenly, then sat down again. The miracle hadn't been a miracle, after all. It was merely common sense.

"Jeder verreckte kennte davon denken!" exclaimed the admiral bluntly.

"Quite right," assented The Thinking Machine. "Any fool could have thought of that—but no other fool did!"

Promptly at noon the wireless operator plucked this from the void:

"Is—letter—satisfactory?"

And the scientist dictated an answer:

"Yes—except—we—require—another—day—to—raise—money."

"Granted—"

"Impossible—put—all—money—one—bag—will—use—three."

"Satisfactory—remember—our—warning."

"You—have—our—pledge."

As the last word of the message went hurtling off into space, The Thinking Machine scrambled down the sea ladder and was rowed ashore. From his own home, half an hour later, he called Hutchinson Hatch on the telephone.

"I want," he said, "three large suit cases, one pair of extra-heavy rubber gloves, ten miles of electric wire well insulated, three Edison transformers, one fast automobile, permission to tap the Abington trolley wire, and two dozen ham sandwiches."

Hatch laughed. He was accustomed to the eccentricities of this little man of science.

"You shall have them," he promised.

"Bring everything to my house at midnight."

"Right!"

Looking back upon it later, Hatch decided he had never worked so hard in his life as he did that night; in addition to which he had the satisfaction of not knowing just what he was doing. There were telephone poles to be climbed, and shallow trenches to be dug and immediately filled in so no trace of their existence remained, and miles of electric wire to be hauled through thickly weeded fields. Dawn was breaking when everything seemed to be done.

"This," remarked The Thinking Machine, "is where the ham sandwiches are useful."

They breakfasted upon them, after which The Thinking Machine went away, leaving Hatch to watch the small dial of some sort of an indicator attached to a wire. At noon the scientist returned, and, without a word, took the reporter's place at the dial. At thirty-three minutes past four the hand of the indicator suddenly shot around to one side, and the scientist arose.

"We have caught a fish," he said. "Come on!"

They were in the automobile, speeding along the highway, before Hatch spoke.

"What sort of fish?" he asked curiously.

"I don't know," was the reply. "A person, or persons, have picked up one or more of those suit cases to the bottom of which our electric wire is connected. He is unable to let go—he, or they, as the case may be. He will be unconscious when we reach him."

"Dead, you mean," said Hatch grimly. "The current from that trolley wire—"

"Unconscious," The Thinking Machine corrected. "The current is reduced. There is a transformer in each of the suit cases. The wiring extends up through the handles where the insulation is stripped off."

Three, four, nearly five, miles they went like the wind; then the motor car stopped with a jerk, and Hatch, taking advantage of his longer legs, galloped off through the open field toward the lone tree in the center. The thing he saw caused him to stop suddenly and raise his hands in horror. Upon the ground in front of him was the convulsed figure of a young man, foreign-looking, distinguished even. His distorted face, livid now, was turned upward, and his hands were gripped to the suit case by the powerful electric current.

"Who is it?" queried the scientist.

"Crown Prince Otto Ludwig, of Germania-Austria!"

"What?" The question came violently, a single burst of amazement. And again: "What?" There was an expression on The Thinking Machine's face the like of which Hatch had never seen there before. "It's a possibility I had never considered. So he wanted the five million—" Suddenly his whole manner changed. "Let's get him to the motor."

With rubber-gloved hands, he cut the wire which held the crown prince prisoner, and the unconscious man fell back limply, as if dead. Five minutes later they had lifted him into the tonneau, and The Thinking Machine bent over him anxiously, with his hand on his wrist.

"Where to?" asked Hatch.

"Anywhere, and fast!" was the reply. "I must think."

Oblivious of the swaying and clatter of the huge car, The Thinking Machine sat silent for minute after minute as it sped on over the smooth road. Finally he seemed satisfied. He leaned forward, and touched Hatch on the shoulder.

"It's all right," he said. "We'll go aboard ship now."

Late that night the crown prince, himself again, but with badly burned hands, explained. He had been stupefied by chloroform, kidnaped, and lowered over the battleship rail in utter darkness. His impression was that he had been taken away in a small boat which had muffled oars. When he recovered, he found himself a prisoner in a deserted country house, with two men on guard. He didn't know the name of either.

Calmly enough, the three of them discussed the affair in all its aspects. They could devise no safe means of communicating with the ship until he suggested the wireless. He even aided in the erection of a station between two tall trees on a remote hill somewhere. One of his guards, meanwhile, had to master the code. He had become fairly proficient when they saw the advertisement in the newspapers.

"But how is it you went to get the money?" the scientist questioned curiously.

"The men feared treachery," was the explanation. "They were willing to take my word of honor that I would get it and return with it, after which I was to be free. A prince of the royal house of Germania-Austria may not break his word of honor."

Tiny corrugations in the domelike brow of the scientist caused Hatch to stare at him expectantly; even as he looked they passed.

"Mr. Hatch," he said abruptly, "I have heard you refer to certain newspaper stories as 'peaches' and 'corkers' and what not. How would you class this?"

"This," said the reporter enthusiastically, "this is a bird!"

"It has only one defect," remarked The Thinking Machine. "It cannot be printed."

One eminent scientist who had achieved the seemingly impossible, and one disgusted newspaper reporter were rowed ashore at midnight.

"What do you think of it all, anyhow?" demanded Hatch suddenly.

"I have no opinion to express," declared The Thinking Machine crabbedly. "The prince has come to his own again; that is sufficient."

Some weeks later Professor Augustus S. F. X. Van Dusen was decorated with the Order of the Iron Eagle by Emperor Gustavus, of Germania-Austria. Reflectively he twisted the elaborate jeweled bauble in his slender fingers; then returned to his worktable under the great electric light. For a minute or more tiny corrugations appeared in his forehead; finally they passed as that strange mind of his became absorbed in the thing he was doing.

A Piece of String

It was just midnight. Somewhere near the center of a cloud of tobacco smoke, which hovered over one corner of the long editorial room, Hutchinson Hatch, reporter, was writing. The rapid click-click of his type writer went on and on, broken only when he laid aside one sheet to put in another. The finished pages were seized upon one at a time by an office boy and rushed off to the city editor. That astute person glanced at them for information and sent them on to the copy desk, whence they were shot down into that noisy, chaotic wilderness, the composing room.

The story was what the phlegmatic head of the copy desk, speaking in the vernacular, would have called a "beaut." It was about the kidnapping that afternoon of Walter Francis, the four-year-old son of a wealthy young broker, Stanley Francis. An alternative to the abduction had been proposed in the form of a gift to certain persons, identity unknown, of fifty thousand dollars. Francis, not unnaturally, objected to the bestowal of so vast a sum upon anyone. So he told the police, and while they were making up their minds the child was stolen. It happened in the usual way—closed carriage, and all that sort of thing.

Hatch was telling the story graphically, as he could tell a story when there was one to be told. He glanced at the clock, jerked out another sheet of copy, and the office boy scuttled away with it.

"How much more?" called the city editor.

"Just a paragraph," Hatch answered.

His type writer clicked on merrily for a couple of minutes and then stopped. The last sheet of copy was taken away, and he rose and stretched his legs.

"Some guy wants yer at the 'phone," an office boy told him.

"Who is it?" asked Hatch.

59

"Search me," replied the boy. "Talks like he'd been eatin' pickles."

Hatch went into the booth indicated. The man at the other end was Professor Augustus S. F. X. Van Dusen. The reporter instantly recognized the crabbed, perpetually irritated voice of the noted scientist, The Thinking Machine.

"That you, Mr. Hatch?" came over the wire.

"Yes."

"Can you do something for me immediately?" he queried. "It is very important."

"Certainly."

"Now listen closely," directed The Thinking Machine. "Take a car from Park-sq., the one that goes toward Worcester through Brookline. About two miles beyond Brookline is Randall's Crossing. Get off there and go to your right until you come to a small white house. In front of this house, a little to the left and across an open field, is a large tree. It stands just in the edge of a dense wood. It might be better to approach it through the wood, so as not to attract attention. Do you follow me?"

"Yes," Hatch replied. His imagination was leading him a chase.

"Go to this tree now, immediately, to-night," continued The Thinking Machine. "You will find a small hole in it near the level of your eye. Feel in that hole, and see what is there—no matter what it is—then return to Brookline and telephone me. It is of the greatest importance."

The reporter was thoughtful for a moment; it sounded like a page from a Dumas romance.

"What's it all about?" he asked curiously.

"Will you go?" came the counter question.

"Yes, certainly."

"Good-by."

Hatch heard a click as the receiver was hung up at the other end. He shrugged his shoulders, said "Good-night" to the city editor, and went out. An hour later he was at Randall's Crossing. The night was dark—so dark that the road was barely visible. The car whirled on, and as its lights were swallowed up Hatch set out to find the white house. He came upon it at last, and, turning, faced

across an open field toward the wood. Far away over there outlined vaguely against the distant glow of the city, was a tall tree.

Having fixed its location, the reporter moved along for a hundred yards or more to where the wood ran down to the road. Here
he climbed a fence and stumbled on through the dark, doing sun-
dry injuries to his shins. After a disagreeable ten minutes he
reached the tree.

With a small electric flash light he found the hole. It was only a
little larger than his hand, a place where decay had eaten its way
into the tree trunk. For just a moment he hesitated about putting
his hand into it—he didn't know what might be there. Then, with a
grim smile, he obeyed orders.

He felt nothing save crumblings of decayed wood, and finally
dragged out a handful, only to spill it on the ground. That couldn't
be what was meant. For the second time he thrust in his hand, and
after a deal of grabbing about produced—a piece of string. It was
just a plain, ordinary, common piece of string—white string. He
stared at it and smiled.

"I wonder what Van Dusen will make of that?" he asked himself.

Again his hand was thrust into the hole. But that was all—the
piece of string. Then came another thought, and with that due regard for detail which made him a good reporter he went looking
around the big tree for a possible second opening of some sort. He
found none.

About three quarters of an hour later he stepped into an all-
night drug store in Brookline and 'phoned to The Thinking Machine. There was an instant response to his ring.

"Well, well, what did you find?" came the query.

"Nothing to interest you, I imagine," replied the reporter
grimly. "Just a piece of string."

"Good, good!" exclaimed The Thinking Machine. "What does it
look like?"

"Well," replied the newspaper man judicially, "it's just a piece
of white string—cotton, I imagine—about six inches long."

"Any knots in it?"

"Wait till I see."

He was reaching into his pocket to take it out, when the startled voice of The Thinking Machine came over the line.

"Didn't you leave it there?" it demanded.

"No; I have it in my pocket."

"Dear me!" exclaimed the scientist irritably. "That's bad. Well, has it any knots in it?" he asked with marked resignation.

Hatch felt that he had committed the unpardonable sin. "Yes," he replied after an examination. "It has two knots in it—just plain knots—about two inches apart."

"Single or double knots?"

"Single knots."

"Excellent! Now, Mr. Hatch, listen. Untie one of those knots—it doesn't matter which one—and carefully smooth out the string. Then take it and put it back where you found it. 'Phone me as soon after that as you can."

"Now, to-night?"

"Now, immediately."

"But—but—" began the astonished reporter.

"It is a matter of the utmost consequence," the irritated voice assured him. "You should not have taken the string. I told you merely to see what was there. But as you have brought it away you must put it back as soon as possible. Believe me, it is of the highest importance. And don't forget to 'phone me."

The sharp, commanding tone stirred the reporter to new action and interest. A car was just going past the door, outward bound. He raced for it and got aboard. Once settled, he untied one of the knots, straightened out the string, and fell to wondering what sort of fool's errand he was on.

"Randall's Crossing!" called the conductor at last.

Hatch left the car and retraced his tortuous way along the road and through the wood to the tall tree, found the hole, and had just thrust in his hand to replace the string when he heard a woman's voice directly behind him, almost in his ear. It was a calm, placid, convincing sort of voice. It said: "Hands up!"

Hatch was a rational human being with ambitions and hopes for the future; therefore his hands went up without hesitation. "I knew something would happen," he told himself.

He turned to see the woman. In the darkness he could only dimly trace a tall, slender figure. Steadily poised just a couple of dozen inches from his nose was a revolver. He could see that without any difficulty. It glinted a little, even in the gloom, and made itself conspicuous.

"Well," asked the reporter at last, as he stood reaching upward, "it's your move."

"Who are you?" asked the woman. Her voice was steady and rather pleasant.

The reporter considered the question in the light of all he didn't know. He felt it wouldn't be a sensible thing to say just who he was.

Somewhere at the end of this thing The Thinking Machine was working on a problem; he was presumably helping in a modest, unobtrusive sort of way; therefore he would be cautious.

"My name is Williams," he said promptly. "Jim Williams," he added circumstantially.

"What are you doing here?"

Another subject for thought. That was a question he couldn't answer; he didn't know what he was doing there; he was wondering himself. He could only hazard a guess, and he did that with trepidation.

"I came from him," he said with deep meaning.

"Who?" demanded the woman suspiciously.

"It would be useless to name him," replied the reporter.

"Yes, yes, of course," the woman mused. "I understand."

There was a little pause. Hatch was still watching the revolver. He had a lively interest in it. It had not moved a hair's breath since he first looked at it; hanging up there in the night it fairly stared him out of countenance.

"And the string?" asked the woman at last.

Now the reporter felt that he was in the mire. The woman herself relieved this new embarrassment.

"Is it in the tree?" she went on.

"Yes."

"How many knots are in it?"

"One."

"One?" she repeated eagerly. "Put your hand in there and hand me the string. No tricks, now!"

Hatch complied with a certain deprecatory manner which he intended should convey to her the impression that there would be no tricks. As she took the string her fingers brushed against his. They were smooth and delicate. He knew that even in the dark.

"And what did he say?" she went on.

Having gone this far without falling into anything, the reporter was willing to plunge—felt that he had to, as a matter of fact.

"He said yes," he murmured without shifting his eyes from the revolver.

"Yes?" the woman repeated again eagerly. "Are you sure?"

"Yes," said the reporter again. The thought flashed through his mind that he was tangling up somebody's affairs sadly—he didn't know whose. Anyhow, it was a matter of no consequence to him, as long as that revolver stared at him that way.

"Where is it?" asked the woman.

Then the earth slipped out from under him. "I don't know," he replied weakly.

"Didn't he give it to you?"

"Oh, no. He—he wouldn't trust me with it."

"How can I get it, then?"

"Oh, he'll fix it all right," Hatch assured her soothingly. "I think he said something about to-morrow night."

"Where?"

"Here."

"Thank God!" the woman gasped suddenly. Her tone betrayed deep emotion; but it wasn't so deep that she lowered the revolver.

There was a long pause. Hatch was figuring possibilities. How to get possession of the revolver seemed the imminent problem. His hands were still in the air, and there was nothing to indicate that they were not to remain there indefinitely. The woman finally broke the silence.

"Are you armed?"

"Oh, no."

"Truthfully?"

"Truthfully."

"You may lower your hands," she said, as if satisfied; "then go on ahead of me straight across the field to the road. Turn to your left there. Don't look back under any circumstances. I shall be behind you with this revolver pointing at your head. If you attempt to escape or make any outcry I shall shoot. Do you believe me?"

The reporter considered it for a moment. "I'm firmly convinced of it," he said at last.

They stumbled on to the road, and there Hatch turned as directed. Walking along in the shadows with the tread of small feet behind him he first contemplated a dash for liberty; but that would mean giving up the adventure, whatever it was. He had no fear for his personal safety as long as he obeyed orders, and he intended to do that implicitly. And besides, The Thinking Machine had his slender finger in the pie somewhere. Hatch knew that, and knowing it was a source of deep gratification.

Just now he was taking things at face value, hoping that with their arrival at whatever place they were bound for he would be further enlightened. Once he thought he heard the woman sobbing, and started to look back. Then he remembered her warning, and thought better of it. Had he looked back he would have seen her stumbling along, weeping, with the revolver dangling limply at her side.

At last, a mile or more farther on, they began to arrive somewhere. A house sat back some distance from the road.

"Go in there!" commanded his captor.

He turned in at the gate, and five minutes later stood in a comfortably furnished room on the ground floor of a small house. A dim light was burning. The woman turned it up. Then almost defiantly she threw aside her veil and hat and stood before him. Hatch gasped. She was pretty—bewilderingly pretty—and young and graceful and all that a young woman should be. Her cheeks were flushed.

"You know me, I suppose?" she exclaimed.

"Oh yes, certainly," Hatch assured her.

And saying that, he knew he had never seen her before.

"I suppose you thought it perfectly horrid of me to keep you with your hands up like that all the time; but I was dreadfully frightened," the woman went on, and she smiled a little uncertainly. "But there wasn't anything else to do."

"It was the only thing," Hatch agreed.

"Now I'm going to ask you to write and tell him just what happened," she resumed. "And tell him, too, that the other matter must be arranged immediately. I'll see that your letter is delivered. Sit here!"

She picked up the revolver from the table beside her and placed a chair in position. Hatch walked to the table and sat down. Pen and ink lay before him. He knew now he was trapped. He couldn't write a letter to that vague "him" of whom he had talked so glibly, about that still more vague "it"—whatever that might be. He sat dumbly staring at the paper.

"Well?" she demanded suspiciously.

"I—I can't write it," he confessed suddenly.

She stared at him coldly for a moment as if she had suspected just that, and he in turn stared at the revolver with a new and vital interest. He felt the tension, but saw no way to relieve it.

"You are an imposter!" she blurted out at last. "A detective?"

Hatch didn't deny it. She backed away toward a bell call near the door, watching him closely, and rang vigorously several times. After a little pause the door opened, and two men, evidently servants, entered.

"Take this gentleman to the rear room up stairs," she commanded without giving them a glance, "and lock him up. Keep him under close guard. If he attempts to escape, stop him! That's all."

Here was another page from a Dumas romance. The reporter started to explain; but there was a merciless gleam, danger even, in the woman's eyes, and he submitted to orders. So, he was led up stairs a captive, and one of the men took a place on guard inside the room.

The dawn was creeping on when Hatch fell asleep. It was about ten o'clock when he awoke, and the sun was high. His guard, wide eyed and alert, still sat beside the door. For several minutes the reporter lay still, seeking vainly some sort of explanation of what was happening. Then, cheerfully:

"Good-morning."

The guard merely glared at him.

"May I inquire your name?" the reporter asked.

There was no answer.

"Or the lady's name?"

No answer.

"Or why I am where I am?"

Still no answer.

"What would you do," Hatch went on casually, "if I should try to get out of here?"

The guard handled his revolver carelessly. The reporter was satisfied. "He is not deaf, that's certain," he told himself.

He spent the remainder of the morning yawning and wondering what The Thinking Machine was about; also he had a few casual reflections as to the mental state of his city editor at his failure to appear and follow up the kidnapping story. He finally dismissed all these ideas with a shrug of his shoulders, and sat down to wait for whatever was coming.

It was in the early afternoon that he heard laughter in the next room. First there was a woman's voice, then the shrill cackle of a child. Finally he distinguished some words.

"You ticky!" exclaimed the child, and again there was the laugh.

The reporter understood "you ticky," coupled with the subsequent peal, to be a sort of abbreviated English for "you tickle." After awhile the merriment died away and he heard the child's insistent demand for something else.

"You be hossie."

"No, no," the woman expostulated.

"Yes, you be hossie."

"No, let Morris be hossie."

"No, no. You be hossie."

That was all. Evidently someone was "hossie," because there was a sound of romping; but finally even that died away. Hatch yawned away another hour or so under the constant eye of his guard, and then began to grow restless. He turned on the guard savagely.

"Isn't anything ever going to happen?" he demanded.

The guard didn't say.

"You'll never convict yourself on your own statement," Hatch burst out again in disgust.

He stretched out on a couch, bored by the sameness which had characterized the last few hours of his adventure. His attention was attracted by some movement at the door, and he looked up. His guard heard, too, and with revolver in hand went to the door, carefully unlocking it. After a few hurriedly whispered words he left the room, and Hatch was meditating an instant rush for a window, when the woman entered. She had the revolver now. She was deathly white and gripped the weapon menacingly. She did not lock the door—only closed it—but with her own person and the attention compelling revolver she blocked the way.

"What is it now?" asked Hatch wearily.

"You must not speak or call, or make the slightest sound," she whispered tensely. "If you do, I'll kill you. Do you understand?"

Hatch confessed by a nod that he understood. He also imagined that he understood this sudden change in guard, and the warning. It was because someone was about to enter or had entered the house. His conjecture was partially confirmed instantly by a distant rapping on a door.

"Not a sound, now!" whispered the woman.

From somewhere below he heard the sound of steps as one of the servants answered the knock. After a short wait he heard two voices mumbling. Suddenly one was raised clearly.

"Why, Worcester can't be that far," it protested irritably.

Hatch knew. It was The Thinking Machine. The woman noted a change in his manner and drew back the hammer of the revolver. The reporter saw the idea. He didn't dare call. That would be suicide. Perhaps he could attract attention, though; drop a key, for instance. The sound might reach The Thinking Machine and be interpreted aright. One hand was in a pocket, and slowly he was drawing out a key. He would risk it. Maybe—

Then came a new sound. It was the patter of small feet. The guarded door was pushed open and a tousle-headed child, a boy, ran in.

"Mama, mama!" he called loudly. He ran to the woman and clutched at her skirts.

"Oh, my baby! what have you done?" she asked piteously. "We are lost, lost!"

"Me 'faid," the child went on.

With the door—his avenue of possible escape—open, Hatch did not drop the key. Instead, he gazed at the woman, then down at the child. From below he again heard The Thinking Machine.

"How far is the car track, then?"

The servant answered something. There was a sound of steps, and the front door closed. Hatch knew that The Thinking Machine had come and gone; yet he was strangely calm about it, quite himself, despite the fact that a nervous finger still lay on the trigger of the pistol.

From his refuge behind his mother's skirts the boy peered around at Hatch shyly. The reporter gazed, gazed, all eyes, and then was convinced. The boy was Walter Francis, the kidnapped boy whose pictures were being published in every newspaper of a dozen cities. Here was a story—the story—the superlative story.

"Mrs. Francis, if you wouldn't mind letting down that hammer—" he suggested modestly. "I assure you I contemplate no harm, and you—you are very nervous."

"You know me, then?" she asked.

"Only because the child there, Walter, called you mama."

Mrs. Francis lowered the revolver hammer so recklessly that Hatch involuntarily dodged. And then came a scene, a scene with tears in it, and all those things which stir men, even reporters. Finally the woman dropped the revolver on the floor and swept the boy up in her arms with a gesture of infinite tenderness. He cuddled there, content. At that moment Hatch could have walked out the door, but instead he sat down. He was just beginning to get interested.

"They sha'n't take you!" sobbed the mother.

"There is no immediate danger," the reporter assured her. "The man who came here for that purpose has gone. Meanwhile, if you will tell me the facts, perhaps—perhaps I may be able to be of some assistance."

Mrs. Francis looked at him, startled. "Help me?"

"If you will explain, perhaps I can do something," said Hatch again.

Somewhere back in a remote recess of his brain he was remembering. And as it became clearer he was surprised that he had not remembered sooner. It was a story of marital infelicity, and its principals were Stanley Francis and his wife—this bewilderingly pretty young woman before him. It had been only eight or nine months back.

Technically she had deserted Stanley Francis. There had been some violent scene and she left their home and little son. Soon afterward she went to Europe. It had been rumored that divorce proceedings would follow, or at least a legal separation, but nothing had ever come of the rumors. All this Mrs. Francis told to Hatch in little incoherent bursts, punctuated with sobs and tears.

"He struck me, he struck me!" she declared with a flush of anger and shame, "and I went then on impulse. I was desperate. Later, even before I went to Europe, I knew the legal status of the affair; but the thought of my boy lingered, and I resolved to come back and get him—abduct him, if necessary. I did that, and I will keep him if I have to kill the one who opposes me."

Hatch saw the mother instinct here, that tigerish ferocity of love which stops at nothing.

"I conceived the plan of demanding fifty thousand dollars of my husband under threat of abduction," Mrs. Francis went on. "My purpose was to make it appear that the plot was that of professional—what would you call it?—kidnappers. But I did not send the letter demanding this until I had perfected all my plans and knew I could get the boy. I wanted my husband to think it was the work of others, at least until we were safe in Europe, because even then I imagined there would be a long legal fight.

"After I stole the boy and he recognized me, I wanted him as my own, absolutely safe from legal action by his father. Then I wrote to Mr. Francis, telling him I had Walter, and asking that in pity to me he legally give me the boy by a document of some sort. In that letter I told how he might signify his willingness to do this; but of course I would not give my address. I placed a string, the one you saw, in that tree after having tied two knots in it. It was a silly, romantic means of communication he and I used years ago in my girlhood when we both lived near here. If he agreed that I should have the child, he was to come or send some one last night and untie one of the two knots."

Then, to Hatch, the intricacies passed away. He understood clearly. Instead of going to the police with the second letter from his wife, Francis had gone to The Thinking Machine. The Thinking Machine sent the reporter to untie the knot, which was an answer of "Yes" to Mrs. Francis's request for the child. Then she would have written giving her address, and there would have been a clue to the child's whereabouts. It was all perfectly clear now.

"Did you specifically mention a string in your letter?" he asked.

"No. I merely stated that I would expect his answer in that place, and would leave something there by which he could signify 'Yes' or 'No,' as he did years ago. The string was one of the odd little ideas of my girlhood. Two knots meant 'No'; one knot meant 'Yes'; and if the string was found by anyone else it meant nothing."

This, then, was why The Thinking Machine did not tell him at first that he would find a string and instruct him to untie one of the knots in it. The scientist had seen that it might have been one of the other tokens of the old romantic days.

"When I met you there," Mrs. Francis resumed. "I believed you were an imposter—I don't know why, I just believed it—yet your answers were in a way correct. For fear you were not what you seemed—that you were a detective—I brought you here to keep you until I got the child's release. You know the rest."

The reporter picked up the revolver and whirled it in his fingers. The action, apparently, did not disturb Mrs. Francis.

"Why did you remain here so long after you got the child?" asked Hatch.

"I believed it was safer than in a city," she answered frankly. "The steamer on which I planned to sail for Europe with my boy leaves to-morrow. I had intended going to New York to-night to catch it; but now—"

The reporter glanced down at the child. He had fallen asleep in his mother's arms. His tiny hand clung to her. The picture was a pretty one. Hatch made up his mind.

"Well, you'd better pack up," he said. "I'll go with you to New York and do all I can."

It was on the New York-bound train several hours later that Hatch turned to Mrs. Francis with an odd smile.

"Why didn't you load that revolver?" he asked.

"Because I was horribly afraid some one would get hurt with it," she replied laughingly.

She was gay with that gentle happiness of possession which blesses woman for the agonies of motherhood, and glanced from time to time at the berth across the aisle where her baby was asleep. Looking upon it all, Hatch was content. He didn't know his exact position in law; but that didn't matter, after all.

Hutchinson Hatch's exclusive story of the escape to Europe of Mrs. Francis and her boy was remarkably complete; but all the facts were not in it. It was a week or so later that he detailed them to The Thinking Machine.

"I knew it," said the scientist at the end. "Francis came to me, and I interested myself in the case, practically knowing every fact from his statement. When you heard me speak in the house where you were a prisoner I was there merely to convince myself that the mother did have the baby. I heard it call her and went away satisfied. I knew you were there, too, because you had failed to 'phone me the second time as I expected, and I knew intuitively what you would do when you got the real facts about Mrs. Francis and her baby. I went away so that the field might be clear for you to act. Francis himself is a detestable puppy. I told him so."

And that was all that was ever said about it.

The Mystery of the Fatal Cipher

For the third time Professor Augustus S. F. X. Van Dusen—so-called The Thinking Machine—read the letter. It was spread out in front of him on the table, and his blue eyes were narrowed to mere slits as he studied it through his heavy eyeglasses. The young woman who had placed the letter in his hands, Miss Elizabeth Devan, sat waiting patiently on the sofa in the little reception room of The Thinking Machine's house. Her blue eyes were opened wide and she stared as if fascinated at this man who had become so potent a factor in the solution of intangible mysteries.

Here is the letter:

To those Concerned:

Tired of it all I seek the end, and am content. Ambition now is dead; the grave yawns greedily at my feet, and with the labor of my own hands lost I greet death of my own will, by my own act.

To my son I leave all, and you who maligned me, you who discouraged me, you may read this and know I punish you thus. It's for him, my son, to forgive.

I dared in life and dare dead your everlasting anger, not alone that you didn't speak but that you cherished secret, and my ears are locked forever against you. My vault is my resting place.

On the brightest and dearest page of life I wrote (7) my love for him. Family ties, binding as the Bible itself, bade me give all to my son.

Good-bye. I die.

Pomeroy Stockton

"Under just what circumstances did this letter come into your possession, Miss Devan?" The Thinking Machine asked. "Tell me the full story; omit nothing."

The scientist sank back into his chair with his enormous yellow head pillowed comfortably against the cushion and his long, steady fingers pressed tip to tip. He didn't even look at his pretty visitor. She had come to ask for information; he was willing to give it, because it offered another of those abstract problems which he always found interesting. In his own field—the sciences—his fame was worldwide. This concentration of a brain which had achieved so much on more material things was perhaps a sort of relaxation.

Miss Devan had a soft, soothing voice, and as she talked it was broken at times by what seemed to be a sob. Her face was flushed a little, and she emphasized her points by a quick clasping and unclasping of her daintily gloved hands.

"My father, or rather my adopted father, Pomeroy Stockton, was an inventor," she began. "We lived in a great, old-fashioned house in Dorchester. We have lived there since I was a child. When I was only five or six years old, I was left an orphan and was adopted by Mr. Stockton, then a man of forty years. I am now twenty-three. I was raised and cared for by Mr. Stockton, who always treated me as a daughter. His death, therefore, was a great blow to me.

"Mr. Stockton was a widower with only one child of his own, a son, John Stockton, who is now about thirty-one years old. He is a man of irreproachable character, and has always, since I first knew him, been religiously inclined. He is the junior partner in a great commercial company, Dutton & Stockton, leather men. I suppose he has an immense fortune, for he gives largely to charity, and is, too, the active head of a large Sunday school.

"Pomeroy Stockton, my adopted father, almost idolized this son, although there was in his manner toward him something akin to fear. Close work had made my father querulous and irritable. Yet I don't believe a better hearted man ever lived. He worked most of the time in a little shop, which he had installed in a large back room on the ground floor of the house. He always worked with the door locked. There were furnaces, moulds, and many things that I didn't know the use of."

"I know who he was," said The Thinking Machine. "He was working to re-discover the secret of hardened copper—a secret which was lost in Egypt. I knew Mr. Stockton very well by reputation. Go on."

"Whatever it was he worked on," Miss Devan resumed, "he guarded it very carefully. He would permit no one at all to enter the room. I have never seen more than a glimpse of what was in it. His son particularly I have seen barred out of the shop a dozen times and every time there was a quarrel to follow.

"Those were the conditions at the time Mr. Stockton first became ill, six or seven months ago. At that time he double-locked the doors of his shop, retired to his rooms on the second floor, and remained there in practical seclusion for two weeks or more. These rooms adjoined mine, and twice during that time I heard the son and the father talking loudly, as if quarreling. At the end of the two weeks, Mr. Stockton returned to work in the shop and shortly afterward the son, who had also lived in the house, took apartments in Beacon Street and removed his belongings from the house.

"From that time up to last Monday—this is Thursday—I never saw the son in the house. On Monday the father was at work as usual in the shop. He had previously told me that the work he was engaged in was practically ended and he expected a great fortune to result from it. About 5 o'clock in the afternoon on Monday the son came to the house. No one knows when he went out. It is a fact, however, that Father did not have dinner at the usual time, 6:30. I presumed he was at work, and did not take time for his dinner. I have known him to do this many times."

For a moment the girl was silent and seemed to be struggling with some deep grief which she could not control.

"And next morning?" asked The Thinking Machine gently.

"Next morning," the girl went on, "Father was found dead in the workshop. There were no marks on his body, nothing to indicate at first the manner of death. It was as if he had sat in his chair beside one of the furnaces and had taken poison and died at once. A small bottle of what I presume to be prussic acid was smashed on the floor, almost beside his chair. We discovered him dead after we had rapped on the door several times and got no answer. Then

Montgomery, our butler, smashed in the door, at my request. There we found Father.

"I immediately telephoned to the son, John Stockton, and he came to the house. The letter you now have was found in my father's pocket. It was just as you see it. Mr. Stockton seemed greatly agitated and started to destroy the letter. I induced him to give it to me, because instantly it occurred to me that there was something wrong about all of it. My father had talked too often to me about the future, what he intended to do and his plans for me. There may not be anything wrong. The letter may be just what it purports to be. I hope it is—oh—I hope it is. Yet everything considered—"

"Was there an autopsy?" asked The Thinking Machine.

"No. John Stockton's actions seemed to be directed against any investigation. He told me he thought he could do certain things which would prevent the matter coming to the attention of the police. My father was buried on a death certificate issued by a Dr. Benton, who has been a friend of John Stockton since their college days. In that way the appearance of suicide or anything else was covered up completely.

"Both before and after the funeral John Stockton made me promise to keep this letter hidden or else destroy it. In order to put an end to this I told him I had destroyed the letter. This attitude on his part, the more I thought of it, seemed to confirm my original idea that it had not been suicide. Night after night I thought of this, and finally decided to come to you rather than to the police. I feel that there is some dark mystery behind it all. If you can help me now—"

"Yes, yes," broke in The Thinking Machine. "Where was the key to the workshop? In Pomeroy's pocket? In his room? In the door?"

"Really, I don't know," said Miss Devan. "It hadn't occurred to me."

"Did Mr. Stockton leave a will?"

"Yes, it is with his lawyer, a Mr. Sloane."

"Has it been read? Do you know what is in it?"

"It is to be read in a day or so. Judging from the second paragraph of the letter, I presume he left everything to his son."

For the fourth time The Thinking Machine read the letter. At its end he again looked up at Miss Devan.

"Just what is your interpretation of this letter from one end to the other?" he asked.

"Speaking from my knowledge of Mr. Stockton and the circumstances surrounding him," the girl explained, "I should say the letter means just what it says. I should imagine from the first paragraph that something he invented had been taken away from him, stolen perhaps. The second paragraph and the third, I should say, were intended as a rebuke to certain relatives—a brother and two distant cousins—who had always regarded him as a crank and took frequent occasion to tell him so. I don't know a great deal of the history of that other branch of the family. The last two paragraphs explain themselves except—"

"Except the figure seven," interrupted the scientist. "Do you have any idea whatever as to the meaning of that?"

The girl took the letter and studied it closely for a moment.

"Not the slightest," she said. "It does not seem to be connected with anything else in the letter."

"Do you think it possible, Miss Devan, that this letter was written under coercion?"

"I do," said the girl quickly, and her face flamed. "That's just what I do think. From the first I have imagined some ghastly, horrible mystery back of it all."

"Or, perhaps Pomeroy Stockton never saw this letter at all," mused The Thinking Machine. "It may be a forgery?"

"Forgery!" gasped the girl. "Then John Stockton—"

"Whatever it is, forged or genuine," The Thinking Machine went on quietly, "it is a most extraordinary document. It might have been written by a poet. It states things in such a roundabout way. It is not directly to the point, as a practical man would have written."

There was silence for several minutes and the girl sat leaning forward on the table, staring into the inscrutable eyes of the scientist.

"Perhaps, perhaps," she said, "there is a cipher of some sort in it?"

"That is precisely correct," said The Thinking Machine emphatically. "There is a cipher in it, and a very ingenious one."

II

It was twenty-four hours later that The Thinking Machine sent for Hutchinson Hatch, reporter, and talked over the matter with him. He had always found Hatch a discreet, resourceful individual, who was willing to aid in any way in his power.

Hatch read the letter, which The Thinking Machine had said contained a cipher, and then the circumstances as related by Miss Devan were retold to the reporter.

"Do you think it is a cipher?" asked Hatch in conclusion.

"It is a cipher," replied The Thinking Machine. "If what Miss Devan has said is correct, John Stockton cannot have said anything about the affair. I want you to go and talk to him, find out all about him and what division of the property is made by the will. Does this will give everything to the son?"

"Also find out what personal enmity there is between John Stockton and Miss Devan, and what was the cause of it. Was there a man in it? If so, who? When you have done all this, go to the house in Dorchester and bring me the family Bible, if there is one there. It's probably a big book. If it is not there, let me know immediately by 'phone. Miss Devan will, I suppose, give it to you, if she has it."

With these instructions Hatch went away. Half an hour later he was in the private office of John Stockton at the latter's place of business. Mr. Stockton was a man of long visage, rather angular and clerical in appearance. There was a smug satisfaction about the man that Hatch didn't quite approve of, and yet it was a trait which found expression only in a soft voice and small acts of needless courtesy.

A deprecatory look passed over Stockton's face when Hatch asked the first question, which bore on his relationship with Pomeroy Stockton.

"I had hoped that this matter would not come to the attention of the press," said Stockton in an oily, gentle tone. "It is something which can only bring disgrace upon my poor father's memory, and his has been a name associated with distinct achievements in the progress of the world. However, if necessary, I will state my knowledge of the affair, and invite the investigation which, frankly, I will say, I tried to stop."

"How much was your father's estate?" asked Hatch.

"Something more than a million," was the reply. "He made most of it through a device for coupling cars. This is now in use on practically all the railroads."

"And the division of this property by will?" asked Hatch.

"I haven't seen the will, but I understand that he left practically everything to me, settling an annuity and the home in Dorchester on Miss Devan, whom he had always regarded as a daughter."

"That would give you then, say, two-thirds or three-quarters of the estate."

"Something like that, possibly $800,000."

"Where is this will now?"

"I understand in the hands of my father's attorney, Mr. Sloane."

"When is it to be read?"

"It was to have been read today, but there has been some delay about it. The attorney postponed it for a few days."

"What, Mr. Stockton, was the purpose in making it appear that your father died naturally, when obviously he committed suicide and there is even a suggestion of something else?" demanded Hatch.

John Stockton sat up straight in his chair with a startled expression in his eyes. He had been rubbing his hands together complacently; now he stopped and stared at the reporter.

"Something else?" he asked. "Pray what else?"

Hatch shrugged his shoulders, but in his eyes there lay almost an accusation.

"Did any motive ever appear for your father's suicide?"

"I know of none," Stockton replied. "Yet, admitting that this is suicide, without a motive, it seems that the only fault I have committed is that I had a friend report it otherwise and avoided a police inquiry."

"It's just that. Why did you do it?"

"Naturally to save the family name from disgrace. But this something else you spoke of? Do you mean that anyone else thinks that anything other than suicide or natural death is possible?"

As he asked the question there came some subtle change over his face. He leaned forward toward the reporter. All trace of the sanctimonious smirk about the thin-lipped mouth had gone now.

"Miss Devan has produced the letter found on your father at death and has said—" began the reporter.

"Elizabeth! Miss Devan!" exclaimed John Stockton. He arose suddenly, paced several times across the room, then stopped in front of the reporter. "She gave me her word of honor that she would not make the existence of that letter known."

"But she has made it public," said Hatch. "And further she intimates that your father's death was not even what it appeared to be, suicide."

"She's crazy, man, crazy," said Stockton in deep agitation. "Who could have killed my father? What motive could there have been?"

There was a grim twitching of Hatch's lips.

"Was Miss Devan legally adopted by your father?" he asked, irrelevantly.

"Yes."

"In that event, disregarding other relatives, doesn't it seem strange even to you that he gives three-quarters of the estate to you—you have a fortune already—and only a small part to Miss Devan, who has nothing?"

"That's my father's business."

There was a pause. Stockton was still pacing back and forth.

Finally he sank down in his chair at the desk, and sat for a moment looking at the reporter. "Is that all?" he asked.

"I should like to know, if you don't mind telling me, what direct cause there is for ill feeling between Miss Devan and you?"

"There is no ill feeling. We merely never got along well together. My father and I have had several arguments about her for reasons which it is not necessary to go into."

"Did you have such an argument on the night before your father was found dead?"

"I believe there was something said about her."

"What time did you leave the shop that night?"

"About 10 o'clock."

"And you had been in the room with your father since afternoon, had you not?"

"Yes."

"No dinner?"

"No."

"How did you come to neglect that?"

"My father was explaining a recent invention he had perfected, which I was to put on the market."

"I suppose the possibility of suicide or his death in any way had not occurred to you?"

"No, not at all. We were making elaborate plans for the future."

Possibly it was some prejudice against the man's appearance which made Hatch so dissatisfied with the result of the interview. He felt that he had gained nothing, yet Stockton had been absolutely frank, as it seemed. There was one last question.

"Have you any recollection of a large family Bible in your father's house?" he asked.

"I have seen it several times," Stockton said.

"Is it still there?"

"So far as I know, yes."

That was the end of the interview, and Hatch went straight to the house in Dorchester to see Miss Devan. There, in accordance with instructions from The Thinking Machine, he asked for the family Bible.

"There was one here the other day," said Miss Devan, "but it has disappeared."

"Since your father's death?" asked Hatch.

"Yes, the next day."

"Have you any idea who took it?"

"Not unless—unless—"

"John Stockton! Why did he take it?" blurted Hatch.

There was a little resigned movement of the girl's hands, a movement which said, "I don't know."

"He told me, too," said Hatch indignantly, "that he thought the Bible was still here."

The girl drew close to the reporter and laid one white hand on his sleeve. She looked up into his eyes and tears stood in her own. Her lips trembled.

"John Stockton has that book," she said. "He took it away from here the day after my father died, and he did it for a purpose. What, I don't know."

"Are you absolutely positive he has it?" asked Hatch

"I saw it in his room, where he had hidden it," replied the girl.

III

Hatch laid the results of the interviews before the scientist at the Beacon Hill home. The Thinking Machine listened without comment up to that point where Miss Devan had said she knew the family Bible to be in the son's possession.

"If Miss Devan and Stockton do not get along well together, why should she visit Stockton's place at all?" demanded The Thinking Machine.

"I don't know," Hatch replied, "except that she thinks he must have had some connection with her father's death, and is investigating on her own account. What has this Bible to do with it anyway?"

"It may have a great deal to do with it," said The Thinking Machine enigmatically. "Now, the thing to do is to find out if the girl told the truth and if the Bible is in Stockton's apartment. Now, Mr. Hatch, I leave that to you. I would like to see that Bible. If you can bring it to me, well and good. If you can't bring it, look at and study the seventh page for any pencil marks in the text, anything whatever. It might be even advisable, if you have the opportunity, to tear out that page and bring it to me. No harm will be done, and it can be returned in proper time."

Perplexed wrinkles were gathering on Hatch's forehead as he listened. What had page 7 of a Bible to do with what seemed to be a murder mystery? Who had said anything about a Bible, anyway? The letter left by Stockton mentioned a Bible, but that didn't seem to mean anything. Then Hatch remembered that same letter carried a figure seven in parentheses which had apparently nothing to do and no connection with any other part of the letter. Hatch's introspective study of the affair was interrupted by The Thinking Machine.

"I shall await your report here, Mr. Hatch. If it is what I expect, we shall go out late to-night on a little voyage of discovery. Meanwhile see that Bible and tell me what you find."

Hatch found the apartments of John Stockton on Beacon Street without any difficulty. In a manner best known to himself he entered and searched the place. When he came out there was a look of chagrin on his face as he hurried to the house of The Thinking Machine nearby.

"Well?" asked the scientist.

"I saw the Bible," said Hatch.

"And page 7?"

"Was torn out, missing, gone," replied the reporter.

"Ah," exclaimed the scientist. "I thought so. To-night we will make the little trip I spoke of. By the way, did you happen to notice if John Stockton had or used a fountain pen?"

"I didn't see one," said Hatch.

"Well, please see for me if any of his employees have ever noticed one. Then meet me here to-night at 10 o'clock."

Thus Hatch was dismissed. A little later he called casually on Stockton again. There, by inquiries, he established to his own satisfaction that Stockton did not own a fountain pen. Then with Stockton himself he took up the matter of the Bible again.

"I understand you to say, Mr. Stockton," he began in his smoothest tone, "that you knew of the existence of a family Bible, but you did not know if it was still at the Dorchester place."

"That's correct," said Stockton.

"How is it then," Hatch resumed, "that that identical Bible is now at your apartments, carefully hidden in a box under a sofa?"

Mr. Stockton seemed to be amazed. He arose suddenly and leaned over toward the reporter with hands clenched. There was a glitter of what might have been anger in his eyes.

"What do you know about this? What are you talking about?" he demanded.

"I mean that you had said you did not know where this book was, and meanwhile have it hidden. Why?"

"Have you seen the Bible in my rooms?" asked Stockton.

"I have," said the reporter coolly.

Now a new determination came into the face of the merchant. The oiliness of his manner was gone, the sanctimonious smirk had been obliterated, the thin lips closed into a straight, rigid line.

"I shall have nothing further to say," he declared almost fiercely.

"Will you tell me why you tore out the seventh page of the Bible?" asked Hatch.

Stockton stared at him dully, as if dazed for a moment. All the color left his face. There came a startling pallor instead. When next he spoke, his voice was tense and strained.

"Is—is—the seventh page missing?"

"Yes," Hatch replied. "Where is it?"

"I'll have nothing further to say under any circumstances. That's all."

With not the slightest idea of what it might mean or what bearing it had on the matter, Hatch had brought out statements which were wholly at variance with facts. Why was Stockton so affected by the statement that page seven was gone? Why had the Bible been taken from the Dorchester home? Why had it been so carefully hidden? How did Miss Devan know it was there?

These were only a few of the questions that were racing through the reporter's mind. He did not seem to be able to grasp anything tangible. If there were a cipher hidden in the letter, what was it? What bearing did it have on the case?

Seeking a possible answer to some of these questions, Hatch took a cab and was soon back at the Dorchester house. He was somewhat surprised to see The Thinking Machine standing on the stoop waiting to be admitted. The scientist took his presence as a matter of course.

"What did you find out about Stockton's fountain pen?" he asked.

"I satisfied myself that he had not owned a fountain pen, at least recently enough for the pen to have been used in writing that letter. I presume that's what inquiries in that direction mean."

The two men were admitted to the house and after a few minutes Miss Devan entered. She understood when The Thinking Machine explained that they merely wished to see the shop in which Mr. Stockton had been found dead.

"And also if you have a sample of Mr. Stockton's handwriting," asked the scientist.

"It's rather peculiar," Miss Devan explained, "but I doubt if there is an authentic sample in existence large enough, that is, to be compared with that letter. He had a certain amount of correspondence, but this I did for him on the typewriter. Occasionally he would prepare an article for a scientific paper, but these were also dictated to me. He has been in the habit of doing so for years."

"This letter seems to be all there is?"

"Of course his signature appears to checks and in other places. I can produce some of those for you. I don't think, however, that there is the slightest doubt that he wrote this letter. It is his hand-writing."

"I suppose he never used a fountain pen?" asked The Thinking Machine.

"Not that I know of," the girl replied. "I have one," and she took it out of a little gold fascinator she wore at her bosom.

The scientist pressed the point of the pen against his thumb nail, and a tiny drop of blue ink appeared. The letter was written in black. The Thinking Machine seemed satisfied.

"And now the shop," he suggested.

Miss Devan led the way through the long wide hall to the back of the building. There she opened a door, which showed signs of having been battered in, and admitted them. Then, at the request of The Thinking Machine, she rehearsed the story in full, showed him where Stockton had been found, where the prussic acid had been broken, and how the servant, Montgomery, had broken in the door at her request.

"Did you ever find the key to the door?"

"No. I can't imagine what became of it."

"Is this room precisely as it was when the body was found? That is, has anything been removed from it?"

"Nothing," replied the girl.

"Have the servants taken anything out? Did they have access to this room?"

"They have not been permitted to enter it at all. The body was removed and the fragments of the acid bottle were taken away, but nothing else."

"Have you ever known of pen and ink being in this room?"

"I hadn't thought of it."

"You haven't taken them out since the body was found, have you?"

"I—I—er—have not," the girl stammered.

Miss Devan left the room, and for an hour Hatch and The Thinking Machine conducted the search.

"Find a pen and ink," The Thinking Machine instructed.

They were not found.

At midnight, which was six hours later, The Thinking Machine and Hutchinson Hatch were groping through the cellar of the Dorchester house by the light of a small electric lamp which shot a straight beam aggressively through the murky, damp air. Finally the ray fell on a tiny door set in the solid wall of the cellar.

There was a slight exclamation from The Thinking Machine, and this was followed immediately by the sharp, unmistakable click of a revolver somewhere behind them in the dark.

"Down, quick," gasped Hatch, and with a sudden blow he dashed aside the electric light, extinguishing it. Simultaneously with this there came a revolver shot, and a bullet was buried in the wall behind Hatch's head.

IV

The reverberation of the pistol shot was still ringing in Hatch's ears when he felt the hand of The Thinking Machine on his arm, and then through the utter blackness of the cellar came the irritable voice of the scientist:

"To your right, to your right," it said sharply.

Then, contrary to this advice Hatch felt the scientist drawing him to the left. In another moment there came a second shot, and by the flash Hatch could see that it was aimed at a point a dozen feet to the right of the point where they had been when the first shot was fired. The person with the revolver had heard the scientist and had been duped.

Firmly the scientist drew Hatch on until they were almost to the cellar steps. There, outlined against a dim light which came down the stairs, they could see a tall figure peering through the darkness toward a spot opposite where they stood. Hatch saw only one thing to do and did it. He leaped forward and landed on the back of the figure, bearing the man to the ground. An instant later his hand closed on the revolver and he wrested it away.

"All right," he sang out. "I've got it."

The electric light which he had dashed from the hand of The Thinking Machine gleamed again through the cellar and fell upon the face of John Stockton, helpless and gasping in the hands of the reporter.

"Well?" asked Stockton calmly. "Are you burglars or what?"

"Let's go upstairs to the light," suggested The Thinking Machine.

It was under these peculiar circumstances that the scientist came face to face for the first time with John Stockton. Hatch introduced the two men in a most matter-of-fact tone and restored to Stockton the revolver. This was suggested by a nod of the scientist's head. Stockton laid the revolver on a table.

"Why did you try to kill us?" asked The Thinking Machine.

"I presumed you were burglars," was the reply. "I heard the noise down stairs and came down to investigate."

"I thought you lived on Beacon Street," said the scientist.

"I do, but I came here to-night on a little business, which is all my own, and happened to hear you. What were you doing in the cellar?"

"How long have you been here?"

"Five or ten minutes."

"Have you a key to this house?"

"I have had one for many years. What is all this, anyway? How did you get in this house? What right had you here?"

"Is Miss Devan in the house to-night?" asked The Thinking Machine, entirely disregarding the other's questions.

"I don't know. I suppose so."

"You haven't seen her, of course?"

"Certainly not."

"And you came here secretly without her knowledge?"

Stockton shrugged his shoulders and was silent. The Thinking Machine raised himself on the chair on which he had been sitting and squinted steadily into Stockton's eyes. When he spoke it was to Hatch, but his gaze did not waver.

"Arouse the servants, find where Miss Devan's room is, and see if anything has happened to her," he directed.

"I think that will be unwise," broke in Stockton quickly.

"Why?"

"If I may put it on personal grounds," said Stockton, "I would ask as a favor that you do not make known my visit here, or your own for that matter, to Miss Devan."

There was a certain uneasiness in the man's attitude, a certain eagerness to keep things away from Miss Devan that spurred Hatch to instant action. He went out of the room hurriedly and ten minutes later Miss Devan, who had dressed quickly, came into the room with him. The servants stood outside in the hall, all curiosity. The closed door barred them from knowledge of what was happening.

There was a little dramatic pause as Miss Devan entered and Stockton arose from his seat. The Thinking Machine glanced from one to the other. He noted the pallor of the girl's face and the frank embarrassment of Stockton

"What is it?" asked Miss Devan, and her voice trembled a little. "Why are you all here? What has happened?"

"Mr. Stockton came here to-night," The Thinking Machine began quietly, "to remove the contents from the locked vault in the cellar. He came without your knowledge and found us ahead of him. Mr. Hatch and myself are here in the course of our inquiry into the matter which you placed in my hands. We also came without your knowledge. I considered this best. Mr. Stockton was very anxious that his visit should be kept from you. Have you anything to say now?"

The girl turned on Stockton with magnificent scorn. Accusation was in her very attitude. Her small hand was pointed directly at Stockton and into his face there came a strange emotion, which he struggled to repress.

"Murderer! Thief!" the girl almost hissed.

"Do you know why he came?" asked The Thinking Machine.

"He came to rob the vault, as you said," said the girl, fiercely. "It was because my father would not give him the secret of his last invention that this man killed him. How he compelled him to write that letter I don't know."

"Elizabeth, for God's sake what are you saying?" asked Stockton with ashen face.

"His greed is so great that he wanted all of my father's estate," the girl went on impetuously. "He was not content that I should get even a small part of it."

"Elizabeth, Elizabeth!" said Stockton, as he leaned forward with his head in his hands.

"What do you know about this secret vault?" asked the scientist.

"I—I—have always thought there was a secret vault in the cellar," the girl explained. "I may say I know there was one because those things my father took the greatest care of were always disposed of by him somewhere in the house. I can imagine no other place than the cellar."

There was a long pause. The girl stood rigid, staring down at the bowed figure of Stockton with not a gleam of pity in her face. Hatch caught the expression and it occurred to him for the first time that Miss Devan was vindictive. He was more convinced than ever that there had been some long-standing feud between these two. The Thinking Machine broke the long silence.

"Do you happen to know, Miss Devan, that page seven of the Bible which you found hidden in Mr. Stockton's place is missing?"

"I didn't notice," said the girl.

Stockton had arisen with the words and now stood with white face and listening intently.

"Did you ever happen to see a page seven in that Bible?" the scientist asked.

"I don't recall."

"What were you doing in my rooms?" demanded Stockton of the girl.

"Why did you tear out page seven?" asked The Thinking Machine.

Stockton thought the question was addressed to him and turned to answer. Then he saw it was unmistakably a question to Miss Devan and turned again to her.

"I didn't tear it out," exclaimed Miss Devan. "I never saw it. I don't know what you mean."

The Thinking Machine made an impatient gesture with his hands; his next question was to Stockton.

"Have you a sample of your father's handwriting?'"

"Several," said Stockton. "Here are three or four letters from him."

Miss Devan gasped a little as if startled and Stockton produced the letters and handed them to The Thinking Machine. The latter glanced over two of them.

"I thought, Miss Devan, you said your father always dictated his letters to you?"

"I did say so," said the girl. "I didn't know of the existence of these."

"May I have these?" asked The Thinking Machine.

"Yes. They are of no consequence."

"Now let's see what is in the secret vault," the scientist went on.

He arose and led the way again into the cellar, lighting his path with the electric bulb. Stockton followed immediately behind, then came Miss Devan, her white dressing gown trailing mystically in the dim light, and last came Hatch. The Thinking Machine went straight to that spot where he and Hatch had been when Stockton had fired at them. Again the rays of the light revealed the tiny door set into the wall of the cellar. The door opened readily at his touch; the small vault was empty.

Intent on his examination of this, The Thinking Machine was oblivious for a moment to what was happening. Suddenly there came again a pistol shot, followed instantly by a woman's scream.

"My God, he's killed himself. He's killed himself."

It was Miss Devan's voice.

V

When The Thinking Machine flashed his light back into the gloom of the cellar, he saw Miss Devan and Hatch leaning over the prostrate figure of John Stockton. The latter's face was perfectly white save just at the edge of the hair, where there was a trickle of red. In his right hand he clasped a revolver.

"Dear me! Dear me!" exclaimed the scientist. "What is it?'"

"Stockton shot himself," said Hatch, and there was excitement in his tone.

On his knees the scientist made a hurried examination of the wounded man, then suddenly—it may have been inadvertently—he flashed the light in the face of Miss Devan.

"Where were you?" he demanded quickly.

"Just behind him," said the girl. "Will he die? Is it fatal?"

"Hopeless," said the scientist. "Let's get him upstairs."

The unconscious man was lifted and with Hatch leading was again taken to the room which they had left only a few minutes before. Hatch stood by helplessly while The Thinking Machine, in his capacity of physician, made a more minute examination of the wound. The bullet mark just above the right temple was almost bloodless; around it there were the unmistakeable marks of burned powder.

"Help me just a moment, Miss Devan," requested The Thinking Machine, as he bound an improvised handkerchief bandage about the head. Miss Devan tied the final knots of the bandage and The Thinking Machine studied her hands closely as she did so. When the work was completed he turned to her in a most matter of fact way.

"Why did you shoot him?" he asked.

"I—I—" stammered the girl, "I didn't shoot him, he shot himself."

"How come those powder marks on your right hand?"

Miss Devan glanced down at her right hand, and the color which had been in her face faded as if by magic. There was fear, now, in her manner.

"I—I don't know," she stammered. "Surely you don't think that I—"

"Mr. Hatch, 'phone at once for an ambulance and then see if it is possible to get Detective Mallory here immediately. I shall give Miss Devan into custody on the charge of shooting this man."

The girl stared at him dully for a moment and then dropped back into a chair with dead white face and fear-distended eyes. Hatch went out, seeking a telephone, and for a time Miss Devan sat silent, as if dazed. Finally, with an effort, she aroused herself and facing The Thinking Machine defiantly, burst out:

"I didn't shoot him. I didn't, I didn't. He did it himself."

The long, slender fingers of The Thinking Machine closed on the revolver and gently removed it from the hand of the wounded man.

"Ah, I was mistaken," he said suddenly, "he was not as badly wounded as I thought. See! He is reviving."

"Reviving," exclaimed Miss Devan. "Won't he die, then?'"

"Why?" asked The Thinking Machine sharply.

"It seems so pitiful, almost a confession of guilt," she hurriedly exclaimed. "Won't he die?"

Gradually the color was coming back into Stockton's face. The Thinking Machine bending over him, with one hand on the heart, saw the eyelids quiver and then slowly the eyes opened. Almost immediately the strength of the heart beat grew perceptibly stronger. Stockton stared at him a moment, then wearily his eyelids drooped again.

"Why did Miss Devan shoot you?" The Thinking Machine demanded.

There was a pause and the eyes opened for the second time. Miss Devan stood within range of the glance, her hands outstretched entreatingly toward Stockton.

"Why did she shoot you?" repeated The Thinking Machine.

"She—did—not," said Stockton slowly. "I—did—it—myself."

For an instant there was a little wrinkle of perplexity on the brow of The Thinking Machine and then it passed.

"Purposely?" he asked.

"I did it myself."

Again the eyes closed and Stockton seemed to be passing into unconsciousness. The Thinking Machine glanced up to find an infinite expression of relief on Miss Devan's face. His own manner changed; became almost abject, in fact, as he turned to her again.

"I beg your pardon," he said. "I made a mistake."

"Will he die?"

"No, that was another mistake. He will recover."

Within a few moments a City Hospital ambulance rattled up to the door and John Stockton was removed. It was with a feeling of pity that Hatch assisted Miss Devan, now almost in a fainting condition, to her room. The Thinking Machine had previously given her a slight stimulant. Detective Mallory had not answered the call by 'phone.

The Thinking Machine and Hatch returned to Boston. At the Park Street subway they separated, after The Thinking Machine had given certain instructions. Hatch spent most of the following day carrying out these instructions. First he went to see Dr. Benton, the physician who issued the death certificate on which Pomeroy Stockton was buried. Dr. Benton was considerably alarmed when the reporter broached the subject of his visit. After a time he talked freely of the case.

"I have known John Stockton since we were in college together," he said, "and I believe him to be one of the few really good men I know. I can't believe otherwise. Singularly enough, he is also one of the few good men who has made his own fortune. There is nothing hypocritical about him.

"Immediately after his father was found dead, he 'phoned to me and I went out to the house in Dorchester. He explained then that it was apparent Pomeroy Stockton had committed suicide. He dreaded the disgrace that public knowledge would bring on an honored name, and asked me what could be done. I suggested the only thing I knew—that was the issuance of a death certificate specifying natural causes—heart disease, I said. This act was due entirely to my friendship for him.

"I examined the body and found a trace of prussic acid on Pomeroy's tongue. Beside the chair on which he sat a bottle of prussic acid had been broken. I made no autopsy, of course. Ethically I may have sinned, but I feel that no real harm has been done. Of course, now that you know the real facts my entire career is at stake."

"There is no question in your mind but what it was suicide?" asked Hatch.

"Not the slightest. Then, too, there was the letter, which was found in Pomeroy Stockton's pocket. I saw that and if there had been any doubt then it was removed. This letter, I think, was then in Miss Devan's possession. I presume it is still."

"Do you know anything about Miss Devan?"

"Nothing, except that she is an adopted daughter, who for some reason retained her own family name. Three or four years ago she had a little love affair, to which John Stockton objected. I believe he was the cause of it being broken off. As a matter of fact, I think at one time he was himself in love with her and she refused to accept him as a suitor. Since that time there has been some slight friction, but I know nothing of this except in a general way from what he has said to me."

Then Hatch proceeded to carry out the other part of The Thinking Machine's instructions. This was to see the attorney in whose possession Pomeroy Stockton's will was supposed to be and to ask him why there had been a delay in the reading of the will.

Hatch found the attorney, Frederick Sloane, without difficulty. Without reservation Hatch laid all the circumstances as he knew them before Mr. Sloane. Then came the question of why the will had not been read. Mr. Sloane, too, was frank.

"It's because the will is not now in my possession," he said. "It has either been mislaid, lost, or possibly stolen. I did not care for the family to know this just now, and delayed the reading of the will while I made a search for it. Thus far I have found not a trace. I haven't even the remotest idea where it is."

"What does the will provide?" asked Hatch.

"It leaves the bulk of the estate to John Stockton, settles an annuity of $5,000 a year on Miss Devan, gives her the Dorchester house, and specifically cuts off other relatives whom Pomeroy Stockton once accused of stealing an invention he made. The letter, found after Mr. Stockton's death—"

"You knew of that letter, too?" Hatch interrupted.

"Oh, yes, this letter confirms the will, except, in general terms, it also cuts off Miss Devan."

"Would it not be to the interest of the other immediate relatives of Stockton, those who were specifically cut off, to get possession of that will and destroy it?"

"Of course it might be, but there has been no communication between the two branches of the family for several years. That branch lives in the far West and I have taken particular pains to ascertain that they could not have had anything to do with the disappearance of the will."

With these new facts in his possession, Hatch started to report to The Thinking Machine. He had to wait half an hour or so. At last the scientist came in.

"I've been attending an autopsy," he said.

"An autopsy? Whose?"

"On the body of Pomeroy Stockton."

"Why, I had thought he had been buried."

"No, only placed in a receiving vault. I had to call the attention of the Medical Examiner to the case in order to get permission to make an autopsy. We did it together."

"What did you find?" asked Hatch.

"What did you find?" asked The Thinking Machine, in turn.

Briefly Hatch told him of the interview with Dr. Benton and Mr. Sloane. The scientist listened without comment and at the end sat back in his big chair squinting at the ceiling.

"That seems to finish it," he said. "These are the questions which were presented: First, In what manner did Pomeroy Stockton die? Second, If not suicide, as appeared, what motive was there for anything else? Third, If there was a motive, to whom does it lead? Fourth, What was in the cipher letter? Now, Mr. Hatch, I think I may make all of it clear. There was a cipher in the letter— what may be described as a cipher in five, the figure five being the key to it.

VI

"First, Mr. Hatch," The Thinking Machine resumed, as he drew out and spread on a table the letter which had been originally placed in his hands by Miss Devan, "the question of whether there was a cipher in this letter was to be definitely decided.

"There are a thousand different kinds of ciphers. One of them, which we will call the arbitrary cipher, is excellently illustrated in Poe's story, 'The Gold Bug'. In that cipher, a figure or symbol is made to represent each letter of the alphabet.

"Then, there are book ciphers, which are, perhaps, the safest of all ciphers, because without a clue to the book from which words may be chosen and designated by numbers, no one can solve it.

"It would be useless for me to go into this matter at any length, so let us consider this particular letter as a cipher possibility. A careful study of the letter develops three possible starting points. The first of these is the general tone of the letter. It is not a direct, straight-away statement such as a man about to commit suicide would write unless he had a purpose—that is, a purpose beyond the mere apparent meaning of the letter itself. Therefore we will suppose there was another purpose hidden behind a cipher.

"The second starting point is that offered by the absence of one word. You will see that the word 'in' should appear between the word 'cherished' and 'secret'. This, of course, may have been an oversight in writing, the sort of thing anyone might do. But further down we find the third starting point.

"This is the figure seven in parentheses. It apparently has no connection whatever with what precedes or follows. It could not have been an accident. Therefore what did it mean? Was it a crude outward indication of a hurriedly constructed cipher?

"I took the figure seven at first to be a sort of key to the entire letter, always presuming there was a cipher. I counted seven words down from that figure and found the word 'binding'. Seven words from that down made the next word 'give'. Together the two words seemed to mean something.

"I stopped there and started back. The seventh word up is 'and'. The seventh word from 'and', still counting backward, seemed meaningless. I pursued that theory of seven all the way through the letter and found only a jumble of words. It was the same way counting seven letters. These letters meant nothing unless each letter was arbitrarily taken to represent another letter. This immediately led to intricacies. I believe always in exhausting simple possibilities first, so I started over again.

"Now what word nearest to the seven meant anything when taken together with it? Not 'family', not 'Bible', not 'son', as the vital words appear from the seven down. Going up from the seven, I did find a word which applied to it and meant something. That was the word 'page'. I had immediately 'page seven'. 'Page' was the fifth word up from the seven.

"What was the next fifth word, still going up? This was 'on'. Then I had 'on page seven'—connected words appearing in order, each being the fifth from the other. The fifth word down from seven I found was 'family'; the next fifth word was 'Bible'; thus, 'on page seven family Bible'.

"It is unnecessary to go further into the study I made of the cipher. I worked upward from the seven, taking each fifth word until I had all the cipher words. I have underscored them here. Read the words underscored and you have the cipher."

Hatch took the letter marked as follows:

To those Concerned:

Tired of it all I seek the end, and am content. Ambition now is dead; the grave yawns greedily at my feet, and with the labor of my own hands lost I greet death of my own will, by my own act.

To my son I leave all, and you who maligned me, you who discouraged me, you may read this and know I punish you thus. It's for him, my son, to forgive.

I dared in life and dare dead your everlasting anger, not alone that you didn't speak, but that you cherished secret, and my ears are locked forever against you. My vault is my resting place.

On the brightest and dearest page of life I wrote (7) my love for him. Family ties, binding as the Bible itself, bade me give all to my son.

Good-bye. I die.

Pomeroy Stockton

Slowly Hatch read this:

"I am dead at the hands of my son. You who read punish him. I dare not speak. Secret locked vault on page 7 family Bible."

"Well, by George!" exclaimed the reporter. It was a tribute to The Thinking Machine, as well as an expression of amazement at what he read.

"You see," explained The Thinking Machine, "if the word 'in' had appeared between 'cherished' and 'secret', as it would naturally have done, it would have lost the order of the cipher, therefore it was purposely left out."

"It's enough to send Stockton to the electric chair," said Hatch.

"It would be if it were not a forgery," said the scientist testily.

"A forgery," gasped Hatch. "Didn't Pomeroy Stockton write it?"

"No."

"Surely not John Stockton?"

"No."

"Well, who then?"

"Miss Devan."

"Miss Devan!" Hatch repeated in amazement. "Then, Miss Devan killed Pomeroy Stockton?"

"No, he died a natural death."

Hatch's head was whirling. A thousand questions demanded an immediate answer. He stared mouth agape at The Thinking Machine. All his ideas of the case were tumbling about him. Nothing remained.

"Briefly, here is what happened," said The Thinking Machine. "Pomeroy Stockton died a natural death of heart disease. Miss Devan found him dead, wrote this letter, put it in his pocket, put a drop of prussic acid on his tongue, smashed the bottle of acid, left the room, locked the door, and next day had it broken down.

"It was she who shot John Stockton. It was she who tore out page seven of that family Bible, and then hid the book in Stockton's room. It was she who in some way got hold of the will. She either has it or destroyed it. It was she who took advantage of her aged benefactor's sudden death to further as weird and inhuman a plot against another as a woman can devise. There is nothing on God's earth as bad as a bad woman, and nothing as good as a good one. I think that has been said before."

"But as to this case," Hatch interrupted. "How? what? why?"

"I read the cipher within a few hours after I got the letter," replied The Thinking Machine. "Naturally I wanted to find out then who and what this son was.

"I had Miss Devan's story, of course—a story of disagreement between father and son, quarreling and all that. It was also a story which showed a certain underlying animosity despite Miss Devan's cleverness. She had so mingled fact with fiction that it was not altogether easy to weed out the truth, therefore I believed what I chose.

"Miss Devan's idea, as expressed to me, was that the letter was written under coercion. Men who are being murdered don't write cipher letters as intricate as that; and men who are committing suicide have no obvious reasons for writing such letters. The line 'I dare not speak' was silly. Pomeroy Stockton was not a prisoner. If he had feared a conspiracy to kill him why shouldn't he speak?

"All these things were in my mind when I asked you to see Stockton. I was particularly anxious to hear what he had to say as to the family Bible. And yet I may say I knew that page seven had been torn out of the book and was then in Miss Devan's possession.

"I may say, too, that I knew that the secret vault was empty. Whatever these two things contained, supposing she wrote the cipher, had been removed or she would not have called attention to them in this cipher. I had an idea that she might have written it from the mere fact that it was she who first called my attention to the possibility of a cipher.

"Assuming then that the cipher was a forgery, that she wrote it, that it directly accused John Stockton, that she brought it to me, I had fairly conclusive proof that if Pomery Stockton had been murdered she had had a hand in it. John Stockton's motive in trying to suppress the fact of a suicide, as he thought it, was perfectly clear. It was, as he said, to avoid disgrace. Such things are done frequently.

"From the moment you told him of the possibility of murder, he suspected Miss Devan. Why? Because, above all, she had the opportunity, because she wanted the bulk of the estate, because there was some animosity against John Stockton.

"This now proves to have been a broken-off love affair. John Stockton broke it off. He himself had loved Miss Devan. She had refused him. Later, when he broke off the love affair, she hated him.

"Her plan for revenge was almost diabolical. It was intended to give her full revenge and the estate at the same time. She hoped, she knew, that I would read that cipher. She planned that it would send John Stockton to the electric chair."

"Horrible!" commented Hatch with a little shudder.

"It was a fear that this plan might go wrong that induced her to try to kill Stockton by shooting him. The cellar was dark, but she

forgot that ninety-nine revolvers out of a hundred leave slight powder stains on the hand of the person who fires them. Stockton said
that she did not shoot him, because of that inexplicable loyalty
which some men show to a woman they love or have loved.

"Stockton made his secret visit to the house that night to get
what was in that vault without her knowledge. He knew of its existence. His father had probably told him. The thing that appeared
on page seven of the family Bible was in all probability the copper
hardening process he was perfecting. I should think it had been
written there in invisible ink. John Stockton knew this was there.
His father told him. If his father told it, Miss Devan probably over-
heard it. She knew it, too.

"Now the actual circumstances of the death. The girl must have
had and used a key to the work room. After John Stockton left the
house that Monday night she entered that room. She found his father dead of heart disease. The autopsy proved this.

"Then the whole scheme was clear to her. She forged that cipher letter—as Pomeroy Stockton's secretary she probably knew
the handwriting better than anyone else in the world—placed it in
his pocket, and the rest of it you know."

"But the Bible in John Stockton's room?" asked Hatch.

"Was placed there by Miss Devan," replied The Thinking Machine. "It was a part of the general scheme to hopelessly implicate
Stockton. She is a clever woman. She showed that when she produced the fountain pen, having carefully filled it with blue instead
of black ink."

"What was in the locked vault?"

"That I can only conjecture. It is not impossible that the inventor had only part of the formula he so closely guarded written on
the Bible leaf and the other part of it in that vault, together with
other valuable documents.

"I may add that the letters which John Stockton had were not
forged. They were written without Miss Devan's knowledge. There
was a vast difference in the handwriting of the cipher letter which
she wrote and those others which the father wrote.

"Of course it is obvious that the missing will is now, or was, in
Miss Devan's possession. How she got it, I don't know. With that

out of the way and this cipher unravelled apparently proving the son's guilt, at least half, possibly all, of the estate would have gone to her."

Hatch lighted a cigarette thoughtfully and was silent for a moment.

"What will be the end of it all?" he asked. "Of course, I understand that John Stockton will recover."

"The result will be that the world will lose a great scientific achievement—the secret of hardening copper, which Pomeroy Stockton had rediscovered. I think it safe to say that Miss Devan has burned every scrap of this."

"But what will become of her?"

"She knows nothing of this. I believe she will disappear before Stockton recovers. He wouldn't prosecute anyway. Remember he loved her once."

John Stockton was convalescent two weeks later, when a nurse in the City Hospital placed an envelope in his hands. He opened it and a little cloud of ashes filtered through his fingers onto the bed clothing. He sank back on his pillow, weeping.

The Mystery of the Golden Dagger

I

"All animals have the same appetites and the same passions. The reasoning faculty is the one thing which lifts man above what we are pleased to call the lower animals. Logic is the essence of the reasoning faculty. Therefore logic is that power which enables the mind of man to reconstruct from one fact a series of incidents leading to a given result. One result may be as surely traced back to its causes as the specialist may reconstruct a skeleton from a fraction of bone."

Thus clearly, pointedly Professor Augustus S. F. X. Van Dusen had once explained to Hutchinson Hatch, reporter, the analytical power by which he had solved some of the most perplexing mysteries that had ever come to the attention of either the police or the press. It was a text from which sermons might be preached. No one knew this better than Hatch.

Professor Van Dusen is the foremost logician of his time. His name has been honored at home and abroad until now it embraces as honorary initials nearly all those letters which had not been included in it in the first place. The Thinking Machine! This phrase applied once in a newspaper to the scientist had clung tenaciously. It was the name by which he was known to the world at large.

In a dozen ways he had proved his right to it. Hatch remembered vividly the scientist's mysterious disappearance from a prison cell once; then there had been the famous automobile mystery, and more lately the strange chain of circumstances whose history has been written as "The Scarlet Thread." This little text, as given above, was one afternoon, when Hatch had casually called on The Thinking Machine. It transpired that a few hours later he had returned to lay before the logician still another mystery.

102

On his return to his office Hatch had been dispatched in a rush on a murder story. In following up the threads of this he had learned every fact the police had, had written his story, and then presented himself at the Beacon Hill home of The Thinking Machine. It was then 11 o'clock at night. The Thinking Machine had received him, and the facts, in substance, were laid before him as follows:

A man who had given the name of Charles Wilkes called at the real estate office of Henry Holmes & Co., on Washington Street on October 14, just thirty-two days prior to the beginning of the story, as Hatch recited it. He was a man of possibly thirty years, stalwart, good-looking and clean-cut in appearance. There had been nothing about him to attract particular attention. He had said that he was eastern agent for a big manufacturing concern, and travelled a great deal.

"I want a six or seven room house in Cambridge," he had explained. "Something quiet, where I won't have too many neighbors. My wife is extremely nervous, and I want to get a couple of blocks from the street cars. If you have a house, say in the middle of a big lot somewhere in the outskirts of Cambridge, I think that will do."

"What price?" a clerk had asked.

"Anywhere from $45 to $60," he replied.

It just happened that Henry Holmes & Co. had such a house. An office man went with Mr. Wilkes to see it. Mr. Wilkes was pleased and paid the first month's rent of $60 to the man who had accompanied him.

"I won't go back to the office with you," he said. "Everything is all right. I'll have my stuff moved out in a couple of days and let your collector come for next month's rent when it is due."

Mr. Wilkes was a very pleasant man; the clerk had found him so and was gratified at the transaction, which gave his firm such a desirable tenant. He did not ask for Mr. Wilkes' address, nor did he think to ask any questions as to where the household goods were at the moment. In the light of subsequent events this lack of caution temporarily hid, at least for a time, it seemed, the key which would have solved a mystery.

The month passed and in the office of Holmes & Co. the matter had been forgotten until the rent came due. Then a collector, Willard Clements, the regular Cambridge collector for the firm went to the Cambridge house. He found the front door locked. The shutters were still over the windows. There was no indication that anyone at all had either occupied the house or used it. That was an impression to be gathered by a casual outside inspection. Clements had gone around the house; the back door stood wide open.

Clements went inside the house and must have remained there for half an hour. When he came out his face was white, his lips quivered, and the madness of terror was in his eyes. He ran staggeringly around the house and down the walk to the street. A few minutes later he rushed into a police station and there poured out a babbling, incoherent story. The usually placid face of the officer in charge was overspread with surprise as he listened.

Three men were detailed to visit the house and investigate Clements' story. Two of these men went with Clements through the back door, which still stood open, and the third, Detective Fahey, began an examination of the premises. Entering through the back door, the kitchen lay to his left. There was nothing to show that it had been occupied for many months. A hurried glance satisfied him, and he passed into the main body of the house. This consisted of a parlor, a dining room and a bedroom. Here, too, he found nothing. The dust lay thick over floors, mantels and window sills.

From the hall, stairs led to three sleeping rooms above. Under these stairs a short flight lead to the cellar. The door stood open, and a damp, chilly breath came up. Utter darkness lay below. The detective shrugged his shoulders and turned to go upstairs where the other men were.

He found them in the smallest of the three rooms, bending over a bed. Clements stood at the door, which had been broken in, still with the pallor of death on his face and his hands working nervously.

"Find anything?" asked the detective briskly.

"My God, no," gasped Clements. "I wouldn't go back in that room for a million dollars."

The detective laughed and passed in.

"What is it?" he asked.

"A girl," was the reply.

"What happened to her?"

"Stabbed," was the laconic answer.

The other two men stood aside and the detective looked down at the body. It was that of a girl possibly twenty or twenty-two years old. She had been pretty, but the hand of death had obliterated many traces of it now. Her hair, of a rich, ruddy gold, mercifully veiled somewhat the ravages of death; her hands lay outstretched on the white of the bed.

She was dressed for the street. Her hat still clung to her hair, fastened by a long, black-headed pin. Her clothing, of dark brown, was good but not rich. A muff lay beside her and her coat was open.

It was not necessary for Detective Fahey to ask the immediate cause of death. A stab wound in the breast showed that.

"Where's the knife?" he asked.

"Didn't find any."

"Any other wounds?"

"Can't tell until the medical examiner arrives. She's just as we found her."

"Here, O'Brien," instructed the detective, "run out and 'phone to Dr. Loyd and tell him to come up as fast as he can get here. It's probably only suicide."

One of the men went out, and the detective picked up and examined the muff. From it he drew out a small purse. He opened this to find a withered rose—nothing else. There was no money, no card, no key—nothing which might immediately throw light on the girl's identity.

After a while Dr. Loyd came. He remained in the room alone for ten minutes or so, while the policemen went carefully over the upper rooms of the house. When the doctor opened the door and stepped out he carried something in his hand.

"It's murder," he told the detective.

"How do you know?"

"There are two wounds in the back, where she could not possibly have inflicted them herself. And I found this beneath the body."

In his open hand lay a dagger—a dagger of gold. The handle was strangely and intricately fashioned and might, from its appearance, have been cut from a solid bar of gold. In the end blazed a single splendid gem—a diamond. It was probably of three or four karats and pure white. The steel blade was bright at the hilt but stained red.

"Great Scott!" exclaimed the detective as he examined it. "With a clue like that, the end is already in sight."

This was the story that Hutchinson Hatch told to The Thinking Machine. The scientist listened carefully, as he lay stretched out in a chair with his enormous yellow head resting easily against a cushion. He asked only three questions.

"How long had the girl been dead?"

"The medical examiner says it is impossible to tell within more than a few days," Hatch replied. "He gave it as his opinion that it was a week or ten days."

"What was in the cellar?"

"I don't know. No one looked."

"Who broke in the door? Clements?"

"Yes."

"I shall go with you to-morrow," said The Thinking Machine. "I want to look at the dagger and also the cellar."

II

It was 10 o'clock next day when Hutchinson Hatch and The Thinking Machine called on Dr. Loyd. The medical examiner willingly displayed the golden dagger, and in technical terms explained just what had caused the girl's death. Minus the medical phraseology his opinion was that the wound in the breast had been the first inflicted and that the dagger point had punctured the heart. One of the wounds in the back had also reached the same vital spot; the other wound was superficial.

The Thinking Machine viewed the body and agreed with the medical examiner. He had, meanwhile, carefully examined the dagger, handle and blade, and had a photograph of it made. Then, with Hatch, he proceeded to the Cambridge house.

"It isn't suicide, is it?" asked Hatch on the way.

"No," was the quick response. "The only question thus far in my mind, is whether or not the girl was killed in that house."

"Why was a man such a fool as to leave a dagger of that value where it would be found—or any dagger for that matter?" Hatch asked.

"A dozen reasons," replied the scientist. "A possible one is, that whoever killed her may have been frightened away before he could regain possession of the weapon. Remember it was found underneath her body. Presumably she fell backwards and covered the dagger. A slight noise—any one of a dozen things—might have caused the person who killed her to run away rather than try to get the weapon again. Against that of course is the value of the dagger. I know little about jewels, but knowing as little as I do, I should say the value was in the thousands."

"The very reason why it wouldn't be left," said Hatch.

"Quite true," said the other. "Yet the value of the dagger may have been the very reason it was left."

Hatch turned quickly and stared at The Thinking Machine with a question in his eyes.

"I mean," The Thinking Machine explained, "that the dagger is nearly as good as the name and the address of its owner, because it can be traced immediately. Its owner would never have left it under any circumstances."

Hatch was puzzled. He did not follow, as yet, the intricate reasoning of the scientist. It seemed that the one solid, substantial clue, as he regarded it, was to be eliminated without a hearing. The Thinking Machine went on:

"Suppose it had been someone's purpose to kill this girl and, on the face of it, immediately direct attention to some other person as the criminal? In that event, what would have done it more effectively than to kill her with a stolen dagger belonging to some other man and leave it?"

"Oh," exclaimed Hatch. "I think I see what you mean. The fact that a person owns this knife is not, then, to be taken against him?"

"On the contrary," said The Thinking Machine sharply. "It's almost a vindication, unless the person who killed her is mad."

A few minutes later, they arrived at the house. It was a two-story frame structure, back thirty or forty feet from the street, in the centre of a small plot of ground. The nearest house was three or four hundred feet away. Hatch was somewhat surprised at the care with which The Thinking Machine examined the premises before he entered the house. Scarcely a foot of ground had not been critically gone over.

Then they entered through the back door. Here, in the kitchen, The Thinking Machine showed the same care in his examination. He squinted aggressively at the sink and casually turned the water on. Then he examined the rusty range. Thence he went to the dining room, where there was the same minute examination. The parlor, hall, and the lower bedroom were examined, after which the two men went up stairs.

"In which room was the girl found?" asked The Thinking Machine.

"The back room," Hatch replied.

"Well, let's examine the other two first," and the scientist led the way to the front of the house. His examination seemed to be confined largely to the water arrangements. He examined each faucet in turn and turned the water on. He went through the same program in the bathroom.

This done, there remained only the room of death. It was precisely as the Medical Examiner had left it, except that the girl's body was gone. The sheets whereon she lay and the pillows were closely scrutinized. Then The Thinking Machine straightened up.

"Any running water in here?" he asked.

"I don't see any," Hatch replied.

"All right, now for the cellar."

The reporter could not even conjecture what The Thinking Machine expected to find in the cellar. It was low ceiling, damp and chilly. By the light of the electric bulb, which the scientist produced, they could see only the furnace, which stood rustily at about the centre. The Thinking Machine examined this for ashes, but found none. Then he wandered aimlessly about the place, taking it all in seemingly in one long, comprehensive squint. Finally he turned to Hatch.

"Let's go," he suggested.

Three-quarters of an hour later, the two men were again in the apartments on Beacon Hill. The scientist dropped into his accustomed place in the big chair and sat silent for a long time. Hatch waited impatiently.

"Has a picture of this dagger been printed yet?" asked The Thinking Machine at last.

"In every newspaper in Boston, to-day."

"Dear me, dear me," exclaimed the scientist. "It would have been perfectly easy to find the owner of the dagger if pictures of it hadn't been printed."

"Do you think it probable that its owner is the criminal?"

"No, unless, as I said, he was insane, but it would have been interesting to know how the knife passed out of his possession. Was it given away? If so, to whom? A thing of that value would never be given to anyone who was not near and dear to the one who gave it. It is not the kind of gift a man would make to a woman, but is rather a kind of gift a King might make to a loyal subject. It is Oriental in appearance and naturally suggests the Orient. But as I said, the person who owned it did not use it to kill the girl."

"Then what did happen to it?" asked Hatch, curiously.

"Probably it was stolen. Here is the problem: A girl whose name we don't know was murdered by a person we don't know. We do know that this dagger was used to kill her. Therefore find the man who owned the dagger originally and learn how it passed out of his hands. That may lead us directly to the man who rented the house. When we find the man who rented the house, we find possibly the man who stole the dagger and the man who may have killed or may know who killed the girl."

"That seems perfectly clear," Hatch remarked smilingly. "That is, the nature of the problem itself is clear, but the solution is as far away as ever."

The Thinking Machine arose abruptly and passed into the adjoining room. After a while Hatch heard the telephone bell. It was half an hour or so before The Thinking Machine returned.

"The person who owns the knife will call to see me this afternoon at 3 o'clock," he announced.

Hatch half rose in his astonishment, then sank down again.

"Whoever it is will be arrested the moment the police learn of it," he said after a pause.

"On what charge?"

"Murder. It's a plain circumstantial case."

"If he is arrested," said the scientist, "there will be some international complications."

"Who is he?" asked Hatch.

"His name will appear in due time. Meanwhile find out for me if there has ever been a report to the police of any robbery, in which a dagger is mentioned in any way."

Wonderingly, Hatch went away to obey instructions. He found no trace of any such robbery for half a dozen years back. There were several entries on the police books, and of these he made a record.

At 1 o'clock that afternoon he was again in Cambridge working with the police and half a dozen reporters in an effort to get some light on the question of the girl's identity. Later he went to the real estate office of Henry Holmes & Co. seeking further light there. It was not forthcoming.

"Did this man, Wilkes, sign anything?" he asked; "a lease, or anything of that sort? A sample of his handwriting might be useful now."

"No," was the reply. "We did not consider a lease necessary."

Meanwhile the police had apparently exhausted every means of finding out who and what Charles Wilkes was. It was clear from the beginning, to them at least, that the name Wilkes was a fictitious one. There was no reason to suppose that if Wilkes rented the house with the deliberate intention of murder that he would give his real name. By the wildest stretch of the imagination they could find no motive for the murder. It was not any of the ordinary things. Yet it was deliberate. They regarded the golden dagger as the key to the entire mystery. There they stopped.

At 3 o'clock Hatch returned to the home of The Thinking Machine. He had hardly been ushered into the little reception room when the doorbell rang and the scientist in person appeared. Accompanying him was a stranger; dark, swarthy and with the coal black beard of the Orient.

Hatch was introduced to him as Ali Hassan. Then The Thinking Machine produced the photograph of the dagger.

"Is this the correct picture?" he asked.

The stranger examined it closely.

"It seems to be," he said at last.

"Is there another dagger like that in existence?"

"No."

"How did it come into your possession?"

"It was a gift to me from the Sultan of Turkey," was the reply.

III

Gravely Mr. Hassan sat down while The Thinking Machine resumed his seat in the big chair opposite. Hatch was leaning forward eagerly to catch every word. The story of the man who owned the wonderful golden dagger was one which the great public would naturally want to know.

"Now," began The Thinking Machine, "would you mind telling us a little of the history of the dagger?"

"It is not a story to be told to infidels," was the reply. "I mean, of course, unbelievers. I will answer any question that you see fit to ask if I can do so."

A little expression of perplexity crept into the squinting eyes of The Thinking Machine; then it passed as suddenly as it came.

"You are a Mohammedan?" he asked.

"Yes."

"Is there any religious significance attached to the dagger?"

"Yes, it is sacred. A gift from the Sultan—my imperial master—and blessed by the royal hand is always sacred to a subject. It may not be even seen by the eyes of an unbeliever."

Hatch straightened up a little, and The Thinking Machine readjusted himself in the big chair.

"You were educated at Oxford?" he asked irrelevantly.

"Yes. I left there in 1887."

"You did not embrace the Christian religion?"

"No. I am a Mohammedan, loyal to my master."

"Would you mind saying for what service the Sultan so honored you?"

"I cannot say that. It was a service to the crown at a time when I was secretary of the Turkish Embassy in England."

"Under what circumstances did this dagger leave your possession?" asked The Thinking Machine quietly.

"It has not left my possession," was the equally quiet reply. "It would be sacrilege if it did. Therefore I still have it—closely guarded."

Frankly, Hutchinson Hatch was amazed. His manner showed it clearly. The Thinking Machine was still leaning back in the chair staring upward.

"I understand then," he said after a little pause, "that the dagger, of which this is a photograph, is in your possession now?"

"It has not been out of my possession at any time since it was given to me," was the startling reply.

"Then how do you account for this photograph?"

"I don't account for it."

"But Dr. Loyd—the dagger—I had it in my hands," Hatch interposed in bewilderment.

"You are mistaken," replied the Turk quietly. "It is still in my possession."

"Will you produce it?" asked The Thinking Machine calmly.

"I will not," was the firm response. "I have explained that it is not to be seen by the eyes of unbelievers."

"If a charge of murder should be laid against you, would you produce it?" insisted The Thinking Machine.

"I would not."

"To avoid an arrest?"

"There is no danger of an arrest," was the still calm response. "I am connected with the Turkish delegation in Washington and I am responsible there. I am entitled to the protection of my own government. If there is any charge against me it must come that way."

There was a long silence. Hatch was bursting with questions, which were silenced by a slight gesture from The Thinking Machine. Under the peculiar circumstances the scientist realized that what Mr. Hassan had said was true. It is one of the idiosyncrasies of international law.

"You know, of course, that a woman has been murdered with that dagger, don't you?" asked the scientist.

"I have heard that a woman has been murdered."

"Do you attribute any magical properties to the weapon?"

"Oh, no."

"Just where is it at present? Would you produce it if your government ordered you to do so?"

"My government will not order me to do so."

Hatch was annoyed. All this was tommyrot. If Mr. Hassan had his dagger, then there were more than one of them in existence. Dr. Loyd had one; the reporter knew that. Whether it was a clever counterfeit he did not know; but the dagger used to kill the girl was certainly in possession of the medical examiner.

"If that dagger should ever by an chance pass out of your possession, Mr. Hassan, what would happen?" asked The Thinking Machine.

"I am sworn to protect it with my life. If it should pass out of my possession I should kill myself. It is customary and so understood in my country."

"Oh," exclaimed the scientist, suddenly. "How long will you be in Boston?"

"For several days, probably," was the reply. "Meanwhile, if I can be of any further service to you, I should do so gladly."

"How long have you been here?"

"About a week."

"Were you ever in Boston before?"

"Once, a couple of years ago, when I first came to this country."

Mr. Hassan arose and took up his hat. He had formally told Hatch and The Thinking Machine good day and was at the door when he turned back.

"I understand," he said, "that this dagger is supposed now to be in the possession of Dr. Loyd, the Medical Examiner?"

"Yes," said the scientist.

Mr. Hassan went away. Hatch sat nursing his wrath a moment, and then came the explosion. It was inevitable; a righteous protest against an insult to his intelligence and that of the eminent scientist who had become interested in the case.

"Mr. Hassan is a liar, else there are two daggers," he burst out.

"Mr. Hassan is a gentleman of the Turkish legation, Mr. Hatch," said The Thinking Machine reprovingly. "Do you know Mr. Loyd very well?"

"Yes."

"'Phone him immediately and ask him to have that dagger secretly removed to a safety deposit vault," instructed the scientist. "Then you had better go out and work with the police to see if they yet have any clue to the girl's identity. Mr. Hassan will produce the dagger if he has it."

The remainder of that day and a part of the next Hatch spent running down the small possibilities, trying to settle some of the minor questions, which were naturally aroused in his mind. There was a result—a very definite result—and when he again appeared before The Thinking Machine, he felt that he had accomplished something.

"It occurred to me," he explained, "that there was a possibility that this man Wilkes had communicated with or advertised for this girl that was dead. I searched the want columns of three newspapers. At last I found this."

He extended a small clipping to The Thinking Machine, who took it and studied it a moment. This clipping was an advertisement for an intelligent young woman as companion and gave the street and number of the house in Cambridge where the girl had been found.

"Very good," said The Thinking Machine, and he rubbed his hands briskly together. "It looks, Mr. Hatch, as if it might be a long tedious work to establish the name of this girl. It may take weeks. I should meanwhile take that clipping and turn it over to the police, and let them make the search. I see it is dated October 19, which is four days form the time Wilkes rented the house. Yet the girl had been dead for not more than ten days. There is a lapse of time in there to be accounted for. Find out if this advertisement appeared more than once, and also get the original copy of it from the newspaper. It might be in Wilkes's handwriting. In that case it would be a substantial clue."

"Have you heard anything more about Hassan's dagger?" inquired the reporter.

"No, but he will produce it. Did you phone Dr. Loyd in reference to it?"

"I 'phoned yesterday, as you suggested, and was then informed that Dr. Loyd had left the city. I 'phoned twice this morning, but got no answer from the house. I presume he has not returned."

"No answer?" asked The Thinking Machine quickly. "No answer? Dear me, dear me!" He arose and paced back and forth across the room twice, then paused before the reporter. "That's bad, bad, bad!" he said.

"Why?" asked Hatch.

The Thinking Machine turned suddenly and entered the adjoining room. When he came out there was a new expression on his face—an expression which Hatch could not read.

"Dr. Loyd was found at 1 o'clock to-day in his home, bound and gagged," he explained shortly. "The only servant there was insensible from some drug. It was burglars. They ransacked the house from top to bottom."

"What—what does that mean?" asked Hatch, wonderingly.

Just then the door from the hall opened and Martha, the aged servant of The Thinking Machine, appeared.

"Mr. Hassan, sir," she said.

The Turk appeared in the door behind her, gravely courteous, suave, and dignified as ever.

"Ah," explained The Thinking Machine. "You have brought the dagger?"

"I talked with the Turkish Minister in Washington by telephone and he explained the necessity of my producing it," said Mr. Hassan. "I have it here to convince you."

"I thought it was in Washington?" Hatch blurted out.

"Here it is," was the Turk's response. He produced a richly jeweled box. In it lay the golden dagger. The Thinking Machine lifted it. The blade was bright and without a trace of a stain. With a quick movement The Thinking Machine twisted the handle and part of it came off. A few drops of a pungent liquid ran out on the floor.

IV

Mr. Hassan left Boston that night for Washington. He took the dagger with him. The Thinking Machine made no objection, and the very existence of the man was as yet unknown to the police.

"When it is necessary to produce that dagger," he explained to Hatch, "it can be done through regular channels, if Hassan is still alive. It seems very probable now that international law may have to take a hand in the case."

"Do you consider it possible that Hassan in person had any connection with the affair?" Hatch asked.

"Anything is possible," was the short reply. "By the way, Mr. Hatch, it might be interesting to know a little more about this real estate collector, Clements, who discovered the girl's body. He might have known about the house being unoccupied. There are still possibilities in every direction, but the real problem hangs on the golden dagger."

"In that event, it seems to come back to Hassan," said the reporter doggedly.

"I would advise you, Mr. Hatch, to settle the points I asked about the advertisement. Then see Dr. Loyd; ask him if he still has the dagger. If you get the original copy of the advertisement, turn it over to the police. You need not mention Hassan to them as yet."

It was early that evening when Hatch saw Dr. Loyd.

"Did the burglars get the dagger?" he asked.

"I have nothing to say," was the reply.

"Have you the dagger now?"

"I have nothing to say."

"Did you turn it over to the District Attorney?"

"I have nothing to say."

The result of this was that Hatch went away firmly convinced that Dr. Loyd did not have the dagger; that the burglars, whoever they were, had taken it away; that they were probably in the employ of Hassan and robbed Loyd's house for the specific purpose of regaining possession of the dagger.

Later Hatch made an investigation of the circumstances attending the publication of the advertisement. It had appeared four times on alternate days. The original copy of it was found and given to him. It was the bold handwriting of a man. This he turned over to the police, with all information as to the advertisement.

Then began a long, minute search, which ultimately resulted in the discovery of the whereabouts of half a dozen girls reported missing. But the fact that they were found immediately removed them as possibilities. From the first, the search for Wilkes had been unceasing. It was generally assumed that the name Wilkes was fictitious.

On the morning of the second day Hatch appeared at his office weary, discouraged and disgusted. But weariness fled when the city editor excitedly approached him.

"They have Wilkes," he said. "They got him late last night in Worcester. The real estate clerk has positively identified him. He will be at police headquarters within an hour or so. Get the story."

"Who is he?" asked Hatch.

"I don't know. He doesn't deny his identity, and insists that his name is Wilkes. He was found at a hotel registered as Charles Wingate."

The first editions of the afternoon papers flamed with the announcement of the capture of the supposed murderer. Meanwhile Hatch and the other reporters had heard Wilkes's story at secondhand. The police saw fit to put as much mystery about it as they could. Having heard this story Hatch immediately went with it to see The Thinking Machine.

"They've caught Wilkes," he explained. "His name is Wilkes, so far as anybody knows. He registered as Wingate because he was frightened. He knows the police of the entire country were looking for him."

"What about the house?" asked The Thinking Machine.

"He tells what appears to be a straight story. He says he rented the house for himself and wife intending to remain there for several months. He did not take a lease. On the day he was to move in his wife grew very ill—a more than usually serious attack of the nervous trouble with which she is afflicted. Then on the advice of physicians he took her away to Cuba rather than to start up housekeeping.

"He inserted the advertisement in the newspaper before he knew how serious this illness was. They remained in Cuba together for two or three weeks, and she is still there, he says. On the day after his return this murder affair came up and he considered it advisable, until it was all cleared up, to stay out of sight."

"What is his business?" asked The Thinking Machine.

"He is Eastern agent for a big cutlery concern in Cleveland. His headquarters are in Boston. He has only recently been appointed and is not known in Boston. Almost from the time of his appointment, he had been travelling. It was an oversight, he says, that he did not notify the real estate people of his determination not to occupy the house. He had rented it by the month anyway."

The Thinking Machine was silent. The blue eyes were turned upward and the long, slender fingers pressed tip to tip. Hatch, eagerly watching his face, saw perplexed wrinkles at times, which immediately disappeared. It was the working of the man's brain.

"Does he know the girl?"

"He is confident that he does not. He never saw, so he says, anyone who answered the advertisement."

"Of course he would say that," snapped The Thinking Machine. "Has he seen the body?"

"He is to see it this afternoon."

"Have the police any idea of the identity of the girl?"

"I think not," said Hatch. "There are the usual boasts about being able to clear it up within a few hours, but it means nothing."

Again there was silence as the scientist sat thoughtfully squinting at the ceiling.

"Doe she know Hassan?" he asked, finally.

"I don't know," Hatch replied. "Remember that no one knows Hassan but you and I, and I haven't seen this man Wilkes yet."

"Will you be able to see him?"

"I don't know. It depends upon the gracious goodness of the police."

"We will go and see him now," declared The Thinking Machine emphatically.

A few minutes later, they were ushered into the office of the chief of the State Police. There were mutual introductions, Hatch officiating. The chief had at various times heard of his distinguished visitor, but had never before met him. Instead he had regarded him as an amusing myth.

"Would it be possible for me to see Mr. Wilkes?" asked The Thinking Machine.

"No, not now," was the reply.

"I thought the purpose of this office was to aid justice," snapped the scientist.

"It is," said the chief, and a flush came to his face.

"Well, I know the man who owns the dagger with which the girl was killed," said the scientist emphatically. "I want to see if this is the man."

The chief arose from his desk in astonishment and stood leaning over it toward his visitors.

"You know—you know—" he began. "Who is it?"

"May I see Wilkes?" insisted the other.

"Well, under the circumstances, I suppose, perhaps—"

"Now," said The Thinking Machine.

The chief pressed a button. After a moment one of his men came in.

"Bring Wilkes in here," directed the police official.

The man went out and after a time returned with Wilkes, who had been undergoing the third degree in another room. The prisoner's face was white and every move indicated his tense nervous condition.

"Mr. Wilkes, when did the dagger pass out of your possession?" asked The Thinking Machine, suddenly, as he extended the photograph of the golden dagger.

"I have never seen such a dagger," was the reply, after a long, deliberate study of the picture.

"Did you not receive an order for a blade for it?" asked The Thinking Machine.

"No."

"Mr. Wilkes, I know possibly more of this affair than the police do as yet. You can supply those facts that I haven't. Now who—who—is the girl who was murdered with this dagger?"

What little color that had been in the prisoner's face was gone now, and he trembled violently. Suddenly he sank down in the chair, burying his face on his arms.

"I don't know, I don't know, I don't know," he sobbed.

Yet that afternoon, when Wilkes stood beside the body of the murdered girl he looked at her long and earnestly then with a wailing cry he lunged forward, half fainting.

"Alice, Alice!" he gasped.

V

Wilkes, or Wingate, as he had been last known, told a story as to his knowledge of the dead girl, which was on its face straight-forward and to the point. In a little room adjoining that in which the body lay he had been revived with a stimulant, and, once himself again, he talked freely. The thing which impressed the police most was the detail which he gave; The Thinking Machine had nothing to say as to what he thought of this recital. He merely observed it without comment.

Briefly here is the story, denuded of extraneous verbiage:

The girl was Alice Gorham. There was no shadow of doubt about the identification. She was the daughter of a man who had been for a long time connected with the Steel Trust offices in Cleveland. Misfortune had finally come to her father and then in her last year at Vassar she had been compelled to return home. Shortly after that her father had died suddenly, leaving her nothing; her mother had died several years previously. She was an only child.

According to his story, Wilkes had been acquainted with her since her childhood.

His father, too, had been in the Steel Trust at one time and had left it to take a partnership in the cutlery concern which he now represented. The girl's age, so far as Wilkes's story went, was about twenty-one years.

Since the death of her father, when she had been thrown upon her own resources, she had been employed as companion to an aged woman in Cleveland. There had been some disagreement between them, and the girl decided to come East. She had been in Boston only a few weeks at the time she was found dead.

"That's all I know about it," said Wilkes in conclusion. "Naturally, the shock was very great when I saw her in there dead. I knew that she had come to Boston. I knew, too, that she had disappeared from where she lived, for both my wife and myself, before we went to Cuba, had called and inquired for her."

"You have no idea where she was from the time she disappeared until the time she was found dead, which was at the most not more than fourteen days ago?" asked The Thinking Machine.

"None," replied Wilkes.

"Do you know of any love affair—any man in the case?" insisted The Thinking Machine.

"No, I never heard of one."

"Of course, you read the newspaper accounts of this affair. Did you, then, from the detailed description of the girl printed, associate her in any way with the girl who was dead?"

"I did, yes, but not directly. The thing which impressed me most in the newspaper accounts was the reiterated statement that the man who rented the house must have been the murderer. This placed it directly to me. Then frankly I got frightened and tried to hide my identity for the moment under another name. It was very foolish, of course, but the circumstances seemed to point so conclusively to me that—that I did what I did."

"When did you last see Miss Gorham?"

"In Cleveland seven months ago."

"That's all," said The Thinking Machine, and he arose as if to go.

"Now what do you know of this?" asked the State police chief.

"I shall call on you to-morrow and explain just what I know and how I learned it," was the reply.

"Who is the man who owned that dagger?" the chief continued.

"You mean the dagger that was stolen from Dr. Loyd?" asked The Thinking Machine. There was a touch of irony in his tone.

"Who—how—what do you know about that?"

"Let's go, Mr. Hatch," said The Thinking Machine suddenly. "I'll see you to-morrow, chief."

Once outside, The Thinking Machine led the way toward the Scollay Square subway.

"Where to now?" asked Hatch.

"To the house in Cambridge," explained The Thinking Machine. "I want to look it over again. I have an idea I overlooked a few things."

"Do you think Wilkes killed Miss Gorham?" asked Hatch.

"I don't know."

"Do you think now that Hassan did it?"

"I don't know."

Further questioning seemed useless, and both men were silent until they stood inside the Cambridge house. Then again, The

Thinking Machine went over the structure from cellar to attic, but more carefully, with more detail than even before. Particularly this was true as to the cellar. Not one square inch of the floor surface escaped his eyes. Once he picked up a small scrap of cloth—black cloth, and examined it. Later, on hands and knees, he studied the soft ground flooring in a remote corner. Hatch stood looking on curiously.

"See this?" The Thinking Machine asked.

Hatch looked by the light of the electric bulb and saw only a few indentations in the soft soil. It was as if something heavy and elaborately carved had been pressed down in the dirt.

"What is it?" he asked.

Without answering The Thinking Machine arose and together they went straight to the room of death upstairs. Here the scientist ruthlessly cut into the smooth wood of the bed. He handed the small chip he removed to the reporter.

"What does that look like?" he asked.

"Mahogany," Hatch replied.

"Good, very good. Now, Mr. Hatch, you go to Boston, see this young man, Willard Clements, the real estate collector. Don't be afraid to ask him questions. Ask him pointedly if he happens to be acquainted with a burglar. It will be an interesting experiment. Find out all you can about him and meet me at my apartments at 8 o'clock to-night. I have a little further work to do here."

"Lord, did he do it?" asked Hatch.

"I don't know," was the reply. "It would be interesting to know what he knows."

Had Hatch not known the peculiar methods of The Thinking Machine, he would have been bewildered by these instructions. As it was, he was merely seeking in his own mind a possible connecting thread between Clements and the mystery. Disregarding Clements for the moment, he could only see Wilkes, who knew the girl, or Hassan, who owned the dagger, in the affair.

Once alone, The Thinking Machine did several things which would have sadly puzzled an outsider. From the back door he examined the ground and even stooped and stared at the grass. Slowly he walked along, half stooping, toward the back of the plot of ground. There he shook the picket fence, which barred his way. It was apparently a new fence, yet a whole panel of it fell. Outside was an alley.

From this point he went to the house of the nearest neighbor and asked many questions about strangers who might have been in the other yard. None had been seen. Finally, he asked the way and was directed to the nearest police station.

"Have many burglaries been reported in this neighborhood lately?" he asked, after he had introduced himself.

"Three of four. Why?"

"Have you heard of any furnished house, at present unoccupied, which has been robbed?"

"Yes, the old Essex estate—about four blocks from here."

"What was stolen, exactly?"

"We don't know. The owners of the house are in Europe now, and we have no means of learning just what is missing. We have caught the men who robbed it."

"What are their name, please?"

"One is called 'Reddy' Blake, the other gave the name of Johnson."

"Where were they caught?"

"In the house. They had a wagon and were trying to move out a heavy mahogany sideboard."

"When was this?"

"Oh, a week or so ago. They got three years each."

"No other similar cases?"

"No."

"Thank you," and The Thinking Machine went away. That night Hutchinson Hatch called on the scientist and found him with a telegram in his hands.

"Did you see Clements?" asked The Thinking Machine, "and did you ask him if he knew a burglar?"

"I did," said Hatch, smiling slightly. "He wanted to fight."

The Thinking Machine unfolded the telegram and handed it to the reporter.

"This might interest you," he said.

Hatch took the yellow slip and read the following:

"Ali Hassan committed suicide this morning."

"Why that's a confession," said the reporter.

VI

There was a gathering of a half a dozen persons in the office of the Chief of Police on the morning of the following day. They were the chief, The Thinking Machine, Charles Wilkes, Detective Fahey, Willard Clements and Hutchinson Hatch. The summons to Clements had been in the nature of a great surprise to that young man. First he had been indignant, but gradually this passed, and there came instead a cowering attitude.

Every one, even the chief, was waiting the pleasure of The Thinking Machine. Hatch, still firmly convinced that Hassan, the Turk, was the criminal, was almost as much surprised as Clements by his presence.

Detective Fahey sat silently by, chewing his cigar and with a slightly amused smile on his face; the chief didn't smile. He had felt the vital power of this diminutive man with the enormous yellow head.

"Now, Mr. Clements," The Thinking Machine began, and the young man started slightly, "I don't believe that you killed Miss Gorham. Perhaps the worst charge that can be laid to you is burglary, or, rather, illicit knowledge of burglary. Your friends, 'Reddy' Blake and this man Johnson have already partially confessed. Now, will you tell the rest of it?"

"Confessed what? What are you talking about?" demanded the young man.

"Never mind, then," said The Thinking Machine, impatiently. He turned to the chief. "Fortune has favored us a good deal in this case," he said. "Particularly is this true in the arrest of Mr. Wilkes. I may compliment you chief on the ability your men displayed in getting Mr. Wilkes."

The chief bowed gravely.

"But he is not the murderer."

The scientist went on:

"By telegraph and cable I have verified his story in full. You may have done so yourself. Here are the answers I received to the wires I sent. I think, perhaps, they will convince you. Meanwhile, you have the real murderer in Charlestown prison now. It is 'Reddy' Blake, or Johnson."

At the second mention of these two names every eye was again turned on Clements. A sudden change had come over his face. He was now frightened; the color was surging back into Wilkes's countenance.

"Proofs, proofs," said the chief, shortly.

"It will be useless," continued The Thinking Machine, "to rehearse Mr. Wilkes's story. It is proven. Therefore, what remains? Let's begin with the dagger and see what it leads to.

"I saw this dagger. It is an extraordinary weapon. Its value must be in the thousands. On it I saw, cut into the handle, the crescent of Turkey, together with half a dozen symbols, religious and otherwise, of that empire. It was a simple matter, comparatively, to call up on the 'phone some one who knew of these things, preferably a Turk. There is a Turk in one of the oriental stores on Boylston Street.

"I talked to him and described the dagger in detail. He is an educated man, knows his country and its customs and was able to say that such a dagger could only have been what I had previously supposed it to have been—a gift from a prince or ruler to a loyal subject for duty well done. I asked if he knew of such a weapon being in this country. He said he did not, but that a certain Turkish gentleman, then in Boston, had once signally served his master, and there was a possibility that he had been rewarded by such a gift. What was his name? Ali Hassan.

"Mr. Hassan was stopping at the Hotel Teutonic. I wrote a note to him. He called and readily identified a photograph of the golden dagger as his property. Remember that this was a photograph of the dagger with which the girl was slain.

"He amazed me a little by stating that the dagger was then in his possession. At the same time he explained that it was a sacred object and not for the eyes of infidels. For a time this was puzzling. Then I asked what would be the result if, by any chance, the dagger should pass out of his possession. He replied that he would kill himself. That was an illuminating point. He had lied; he did not have the dagger. If any one else had known that he did not have it, it would have been his death. He saved his life thus far by lying. It has been done before. I may say, too, that the idea of a duplicate dagger was not tenable."

"If this man owns the dagger and admits it," interrupted the chief, "I will have him immediately arrested."

"There are two reasons why you can't do that," said The Thinking Machine, quietly. "The first is that Mr. Hassan was a secretary of the Turkish legation in Washington; the second, he is dead."

There was a pause while the chief and the remainder of the party absorbed this.

"Dead," exclaimed the chief. "How?"

"Suicide by poison," was the brief response. "Anyway, I had established the ownership of the dagger. I also learned that Hassan had been in Boston only five days at the time the body was found. The girl had been dead for a week or ten days—possibly ten days. Therefore, Hassan did not kill Miss Gorham. That was conclusive.

"Then came the question of how the dagger passed out of his possession. Obviously it was not a gift. Stolen? Probably. When? Mr. Hassan showed in a way that he had not been in Boston for two years. But burglars operate all over the country. Therefore, burglars. It is perfectly possible that the dagger was stolen some time in Washington by 'Reddy' Blake and his gang, and for some reason they kept it instead of selling it. No man, not even a 'fence,' would have tried to dispose of a four-carat diamond. In the second place, Mr. Hassan would not have dared to report the loss of the dagger to the police. Blake, of course, could not know this. He kept the weapon. The safest place for it was on his person."

The Thinking Machine lay back in his chair, squinting at the ceiling, while his listeners leaned forward eagerly. The chief was fascinated, amazed by the strange story. The scientist resumed:

"It was stated in the hearing of Mr. Hassan and also published that the dagger was in the possession of Medical Examiner Loyd. It is easy to see how employees of this man burglarized Loyd's home and recovered the weapon. Its possession meant life to Hassan. Immediately after this burglary he returned to Washington. There he committed suicide, probably by order of his superiors. I had wired the facts, not intending to cause his death, of course, but to have the dagger produced here when necessary. That disposes, I think, of the ownership of the weapon, and places it in the hands of 'Reddy' Blake or his pals."

The Thinking Machine turned suddenly on Clements.

"As collector for Henry Holmes & Co. you know Cambridge well, I should imagine. You have opportunities, which fall to few men— legitimately—to know where rich hauls may be made. You were also in a position to know practically every vacant house in Cambridge. Knowing this you might know, too, the best vacant house for a rendezvous for thieves. In passing, you might have learned that the house rented by Mr. Wilkes had not been occupied. It is perfectly possible that you did not even know the house had been rented until the bill for rent was placed in your hands. These are possibilities; now here are facts.

"You went to that house to collect rent. The front door was locked and the shutters up. In the natural course of events you would have satisfied yourself that it was unoccupied. You might have shouted to attract someone's attention, but in the ordinary course of events you would not have gone upstairs to look further, unless you had asked something. You found something in a back room and probably behind a door that was closed. You broke open that door. Why did you go to that room? Why did you break down that door?

"Let's see. Suppose for a moment that you were one of the most valued members of a gang of burglars—valued because you appear the gentleman and can go places and learn things without attracting attention. Suppose this house was a hiding place for stolen goods. Suppose the girl, answering Mr. Wilkes's advertisement for a companion, should have gone to that house and found it locked. It is not improbable that she should have gone around the house, believing it to be occupied, to find someone.

"Suppose she had come upon a party of thieves. It would have been a natural consequence for them to fear a spy and attempt to get rid of her.

"What more possible than that they should have locked her up? She was at least four hundred feet from the nearest house, and forty, fifty or sixty feet from the street and behind thick walls. Her screams would not have been heard.

"There we have the girl a prisoner in the hands of the men who had the golden dagger. The murder may have followed at any time. It happened but a few days ago. Meanwhile the burglars had taken from their loot a bed and its furnishings, providing a place for the girl to sleep. You, Mr. Clements, knew that the girl had been a prisoner upstairs. That is why you went to that room. I will not say that you knew of the murder at that time. You discovered that. You were frightened at this hideous ending of an affair in which you had been interested. Perhaps you were a little angry, too. It may have been that the burglars had taken away the stolen stuff, sold it and left you out in the division. Is that right?"

Clements stared at him with glassy eyes, then suddenly leaned forward with his head in his hands, and sobbed bitterly. It was practically a confession.

"How did it come that you considered burglars in the first place?" asked the chief.

"I made two examinations of the house. The first was not thorough. I examined the faucets to see if the water was on, and if there was a possible trace of blood on them anywhere. It was not impossible that the murderer of Miss Gorham got blood on his hands and left a thumb or finger print when he washed it off. I found none. He was careful.

"On the second examination I looked particularly for a trace of burglars in the cellar. There I found, freshly pressed down in the soft soil, the imprint of what must have been a carved piano leg and beside it a large imprint indicating that a grand piano had been leaned against the wall. People don't keep pianos in the cellar. Therefore, if one were there, it was hidden. Naturally burglars. The bed was not handsome, but was of mahogany. Nobody moving out would leave a mahogany bed. Still burglars. There is no path leading from the back of the house to the back fence. Yet there is a straight line across the grass to a certain panel in that fence where people have walked frequently. That panel of the fence fell out when I shook it; there is no gate. Burglars, even at night, would not move their loot in at the front; it would be comparatively easy to bring in large objects, such as a piano, through the alley, tearing down a fence panel and then to the house. Therefore burglars.

"Now, burglars do not steal pianos and mahogany beds in a wagon from a house that is occupied. The police informed me that burglars— 'Reddy' Blake, among them—had been robbing an unoccupied furnished house. They could have stolen a piano or anything else. Therefore the chain is complete."

"Admitting that is all true," interrupted the chief, "how did you explain the fact that the man who killed Miss Gorham left the dagger? If he had been a burglar, as you say, wouldn't he have been the last man to leave a thing of that value?"

"All men are fools when they kill people," said The Thinking Machine. "They are frightened, half-witted, and do all kinds of inexplicable things. Suppose there had been a sudden violent noise in the house, made by one of his pals just at the moment the girl fell backward, covering the knife with her body. The murderer might have run, leaving it where it was. I don't state this as a fact, but as a strong probability. He might have intended to return for the knife, but if he had meanwhile been arrested, as Blake and Johnson were, this would have been impossible. I think that is all."

"Why is it that Mr. Wilkes did not see the stolen goods when he went to look at the house?" asked the chief.

"Because they were in the cellar. You didn't go into the cellar, did you, Mr. Wilkes?"

"No; oh, no," Wilkes replied.

"And remember, the girl wasn't in the house then," The Thinking Machine added. "She went to answer the advertisement which appeared after Mr. Wilkes had rented the house."

Then Hutchinson Hatch, who had been an interested listener, had a question.

"Why did you ask Mr. Wilkes if he had ever seen the knife or had given an order for a blade for it?"

"The blade in the dagger was of American make," replied the scientist. "The original had been broken. Peculiarly enough the new blade was made by the cutlery company which Mr. Wilkes represents. It was not impossible, therefore, that this dagger had been in his possession."

There was a long silence. The chief and Detective Fahey removed their half-chewed cigars and looked inquiringly at each other. Fahey shook his head—he had no questions. At last the chief turned to The Thinking Machine:

"If, as you say, Blake or Johnson killed Miss Gorham, how can we prove it? This is not proof—it is theory."

"Simply enough. Do the men occupy the same cell in Charlestown?"

"I hardly think so. Members of a gang that way are rarely kept in the same cell."

"In that case," said The Thinking Machine, "let the warden go to each man and tell him that the other has turned state's evidence, accusing his pal of the murder."

Johnson confessed.

The Mystery of the Grip of Death

I

Deep silence, then a long shuddering wail of terror, a stifled, strangling cry for help, the sound of a body falling, and again deep silence. A pause, and after awhile the tramp, tramp of heavy shoes through a lower hall. A door slammed and a man staggered out into a deserted street, haggard, trembling and with lips hard set. He reeled down the street and turned the first corner, waving his trembling hands fantastically.

Another pause, and spears of light flashed through the black night from the second floor of a great six-story tenement in South Boston, then came the sound of stockinged feet hurrying along the hall. Half a dozen horror-stricken men and women gathered at the door of the room whence had come the cry, helplessly gazing into one another's eyes, waiting, waiting, listening.

Finally, from inside the room, they heard a faint whispering sound as of wind rustling through dead leaves, or the silken swish of skirts, or the gasp of a dying man. They listened with strained attention until the noise stopped.

At last one of the men rapped on the door lightly. There was no answer, no sound. Again he rapped, this time louder; then he beat his fists on the door and called out. Still a silence that was terrifying. Mute inquiry lay in the eyes of all.

"Break in the door," said some one at length, in an awed whisper.

"Send for the police," said another.

The police came. They smashed in the door, old and rotting from age, and two of them entered the dark room. One of them used his lantern and those who crowded the door heard an exclamation.

"He's dead!"

Peering curiously around the corner of the door the white-faced watchers in the hall saw a man, dressed for bed, lying still on the floor. Two chairs had been over-turned; the bed clothing was disarranged. One of the policemen was bending over the body, making a hurried examination. He finally arose.

"Strangled to death with a rope—but no rope here," he explained to the other. "This is a case for a medical examiner and detectives."

"What's his name?" asked one of the policemen of a man who stood looking in curiously.

"Fred Boyd," was the reply.

"Have a room-mate?"

"No."

The other policeman was fumbling about the table with his light. At last he turned and held up something in his hand.

"Look here," he said.

It was a new wedding ring. The bright gold glittered in the lantern light.

An hour later a man turned from a side street into the avenue where stood the big tenement house, and swung along in that direction. It was the man who had left the lower door soon after the cries were heard on the second floor. Then his face had been haggard, distorted; now it was calm. One might even trace a line of melancholy and regret there.

Around the street door of the tenement was gathered a crowd of half a hundred curious ones, half-clad and shivering in the chill of the night, all craning their necks to see into the hall over the broad shoulders of a policeman who barred the door.

From a score of windows the heads of other curious ones were thrust out; there was the hum of subdued conversation.

The stranger paused on the outskirts of the little knot and peered curiously into the hall, as others were doing. He saw nothing, and turned to a bystander.

"What is it?" he asked.

"Man murdered inside," was the short response.

"Murdered?" exclaimed the stranger, "who was it?"

"Fellow named Fred Boyd."

A flash of horror passed over the stranger's face and he made an involuntary motion with his hand toward his heart. Then he steadied himself with an effort.

"How was he—he murdered?" he asked.

"Choked to death," said the other. "Somebody heard him yell for help a little while ago, and when a policeman came he smashed in the door and found him dead. The body was still warm."

The stranger's face was white as death now and his lips moved nervously. His hands, thrust deep into his pockets, were clenched until the nails cut the flesh.

"What time did it happen?" he said.

"The cop says about fifteen minutes to eleven," was the reply. "One of the tenants who lived on the second floor, where Boyd had a room, looked at his clock when he got up after he heard Boyd shout, so they know just when it was."

Uncontrollable terror glittered in the stranger's eyes, but none noted it. All were intently looking into the hall waiting for something.

"Medical Examiner Barry and Detective Mallory are up there now," volunteered the bystander. "The body will be coming out in a minute."

Then an awed whisper went around: "It's coming."

The stranger stood peering on as the others did.

"Do they know who did it?" he asked. His voice was tense, and he fiercely repressed a quaver in it.

"No," said his informant. "I heard, though, that a fellow had been up in Boyd's room to-night, and the man who had the next room heard them talking very loud. They had been playing cards."

"Did the man go out?" asked the stranger.

"Nobody saw him if he did," was the reply. "I guess, though, the police know who he was, and they're probably looking for him by this time. If they don't know, Mallory'll find him out all right."

"Great God!" exclaimed the stranger between his tightly compressed lips.

The other man turned and looked at him curiously.

"What's the matter?" he asked.

"Nothing, nothing," said the stranger, hurriedly. "Look, there it comes—that's all. It's awful, awful, awful."

The big policeman in the door stepped to one side, and men came out bearing a litter, on which lay a grim, grisly something that had been a man. It was covered with a sheet. Beside it were Detective Mallory and Medical Examiner Barry. The little knot of onlookers was silent in the presence of death.

The stranger looked, looked as if fascinated by the horrid thing which lay there, watched them put the litter into the police ambulance, heard the Medical Examiner give some instructions and then Detective Mallory re-entered the house. The wagon drove away.

Turning suddenly, the stranger strode quickly down the avenue to the first corner. There he turned away and was swallowed up in the darkness. After a moment, from a distance, came the sound of a man's footsteps, running.

II

Several newspaper men, among them Hutchinson Hatch, went over the scene of the crime with Detective Mallory. It was a square, corner room on the second floor. The furniture consisted only of a bed, a table, a wash stand, chairs, there was no carpet to cover the gaping cracks in the floor, no curtains on the two windows.

The building was old and poorly constructed. Here a part of the cornice was sagging and broken, there the walls were mouldy; the ceiling was blotched with smoke, over by the steam radiator rats had gnawed a hole big enough to put one's fist in, the single-stemmed gas jet was grimy with dirt.

Of the two windows one was in the back wall and one in the side. Hutchinson Hatch trailed around the room with Detective Mallory. He saw that the two windows were securely fastened down with a sliding catch over the middle of the lower sash; there were no broken panes so that one leaving by the window might have reached in and fastened it after him.

Mr. Mallory explored the closet, but found only the things that belong to a poor man: clothing, an old hat, a battered trunk. There was no opening, the walls were solid. Then Mr. Mallory went to the door that had been smashed in. It was the only door except that of the closet. There was no transom.

Mr. Mallory and the reporter looked at this door a long time. It had been fastened when the police came—barred with an iron rod from one side to the other—held in round, iron sockets, set in the door facing. Neither of the sockets was open at the top; the bar had to be pushed through one straight on across the door into the other.

Thus early in the investigation Hutchinson Hatch saw this problem. If the windows were fastened inside and the murderer could not have passed out that way; if the door was fastened inside with an iron bar in both sockets and the murderer could not have gone that way—What then?

Hatch thought instinctively of a certain scientist and logician of note. Professor Augustus S. F. X. Van Dusen, Ph. D., M. D., LL. D., etc., so-called The Thinking Machine, whom he had occasion to know well because of certain previous adventures in which the scientist had accomplished seemingly impossible things.

"And I think this would stump even him," Hatch said to himself with a grim smile.

Then he listened as Detective Mallory questioned the various tenants of the house. Briefly the detective brought out these facts:

A man, whose description the detective carefully noted, had called to see Boyd that evening about half past eight o'clock. He had been there many times before. Four persons had seen him this evening in Boyd's room, but no one of these knew his name. Some one passing had seen Boyd playing cards with him.

Shortly after 10 o'clock, when practically every one in the house had gone to bed, a man and woman in the next room heard Boyd's voice and that of his caller raised suddenly as if in argument. This continued for five minutes or so, then it quieted down. Such things were common in the tenement and the man and woman dropped off to sleep, thinking nothing of it.

Some time later, evidently only a few minutes, they were awakened by that pitiful, terror-stricken cry which made them shudder. With others in the house who had been aroused they dressed hurriedly. It was then they heard heavy foot steps in the hall below and the street door opened with a bang.

Both were of the opinion not five minutes could not have elapsed from the time they heard the cry until they stood outside the door where the man lay. They would have heard, they thought, anyone leave Boyd's room after they were awakened by the cry, yet there was no sound from there when they stood in the hall. Then they heard—what?

"It was a peculiar sound," the man explained. "It struck me first that it was the swish of silk skirt, then, of course, as no woman was in the room, it must have been the dying man breathing."

"Silk skirt! Woman! woman! wedding ring!" Hatch thought. Whose was it? How could a woman have escaped from the room when it seemed that it would have been impossible for a man to escape? The questionings concluded, Detective Mallory turned graciously to the representatives of the press who were waiting impatiently. It was after midnight, dangerously near the first edition time, and the reporters were anxious for the detective's comment.

He was about to begin when another reporter, one of Hatch's fellow workers, entered, called Hatch to one side and said something quickly. Hatch nodded his head and idly fingered a pack of playing cards he had taken from the table.

"Good," he said, "Go back to the office and write the story. I'll 'phone Mallory's statement and tell him that other thing. I want to do a little more work, but I'll be at the office by half-past 2 o'clock."

The reporter went out hurriedly.

"I suppose you boys want to know something about how all this happened?" the detective was saying. He lighted a cigar and spread his feet wide apart. "I'll tell you all I can—not all I know, mind you, because that wouldn't be wise, but how the murder happened, and you can put in the thrill and all that to suit yourself.

"About half-past 8 o'clock to-night a man called here to see Boyd. He knew Boyd very well—was probably a friend of several years' standing—and had called here frequently. We have an accurate description of him. He was seen by several persons who knew him by sight, therefore will be able to absolutely identify him when we arrest him.

"Now, those two men were together in this room for possibly two hours. They were playing cards. More than half the murders on record are committed in the heat of passion. These men quarrelled over their game, probably 'pitch' or 'casino'—"

"It's a pinochle pack," said Hatch.

"Then the crime was committed," the detective went on, not heeding the interruption, "the unknown man was sitting here," and Mallory indicated an overturned chair to his right.

"He leaped like this," and the detective, with a full eye for dramatic effect, illustrated, "seized Boyd by the throat, there was a struggle, notice the other overturned chair—and the unknown man bore Boyd down gripping his throat. He choked him to death."

"I thought the dead man was undressed when he was found?" asked Hatch. "The bed, too," and he indicated its disordered condition.

"He was, but—but it must have happened as I said," said the detective. He didn't like reporters who asked embarrassing questions. "His victim dead, the murderer went out by that door," and he pointed dramatically.

"Through the keyhole, I suppose?" said Hatch, quietly. "That door was fastened inside as no mere mortal could fasten it after he left the room."

"It's an old burglar's trick to fasten a door after you leave the room," said the detective, loftily.

"How about the wedding ring?"

"Ah!" and the detective looked wise. "There's nothing to be said of that now." He saw suddenly that he had made one mistake and he felt his prestige slipping away. The reporters turned a flood of questions upon him: "How did it happen Boyd was undressed?" "Who put out the gas?" "How would a burglar replace an iron bar like that?" "Do you suspect a burglar?"

Mr. Mallory raised his hand. "I will say absolutely nothing else about the case."

"Let's see if we understand you," said Hatch, and there was a mocking smile on his lips. "The police theory briefly is this: A man came here, there was a quarrel, a struggle; Boyd was killed, choked; then the murderer left this room by that door, possibly through the keyhole or a convenient crack. Then, being dead, Boyd got up, took off his clothes, turned out the gas, lay down on the floor, screamed for help and died again. Is that right?"

"Bah!" thundered Mr. Mallory, on the verge of apoplexy. "Perhaps," he added scornfully, "you know more about it than I do."

"Well, yes, I'll confess that," said Hatch. "I know at least the name of the man who was here to-night, and these other reporters will know it when their outside men come in."

"You do, eh," demanded Mr. Mallory. "Who is it?"

"His name is Frank Cunningham, a watchmaker of No. 213 — Street."

"Then he is Boyd's murderer," Mr. Mallory declared. "We'll have him under arrest in an hour."

"He has disappeared," said Hatch, and he left the room.

III

From the South Boston tenement house Hutchinson Hatch went to the undertaking establishment where the body of Fred Boyd lay, made a careful examination of the mark which showed that he had been throttled, and then went in a cab to the home of Professor Van Dusen, The Thinking Machine. As he drove up he noticed a bright light in the professor's laboratory. It was just fifteen minutes past 1 o'clock when he ascended the steps.

The Thinking Machine in person answered the door bell, the leonine head with its shock of yellow hair, the clean shaven face, and the perpetually squinted eyes behind thick glasses standing out boldly and grotesquely in the light from a nearby arc.

"Who is it?" asked The Thinking Machine.

"Hutchinson Hatch," said the reporter. "I saw your light and I was particularly anxious for a little advise, so I thought—"

"Come in," said the scientist, and he extended his long, slender fingers cordially.

Hatch followed the thin, bowed figure of the scientist, which seemed that of a child, into the laboratory where he was motioned to a seat. Then Hatch told the story of the crime, so far as it was known, while the professor sat squinting steadily at him, his long taper fingers pressed together.

"Did you see the man?" asked The Thinking Machine.

"Yes."

"What kind of marks, exactly, were those on his neck?"

"They seemed to be such marks as would be made by a large rope drawn about the throat."

"Was the skin broken?"

"No, but whoever strangled him must have had tremendous strength," said the reporter. "The pressure seemed to have been all around."

The Thinking Machine sat silent for several minutes.

"Door fastened inside with iron bar," he mused, "and no transom, so the bar was not placed back in position. Both windows fastened inside."

"It would have been absolutely impossible for any person to leave that room after Boyd was dead," said the reporter, emphatically.

"Nothing is impossible, Mr. Hatch," said The Thinking Machine, testily. "I thought I had demonstrated that clearly, once. The worst anything can be is extremely difficult—not impossible."

Hatch bowed gravely. He had walked over one of The Thinking Machine's pet hobbies.

"Man was undressed," went on The Thinking Machine. "Bed disordered, chairs overturned, gas out." He paused a moment, then asked: "You reason that the man must have gone to bed after putting out the light, and that his murderer came upon him unawares?"

"That seems to be the only possible thing to imagine," said Hatch.

"And in that case the other man—Cunningham—would not have been there?"

"Precisely."

"What sort of a wedding ring was it?"

"Perfectly new. It didn't seem to have ever been worn."

The Thinking Machine arose from his seat and took down a heavy volume, one of hundreds which lined his walls.

"You don't believe it probable that Cunningham left the room while angry and returned after Boyd was asleep and killed him?" asked The Thinking Machine as he fingered the leaves.

"He couldn't have come back if that door was fastened," said Hatch, doggedly.

"He could have, of course," said The Thinking Machine, "but it is hardly probable. Do you think it reasonable to suppose then that someone hidden in the closet waited until Cunningham was gone and then killed Boyd?"

"That sounds more plausible," said Hatch, after a moment's consideration. "But he couldn't have gone out of that room and fastened the door or window behind him."

"Of course he could have," said The Thinking Machine, irritably. "Don't keep saying he couldn't have done anything. It annoys me exceedingly."

Properly rebuked Hatch sat silent while The Thinking Machine sought something in the book.

"In the event, of course, that somebody was hidden in the room it would make it a premeditated murder, wouldn't it?" asked the scientist.

"Yes, unquestionably," replied the reporter.

"Here is something," said The Thinking Machine, as he squinted into the volume he held. "It is logic reduced to figures. Criminologists agree, practically, that thirty and one-third per cent of all premeditated crimes are committed because of money, directly or indirectly; that two per cent are committed because of insanity; and that the others, sixty-seven and two-thirds per cent, are committed because of women."

Hatch nodded.

"We'll shut out for the time being the matter of insanity—it is only a remote chance; money would hardly enter into the case because of the fact that both men were poor. Therefore, there remains a woman. The wedding ring found in the room also indicates a woman, though in what connection is not clear.

"Now, Mr. Hatch," he continued, glaring at the reporter almost fiercely, "find out all you can about the private life of this man Boyd—it will probably be like every other man of his class—and particularly his love affairs; find out also all you can about Cunningham and his love affairs. If the name of any woman appears in the case at all, find out all about her—and her love affairs. You understand?"

"Yes," was the reply.

"Don't delude yourself with the thought that it was impossible for anyone to leave that room after Boyd was dead," went on the scientist, with the stubborn persistence of a child. "Suppose this—I don't offer it as a solution—suppose that Boyd had been engaged to be married, that someone else loved the girl he was to marry, that that someone else had hidden in his room until Cunningham went away, then—you see?"

"By George!" exclaimed the reporter. "I never thought of that. But how did he get out?" he added helplessly.

"If a man did do such a thing he would have made every arrangement to leave that room in a manner calculated to puzzle anyone who came after. Mind, I don't say this is what happened at all—I merely suggest it as a possibility until I find more to work on."

Hatch arose, stretched his long legs and thanked The Thinking Machine as he pulled on his gloves.

"I'm sorry I could not have been of any more direct assistance," said the scientist. "When you do these things I ask come back to see me—I may be able to help you then. You see I'm at a tremendous disadvantage in not having seen the place where Boyd was killed. There is one thing, though, which I particularly would like for you to find out for me now—to-night."

"What is it?" asked Hatch.

"This tenement is an old building, I understand. I should like to know if the occupants have ever been annoyed by rats and mice, and if they are so annoyed now?"

"I don't quite see—" began the reporter in surprise.

"Of course not," said The Thinking Machine petulantly. "But I should like to know just the same."

"I'll find out for you."

Hutchinson Hatch had still nearly an hour, and he drove to the tenement in South Boston, to wake up its occupants and ask them—of all the silly questions in the world— "Are you annoyed by mice?" He set his teeth grimly and smiled.

When he reached the tenement he went straight on to the second floor. The steps ended within a few feet of the door where the crime had been committed. Hatch looked at the door curiously; the police had gone, the room was silent again, hiding its own mystery.

As he stood there he heard something which startled him. It came from the room where Boyd had been found dead. There was no question of that. It was a faint whispering sound as of wind rustling through dead leaves, or the silken swish of skirts, or the gasp of a dying man.

With blood tingling, Hatch rushed to the door and threw it open. He stepped inside, lighting a match as he did so. The room was empty save for the poor furniture. No sign of as living thing!

IV

Straining his ears to catch every sound, Hatch stood still, peering this way and that until the match burned his fingers. Then he lighted another and still another, but there was no repetition of the noise. At last the ghostly quiet of the room, its gloom and thoughts of the mystery which its walls had witnessed began to press on his nerves. He laughed shortly.

"A very pronounced case of enlargement of the imagination," he said to himself, and he passed out. "This thing is getting on my nerves."

Then, feeling very foolish, he aroused several persons and inquired solicitously as to whether or not they had ever been troubled with mice or rats, and when this annoyance had stopped, if it had stopped.

The concensus of opinion was that it was a silly thing to ask, but that up to a fortnight ago the rodents had been very bad. Since then no one had noticed particularly. These things, in so far as they related to rodents of any kind, were telephoned to The Thinking Machine.

"Uh, huh," he said over the 'phone. "Thanks. Good night."

From that point on every effort of the police and the press was directed to finding Frank Cunningham, who was openly charged with the murder of Fred Boyd. His disappearance had been complete. If there had been any doubt whatsoever of his guilt, this was convincing—to the police.

It was Hatch's personal efforts that uncovered the fact that Cunningham had had a bank account of $287 in a small institution, that on the morning following the mysterious crime in the

South Boston tenement a check to "cash" had been presented for the full sum and that check had been honored. This began to look conclusive.

It was also due to Hatch's personal efforts that the police learned Cunningham was to have been married a week after his disappearance to Caroline Pierce, a working girl of the West End. Then Hatch discovered that Caroline Pierce had also disappeared; that she went away presumably to work on the morning after the murder of Boyd. Where had she gone? No one knew, not even Miss Jerrod, the girl who, with her, occupied a suite of three rooms in the West End. Why had she gone? No one knew that. When had she gone? Still no one knew. When would she return? Again the same answer.

To the reporter there seemed only one plausible explanation. This was that Cunningham had drawn his money from the bank—which he had saved to make a little home for the girl he loved—and they had gone away together. In the natural course of his duty Hatch printed this, and it came to the eyes of the police. Detective Mallory smiled.

But the wedding ring in Boyd's room?

There was no explanation of that. Boyd had had no love affair so far as any one knew. He had been a hard-working, steady-going man in his trade—electrician employed by a telephone company—and he and Cunningham had been friends since boyhood.

All these things, while interesting in themselves, still threw no light on the actual crime. Who killed Boyd, and why? How did the murderer get away? Hatch had put the question to himself time and again. There was no answer. Thus the intangible pall of mystery which lay over the happenings in the South Boston tenement was still impenetrable.

On the second day after the crime Hatch again consulted The Thinking Machine. The scientist listened patiently and carefully, but without any enthusiastic interest to the reporter's recital of what he had discovered.

"Have you a man watching the place where the girl lives?" he asked.

"No," Hatch replied. "I think she's gone for good."

"I don't think so," said The Thinking Machine. "I should send a man there to see if she returns."

"If you think best," said Hatch. "But don't you think now this man Cunningham must have been the criminal?"

The scientist squinted at the reporter a long time, seemingly having heard nothing of the question.

"It looks that way to me," Hatch went on, hesitatingly. "But frankly, I can't imagine a way that he might have left that room after Boyd was dead."

Still the scientist was silent, and the reporter nervously fingered his hat. "That information you gave me about the rats was very interesting," said The Thinking Machine at last, irrelevantly.

"Perhaps, but I don't see how it applies."

"Looking out the windows of the room where Boyd was found, what did you see?" the scientist interrupted.

Hatch did not recall that he had ever looked out either of the windows; he had merely satisfied himself that neither had been used as a means of exit. Now he blushed guiltily.

"I'm afraid you haven't looked," said The Thinking Machine, testily. "I thought probably you wouldn't have. Suppose we go to South Boston this afternoon and see that room."

"If you only would," said Hatch, delightedly. Here was better luck than he dreamed of. "If you only would," he repeated.

"We'll go now," said The Thinking Machine. He left the room and returned a moment later dressed for the street. The slender, bent figure and the great head seemed more grotesque than ever.

"Before we go," he instructed, "telephone to your office and have a reliable man sent to watch the girl's house. Tell him under no circumstances to try to enter or speak with anyone there until he hears from us."

The Thinking Machine stood waiting impatiently while Hatch did this. Then they took a cab to the tenement in South Boston.

"Dear me, what an old, ramshackle affair it is!" commented the scientist as they climbed the stairs.

The door of Boyd's room was not locked. The furniture and the personal effects of the man had been moved out—taken in charge by the Medical Examiner for possible use at an inquest.

"Just how was this room fastened when Boyd was found?" asked the scientist.

Hatch showed him, at the door and windows. The Thinking Machine was interested for a moment and then looked out the side window. Straight down fifteen feet was a wilderness of ash barrels and boxes and papers—a typical refuse heap of a cheap tenement. Then The Thinking Machine squinted out the back window. There he saw an open space, a rough baseball diamond, intersected at two places by the trampled down rings of a circus.

Perfunctorily he peered into the closet, after which his eyes swept the room in one comprehensive squint. He noted the begrimed condition of the place; the drooping cornice, the smoky ceiling, the gaping cracks in the floor, the rat holes beside the radiator, the dirty gas pipe leading down to a single jet. He leaned against a wall and wrote for several minutes on a sheet of paper torn from his notebook.

"Have you an envelope?" he asked.

Hatch produced one. The Thinking Machine put what he had written into the envelope, sealed it and handed it back.

"There's something that may interest you some time," he said, "but don't open it until I give you permission to do so."

"Certainly not," said the reporter, puzzled but without question. "But may I ask—"

"What it is?" snapped the scientist. "No, I will tell you when to open it."

They descended the stairs together.

"Somewhere to a public telephone," were The Thinking Machine's instructions to the cabby. At a nearby drug store, he disappeared into a telephone booth and remained for five minutes. When he came out he asked for the envelope he had given Hatch and in a little crabbed hand wrote on it:

"November 9-10."

"Keep it," he commanded, as he returned it to the reporter. "Now we'll drive to the girl's place."

When the cab reached the West End address it was a little later than dusk. Caroline Pierce and her girl chum occupied a front apartment on the ground floor. As The Thinking Machine and

Hatch were about to enter the building, Tom Manning, another reporter on Hatch's paper, approached them.

"The girl hasn't returned," he reported. "The other girl—Miss Jerrod—came back home from work just a few minutes ago."

"We'll see her," said The Thinking Machine. Then to Manning: "At the end of two minutes, by your watch, after I enter this apartment, ring the bell several times. Don't be afraid. Ring it! If any person runs out, man or woman, hold him. Mr. Hatch, you go to the back entrance of this apartment. Stop any person, man or woman, coming from this suite."

"You believe then—" Hatch began.

"I'll give you two minutes to get to the back door," snapped The Thinking Machine.

Hatch disappeared hurriedly, and for just two minutes, not a second more, The Thinking Machine waited. Then he rang the bell of the apartment. Miss Jerrod appeared at the door. He followed her into the suite.

Manning at the front door waited, watch in hand. When the two minutes were up he rang the bell time after time, long, insistent rings. He could hear it tinkling furiously. Then he heard something else. It was the slamming of a door, a rush of feet and a struggle. Then The Thinking Machine appeared before him.

"Come in," he said, modestly. "We have Cunningham inside."

V

A little drama of human emotion was being enacted in the tiny front suite. Frank Cunningham, wanted for the murder of Fred Boyd, sat wearily resigned in the corner furthest from the door under the watchful eye of Hutchinson Hatch. The man was unshaven, haggard, and there lay in his eyes the restless, feverish look of one who lives his life in terror of the law. Caroline Pierce, who was to have been his wife, had flung herself on a couch, weeping hysterically.

Towering above the slender, shrinking figure of The Thinking Machine, Miss Jerrod was bitterly denouncing him for a trick which had given Cunningham into his hands. The scientist listened patiently, albeit unhappily. He couldn't help himself.

"You told me," stormed Miss Jerrod, "that you believed him innocent, and now this—this."

"Well?" said The Thinking Machine meekly.

Miss Jerrod was about to say something else when Cunningham stopped her with a gesture.

"I'm rather glad of it," he said, "or rather I would be if it were not for her," and he indicated Caroline Pierce. "I have never spent such hours of mortal fear as those since the murder of Fred Boyd. Now, somehow, it's a relief to know it must all come out."

"You know you were a fool to try to hide, anyway," said The Thinking Machine, frankly.

"I know I made a mistake—now," replied Cunningham. "But we were afraid—Caroline and I—and I couldn't help it."

"Well, go on with your story," commanded the scientist testily.

Manning, the other reporter, crossed the room and sat beside Hatch, while Cunningham moved over, took a seat beside the couch where the girl lay weeping and gently stroked her hair.

"I'll tell what story I can," he said at last. "I don't know what you'll think of it, but—"

"Pardon me just a moment," said The Thinking Machine. He went to Cunningham and ran his long, slender fingers over the prisoner's head several times. Suddenly he leaned forward and squinted at Cunningham's head.

"What is this?" he asked.

"That is where a silver plate was put in," Cunningham replied. "I was badly injured by a fall when I was about fourteen years old."

"Yes, yes," said the scientist. "Go on with your story."

"I have known Boyd since we were boys together up in Vermont," Cunningham began, "and there, too, I knew Caroline. All three of us came from the same little town—Caroline only two years ago. Boyd and I had been in Boston for seven years when she came. Boyd lived for five years in that—that room in South Boston, where—"

"Never mind," said The Thinking Machine. "Go on."

"Well, Caroline came here two years ago as I said and I believe that Boyd loved her as well as I do," said Cunningham. "But she promised to be my wife and we were to be married next Wednesday—"

"But the night Boyd was killed," interrupted The Thinking Machine impatiently. "Come down to that."

"I went to Boyd's room that night at a few minutes after eight o'clock. We sat for an hour or more and talked of our work, our plans and various things as we played cards—pinochle it was. Neither of us was particularly interested in the game.

"Boyd didn't know of my coming marriage to Caroline and finally I happened to mention her name. I also showed him the wedding ring I had bought that day for her. He looked at it, and asked me what I intended to do with it. I then told him that Caroline and I were to be married.

"He was surprised. I think any man in his position would have been surprised, because I think it was his intention to ask her to marry him. Well, at any rate, he grew angry about it, and I tried to placate him.

"I guess he was pretty hard hit—worse than I thought—for several times between the deals he picked up the ring and looked at it, then he'd put it down each time on his side of the table.

"After awhile he threw down his hand with the remark that he didn't care to play. 'Now look here, Fred,' I said, 'I didn't think of the thing hitting you so hard.' He replied something about it not being fair to him, though just what he meant I didn't know.

"Then word led to word, until finally I was in a fury at a careless reference he made to Caroline—a thing he would never thought of doing in his proper senses—and demanded an apology. He grew ugly and said still more, and then, somehow, I don't know quite what happened. I know that I had an insane desire to take hold of him—but—"

Cunningham paused and gently stroked the hand of the girl.

"And then?" asked The Thinking Machine.

"You know this hurt on my head was more serious than you may imagine," said Cunningham. "There are times, in moments of anger particularly, when things are not clear to me. I lose myself, I don't know what to do. A surgeon once explained to me why it was but I don't remember."

"I understand," said The Thinking Machine. "Go on."

"Well, from the moment the quarrel became really serious I would not swear to anything that happened," Cunningham resumed.

"I know at last I found myself in the lower hall after what seemed a long time, and I remember leaving there, slamming the door behind me.

"I went down the avenue and was almost home when it occurred to me that the ring was in Boyd's room. By that time, too, I was seeing things more clearly. I wanted to go back and talk to Boyd more calmly and see if both of us hadn't said things we should not have said. It was with this double purpose of seeing him and getting the ring that I started back to the tenement.

"Outside, I found a crowd. I wondered why, and asked. One man told me Boyd had been murdered—choked to death; that the police knew who did it and were searching for him. I was terror-stricken, and after the body was taken out I walked away. The terror was on me, and after I turned into a side street I broke into a run. I knew myself, you see, and my own irresponsibility.

"Then, although it was midnight, I came straight here, aroused Caroline and Miss Jerrod and told them both what had happened so far as I knew. There seemed to be nothing else to do but hide; I did it. I remained here, as I thought safely enough. Two or three reporters came and asked questions, and once a detective was here, but Miss Jerrod answered their inquiries satisfactorily and that seemed to be all—until now. To-morrow Caroline and I were going back to Vermont."

There was a long pause. Caroline pressed the hand of the man she loved to her cheek with a gesture of infinite confidence. The Thinking Machine sat silent with the tips of his long, slender fingers together.

"Mr. Cunningham," he said at last, "you have not told us the one vital thing. Did you or did you not kill Fred Boyd?"

"I don't know," was the reply. "If I only could know!"

"Uh," grunted The Thinking Machine. "I was afraid you wouldn't know."

VI

Hutchinson Hatch and Manning, the other reporter, gazed at Cunningham thunderstruck, and from him to The Thinking Machine.

"Don't know whether or not you killed a man?" asked Hatch incredulously.

"It's perfectly possible, Mr. Hatch," said The Thinking Machine, curtly. "I understand, Mr. Cunningham," he explained. "I suppose you would be perfectly willing to go with me now?"

"No, no, no," exclaimed Caroline Pierce suddenly, in evident terror.

"Not to the police, Miss Pierce," said The Thinking Machine. He paused a moment and looked at the girl curiously. Of women he knew nothing, and knew he knew nothing. "Perhaps it would assure you, Miss Pierce, if I told you I know that Mr. Cunningham did not kill Boyd."

"You believe he didn't, then?" she asked eagerly.

"I know he didn't," said The Thinking Machine tersely. "Two and two make four not some times, but *all* the time," he went on enigmatically. "If Mr. Cunningham will come with me now we will establish beyond all doubt the cause of Boyd's death. Do you believe me?"

"Yes," said the girl slowly, and she looked steadily into the squint eyes of the scientist. "I—I have faith in you."

The Thinking Machine coughed, slightly embarrassed, and turned to Hatch with a faint color in his cheeks.

"Well, who did kill Boyd?" asked Hatch, amazed.

"That's what we will now demonstrate," was the reply. "Come on."

After Cunningham had himself assured the girl of his safety the four men passed out into the night—it was nearly 10 o'clock—entered a cab and were driven to the tenement in South Boston. There they passed up the one flight of stairs into the room where Boyd had been found, and after lighting the gas the scientist made one quick survey of the room.

"These walls are awfully thin," he commented petulantly. "If I should fire a pistol in here I might kill someone in another room. Yes, a knife would do better. Have any of you gentlemen a knife—one with a blade that won't break easily?"

"Will this do?" asked Cunningham, and he produced one.

The Thinking Machine examined it and nodded his satisfaction.

"Now a revolver," he said.

Manning went out to get one. While he was gone The Thinking Machine gave some formal instructions to Cunningham and Hatch.

"I'm going to put out this light and remain in this room alone," he said. "I may be here fifteen minutes or I may be here till daylight. I don't know. But I want you three to remain quietly outside the door and listen. When I need you I shall need you quickly. My life may be in danger, and I am not a strong man."

"What is it anyway?" asked Hatch curiously.

"After awhile you will hear something inside, I have no doubt," went on the scientist, paying no attention to the question. "But don't enter the room under any circumstances until I call out or you hear a struggle."

"But what is it?" asked Hatch again. "I don't understand at all."

"I'm going to find the murderer of Fred Boyd," said the scientist. "Please do not ask so many absurd questions. They annoy me exceedingly. I may have to kill him," he added reflectively.

"Kill him?" gasped Hatch. "Who, the murderer?" He couldn't help it.

"Yes, the murderer," was the tart reply.

Manning returned with the revolver, which The Thinking Machine examined and handed to Hatch.

"You will know what to do with it when you enter the room," he instructed. "You, Manning, come in with these other two and light this gas. Keep your matches in your hand."

Then the two reporters and Cunningham passed out of the room, closing the door, but not fastening it. Pressed close against the panels outside, listening, Hatch started to explain to Manning in a whisper when they heard the irritated voice of the scientist.

"Keep silent," was the sharp command.

Five minutes, ten minutes, half an hour of utter silence, save for a distant sound of some sort in the big tenement. But no one came up the stairs. The dim gas light fluttered weirdly down the hall.

A full hour passed, still nothing. Hatch could hear his heart beat, also he thought the regular breathing of The Thinking Machine. At last there came a slight sound, and Hatch started. The other men heard, too.

It was a faint whispering sound, as of the wind rustling through dead leaves, or the silken swish of skirts or the gasp of a dying man.

Hatch clutched the revolver more firmly and set his teeth hard together. He was going to face something—a deadly, terrible something—and had not the faintest idea of what it might be. Manning held a match ready for instant use.

Then, as they listened, there was another sound, still faint, as of something sliding over the floor. Suddenly there was a heavy thump, a half-strangled cry from The Thinking Machine and the sounds of a fearful struggle. Hatch rushed into the room with revolver raised; Manning was just behind him. A match flared up and they saw a struggling heap on the floor. The arm of the scientist rose and fell thrice, burying the knife each time in flesh.

In the light of the gas, which hissed into a brilliant light under the match, the reporter placed the revolver flat against the head of a writhing, twisting body and fired. For the second time he fired, and the struggling bodies lay still.

Then for the first time Hatch realized what had happened. A giant boa constrictor held The Thinking Machine in its coils and was in its death struggle almost crushing the life out of him. It required the combined efforts of the three men to release the scientist from the deadly folds. He lay still for a moment, but finally the life came back into his frail body with a rush. He raised up from Hatch's arms and looked curiously at the snake.

"Dear me, dear me," he commented. "What a brain would have been lost to scientific inquiry if that snake had killed me."

Occupants of the house, aroused by the two pistol shots, rushed again terror-stricken to the room, and after awhile the police came and rescued the four men from the besieging mob of questioners. All went to the police station, and there The Thinking Machine, with several caustic comments on the police in general, told his story. The body of the giant retile lay full length on the floor.

"Mr. Hatch here asked for my advice in the matter," he explained to the police captain, "and I did what I could to assist him. When he explained the condition of the body and the room when it was broken open—the fact the door and both windows were fastened securely inside—it instantly occurred to me that, with suicide removed as a possibility, the thing which had killed Boyd was still in the room or else had escaped only after the body was found.

"It was not unreasonable to suppose that any animal, a snake for instance, would have attempted to leave the room while a crowd of people blocked the door; in fact it was not unreasonable to suppose that such a snake, snuggly fixed in a large, tumble-down building, with the infinite possibility of feeding on rats and mice, would attempt to leave the building at all. It could get water easily from a dozen places.

"Therefore I presumed it was a snake, and I asked Mr. Hatch to ascertain for me first if the people in the house had ever been greatly annoyed by rodents; if they were now, and if not, when they had noticed that they were not. He reported to me that they had been annoyed up to a fortnight preceding the crime, but since they had not noticed. Of course a boa constrictor can live on rodents, therefore they would leave the building or be eaten out of it gradually.

"A fortnight since they missed the rodents? That meant that the snake must have been in the building at least that long. All these conclusion I reached before I personally went over the scene. If it were a snake, as I thought possible, it must have come from somewhere. Where, then?"

The Thinking Machine paused and looked from one to another of his hearers. Each in turn shook his head, Hatch being the last to do so.

"And yet your own paper published a full solution of the mystery before it ever occurred," said the scientist sharply. "Looking from the back window of the room there, perfectly visible, were three banked rings, plainly where a circus had been. Possibly the snake escaped from that circus and crept into the house.

"I called up your office on the 'phone, Mr. Hatch, and ascertained that there had been a circus on that place two weeks before, November 9 and 10, and further I found that a boa constrictor had escaped from that circus. You printed a column of it on the first page."

"Lord, and we really thought that was a press agent's yarn," remarked Hatch sadly.

"To-night when we went to the room it was my intention to allow the snake to creep out of that large hole near the radiator—I suppose you noticed there was one there?—then to pass between the snake and the hole and call for Mr. Hatch and these other gentlemen who were waiting outside the door.

"If the snake attacked me I had a knife and Mr. Hatch had a revolver.

"But I'm afraid I didn't give the snake credit for quickness and such enormous strength," he went on ruefully. "I heard the snake come out of the hole, and then instantly almost I felt its folds crushing me. Then these gentlemen rushed in. I can readily understand how it choked Boyd, he having no way to defend himself, and then crawled away when those people knocked on the door. It nearly crushed the life out of me."

That seemed to be all, and The Thinking Machine stopped.

"But Frank Cunningham?" asked the police captain. "Why did he run away, and where is he now?"

"Cunningham?" repeated the scientist, puzzled.

"Yes," said the captain. "Where is he?"

"Why here he is," and The Thinking Machine indicated the accused man. "Mr. Cunningham permit me to introduce you to Captain—er—er. I don't know his name."

The captain was not surprised; he was nonplussed. It had never occurred to him to ask the name of the fourth member of the party; he knew the two newspaper men.

"How—where—when did you—" he began.

"Not knowing whether or not he had killed his friend Boyd," explained the scientist, "he was hiding in the suite of Miss Caroline Pierce, his fiancé. His lack of knowledge was due entirely to a queer mental condition. He was badly hurt at one time and wears a silver plate in his head. That accounts for many things."

"How did you get him?" asked the captain, amazed.

"I walked into Miss Pierce's suite after I had put a man at the back and front to stop any one who ran out, and told Miss Pierce's friend, Miss Jerrod, that I believed—in fact knew—that Cunningham was innocent, and that I had come merely to warn him," said The Thinking Machine.

"I told her then that three policemen were at the front door, and then Mr. Manning here rang the bell violently, as I had instructed him, and Cunningham dashed out of a rear room and started out the back way. Mr. Hatch got him there. It was perfectly simple—that part of it. Of course, there was a chance that he wasn't there at all—but he was."

The Thinking Machine arose.

"Is that all?" he asked.

"Why did you examine Cunningham's head before he told us his story?" asked Hatch.

"I have some idea of the cranial formation of criminals and I merely wanted to satisfy myself," said the scientist. "It was then that I discovered the silver plate in his head."

"And this?" asked Hatch. He took from his pocket the sealed envelope which The Thinking Machine had given him in the tenement room immediately after he had inspected the room. On this envelope was written "November 9-10", this being the date the circus was in South Boston.

"Oh, that?" said Professor Van Dusen a little impatiently, "that is merely a solution to the mystery."

Hatch opened the envelope and looked at it. There were only a few words:

"Snake. Came through hole near radiator. Lived in walls. Escaped from circus. Cunningham innocent."

"That all?" again asked The Thinking Machine.

There was no answer, and the scientist and the two newspaper men left the police station, followed by Cunningham.

The Problem of Convict No. 97

Martha opened the door. Her distinguished master, Professor Augustus S. F. X. Van Dusen—The Thinking Machine—lay senseless on the floor. His upturned face, always drawn and pale, was deathly white now, the thin straight lips were colorless, the eyelids drooping, and the profuse yellow hair was tumbled back from the enormous brow in disorder. His arms were outstretched on either side helplessly, and the slender white hands were still and inert. The fading light from the windows over the laboratory table beat down upon the pitifully small figure, and so for the moment Martha stood with distended eyes gazing in terror and apprehension. She was not of the screaming kind, but a great lump rose in her old throat. Then, with fear tearing at her heart, she swooped the slender, child-like figure up in her strong arms and laid it on a couch.

"Glory be!" she exclaimed, and there was devotion in the tone—devotion to this eminent man of science whom she had served so long. "What could have happened to the poor, poor man?"

For another moment she stood looking upon the pallid face, then the necessity of action impressed itself upon her. The heart was still beating,—she convinced herself of that,—and he was breathing. Perhaps he had only fainted. She grasped at the idea hopefully, and turned, seeking water. There was a faucet over a sink at the end of the long table, and innumerable graduated glasses; but even in her excited condition Martha knew better than to use one of them. All sorts of chemicals had been in them—poisons too. With another quick glance at the little scientist she rushed out of the room, as she had entered, bent on getting water.

When she appeared again at the open door with pitcher and drinking glass she paused a second time in amazement. The distinguished scientist was sitting cross legged on the couch, thoughtfully caressing the back of his head.

"Martha, did anyone call?" he inquired.

"Lor', sir! what did happen to you?" she burst out amazedly.

"Oh, a little accident," he explained irritably. "Did anyone call?"

"No, sir. How do you feel now, sir?"

"Don't disturb yourself about me, my good woman; I'm all right," The Thinking Machine assured her, and put his feet to the floor. "You are sure no one was here?"

"Yes, sir. Lor'! you was that white when I picked you up from the floor there—"

"Was I lying on my back or my face?"

"Flat of your back, sir, all sprawled out. I thought you was dead, sir."

Again The Thinking Machine thoughtfully caressed the back of his head, and Martha rattled on verbosely, indicating just where and how he had been lying when she opened the door.

"Are you sure that you didn't hear any sound?" again queried the scientist.

"Nothing, sir."

"Any sudden jar?"

"Nothing, sir, nothing. I was just laying the tea things, sir, and opened the door to tell you it was ready."

She poured a glass of water from the pitcher, and The Thinking Machine moistened his lips, to which the color was slowly returning.

"Martha," he directed, "go see if the front door is closed, please."

Martha went out. "Yes, sir," she reported on her return.

"Locked?"

"Yes, sir."

The Thinking Machine arose and straightened up, almost himself again. Then he went over to the laboratory table and peered squintingly into a mirror which hung there, after which he wandered all over his apartments, examining windows, trying doors, and stopping occasionally to stare curiously about at objects which had been familiar for years. He turned; Martha was just behind him, looking on wonderingly.

"Lost something, sir?" she asked solicitously.

"You are sure you didn't hear any sound of any sort?" he asked in turn.

"Not a thing, sir."

Then The Thinking Machine went to the telephone. In a minute or so he was in conversation with Hutchinson Hatch, newspaper reporter.

"Heard of any jail delivery at Chisholm prison?" he inquired.

"No," replied the reporter. "Why?"

"There has been an escape," said the scientist positively.

"Who was it?" demanded the reporter eagerly. "How did it happen?"

"The prisoner's name is Philip Gilfoil. I don't know how he got out, but he is out."

"Philip Gilfoil?" Hatch repeated. "He's the forger who—"

"Yes, the forger," said The Thinking Machine abruptly. "He's out. You might go over and investigate, then come by and see me."

Hatch spoke to his city editor and rushed out. Half an hour later he was at Chisholm prison, a vast spreading structure of granite in the suburbs, and in conversation with the warden, an old acquaintance.

"Who was it that escaped?" Hatch began briskly.

"Escaped?" repeated the warden with a momentary start, and then he laughed. "Nobody."

"You have been keeping Philip Gilfoil here, haven't you?"

"I am keeping Philip Gilfoil here," was the grim response. "He is No. 97, and is now in Cell 9."

"How long since you have seen him?" the reporter insisted.

"Ten minutes," was the ready response.

The reporter was staring at him steadily; but the warden's eyes met his frankly. There have been instances where denials of this sort have been made offhand with the idea of preventing the public from knowing the truth as long as possible. Hatch knew of several.

"May I see Gilfoil?" he inquired coldly.

"Sure," replied the warden cheerfully. "Come on and I'll show you."

He escorted the newspaper man along the corridor to Cell 9. "Ninety-seven, are you there?" he called.

"Where'd you expect I'd be?" grumbled some one inside.

"Come to the door for a minute."

There was a movement inside the cell, and the figure of a man approached the door out of the gloom. It had been several months since Hatch had seen Philip Gilfoil; but there was not the slightest question in his mind about the identity of this man. It was Gilfoil—the same sharp, hooked nose, the same thin lipped mouth, everything the same save now that the prison pallor was upon him. There was frank surprise in the reporter's face.

"Do you know me, Gilfoil?" he inquired.

"I'll never forget you," replied the prisoner. There was anything but a kindly expression in the voice. "You're the fellow who helped to send me here—you and the old professor chap."

Hatch led the way back to the warden's office. "Look here, warden!" he remarked pointedly, accusingly. "I want to know the real facts. Has that man been out of his cell since he has been here?"

"No, except for exercise," was the reply. "All the prisoners are allowed a certain time each day for that."

"I mean has he never been out of the prison?"

"Not on your life!" declared the warden. "He's in for eight years, and he doesn't get out till that's up."

"I have reason to believe—the best reason in the world to believe—that he has been out," insisted the reporter.

"You are talking through your hat, Hatch," said the warden, and he laughed with the utmost good nature. "What's the matter, anyway?"

Hatch didn't choose to tell him. He went instead to a telephone and called up The Thinking Machine.

"You are mistaken about Gilfoil having escaped," he told the scientist. "He is still in Chisholm prison."

"Did you see him?" came the irritable demand.

"Saw him and talked to him," replied the reporter. "He was in Cell 9 not five minutes ago."

There was a long silence. Hatch could imagine what it meant—The Thinking Machine was turning this over and over in his mind.

"You are mistaken, Mr. Hatch," came the surprising statement at last in the same irritable, querulous voice. "Gilfoil is not in his cell. I know he is not. There is no need to argue about it. Good by."

It so happened that Professor Augustus S. F. X. Van Dusen was well acquainted with the warden of Chisholm prison. Thus it was that when he called at the prison half an hour or so after Hatch had gone he was received with more courtesy and attention than would have been the case if he had been a casual visitor. The warden shook hands with him and there was a pleasant reminiscent grin on his face.

"I want to find out something about this man Gilfoil," the scientist began abruptly.

"You too?" remarked the warden. "Hutchinson Hatch was here a little while ago inquiring about him."

"Yes, I sent him," said the scientist. "He tells me that Gilfoil is still here?"

"He is still here," said the warden emphatically. "He's been here for nearly a year, and will remain here for another seven years. Hatch seemed to have an impression that he had escaped. Do you happen to know where he got that idea?"

The Thinking Machine squinted into his face for an instant inscrutably, then glanced up at the clock. It was eighteen minutes past eight o'clock.

"Are you sure that Gilfoil is in his cell?" he demanded curtly.

"I know he is—in Cell 9." The warden tilted his cigar to an angle which was only a little less than aggressive, and glared at his visitor curiously. This constant questioning as to Convict 97, and the implied doubt behind it, was anything but soothing. The Thinking Machine dropped back into a chair, and the watery blue eyes were turned upward. The warden knew the attitude.

"How long have you had Gilfoil?" queried The Thinking Machine after a moment.

"A little more than ten months."

"Well behaved prisoner?"

"Well, yes, now he is. When he first came he was rather an unpleasant customer, and was given to profanity, but lately he has realized the uselessness of it all, and now, I may say, he is a model of decency. That's the usual course with prisoners; they are bad at first, and then in nine cases out of ten they settle down and behave themselves."

"Naturally," mused the scientist. "Just when did you first notice this change for the better in his conduct?"

"Oh, a month or six weeks ago," was the reply.

"Was it a gradual change or a sudden change?"

"I couldn't say, really," responded the wondering warden. "I suppose it might be called a sudden change. I noticed one day that he didn't swear at me as I passed his cell, and that was unusual."

The Thinking Machine straightened up in his chair suddenly and squinted belligerently at the official for an instant. Then he sank back again, and his eyes wandered upward.

"Do you happen to remember that first date he didn't swear at you?"

The warden laughed. "It didn't make any particular impression on my mind. It was a month or six weeks ago."

"Has he sworn at you since?" the scientist went on.

"No, I don't think anyone has heard him swear since. He's been remarkably well behaved."

"Any callers?"

"Well, not for a long time. A physician came here to see him twice. There was something the matter with his throat, I think."

"How did it happen that the prison physician didn't attend him?" demanded The Thinking Machine curiously.

"He asked that an outside physician be called," was the response. "He had twelve or fifteen dollars here in the office, and I paid the physician out of that."

Some new line of thought had evidently been awakened in the scientist's mind; for there came a subtle change in the drawn face, and for a long time he was silent.

"Do you happen to remember," he asked slowly at last, "if the physician was called in before or after he stopped swearing?"

"After, I think," the warden replied wearily. "What the deuce is all this about, anyway?" he demanded flatly after a moment.

"Throat trouble, you said. How did it affect him?"

"Made him a little hoarse, that's all. The doctor told me it wasn't anything particularly—probably the dampness in the cell or something."

"And did you know the doctor who was called—know him personally?" demanded The Thinking Machine, and there was a strange, new gleam in the narrow eyes.

"Yes, quite well. I've known him for years. I let him in and let him out."

The crabbed little scientist seemed almost disappointed. He dropped back again into the depths of the chair.

"Do you want to see Gilfoil?" asked the warden.

"Not yet," was the reply; "but I should like you to walk down the corridor very, very softly and flash your light in Cell 9 and see if Convict 97 is there?"

The warden came to his feet suddenly. There was something in the tone which startled him; but the momentary shock was followed instantly by a little nervous laugh. No man knew better than he that Convict 97 was still there, yet to please this whimsical visitor he lighted his dark lantern and went out. He was gone only a couple of minutes, and when he returned there was a queer expression on his face—almost an awed expression.

"Well?" queried the scientist. "Was he asleep."

"No," replied the warden, "he wasn't. He was down on his knees beside his cot, praying."

The Thinking Machine arose and paced back and forth across the office two or three times. At last he turned to the warden. "Really, I hate to put you to so much trouble," he said; "but believe me it is in the interests of justice. I should like personally to visit Cell 9 say in an hour from now after Convict 97 is asleep. Meanwhile, don't let me disturb you. Go on about your affairs; I'll wait."

And then and there The Thinking Machine gave the warden a lesson in perfect repose. He glanced at the clock,—the hands indicated eight-forty,—then sat down again, and for one hour he sat there without the slightest movement to indicate even a casual interest in anybody or anything. The warden, busy with some accounts, glanced around curiously at the diminutive figure half a dozen times; once or twice he imagined his visitor had fallen asleep, but the blue eyes behind the thick spectacles, narrow as they were, belied this idea. It was precisely twenty-one minutes of ten o'clock when The Thinking Machine arose.

"Now, please," he requested.

Without a word of protest the warden relighted the dark lantern, opened the doors leading into the corridor of the prison, and they went on to Cell 9. They paused at the door. There was utter silence in the huge prison, broken only by the regular, rhythmic breathing of Convict 97. At a motion from The Thinking Machine the warden softly unlocked the cell door, and they entered.

"Silence, please," whispered the scientist.

He took the lantern from the warden's unresisting hand, and going softly to the cot turned the light full into the face of the sleeping man. For a second or so he gazed steadily at the features upturned thus to him, then the brilliant light seemed to disturb the sleeper, for his eyelids twitched, and finally opened with a start.

"Do you know me, Gilfoil?" demanded The Thinking Machine suddenly, and he leaned forward so that the cutting rays of light should illumine has own features.

"Yes," the prisoner replied shortly.

"What's my name?" insisted the scientist.

"Van Dusen," was the prompt reply. "I know you, all right." Convict 97 raised himself on an elbow and met the eyes of the other two men without a quiver.

"What size shoe do you wear?" demanded the scientist.

"None of your business!" growled the convict.

The Thinking Machine turned the lantern to the floor and found the shoes the prisoner had laid aside on retiring. He picked them up and examined them carefully, after which he replaced them, nodded to the warden, and they went out. The prisoner lay for a long time, resting on his elbow, seeking to pierce the gloom of the cell and corridor beyond with wide awake eyes, then, sighing, lay down again.

"Let me see Gilfoil's pedigree, and I shall not annoy you further," The Thinking Machine requested, once they were in the warden's office again. The record book was forthcoming. The scientist copied, accurately and at length, everything written therein concerning Philip Gilfoil. "And last," he requested, "the name, please, of the physician who called to see Convict 97?"

"Dr. Heindell," replied the Warden,— "Dr. Delmore L. Heindell."

The Thinking Machine replaced his notebook in his pocket, planted his hat more firmly on the great shock of yellow hair, and slowly began to draw on his gloves.

"What is all this thing about Gilfoil, anyhow?" demanded the warden desperately. "Be good enough to inform me what the deuce you and Hatch have been driving at?"

"You are, I believe, an able, careful, conscientious man," said The Thinking Machine, "and I don't know that under the circumstances you can be blamed for what has happened; but the man you have in Cell 9 is not Philip Gilfoil. I don't know who your Convict 97 is; but Philip Gilfoil hasn't been in Chisholm prison for weeks. Good night."

And the crabbed little scientist went on his way.

For the third time Hutchinson Hatch rapped upon the little door. The echo reverberated through the house; but there came no answering sound. The modest cottage in a quiet street of a fashionable suburb seemed wholly deserted, yet as he stepped back to the edge of the veranda he could see a faint light trickling through closely drawn shutters on the second floor.

Surely there must be some one there, the reporter reasoned, or that light would not be burning. And if some one was there, why wouldn't they answer? As he looked the trickling light remained still, and then he went to the door and tried it. It was unlocked. He merely ascertained that the door yielded readily under his hand, then he rapped for the fourth time. No answer yet.

He was just turning away from the door, when suddenly it opened before him, a single arm shot out from the gloom of the hall, and before he could retreat had closed on the collar of his coat. He was hauled into the house despite an instinctive resistance, then the door banged behind him. He could see nothing; the darkness was intense. But still that powerful hand gripped his collar.

"I'll fix your clock, young fellow, right now!" said a man's voice.

Then, even as he struggled, he was conscious of a heavy blow on the point of the chin, strange lights dancing fantastically before his eyes; he felt himself sinking, sinking, and then he knew no more.

When he recovered consciousness he lay stretched full length upon a couch on a strange room. His head seemed bursting, and the rosy light of dawn through the window caused a tense pain in his eyes. For half a minute he lay still, until he had remembered those singular events which had preceded this, and then he started up. He was leaning on one elbow surveying the room, when he became conscious of the rustling of skirts. He turned; a woman was advancing toward him—a woman of apparently thirty years, in whose sweet face lay some heavy, desperate grief.

Involuntarily Hatch struggled to his feet—perhaps it was a spirit of defense, perhaps a natural gallantry. She paused and stood looking at him.

"What happened?" he demanded flatly. "What am I doing here?"

The woman's eyes grew suddenly moist, and her lips trembled. "I'm glad it was no worse," she said hopelessly.

"Who are you?" Hatch asked curiously.

"Please don't ask," she pleaded. "Please don't! If you are able to go, please go now while you may."

The reporter wasn't at all certain that he wanted to go. He was himself again now, confident, alert, with new strength rushing through his veins, and a naturally inquisitive mind fully aroused. If it was only a poke in the jaw he got, it didn't matter much. He had had those before, and besides here was something which demanded an explanation.

"Who was the man who struck me last night?" he asked.

"Please go!" the woman pleaded. "Believe me, you must. I can't explain anything—it's all horrible and unreal and hideous!" Tears were streaming down the wan cheeks now, and the hands closed and unclosed spasmodically.

Hatch sat down. "I am not going yet," he said. "Tell me about it."

"There is nothing I can tell—nothing!" the woman sobbed.

She buried her face in her hands and wept softly. Then Hatch saw a great bruised spot across her cheek and neck—it might have been the mark of a lash. Whatever particular kind of trouble he was in, he told himself, he was not alone, for she too was a victim.

"You must tell me about it," he insisted.

"I can't, I can't!" she wailed.

And then a cringing, awful fear came into her tear stained face, as she lifted her head to listen. There was the sound of footsteps outside the door.

"He'll kill you, he'll kill you!" whispered the woman.

Hatch set his lips grimly, motioned her to silence, and stepped toward the door. A heavy chair stood there. He weighed it judicially in his hands, and glanced toward the woman reassuringly. She had dropped down on the couch and had buried her face in a pillow; her slender form was shaking with sobs. Hatch raised the chair above his head and closed his hands on it fiercely.

There was a slight rattle as some one turned the knob of the door. Then it opened and a man entered. Hatch stared at the profile with amazed eyes.

"By George!" he exclaimed.

Then he brought the chair down with all the strength of two well muscled arms. The man sank to the floor without a sound; the woman straightened up, screamed once, and fell forward in a dead faint.

It was about ten o'clock that morning when The Thinking Machine and Hutchinson Hatch, together with a powerful cabman, dragged a man into the warden's office at Chisholm prison.

"Here's your man, Philip Gilfoil," said The Thinking Machine tersely.

"Gilfoil!" the warden almost shouted. "Did he escape?"

And a moment later two guards came into the warden's office with Convict 97 between them. There were two Philip Gilfoils, if one might trust the evidence of a sense of sight; the first with dissipated, brutally lined face, and the other with the prison pallor upon him and with deep grief written indelibly in his eyes.

"They are brothers, gentlemen—twin brothers," explained The Thinking Machine. He turned to the man in prison garb, the man from Cell 9. "This is the Rev. Dr. Phineas Gilfoil, pastor of a fashionable little church in a suburb, and," he turned upon the man whom they had brought there in the cab, "this is Philip Gilfoil, forger—this is Convict 97."

The warden and the prison guards stood stupefied, gazing from one to the other of the two men. The facial lines were identical; physically they had been cast in the same mold.

"The only real difference between them, except a radical mental difference, is the size of their feet," The Thinking Machine went on. "Philip Gilfoil, the forger, the real Convict 97, who has been out of this prison for five weeks and four days, wears a number eight and a half shoe, according to your own records Mr. Warden; the Rev. Phineas Gilfoil, who has been in his brothers place, Cell 9, for five weeks and four days, wears a number seven shoe. See here!"

He stooped suddenly, lifted one of Dr. Gilfoil's feet and slipped one shoe off without even untying it. It showed no impression of the foot at all in the upper part, it was so large. Dr. Gilfoil dropped back weakly into a chair without a word and buried his face in his hands; Philip Gilfoil, the forger, his head still awhirl with the fumes of liquor, took one step toward his brother, then sat down and glared from one to the other defiantly.

"But how—what—when did they change places?" demanded the warden stammeringly. The whole thing was a nightmare to him.

"Precisely five weeks and four days ago," replied The Thinking Machine. "Your records show that. On your own books, in your own handwriting, is a complete solution of the problem, although you didn't know it," he added magnanimously. "Everything is there. Let me see the book a moment."

The squint eyes ran rapidly down a page, and stopped at a written entry opposite the pedigree record.

"'Sept. 3.—Miss P. Gilfoil, sister, permitted half-hour's conversation with 97 in afternoon. Brought permission from chairman of Prison Commission.'

"That's the record of the escape," continued The Thinking Machine. "Philip Gilfoil has no sister, therefore the person who called was the Rev. Dr. Phineas Gilfoil, an only brother, and he wore woman's clothing. He went to that cell willingly and for the specific purpose of changing places with his brother,—the motive doesn't appear,—and was to remain in the cell for a time agreed upon. The necessary changes of clothing were made, instructions which were to enable the minister to impersonate his brother were given,—and they were elaborate,—then Philip Gilfoil, Convict 97, walked out as a woman. I dare say he invited a close scrutiny; it was perfectly safe because of his remarkable resemblance to the man he had left behind."

Amazement in the warden's eyes was giving way to anger at the trick of which he had been the victim. He turned to the guards who had stood by silently.

"Take this man back!" he directed, and indicated Philip Gilfoil. "Put him where he belongs!" Then he turned toward the white faced minister. "I shall deliver you over to the police."

Philip Gilfoil was led away; then the warden reached for the telephone receiver.

"Now, just a moment, please," requested The Thinking Machine, and he sat down. "You have your prisoner now, safely enough, and here you are about to turn over to the police a man whose every act of life has been a good one. Remember that for a moment, please."

"But why should he change places with my prisoner?" blazed the warden. "That makes him liable too. The statutes are specific on—"

"The Rev. Dr. Gilfoil has done one of the most amazing, not to say heroic, things that I ever heard of," interrupted the scientist. "Now, wait a minute. He, a man of position, of reputation, of unquestioned morals, a good man, deliberately incarcerates himself for the sake of a criminal brother who, in this man's eyes, must be free for a short time at any rate. The reason of this, the necessity, while urgent, still doesn't appear. Dr. Gilfoil trusted his brother, criminal though he was, to return to his cell in four weeks and finish his sentence. The exchange of prisoners then was to be made in the same manner. That the criminal brother did not return, as he agreed, but that Dr. Gilfoil was loyal to him even then and lived up to the lie, can only reflect credit upon Dr. Gilfoil for a self sacrifice which is almost beyond us prosaic people of this day."

"I did it because—" Dr. Gilfoil began hoarsely, his voice quivering with emotion. It was the first time he had spoken.

"It doesn't matter why you did it," interrupted The Thinking Machine. "You did it for love of a brother, and he betrayed you—betrayed you to the point of his taking possession of your house while maudlin from drink, to the point of striking your wife like the coward he is, and of making a temporary prisoner of Mr. Hatch here, who had gone to your home to investigate. It is due to Mr. Hatch's personal courage that your wife is freed from him,—she was practically a prisoner,—and that he is now in his cell again."

Dr. Gilfoil's face went pallid for an instant, and he staggered to his feet, with lips tightly pressed together, fighting back an emotion which nearly overwhelmed him. After a moment came a strange softening of his features, and he stood staring out the window into the prison yard with upraised eyes.

"That's all of it," said the scientist, after a moment. "I don't think, Mr. Warden, that justice would demand the imprisonment of this man. I believe it would be far better to let the matter remain just between ourselves. It will not happen again, and—"

"But it was a crime," interrupted the warden.

"Technically, yes," admitted The Thinking Machine; "but we can overlook even a crime, if it does no harm, and if it is inspired by the motive which prompted this one. Think of it for a moment in that light."

There was a long silence in the little office. The Thinking Machine sat with upturned eyes and fingers pressed tip to tip; Dr. Gilfoil's eyes roved from the drawn, inscrutable face of the scientist to the warden; Hatch's brow was furrowed with wrinkles of perplexity.

"How did you find out about this escape first?" asked the reporter curiously.

"I knew Philip Gilfoil had escaped, because I saw him," replied The Thinking Machine tersely. "He came to my place, evidently to kill me. I was in my laboratory. He came up behind me to strike me down. I glanced into a mirror above my work table, saw him, and tried to avoid the blow. It caught me in the back of the head, and I fell unconscious. Martha made some noise outside which must have frightened Gilfoil, for he fled. The front door locked behind him—it's a spring lock. But I had recognized the escaped prisoner perfectly,—I never forget faces,—and I knew he had the motive to kill me because I had been instrumental in sending him here.

"I told you merely that Gilfoil had escaped and sent you here to inquire. Afterward I came myself, because I knew Philip Gilfoil was not in that cell. I found out many additional facts, among them a sudden change for the better in the prisoner's behavior, which confirmed my knowledge that it was Philip Gilfoil who had attacked me. I sought to surprise Dr. Gilfoil here into a betrayal of identity by a visit to his cell at night. But his loyalty to his brother and his perfect self possession enabled him to play the role. He recognized me as he recognized you, Mr. Hatch, because we can imagine that Philip Gilfoil had been careful in his plans and had instructed him to look out for us.

"Everything else came from the record book. This gave me Philip Gilfoil's pedigree, mentioned Phineas Gilfoil, without stating his vocation, and gave a clue to his place of residence. You followed up that end, Mr. Hatch, while I called on Dr. Heindell who had treated the prisoner for a bad throat. He informed me that there was nothing at all the matter with the prisoner's throat, so a plain problem in addition brought me a definite knowledge of what had happened. In conclusion, I may say that Dr. Gilfoil planned only a four weeks' stay here. I know that because you told me he had gone on a four weeks' vacation."

The minister's eyes again settled on the face of the warden. That official had been turning the matter over in his mind, evidently at length, as he listened. Finally he spoke.

"You had better go back to the cell, Dr. Gilfoil," he said respectfully, "and change clothing with your brother. You couldn't wear that prison suit in the street safely."

The Problem of the Auto Cab

Hutchinson Hatch gathered up his overcoat and took the steps coming down two at a time. There was no car in sight, nothing on wheels in fact, until—yes, here was an automobile turning the corner, an automobile cab drifting along apparently without purpose. Hatch hailed it.

"Get me out to Commonwealth Avenue and Arden Street in a hurry!" he instructed. "Take a chance with the speed law, and I'll make it worth while. It's important."

He yanked open the door, stepped in, and closed it with a slam. The chauffeur gave a twist to his lever, turned the car almost within its length, and went scuttling off up street.

Safely inside, Hatch became suddenly aware that he had a fellow passenger. Through the gloom he felt, rather than saw, two inquisitive eyes staring out at him, and there was the faintest odor of violets.

"Hello!" Hatch demanded. "Am I in your way?"

"Not in the slightest," came the voice of a woman. "Am I in yours?"

"Why—I beg your pardon," Hatch stammered. "I thought I had the cab alone—didn't know there was a passenger. Perhaps I'd better get out?"

"No, no!" protested the woman quickly. "Don't think of it."

Then from outside came the bellowing voice of a policeman. "Hey, there! I'll report you!"

Glancing back, Hatch saw him standing in the middle of the street jotting down something in a note book. The chauffeur made a few uncomplimentary remarks about bluecoats in general, swished round a corner, and sped on. With a half smile of appreciation on his lips, Hatch turned back to his unknown companion.

"If you will tell me where you are going," he suggested, "I'll have the chauffeur set you down."

"It's of no consequence," replied the woman a little wearily. "I am going no place particularly—just riding about to collect my thoughts."

A woman unattended, riding about in an automobile at fifteen minutes of eleven o'clock at night to collect her thoughts! And the chauffeur didn't know he had a passenger! The reporter sat oblivious of the bumping, grinding, of the automobile, trying to consider this unexpected incident calmly.

"You are a reporter?" inquired the woman.

"Yes," Hatch replied. "How did you guess it?"

"From seeing you rush out of a newspaper office in such a hurry at this time of night," she replied. "Something important, I dare say?"

"Well, yes," Hatch agreed. "A jewel robbery at a ball. Don't know much about it yet. Just got a police bulletin stating that Mrs. Windsor Dillingham had been robbed of a necklace worth thirty thousand dollars at a big affair she is giving to-night."

The inside of the cab was lighted brilliantly by the electric arc outside, and Hatch had an opportunity of seeing the woman face to face at close range. She was pretty; she was young; and she was well dressed. From her shoulders she was enveloped in some loose cloak of dark material; but it was not drawn together at her throat, and her bare neck gleamed.

There being nothing whatever to say, Hatch sat silently staring out of the window as the automobile whirled into Commonwealth Avenue and slowed up as it approached Arden Street.

"Will you do me one favor, please?" asked the woman.

"Yes, if I can," was the reporter's reply.

"Allow me, please, to get out of the automobile on the side away from the curb, and be good enough to attract the attention of the chauffeur to yourself while I am doing it. Here is a bill," and she pressed something into Hatch's hand. "You may pay the chauffeur a tip for the passenger he didn't know he had."

Hatch agreed in a dazed sort of way, and the automobile came to a stop. He stepped out on the curb, and slammed the door as the chauffeur leaped down from his seat. From the other side came an answering door slam, as if an echo.

Five minutes later Hatch joined Detective Mallory inside. At just that moment the detective was listening to the story of Mrs. Dillingham's maid.

"There's nothing missing but the necklace," she explained; "so far, at least, as we have been able to find out. Mrs. Dillingham began dressing at about half-past eight o'clock, and I assisted her as usual. I suppose it was half-past nine when she finished. All that time the necklace was in the jewel box on her dressing table. It was the only article of jewelry in the box.

"Well, the butler came up about half-past nine o'clock for his final instructions, and Mrs. Dillingham went into the adjoining room to talk to him. It was not more than a minute later when she sent me down to the conservatory for a rose for her hair. She was still talking to him when I returned five minutes later. I put the rose in her hair, and she sent me into her dressing room for her necklace. When I looked into the jewel box, the necklace was gone. I told Mrs. Dillingham. The butler heard me. That's all I know of it, except that Mrs. Dillingham went into hysterics and fainted, and I telephoned for a doctor."

Detective Mallory regarded the girl coldly; Hatch knew perfectly what was coming. "You are quite sure," asked the detective, "that you did not take the necklace with you when you went down to the conservatory, and pass it to a confederate on the outside."

The sudden pallor of the girl, her abject, cringing fright, answered the question to Hatch's satisfaction even before she opened her lips with a denial. Hatch himself was about to ask a question, when a footman entered.

"Mrs. Dillingham will see you in her boudoir," he announced.

From the lips of Mrs. Dillingham they heard identically the same story the maid had told. Mrs. Dillingham did not suspect anyone of her household. For half an hour the detective interrogated her; then there came a rap at the door, and a woman entered.

"Why, Dora!" exclaimed Mrs. Dillingham

The young woman went straight to her, put her arms about her shoulders protectingly, then turned to glare defiantly at Detective

Mallory and Hutchinson Hatch. The reporter gasped—it was the mysterious woman of the automobile. An exclamation was on his lips; but something in her eyes warned him, and he was silent.

When, on the following day, Hutchinson Hatch related the circumstances of the theft of Mrs. Dillingham's necklace to Professor Augustus S. F. X. Van Dusen—The Thinking Machine—he did not mention the mysterious woman in the automobile. However curious those incidents in which he and she had figured were, they were inconsequential, and there was nothing to connect them in anyway with the problem in hand. The strange woman's meeting with Mrs. Dillingham in the reporter's presence had convinced him that she was an intimate friend.

"Just what time was the theft discovered?" inquired The Thinking Machine.

"Within a few minutes of half-past nine."

"At what time did most of the guests arrive?"

"Between half-past nine and ten."

"Then at half-past nine," continued the scientist, "there could not have been many persons there?"

"Perhaps a dozen," returned the reporter.

"And who were they?"

"Their names, you mean? I don't know."

"Well, find out," directed The Thinking Machine crustily. "If the servants are removed from the case, and there were a dozen other persons in the house, common sense tells us to find out who and what they were. Suppose, Mr. Hatch, you had attended that ball and stolen that necklace; what would have been your natural inclination afterward?"

Hatch stared at him blankly for a minute, then smiled whimsically. "You mean how would I have tried to get away with it?" he asked.

"Yes. When would you have left the place?"

"That's rather hard to say," Hatch declared thoughtfully. "But I think I should either have gone before anybody else did, through fear of discovery, or else I should have been one of the last, through excess of caution."

"Then proceed along those lines," instructed The Thinking Machine. "You might almost put that down as a law of criminology. It will enable you in the beginning, therefore, to narrow down the dozen or so guests to the first and last who left."

Deeply pondering this little interjection of psychology into a very material affair, Hatch went his way. In the course of events he saw Mrs. Dillingham, who, out of consideration for her guests, flatly refused to give their names.

Luckily for Hatch, the butler didn't feel that way about it at all. This was due partly to the fact that Detective Mallory had given him a miserable half-hour, and partly, perhaps, to the fact that the reporter oiled his greedy palm with a bill of two figures.

"To begin with," said the reporter, "I want to know the names of the first dozen or so persons who arrived here that evening—I mean those who were here when you went up to speak with Mrs. Dillingham."

"I might find out, sir. Their cards were laid on the salver as they arrived, and that salver, I think, has remained undisturbed. Therefore, the first dozen cards on it would give you the names you want."

"Now, that's something like," commented the reporter enthusiastically. "And do you remember any person who left the house rather early that evening?"

"No, sir," was the reply. Then suddenly there came a flash of remembrance across the stoical face. "But I remember that one gentleman arrived here twice. It was this way. Mr. Hawes Campbell came in about eleven o'clock, and passed by without handing me a card. Then I remembered that he had been here earlier and that I had his card. But I don't recall that anyone went out, and I was at the door all evening except when I was up stairs talking to Mrs. Dillingham."

On a bare chance, Hatch went to find Campbell. Inquiry at his two clubs failed to find him, and finally Hatch called at his home.

At the end of five minutes, perhaps, Hatch caught the swish of skirts in the hallway, then the portieres were thrust aside, and—again he was face to face with the mysterious woman of the automobile.

"My brother isn't here," she said calmly, without the slightest sign of recognition. "Can I do anything for you?"

Her brother! Then she was Miss Campbell, and Mrs. Dillingham had called her Dora—Dora Campbell!

"Well—er—" Hatch faltered a little, "it was a personal matter I wanted to see him about."

"I don't know when he will return," Miss Campbell announced.

Hatch stared at her for a moment; he was making up his mind. At last he took the bit in his teeth. "We understand, Miss Campbell," he said at last slowly and emphatically, "that your brother, Hawes Campbell has some information which might be of value in unraveling the mystery surrounding the theft of Mrs. Dillingham's necklace."

Miss Campbell dropped into a chair, and unconsciously Hatch assumed the defensive.

"Mrs. Dillingham is very much annoyed, as you must know," Miss Campbell said, "about the publicity given to this affair; particularly as she is confident that the necklace will be returned within a short time. Her only annoyance, beyond the wide publicity, as I said, is that it has not already been returned."

"Returned?" gasped Hatch.

Miss Campbell shrugged her shoulders. "She knows," she continued, "that the necklace is now in safe hands, that there is no danger of its being lost to her; but the situation is such that she cannot demand its return."

"Mrs. Dillingham knows where the necklace is, then?" he asked.

"Yes," replied Miss Campbell.

"Perhaps you know?"

"Perhaps I do," she responded readily. "I can assure you that Mrs. Dillingham is going to take the affair out of the hands of the police, because she knows her property is safe—as safe as if it was in your hands, for instance. It is only a question of time when it will be returned."

"Where is the necklace?" Hatch demanded suddenly.

Again Miss Campbell shrugged her shoulders.

"And what does your brother know about the affair?"

"I can't answer that question, of course," was the response.

"Well, why did he go to Mrs. Dillingham's early in the evening, then go away, and return about eleven o'clock?" insisted the reporter bluntly.

For the first time there came a change in Miss Campbell's manner, a subtle, indefinable something which the reporter readily saw but to which he could attach no meaning.

"I can't say more than I have said," she replied after a moment. "Believe me," and there was a note of earnestness in her voice, "it would be far better for you to drop the matter, because otherwise you may be placed in—in a ridiculous position."

And that was all—a threat, delicately veiled it is true, but a threat nevertheless. She arose and led the way to the door.

Hatch didn't realize the significance of that remark then, nor did it occur to him that the mysterious affair in the automobile had not been mentioned between them; for here was material, knotty, incoherent, inexplicable material, for The Thinking Machine, and there he took it. Again he told the story; but this time all of it—every incident from the moment he hailed the automobile in front of his office on the night of the robbery until Miss Campbell closed the door.

"Why didn't you tell me all of it before?" demanded The Thinking Machine irritably.

"I couldn't see that the affair in the automobile had any connection with the robbery," explained the reporter.

"Couldn't see!" stormed the eminent man of science. "Couldn't see! Every trivial happening on this whole round earth bears on every other happening, no matter how vast or how disconnected it may seem; the correlation of facts makes a perpetually unbroken chain. In other words, if Mrs. Leary hadn't kept a cow, Chicago would not have been destroyed by fire. Couldn't see!"

For an instant The Thinking Machine glared at him; and the change from petulant annoyance to deep abstraction, as that singular brain turned to the problem in hand, was almost visible. It was uncanny. Then the scientist dropped back into his chair with eyes turned upward, and long slender fingers pressed tip to tip. Ten minutes passed, twenty, thirty, and he turned suddenly to the reporter.

"What was the number of that automobile?" he demanded.

Hatch grinned in sheer triumph. Of all the questions he could have anticipated this was the most unlikely, and yet he had the number set down in his note book where it would ultimately become a voucher in his expense account. He consulted the book.

"Number 869019," he replied.

"Now, find that automobile," directed The Thinking Machine. "It is important that you do so at once."

"You mean that the necklace—" Hatch began breathlessly.

"When you bring the automobile here, I will produce the necklace," declared The Thinking Machine emphatically.

Hatch returned half a dozen hours later with troubled lines in his face.

"Automobile No. 869019 has disappeared, evaporated into air," he declared with some heat. "There was one that night, because I was in it, and the highway commission's records show a private cab license granted to John Kilrain under the number; but it has disappeared."

"Where is Kilrain?" inquired The Thinking Machine.

"I didn't see him; but I saw his wife," explained the reporter. "She didn't know anything about automobile No. 869019, or said she didn't. She said his auto car was—"

"No. 610698," interrupted The Thinking Machine. It was not a question; it was the statement as of one who knew.

Hatch stared from the scientist to the note book where he had written down the number the woman gave him, and then he looked his utter astonishment.

"Of course, that is the number," continued The Thinking Machine, as if some one had disputed it. "It is past midnight now, and we won't try to find it; but I'll have it here to-morrow at noon. We shall see for ourselves how safely the necklace has been kept."

Detective Mallory entered and glanced about inquiringly. He saw only The Thinking Machine and Hutchinson Hatch.

"I sent for you," explained the scientist, "because in half an hour or so I shall either place the Dillingham necklace in your hands, or turn over to you the man who knows where it is. You may use your own discretion as to whether or not you will prosecute. Under all the circumstances, I believe the case is one for a sanatorium, rather than prison. In other words, the person who took the necklace is not wholly responsible."

"Who is it?" demanded the detective.

"You don't happen to know all the facts in this case," continued The Thinking Machine without heeding the question. "I got them all, only after Mr. Hatch, at my suggestion, had located the thief. Originally I began where you left off. I believed you had eliminated the servants, and presumed there was not a burglary. Ultimately this led to Hawes Campbell in a manner which is of no interest to you. Then I got all the facts.

"When Mr. Hatch left his office to go to Mrs. Dillingham's, he took an automobile which happened to be passing," resumed the scientist. "It was a cab, No. 869019. Inside that cab he found, much to his astonishment, a woman—a young woman in evening dress. She made the surprising statement that the chauffeur didn't know she was there, and that she was not going anywhere—was merely riding around to collect her thoughts. And this was, please remember, about eleven o'clock at night. On its face this incident had no connection with the jewel theft; but by a singular chain of coincidences, subsequently developed, it seemed that Mr. Hatch had arrived at the solution of the mystery before he even knew the circumstances of the theft."

Detective Mallory nodded doubtfully. "But how does that connect with the—" he began.

"Subsequent developments establish a direct connection," interrupted The Thinking Machine. "We have the woman in the automobile. We shall presume that she must have had some strong motive for leaving a house at that time of night and doing the apparently purposeless things that she did do. We don't know this motive from these facts—we only know there was a motive.

"Now when you and Mr. Hatch were talking to Mrs. Dillingham, a woman entered the room. Mr. Hatch recognized her immediately as the woman in the automobile. Everything indicated that she was an intimate friend of Mrs. Dillingham's. So we pass on to the point where Mr. Hatch found that Hawes Campbell arrived at the ball early, went away again, then returned after eleven o'clock. Mr. Hatch wanted to know why he left, and went to his home to inquire. Campbell's sister met him there. She was the woman he had met in the automobile. So we have Campbell leaving the ball, immediately after the theft, say, and his sister running away from her home sometime between nine-thirty and eleven, and secreting herself in an automobile.

"Why? I have said, Mr. Mallory, that imagination—the ability to bridge gaps temporarily—is the most essential part of the logical mind. Now, if we imagine that Campbell stole the necklace, that he went home, that his sister found it out, that there was some sort of scene which terminated in her flight with the necklace, we account for absolutely every incident preceding and following Mr. Hatch's arrival at the Dillingham place.

"I have made inquiries. The Campbells are worth, not thousands, but millions. Therefore, the question. Why should Hawes Campbell steal a necklace? The answer, kleptomania. And again, it was known to the sister, who tried in her own manner to return the stolen property and avoid the scandal. When she was in the automobile, she was trying to collect her thoughts—trying to invent a way to return the necklace. It was the merest chance that Mr. Hatch happened to get into that particular vehicle.

"Now, we come to the most difficult part of the problem," and The Thinking Machine dropped back still further into the cavernous depths of his chair. "What would a frightened, perhaps hysterical, woman do with that necklace? From the fact that it has not been returned, we know that she didn't venture into the house with it, and leave it casually in any one of a hundred places where it might have been discovered without danger to herself. Yet everything indicates that she had it while in the cab. The obvious thing which suggests itself is that she hid it in the cab, intending to regain possession of it later and return it. Now, that cab number was 869019. Strangely enough, after Mr. Hatch left the cab it seems to have disappeared. The chauffeur, John Kilrain, has another cab number now, 610698—that is, auto cab No. 869019 was made to disappear by the simple act of turning the number board upside down, giving us 610698."

"Well, by George!" exclaimed Detective Mallory. No mere words would convey the reporter's astonishment; he gasped.

"Now," continued The Thinking Machine after a moment, "there are two reasons, both good, why auto cab number 869019 should have disappeared. The vital one, it seems to me, is that Kilrain discovered the necklace inside and kept it; the other is that he was threatened with arrest by the policeman who took his number for speeding, and to avoid a fine disguised the identity of his cab. There are one or two other possibilities; but if the necklace isn't found in the automobile, I should advise, not arrest, but a close watch on Kilrain, both at his home and in his intercourse with other chauffeurs at the various cab stands."

There was a rap at the door, and Martha appeared. "Did you want an automobile, sir?"

"We'll be right out," returned the scientist.

And so it came about that The Thinking Machine, Detective Mallory, and Hutchinson Hatch searched the very vitals of auto cab No. 869019, temporarily masquerading as No. 610698, while Kilrain stood by in perturbed amazement. At the end he was allowed to go.

"Remember, please, what I advised you to do," The Thinking Machine reminded Detective Mallory.

With eyes that were heavy with sleep Hutchinson Hatch crawled out of bed and answered the insistent ringing of his telephone. The crabbed voice of The Thinking Machine came over the wire, in a question.

"If Miss Campbell was so anxious to return the necklace that night, she couldn't have done better, could she, than to have handed it to a reporter who was going to the house to investigate the robbery?"

"I don't think so," Hatch replied wonderingly.

"Did you have on your overcoat that night?"

"I had it with me."

"Suppose you go look in the pockets, and—"

Hatch dropped the receiver, already inspired by the suggestion, and dragged his overcoat out of the closet. In the left hand lower pocket was a small package. He opened it with trembling fingers. There before his eyes lay the iridescent, gleaming bauble. It had been in his possession from an hour after it was stolen until this very instant. He rushed back to the telephone.

"I've got it!" he shouted.

"Silly of me not to have thought of it in the first place," came the querulous voice of The Thinking Machine. "Good night."

The Problem of the Broken Bracelet

The girl in the green mask leaned against the foot of the bed and idly fingered a revolver which lay in the palm of her daintily gloved hand. The dim glow of the night lamp enveloped her softly, and added a sinister glint to the bright steel of the weapon. Cowering in the bed was another figure—the figure of a woman. Sheets and blankets were drawn up tightly to her chin, and startled eyes peered anxiously, as if fascinated, at the revolver.

"Now please don't scream!" warned the masked girl. Her voice was quite casual, the tone in which one might have discussed an affair of far removed personal interest. "It would be perfectly useless, and besides dangerous."

"Who are you?" gasped the woman in the bed, staring horror stricken at the inscrutable mask of her visitor. "What do you want?"

A faint flicker of amusement lay in the shadowy eyes of the masked girl, and her red lips twitched slightly. "I don't think I can be mistaken," she said inquiringly. "This is Miss Isabel Leigh Harding?"

"Y-yes," was the chattering reply.

"Originally of Virginia?"

"Yes."

"Great-granddaughter of William Tremaine Harding, an officer in the Continental Army about 1775?"

The inflection of the questioning voice had risen almost imperceptibly; but the tone remained coldly, exquisitely courteous. At the last question the masked girl leaned forward a little expectantly.

"Yes," faltered Miss Harding faintly.

"Good, very good," commented the masked girl, and there was a note of repressed triumph in her voice. "I congratulate you, Miss

Harding, upon your self possession. Under the same circumstances most women would have begun by screaming. I should have myself."

"But who are you?" demanded Miss Harding again. "How did you get in here? What do you want?"

She sat bolt upright in bed, with less of fear now than curiosity in her manner, and her luxuriant hair tumbled about her semi-bare shoulders in profuse dishevelment.

At the sudden movement the masked girl took a firmer grip on the revolver, and moved it forward a little threateningly. "Now please don't make any mistake!" she advised Miss Harding pleasantly. "You will notice that I have drawn the bell rope up beyond your reach and knotted it. The servants are on the floor above in the extreme rear, and I doubt if they would hear a scream. Your companion is away for the night, and besides there is this." She tapped her weapon significantly. "Furthermore, you may notice that the lamp is beyond your reach; so that you cannot extinguish it as long as you remain in bed."

Miss Harding saw all these things, and was convinced.

"Now as to your question," continued the masked girl quietly. "My identity is of absolutely no concern or importance to you. You would not even recognize my name if I gave it to you. How did I get here? By opening an unfastened window in the drawing room on the first floor and walking in. I shall leave it unlatched when I go; so perhaps you had better have some one fasten it, otherwise thieves may enter." She smiled a little at the astonishment in Miss Harding's face. "Now as to why I am here and what I want."

She sat down on the foot of the bed, drew her cloak more closely about her, and folded her hands in her lap. Miss Harding placed a pillow and lounged against it comfortably, watching her visitor in astonishment. Except for the mask and the revolver, it might have been a cozy chat in any woman's boudoir.

"I came here to borrow from you—borrow, understand," the masked girl went on, "the least valuable article in your jewel box."

"My jewel box!" gasped Miss Harding suddenly. She had just thought of it, and glanced around at the table where it lay open.

"Don't alarm yourself," the masked girl remarked reassuringly; "I have removed nothing from it."

The light of the lamp fell full upon the open casket whence radiated multicolored flashes of gems. Miss Harding craned her neck a little to see, and seeing sank back against her pillow with a sigh of relief.

"As I said, I came to borrow one thing," the masked girl continued evenly. "If I cannot borrow it, I shall take it."

Miss Harding sat for a moment in mute contemplation of her visitor. She was searching her mind for some tangible explanation of this nightmarish thing.

After awhile she shook her head, meaning thereby that even conjecture was futile. "What particular article do you want?" she asked finally.

"Specifically by letter, from the prison in which he was executed by order of the British commander, your great-grandfather, William Tremaine Harding, left a gold bracelet, a plain band, to your grandfather," the masked girl explained; "Your grandfather, at that time a child, received the bracelet, when twenty-one years old, from the persons who held it in trust for him, and on his death, March 25, 1853, left it to your father. Your father died intestate in April, 1898, and the bracelet passed into your mother's keeping, there being no son. Your mother died within the last year. Therefore, the bracelet is now, or should be, in your possession. You see," she concluded, "I have taken pains to acquaint myself with your family history."

"You have," Miss Harding assented. "And may I ask why you want this bracelet?"

"I should answer that it was no concern of yours."

"You said borrow it, I believe?"

"Either I will borrow it or take it."

"Is there any certainty that it will ever be returned? And if so, when?"

"You will have to take my word for that, of course," replied the masked girl. "I shall return it within a few days."

Miss Harding glanced at her jewel box. "Have you looked there?" she inquired.

"Yes," replied the masked girl. "It isn't there."

"Not there?" repeated Miss Harding.

"If it had been there I should have taken it and gone away without disturbing you," the masked girl went on. "Its absence is what caused me to wake you."

"Not there!" said Miss Harding again wonderingly, and she moved as if to get up.

"Don't do that, please!" warned the masked girl quickly. "I shall hand you the box if you like."

She arose and passed the casket to Miss Harding, who spilled out the contents in her lap.

"Why, it is gone!" she exclaimed.

"Yes, from there," said the other a little grimly. "Now please tell me immediately where it is. It will save trouble."

"I don't know," replied Miss Harding hopelessly.

The masked girl stared at her coldly for a moment, then drew back the hammer of the revolver until it clicked.

Miss Harding stared in sudden terror.

"All this is merely time wasted," said the masked girl sternly, coldly. "Either the bracelet or this!" Again she tapped the revolver.

"If it is not here, I don't know where it is," Miss Harding rushed on desperately. "I placed it here at ten o'clock to-night—here in this box—when I undressed. I don't know—I can't imagine—"

The masked girl tapped the revolver again several times with one gloved finger. "The bracelet!" she demanded impatiently.

Fear was in Miss Harding's eyes now, and she made a helpless, pleading gesture with both white hands. "You wouldn't kill me—murder me!" she gasped. "I don't know. I—Here, take the other jewels. I can't tell you."

"The other jewels are of absolutely no use to me," said the girl coldly. "I want only the bracelet."

"On my honor," faltered Miss Harding, "I don't know where it is. I can't imagine what has happened to it. I—I—" she stopped helplessly.

The masked girl raised the weapon threateningly, and Miss Harding stared in cringing horror.

"Please, please, I don't know!" she pleaded hysterically.

For a little while the masked girl was thoughtfully silent. One shoe tapped the floor rhythmically; the eyes were contracted. "I believe you," she said slowly at last. She arose suddenly and drew her coat closely about her. "Good night," she added as she started toward the door. There she turned back. "It would not be wise for you to give an alarm for at least half an hour. Then you had better have some one latch the window in the drawing room. I shall leave it unfastened. Good night."

And she was gone.

Hutchinson Hatch, reporter, had just finished relating the story to The Thinking Machine, incident by incident, as it had been reported to Chief of Detectives Mallory, when the eminent scientist's aged servant, Martha, tapped on the door of the reception room and entered with a card.

"A lady to see you, sir," she announced.

The scientist extended one slender white hand, took the card, and glanced at it.

"Your story is merely what Miss Harding told the police?" he inquired of the reporter. "You didn't get it from Miss Harding herself?"

"No, I didn't see her."

"Show the lady in, Martha," directed The Thinking Machine. She turned and went out, and he passed the card to the reporter.

"By George! it's Miss Harding herself!" Hatch exclaimed. "Now we can get it all straight."

There was a little pause, and Martha ushered a young woman into the room. She was girlish, slender, daintily yet immaculately attired, with deep brown eyes, firmly molded chin and mouth, and wavy hair. Hatch's expression of curiosity gave way to one of frank admiration as he regarded her. There was only the most impersonal sort of interest in the watery blue eyes of The Thinking Machine. She stood for a moment with gaze alternating between the distinguished man of science and the reporter.

"I am Mr. Van Dusen," explained The Thinking Machine. "Allow me, Miss Harding—Mr. Hatch."

The girl smiled and offered a gloved hand cordially to each of the two men. The Thinking Machine merely touched it respectfully; Hatch shook it warmly. The eyes were veiled demurely for an instant, then the lids were lifted suddenly, and she favored the newspaper man with a gaze that sent the blood to his cheeks.

"Be seated, Miss Harding," the scientist invited.

"I hardly know just what I came to say, and just how to say it," she began uncertainly, and smiled a little. "And anyway I had hoped that you were alone; so—"

"You may speak with perfect freedom before Mr. Hatch," interrupted The Thinking Machine. "Perhaps I shall be able to aid you; but first will you repeat the history of the bracelet as nearly as you can in the words of the masked woman who called upon you so—so unconventionally."

The girl's brows were lifted inquiringly, with a sort of start.

"We were discussing the case when your card was brought in," continued The Thinking Machine tersely. "We shall continue from that point, if you will be so good."

The young woman recited the history of the bracelet, slowly and carefully.

"And that statement of the case is correct?" queried the scientist.

"Absolutely, so far as I know," was the reply.

"And as I understand it, you were in the house alone; that is, alone except for the servants?"

"Yes; I live there alone, except for a companion and two servants. The servants were not within the sound of my voice, even if I had screamed, and Miss Talbott, my companion, it happened, was out for the night."

The Thinking Machine had dropped back into his chair, with squint eyes turned upward, and long white fingers pressed tip to tip. He sat thus silently for a long time. The girl at last broke the silence.

"Naturally I was a little surprised," she remarked falteringly, "that I should have appeared just in time to interrupt a discussion of the singular happenings in my home last night; but really—"

"This bracelet," interrupted the little scientist again. "It was of oval form, perhaps, with no stones set in it, or anything of that sort—merely a band that fastened with an invisible hinge. That's right, I believe?"

"Quite right, yes," replied the girl readily.

It occurred to Hatch suddenly that he himself did not know—in fact, had not inquired—the shape of the bracelet. He knew only that it was gold, and of no great value. Knowing nothing about what it looked like, he had not described it to The Thinking Machine; therefore he raised his eyes inquiringly now. The drawn face of the scientist was inscrutable.

"As I started to say," the girl went on, "the bracelet and the events of last night have no direct connection with the purpose of my visit here."

"Indeed?" commented the scientist.

"No; I came to see if you could assist me in another way. For instance," and she fumbled in her pocket book, "I happened to know, Professor Van Dusen, of some of the remarkable things you have accomplished, and I should like to ask if you can throw any light on this for me."

She drew from the pocketbook a crumpled, yellow sheet of paper—a strip perhaps an inch wide, thin as tissue, glazed, and extraordinarily wrinkled. The Thinking Machine squinted at its manifold irregularities for an instant curiously, nodded, sniffed at it, then slowly began to unfold it, smoothing it out carefully as he went. Hatch leaned forward eagerly and stared. He was a little more than astonished at the end to find that the sheet was blank. The Thinking Machine examined both sides of the paper thoughtfully.

"And where did you find the bracelet at last?" he inquired casually.

"I have reason to believe," the girl rushed on suddenly, regardless of the question, "that this strip of paper has been substituted for one of real value,—I may say one of great value,—and I don't know how to proceed, unless—"

"Where did you find the bracelet?" demanded The Thinking Machine again impatiently.

Hatch would have hesitated a long time before he would have said the girl was disconcerted at the question, or that there had been any real change in the expression of her pretty face. And yet—

"After the masked woman had gone," she went on calmly, "I summoned the servants and we made a search. We found the bracelet at last. I thought I had tossed it into my jewel box when I removed it last night; but it seems I was careless enough to let it fall down behind my dressing table, and it was there all the time the—the masked woman was in my room."

"And when did you make this discovery?" asked The Thinking Machine.

"Within a few minutes after she went out."

"In making your search, you were guided, perhaps, by a belief that in the natural course of events the bracelet could not have disappeared from your jewel box unless some one had entered the room before the masked woman entered; and further that if any-one had entered you would have been awakened?"

"Precisely." There was another pause. "And now please," she went on, "what does this blank strip of paper mean?"

"You had expected something with writing on it, of course?"

"That's just what I had expected," and she laughed nervously. "You may rest assured I was considerably surprised at finding that."

"I can imagine you were," remarked the scientist dryly.

The conversation had reached a point where Hatch was hope-lessly lost. The young woman and the scientist were talking with mutual understanding of things that seemed to have no connec-tion with anything that had gone before. What was the paper any-way? Where did it come from? What connection did it have with the affairs of the previous night? How did—

"Mr. Hatch, a match, please," requested The Thinking Machine.

Wonderingly the reporter produced one and handed it over. The imperturbable man of science lighted it and thrust the mysterious paper into the blaze. The girl arose with a sudden, startled cry, and snatched at the paper desperately, extinguishing the match as she did so. The Thinking Machine turned disapproving eyes on her.

"I thought you were going to burn it!" she gasped.

"There is not the slightest danger of that, Miss Harding," de-clared The Thinking Machine coldly. He examined the blank sheet again. "This way, please."

He arose and led the way into his tiny laboratory across the narrow hall, with the girl following. Hatch trailed behind, won-dering vaguely what it was all about. A small brazier flashed into flame as The Thinking Machine applied a match, and curious eyes peered over his shoulders as he held the blank strip, now smoothed out, so that the rising heat would strike it.

For a long time three pairs of eyes were fastened on the mysterious paper, all with understanding now, but nothing appeared. Hatch glanced round at the young woman. Her face wore an expression of tense excitement. The red lips were slightly parted in anticipation, the eyes sparkling, and the cheeks flushed deeply. In staring at her the reporter forgot for the instant everything else, until suddenly:

"There! There! Do you see?"

The exclamation burst from her triumphantly, as faint, scrawly lines grew on the strip suspended over the brazier. Totally oblivious of their presence apparently, The Thinking Machine was squinting steadily at the paper, which was slowly crinkling up into wavy lines under the influence of the heat. Gradually the edges were charring, and the odor of scorched paper filled the room. Still the scientist held the paper over the fire. Just as it seemed inevitable that it would burst into flame, he withdrew it and turned to the girl.

"There was no substitution," he remarked tersely. "It is sympathetic ink."

"What does it say?" demanded the young woman abruptly. "What does it mean?"

The Thinking Machine spread the scorched strip of paper on the table before them carefully, and for a long time studied it minutely.

"Really, my dear young woman, I don't know," he said crabbedly at last. "It may take days to find out what it means."

"But something's written there! Read it!" the girl insisted.

"Read it for yourself," said the scientist impatiently. "I am frank to say it's beyond me as it is now. No, don't touch it. It will crumble to pieces."

Faintly, yet decipherable under a magnifying glass, the three were able to make out this on the paper:

Stonehedge—idim-sérpa'l ed serueh siort tnaeG ed etéT
al rap eétej erbmo'l ed tniop ud zerit sruO'd rehcoR ud
eueuq ud dron ua sdeip tnec.   W.F.H.

"What does it mean? What does it mean?" demanded the young woman impatiently. "What does it mean?"

The sudden hardening of her tone caused both Hatch and The Thinking Machine to turn and stare at her. Some strange change had come over her face. There was chagrin, perhaps, and there was more than that,—a merciless glitter in the brown eyes, a grim expression about the chin and mouth, a greedy closing and unclosing of the small, well shaped hands.

"I presume it's a cipher of some sort," remarked The Thinking Machine curtly. "It may take time to read it and to learn definitely just where the treasure is hidden, and you may have to wait for—"

"Treasure!" exclaimed the girl. "Did you say treasure? There is treasure, then?"

The Thinking Machine shrugged his shoulders. "What else?" he asked. "Now, please, let me see the bracelet."

"The bracelet!" the girl repeated, and again Hatch noted that quick change of expression on the pretty face. "I—er—must you see it? I—er—" And she stopped.

"It is absolutely necessary, if I make anything of this," and the scientist indicated the charred paper. "You have it in your pocketbook, of course."

The girl stepped forward suddenly and leaned over the laboratory table, intently studying the mysterious strip of paper. At last she raised her head as if she had reached a decision.

"I have only a—a part of the bracelet," she announced, "only half. It was unavoidably broken, and—"

"Only half?" interrupted The Thinking Machine, and he squinted coldly into the young woman's eyes.

"Here it is," she said at last, desperately almost. "I don't know where the other half is; it would be useless to ask me."

She drew an aged, badly scratched half circlet of gold from her pocketbook, handed it to the scientist, then went and looked out the window. He examined it—the delicate decorative tracings, then the invisible hinge where the bracelet had been rudely torn apart. Twice he raised his squint eyes and stared at the girl as she stood silhouetted against the light of the window. When he spoke again there was a deeper note in his voice—a singular softening, an unusual deference.

"I shall read the cipher of course, Miss Harding," he said slowly. "It may take an hour, or it may take a week, I don't know." Again he scrutinized the charred paper. "Do you speak French?" he inquired suddenly.

"Enough to understand and to make myself understood," replied the girl. "Why?"

The Thinking Machine scribbled off a copy of the cipher and handed it to her.

"I'll communicate with you when I reach a conclusion," he remarked. "Please leave your address on your card here," and he handed her the card and pencil.

"You know my home address," she said. "Perhaps it would be better for me to call this afternoon late or to-morrow."

"I'd prefer to have your address," said the scientist. "As I say, I don't know when I shall be able to speak definitely."

The girl paused for a moment and tapped the blunt end of the pencil against her white teeth thoughtfully with her left hand. "As a matter of fact," she said at last, "I am not returning home now. The events of last night have shaken me considerably, and I am now on my way to Blank Rock, a little sea shore town where I shall remain for a few days. My address there will be the High Tower."

"Write it down, please!" directed The Thinking Machine tersely. The girl stared at him strangely, with a challenge in her eyes, then leaned over the table to write. Before the pencil had touched the card, however, she changed her mind and handed both to Hatch, with a smile.

"Please write it for me," she requested. "I write a wretched hand anyway, and besides I have on my gloves." She turned again to the little scientist, who stood squinting over her head. "Thank you so much for your trouble," she said in conclusion. "You can reach me at this address either by wire or letter for the next fortnight."

And a few minutes later she was gone. For awhile The Thinking Machine was silent as he again studied the faint writing on the strip of paper.

"The cipher," he remarked to Hatch at last, "is no cipher at all; it's so simple. But there are some other things I shall have to find out first, and—suppose you drop by early to-morrow to see me."

Half an hour later The Thinking Machine went to the telephone, and after running through the book called a number.

"Is Miss Harding home yet?" he demanded, when an answer came.

"No, sir," was the reply, in a woman's voice.

"Would you mind telling me, please, if she is left handed?"

"Why, no, sir. She's right handed. Who is this?"

"I knew it, of course. Good by."

The Thinking Machine was squinting into the inquiring eyes of Hutchinson Hatch.

"The reason why the police are so frequently unsuccessful in explaining the mysteries of crime," he remarked, "is not through lack of natural intelligence, or through lack of a birth-given aptitude for the work, but through the lack of an absolutely accurate knowledge which is wide enough to enable them to proceed. Now here is a case in point. It starts with a cipher, goes into an intricate astronomical calculation, and from that into simple geometry. The difficulty with the detectives is not that they could not work out each of these as it was presented, perhaps with the aid of some outsider, but that they would not recognize the existence of the three phases of the problem in the first place.

"You have heard me say frequently, Mr. Hatch, that logic is inevitable—as inevitable as that two and two make four not sometimes, but *all* the time. That is true; but it must have an indisputable starting point,—the one unit which is unassailable. In this case unit produces unit in order, and the proper array of these units gives a coherent answer. Let me demonstrate briefly just what I mean.

"A masked woman, employing the method at least of a thief, demands a certain bracelet of this Miss—Miss Harding. (Is that her name?) She doesn't want jewels; she wants that bracelet. Whatever other conjectures may be advanced, the one dominant fact is that that bracelet, itself of little comparative value, is worth more than all the rest to her,—the masked woman, I mean,—and she has endangered liberty and perhaps life to get it. Why? The history of the bracelet as she herself stated it to Miss Harding gives the answer. A man in prison, under sentence of death, had that bracelet at one time. We can conjecture immediately, therefore, that the masked woman knew that the fact of its having been in this man's possession gave him an opportunity at least of so marking the bracelet,— or of confiding in it, I may say, a valuable secret. One's first thought, therefore, is of treasure—hidden treasure. We shall go further and say treasure hidden by a Continental officer to prevent its falling into other hands as loot. This officer under sentence of death, and therefore cut off from all communication with the outside, took a desperate means of communicating the location of the treasure to his heirs. That is clear, isn't it?"

The reporter nodded.

"I described the bracelet,—you heard me,—and yet I had never seen it, nor had I a description of it. That description was merely a forward step, a preliminary test of the truth of the first assumptions. I reasoned that the bracelet must be of a type which could be employed to carry a message safely past prying eyes; and there is really only one sort which is feasible, and that is the one I described. These bracelets are always hollow, the invisible hinges hold them together on one side, and they lock on the other. It would be perfectly possible, therefore, to write the message the prisoner wanted to send out on a strip of tissue paper, or any thin paper, and cram it into the bracelet at the lock end. In that event it would certainly pass minute inspection; the only difficulty would be for the outside person to find it. That was a chance; but it was all a chance anyway.

"When the young woman came here and produced a strip of thin paper, apparently blank, with the multitude of wrinkles in it, I immediately saw that that paper had been recovered from the bracelet. It was old, yellow, and worn. Therefore, blank or not, that was the message which the prisoner had sent out. You saw me hold it over the brazier, and saw the characters appear. It was sympathetic ink, of course.

"Hard to make in prison, you say? Not at all. Writing either with lemon juice or milk, once dry, is perfectly invisible on paper; but when exposed to heat at any time afterward, it will appear. That is a chemical truth.

"Now the thing that appeared was a cipher—an absurd one, still a cipher. Extraordinary precaution of the prisoner who was about to die! This cipher—let me see exactly," and the scientist spelled it out:

"'Stonehedge—idim-sérpa'l ed serueh siort tnaeG ed etéT al rap eétej erbmo'l ed tniop ud zerit sruO'd rehcoR ud eueuq ud dron ua sdeip tnec.'

"If you know anything of languages, Mr. Hatch," he continued, "you know that French is the only language where the apostrophe and the accent marks play a very important part. A moment's study of this particular cipher therefore convinced me that it was in French. I tried the simple expedient of reading it backward, with this result:

"'Stonehedge. Cent pieds au nord du queue du Rocher d'Ours tirez du point de l'ombre jetée par La Téte de Geant trois heures de l'aprés-midi.'

"Here, therefore, was a sensible statement in French, which translated freely into English is simply:

"'Stonehedge. Hundred feet due north from tail Bear Rock through apex (or point) of shadow cast by Giant's Head, three p.m.'

"I had read the cipher and knew its English before I gave a copy of it to the young woman who was here. I specifically asked her if she knew French, to give her a clue by which she might interpret the cipher herself. And thus I blazed the way within a few minutes to the point where astronomical and geometrical calculations were next. Please bear in mind that this message from the dead was not dated.

"Now, about the young woman herself," continued the scientist after a moment. "The statement of how she came to find the bracelet was obviously untrue; particularly are we convinced of this when she cannot, or will not, explain how it was broken. Therefore, another field is open for scrutiny. The bracelet was broken. If we assume that it is the bracelet, and there is no reason to doubt it, and we know it is in her possession, we know also that more than one person had been searching for it. We know positively that that other person—not the masked girl, but the one who had preceded her to Miss Harding's room on the same night—got the bracelet from Miss Harding, and we are safe in assuming that it passed out of that other person's hand by force. The bracelet had been literally torn apart at the hinge. In other words, there had been a physical contest, and one piece of the circlet—the piece with the message—passed out of the hands of the person who had preceded the masked woman and stolen the bracelet.

"But this is by the way. Stonehedge is the name of the old Tremaine Harding estate, about twenty miles out, and there the Tremaine Harding family valuables were hidden by William Tremaine Harding, who died by bullet, a martyr to the cause of freedom. We shall get the treasure this afternoon, after I have settled one or two dates and made the astronomical and geometrical calculations which are necessary."

There was silence for a minute or more, broken at last by the impatient "Honk, honk!" of an automobile outside.

"We'll go now," announced The Thinking Machine as he arose. "There is a car for us."

He led the way out, Hatch following. A heavy touring car, with three seats, driven by a young woman, was waiting at the door. The woman was a stranger to the reporter; but there was no introduction.

"Did you get the date of Captain Harding's imprisonment?" asked The Thinking Machine.

"Yes," was the reply,— "June 3, 1776."

The Thinking Machine clambered in, Hatch following silently, and the car rushed away. It paused in a suburb long enough to pick up two workmen with picks and shovels, who took their places in the back seat, and then the automobile with its strange company— a pretty woman, a newspaper reporter, a distinguished scientist, and two laborers—proceeded on its way. Hatch, alone in the second seat, heard only one remark by the scientist, and this was:

"Of course she was clever enough to read the cipher, after I gave her the hint that it was in French; so we shall find that the place has been dug over; but there is only one chance in three hundred and sixty-five that the treasure was found. I give her credit for extraordinary cleverness; but not enough to make the necessary astronomical calculations."

A run of an hour and a half brought them to Stonehedge, a huge old estate with ramshackle dwelling and acres of rock ridden ground. Away off in the northwest corner were two large stones— Bear Rock and Giants Head—rising fifteen or twenty feet above the ground. The car was driven over a rough road and stopped near them.

"You see, she did read the cipher," remarked the scientist placidly. "Workmen have already been here."

Straight ahead of them was an excavation ten feet or more square. Hatch peered into it, while The Thinking Machine busied himself by planting a stake at the so-called tail of Bear Rock. Then he glanced at his watch,—it was half past two o'clock,—and sat down with the young woman in the shadow of Giants Head. Hatch lounged on the ground near them, and the workmen made themselves comfortable in their own way.

"We can't do anything till three o'clock," remarked The Thinking Machine.

"And just what shall we do then?" inquired the young woman expectantly. It was the first time she had spoken since they started.

"It is rather difficult to explain," said The Thinking Machine. "The hole there proves that the young woman read the cipher, of course. Now here briefly is why the treasure was not found. To-day is September 17. A measurement was made, according to instructions, from the tail of Bear Rock through the apex of the shadow of Giants Head precisely at three o'clock yesterday, one hundred feet due north, or as near north as possible. The hole shows the end of the hundred-foot line. Now, we know that Captain Harding was imprisoned on June 3, 1776; we know he buried the treasure before that date; we have a right to assume that it was only shortly before. On June 3 of any year the apex of the shadow will be in a totally different place from September 17, because of the movement of the earth about the sun and the relative changes in the sun's position. What we must do now is to find precisely where the shadow falls at three o'clock today, then make our calculations to show where it will fall say one week before June 3. Do you follow me? In other words, a difference of half a foot in the location of the apex of the shadow will make a difference of many feet at the end of one hundred feet when we follow the cipher."

At precisely three o'clock The Thinking Machine noted the position of the shadow, and then began a calculation which covered two sheets of blank paper which Hatch had in his pocket.

"This is correct," said The Thinking Machine at last as he arose and planted another stake in the ground. "There is a chance of course that we miss fire the first time because of possible seismic disturbances at sometime past or of a change in the surface of the ground; but this is mathematically correct."

Then, with the assistance of the newspaper man and the young woman, he drew his hundred-foot line, and planted a third stake.

"Dig here!" he told the workmen.

One hour later the long lost family plate and jewels of the ancient Harding family had been unearthed. The Thinking Machine and the others stooped over the rotting box which had been brought to the surface and noted the contents. Roughly the value was above two hundred thousand dollars.

"And I think that is all, Miss Harding," said the scientist at last. "It is yours. Load it into your car there and drive home."

"Miss Harding!" Hatch repeated quickly, with a glance at the young woman. "Miss Harding?"

The Thinking Machine turned and squinted at the reporter for a moment. "Didn't you know that the young woman who called on me was not Miss Harding?" he demanded. "It was evident in her every act,—in her failing to explain the broken bracelet; and in the fact that she was left handed. You must have noticed that. Well, this is Miss Harding, and she is right handed."

The girl smiled at Hatch's astonishment.

"Then the other young woman merely impersonated Miss Harding?" he asked at last.

"That is all, and cleverly," replied The Thinking Machine. "She merely wanted me to read the cipher for her. I put her on the track of reading it herself purposely, and she and the persons associated with her are responsible for the excavation over there."

"But who is the other young woman?"

"She is the one who visited Miss Harding, wearing a mask."

"But what is her name?"

"I'm sure I haven't the faintest idea, Mr. Hatch," responded the little scientist shortly. "We have her to thank, however, for placing a solution of the affair into our hands. Who she is and what she is, is of no real consequence, particularly as Miss Harding has this."

The scientist indicated the box with one small foot, then turned and clambered into the waiting automobile.

The Problem of the Cross Mark

It was an unsolved mystery, apparently a riddle without an answer, in which Watson Richards, the distinguished character actor, happened to play a principal part. The story was told at the Mummers Club one dull afternoon. Richards' listeners were three other actors, a celebrated poet, and a newspaper reporter named Hutchinson Hatch.

"You know there are few men in the profession to-day who really amount to anything who haven't had their hard knocks. Well, my hard times came early, and lasted a long time. So it was just about three years ago to a day that a real crisis came in my affairs. It seemed the end. I had gone one day without food, had bunked in the park that night, and here it was two o'clock in the afternoon of another day. It was dismal enough.

"I was standing on a corner, gazing moodily across the street at the display window of a restaurant, rapidly approaching the *don't care* stage. Some one came up behind and touched me on the shoulder. I turned listlessly enough, and found myself facing a stranger—a clean cut, well groomed man of some forty years.

"'Is this Mr. Watson Richards, the character actor?' he asked.

"'Yes,' I replied.

"'I have been looking for you everywhere,' he explained briefly. 'I want to engage you to do a part for one performance. Are you at liberty?'

"You chaps know what that meant to me just at that moment. Certainly the words dispelled some unpleasant possibilities I had been considering.

"'I am at liberty—yes,' I replied. 'Be glad to do it. What sort of part is it?'

"'An old man,' he informed me. 'Just one performance, you know. Perhaps you'd better come up town with me and see Mr. Hallman right now.'

"I agreed with a readiness which approached eagerness, and he called a passing cab. Hallman was perhaps the manager, or stage manager, I thought. We had driven on for a block in the general direction of up town, my companion chatting pleasantly. Finally he offered me a cigar. I accepted it. I know now that cigar was drugged, because I had hardly taken more than two or three puffs from it when I lost myself completely.

"The next thing I remember distinctly was of stepping out of the cab—I think the stranger assisted me—and going into a house. I don't know where it was—I didn't know then—didn't know even the street. I was dizzy, giddy. And suddenly I stood before a tall, keen faced, clean shaven man. He was Hallman. The stranger introduced me and then left the room. Hallman regarded me keenly for several minutes, and somehow under that scrutiny my dormant faculties were aroused. I had thrown away the cigar at the door.

"'You play character parts?' Hallman began.

"'Yes, all the usual things,' I told him. 'I'm rather obscure, but—'

"'I know,' he interrupted; 'but I have seen your work, and like it. I have been told too that you are remarkably clever at make-up.'

"I think I blushed,—I hope I did, anyway,—I know I nodded. He paused to stare at me for a long time.

"'For instance,' he went on finally, 'you would have no difficulty at all in making up as a man of seventy-five years?'

"'Not the slightest,' I answered. 'I have played such parts.'

"'Yes, yes, I know,' and he seemed a little impatient. 'Well, your make-up is the matter which is most important here. I want you for only one performance; but the make-up must be perfect, you understand.' Again he stopped and stared at me. 'The pay will be one hundred dollars for the one performance.'

"He drew out a drawer of a desk and produced a photograph. He looked at it, then at me, several times, and finally placed it in my hands.

"'Can you make up to look precisely like that?' he asked quietly.

"I studied the photograph closely. It was that of a man about seventy-five years old, of rather a long cast of features, not unlike the general shape of my own face. He had white hair, and was clean shaven. It was simple enough, with the proper wig, a make-up box, and a mirror.

"'I can,' I told Hallman.

"'Would you mind putting on the make-up here now for my inspection?' he inquired.

"'Certainly not,' I replied. It did not strike me at the moment as unusual. 'But I'll need the wig and paints.'

"'Here they are,' said Hallman abruptly, and produced them. 'There's a mirror in front of you. Go ahead.'

"I examined the wig and compared it with the photograph. It was as near perfect as I had ever seen. The make-up box was new and the most complete I ever saw. It didn't occur to me until a long time afterward that it had never been used before. So I went to work. Hallman paced up and down nervously behind me. At the end of twenty minutes I turned upon him a face which was so much like the photograph that I might have posed for it. He stared at me in amazement.

"'By George!' he exclaimed. 'That's it! It's marvelous!' Then he turned and opened the door. 'Come in, Frank,' he called, and the man who had conducted me there entered. Hallman indicated me with a wave of his hand. 'How is it?' he asked.

"Frank, whoever he was, also seemed astonished. Then that passed and a queer expression appeared on his face. You may imagine that I awaited their verdict anxiously.

"'Perfect—absolutely perfect,' said Frank at last.

"'Perhaps the only thing,' Hallman mused critically, 'is that it isn't quite pale enough.'

"'Easily remedied,' I replied, and turned again to the make-up box. A moment later I turned back to the two men. Simple enough, you know—it was one of those pallid, pasty faced make-ups—the old man on the verge of the grave, and all that sort of thing—good deal of pearl powder.

"'That's it!' the two men exclaimed.

"The man Frank looked at Hallman inquiringly.

"'Go ahead,' said Hallman, and Frank left the room.

"Hallman went over, closed and locked the door, after which he came back and sat down in front of me, staring at me for a long time in silence. At length he opened an upper drawer of the desk and glanced in. A revolver lay there, right under his hand. I know now he intended that I should see it.

"'Now, Mr. Richards,' he said at last very slowly, 'what we want you to do is very simple, and as I said there's a hundred dollars in it. I know your circumstances perfectly—you need the hundred dollars.' He offered me a cigar, and foolishly enough I accepted it. 'The part you are to play is that of an old man, who is ill in bed, speechless, utterly helpless. You are dying, and you are to play the part. Use your eyes all you want; but don't speak!'

"Gradually the dizziness I had felt before was coming upon me again. As I said, I know now it was the cigar; but I kept on smoking.

"'There will be no rehearsal,' Hallman went on, and now I knew he was fingering the revolver I had seen in the desk; but it made no particular impression on me. 'If I ask you questions, you may nod an affirmative, but don't speak! Do only what I say, and nothing else!'

"Full realization was upon me now; but everything was growing hazy again. I remember I fought the feeling for a moment; then it seemed to overwhelm me, and I was utterly helpless under the dominating power of that man.

"'When am I to play the part?' I remember asking.

"'Now!' said Hallman suddenly, and he rose. 'I'm afraid you don't fully understand me yet, Mr. Richards. If you play the part properly, you get the hundred dollars; if you don't, this!'

"He meant the revolver. I stared at it dumbly, overcome by a helpless terror, and tried to stand up. Then there came a blank, for how long I don't know. The next thing I remember I was lying in bed, propped up against several pillows. I opened my eyes feebly enough, and there wasn't any acting about it either, because whoever drugged those cigars knew his business.

"There in front of me was Hallman, with a grief stricken expression on his face which made all my art seem amateurish. There was another man there too (not Frank), and a woman who seemed

to be about forty years old. I couldn't see their faces—I wouldn't
even be able to suggest a description of them, because the room
was almost dark. Just the faintest flicker of light came through the
drawn curtains; but I could see Hallman's devilish face all right.
These three conversed together in low tones—sick room voices—
but I couldn't hear, and doubt if I could have followed their conversation if I had heard.

"Finally the door opened and a girl entered. I have seen many
women, but—well, she was peculiarly fascinating. She gave one
little cry, rushed toward the bed impulsively, dropped on her knees
beside it, and buried her face in the sheets. She was shaking with sobs.

"Then I knew—intuitively, perhaps, but I knew—that in some
way I was being used to injure that girl. A sudden feeling of fearful
anger seized upon me, but I couldn't move to save my soul. Hallman
must have caught the blaze in my eyes, for he came forward on the
other side of the bed, and, under cover of a handkerchief which he
had been using rather ostentatiously, pressed the revolver against
my side.

"But I wouldn't be made a tool of. In my dazed condition I know
I was seized with a desperate desire to fight it out—to make him
kill me if he had to, but I would not deceive the girl. I knew if I
could jerk my head down on the pillow it would disarrange the wig,
and perhaps she would see. I couldn't. I might pass my hands across
my make-up and smear it. But I couldn't lift my hands. I was struggling to speak, and couldn't.

"Then somehow I lost myself again. Hazily I remember that
somebody placed a paper in front of me on a book—a legal-looking
document—and guided my hand across it; but that isn't clear. I
was helpless, inert, so much clay in the hands of this man Hallman.
Then everything faded—slowly, slowly. My impression was that I
was actually dying; my eyelids closed of themselves; and the last
thing I saw was the shining gold of that girl's hair as she sobbed
there beside me.

"That's all of it. When I became fully conscious again a policeman was shaking me. I was sitting on a bench in the park. He swore
at me volubly, and I got up and moved slowly along the path with
my hands in my pockets. Something was clenched in one hand. I

drew it out and looked at it. It was a hundred-dollar bill. I remember I got something to eat; and I woke up in a hospital.

"Well, that's the story. Make what you like of it. It can never be solved, of course. It was three years ago. You fellows know what I have done in that time. Well, I'd give it all, every bit of it, to meet that girl again (I should know her), tell her what I know, and make her believe that it was no fault of mine."

Hutchinson Hatch related the circumstances casually one afternoon a day or so later to Professor Augustus S. F. X. Van Dusen—The Thinking Machine.

That eminent man of science listened petulantly, as he listened to all things. "It happened in this city?" he inquired at the end.

"Yes."

"But Richards has no idea what part of the city?"

"Not the slightest. I imagine that the drugged cigar and a naturally weakened condition made him lose his bearings while in the cab."

"I dare say," commented the scientist. "And of course he has never seen Hallman again?"

"No—he would have mentioned it if he had."

"Does Richards remember the exact date of the affair?"

"I dare say he does, though he didn't mention it," replied the reporter.

"Suppose you see Richards and get the date—exactly, if possible," remarked The Thinking Machine. "You might telephone it to me. Perhaps—" and he shrugged his slender shoulders.

"You think there is a possibility of solving the riddle?" demanded the reporter eagerly.

"Certainly," snapped The Thinking Machine. "It requires no solution. It is ridiculously simple,—obvious, I might say,—and yet I dare say the girl Richards referred to has been the victim of some huge plot. It's worth looking into for her sake."

"Remember, it happened three years ago," Hatch suggested tentatively.

"It wouldn't matter particularly if it happened three hundred years ago," declared the scientist. "Logic, Mr. Hatch, remains the same through all the ages—from Adam and Eve to us. Two and two made four in the Garden of Eden just as they do now in a counting house. Therefore, the solution, I say, is absurdly simple. The only problem is to discover the identity of the principals in the affair— and a child could do that."

Later that afternoon Hatch telephoned to The Thinking Machine from the Mummers Club.

"That date you asked for was May 19, three years ago," said the reporter.

"Very well," commented The Thinking Machine. "Drop by tomorrow afternoon. Perhaps we can solve the riddle for Richards."

Hatch called late the following afternoon, as directed, but The Thinking Machine was not in.

"He went out about nine o'clock, and hasn't returned yet," the scientist's aged servant, Martha, informed him.

That night about ten o'clock Hatch used the telephone in a second attempt to reach The Thinking Machine.

"He hasn't come in yet," Martha told him over the wire. "He said he would be back for luncheon; but he isn't here yet."

Hatch replaced the receiver thoughtfully on the hook. Early the following morning he again used the telephone, and there was a note of anxiety in Martha's voice when she answered.

"He hasn't come yet, sir," she explained. "Please, what ought I to do? I'm afraid something has happened to him."

"Don't do anything yet," replied Hatch. "I dare say he'll return to-day."

Again at noon, at six o'clock, and at eleven that night Hatch called Martha on the telephone. Still the scientist had not appeared. Hatch too was worried now; yet how should he proceed? He didn't know, and he hesitated to think of the possibilities. On the morrow, however, something must be done—he would take the matter to Detective Mallory at police headquarters if necessary.

But this was made unnecessary unexpectedly by the arrival next morning of a letter from The Thinking Machine. As he read, an expression of utter bewilderment spread over Hatch's face. Tersely the letter was like this:

Employ an expert burglar, a careful, clever man. At two o'clock of the night following the receipt of this letter go with him to the alley which runs behind No. 810 Blank Street. Enter this house with him from the rear, go up two flights of stairs, and let him pick the lock of the third door on the left from the head of the stairs. Silence above everything. Don't shoot if possible to avoid it.

Van Dusen.

P.S. Put some ham sandwiches in your pocket.

Hatch stared at the note in blank bewilderment for a long time; but he obeyed orders. Thus it came to pass that at ten minutes of two o'clock that night he boosted the notorious Blindy Bates—a man of rare accomplishments in his profession, who at the moment happened to be out of prison—to the top of the rear fence of No. 810 Blank Street. Bates hauled up the reporter, and they leaped down lightly inside the yard.

The back door was simplicity itself to the gifted Bates, and yielded in less than sixty seconds from the moment he laid his hand upon it. Then came a sneaking, noiseless advance along the lower hall, to the accompaniment of innumerable thrills up and down Hatch's spinal column; up the first flight safely, with Blindy Bates leading the way; then along the hall and up the second flight. There was absolutely not a sound in the house—they moved like ghosts.

At the top of the second flight Bates shot a gleam of light from his dark lantern along the hall. The third door it was. And a moment later he was concentrating every faculty on the three locks of this door. Still there had been not the slightest sound. The one spot in the darkness was the bull's eye of the lantern as it illuminated the lock. The first lock was unfastened, then the second, and finally the third. Bates didn't open the door—he merely stepped back—and the door opened as of its own volition. Involuntarily Hatch's hand closed fiercely on his revolver, and Bates's ready weapon glittered a little in the darkness.

"Thanks," came after a moment, in the quiet, querulous voice of The Thinking Machine. "Mr. Hatch, did you bring those sandwiches?"

Half an hour later The Thinking Machine and Hatch appeared at police headquarters. Being naturally of a retiring, unostentatious disposition, Bates did not accompany them; instead, he went his way fingering a bill of moderately large denomination.

Detective Mallory was at home in bed; but Detective Cunningham, another shining light, received his distinguished visitor and Hatch.

"There's a man named Howard Guerin now asleep in his state room aboard the steamer *Austriana*, which sails at five o'clock this morning—just an hour and a half from now—for Hamburg," began The Thinking Machine without any preface. "Please have him arrested immediately."

"What charge?" asked the detective.

"Really, it's of no consequence," replied The Thinking Machine. "Attempted murder, conspiracy, embezzlement, fraud—whatever you like. I can prove any or all of them."

"I'll go after him myself," said the detective.

"And there is also a young woman aboard," continued The Thinking Machine,— "a Miss Hilda Fanshawe. Please have her detained, not arrested, and keep a close guard on her—not to prevent escape, but to protect her."

"Tell us some of the particulars of it," asked the detective.

"I haven't slept in more than forty-eight hours," replied The Thinking Machine. "I'll explain it all this afternoon, after I've rested a while."

The Thinking Machine, for the benefit of Detective Mallory and his satellites, recited briefly the salient points of the story told by the actor, Watson Richards. His listeners were Howard Guerin, tall, keen faced, and clean shaven; Miss Hilda Fanshawe, whose pretty face reflected her every thought; Hutchinson Hatch, and three or four headquarters men. Every eye was upon the drawn face of the diminutive scientist, as he sat far back in his chair, with squint eyes turned upward, and fingertips pressed together.

"From the facts as he stated them, we know beyond all question, in the very beginning, that Mr. Richards was used as a tool to further some conspiracy or fraud," explained The Thinking Machine. "That was obvious. So the first thing to do was to learn the identity of those persons who played the principal parts in it. From Mr. Richards' story we apparently had nothing, yet it gave us practically the names and addresses of the persons at the bottom of the thing.

"How? To find how, we'll have to consider the purpose of the conspiracy. An actor—an artist in facial impersonation, we might say—is picked up in the street and compelled to go through the mummery of a death bed scene while stupefied with drugs. Obviously this was arranged for the benefit of some person who must be convinced that he or she had witnessed a dissolution and the signature of a will, perhaps,—and a will signed under the eyes of that person for whose benefit the farce was acted.

"So we assume a will was signed. We know, within reason, that the mummery was arranged for the benefit of a young woman—Miss Fanshawe here. From the intricacy and daring of the plot, it was pretty safe to assume that a large sum of money was involved. As a matter of fact, there was—more than a million. Now, here is where we take an abstract problem and establish the identity of the actors in it. That will was signed by compulsory forgery, if I may use the phrase, by an utter stranger—a man who could not have known the handwriting of the man whose name he signed, and who was in a condition that makes it preposterous to imagine that he even attempted to sign that name. Yet the will was signed, and the conspirators had to have a signature that would bear inspection. Now, what have we left?

"When a person is incapable of signing his or her name, physically or by reason of no education, the law accepts a cross mark as a signature, when properly witnessed. We know Mr. Richards couldn't have known or imitated the signature of the old man he impersonated; but he did sign—therefore a cross mark, which could have been established beyond question in a court of law. Now, you see how I established the identity of the persons in this fraud. I got the date of the incident from Mr. Richards, then a trip to the surrogate's office told me all I wanted to know. What will had been filed for probate about that date which bore the cross mark as a signature? The records answered the question instantly—John Wallace Lawrence.

"I glanced over the will. It specifically allowed Miss Hilda Fanshawe a trivial thousand dollars a year, and yet she was Lawrence's adopted daughter. See how the joints began to fit together? Further, the will left the bulk of the property to Howard Guerin, a Mrs. Francis,—since deceased, by the way,—and one Frank Hughes. The men were his nephews, the woman his niece. The joints continued to fit nicely, therefore the problem was solved. It was an easy matter to find these people, once I knew their names. I found Guerin—Mr. Richards knew him as Hallman—and asked him about the matter. From the fact that he locked me up in a room of his house and kept me prisoner for two days I was convinced that he was the principal conspirator, and so it proves."

Again there was silence. Detective Mallory took three long breaths, and asked a question. "But where was John Wallace Lawrence when this thing happened?"

"Miss Fanshawe had been in Europe, and was rushing home, knowing that her adopted father was dying," The Thinking Machine explained. "As a matter of fact, when she returned Mr. Lawrence was dead—he died the day before the farce which had been arranged for her benefit, and at the moment his body lay in an up stairs room. He was buried two days later—a day after the farce had been played—and she attended his funeral.

"You see there was no reason why she should have suspected anything. I don't happen to know the provisions of Lawrence's real will, but I dare say it left practically everything to her. The thousand-dollar allowance by the conspirators was a sop to stop possible legal action."

The door of the room opened, and a uniformed man thrust his head in. "Mr. Richards wants to see Professor Van Dusen," he announced.

Immediately behind him came the actor. He stopped in the door and stared at Guerin for a moment.

"Why, hello, Hallman!" he remarked pleasantly. Then his eyes fell upon the girl, and a flash of recognition lighted them.

"Miss Fanshawe, permit me, Mr. Richards," said The Thinking Machine. "You have met before. This is the gentleman you saw die."

"And where is Frank Hughes?" asked Detective Mallory.

"In South Africa," replied the scientist. "I learned a great deal while I was a prisoner."

A deeply troubled expression suddenly appeared on Hutchinson Hatch's face that night when he was writing the story for his newspaper, and he went to the telephone and called The Thinking Machine.

"If you were guarded so closely as a prisoner in that room, how on earth did you mail that letter to me?" he inquired.

"Guerin came in to say some unpleasant things," came the reply, "and placed several letters he intended to post on the table for a moment. The letter for you was already written and stamped, and I was seeking a way to mail it, so I put it with his letters and he mailed it for me."

Hatch burst out laughing.

The Problem of the Ghost Woman

Ruby Reagan, expert cracksman, was busily, albeit quietly, engaged in the practice of his profession. His rubber soles fell silently upon the deep carpet as he stepped into the utter gloom of the study and closed the door noiselessly behind him. For a long time he stood perfectly still, listening, feeling with that vague single sense for the presence of some one else; then he flashed his electric light. A flat topped library table was directly in front of him, littered over with books, and to his left were the bulky outlines of a roll top desk. There were some chairs, a cabinet or so, and rows of bookcases.

His scrutiny, brief but comprehensive, seemed to satisfy Reagan; for the light went out suddenly, and, turning in his tracks, he slid the bolt of the door into its socket slowly, to avoid even a click. Next he released the grips on one of the windows, for it might be necessary to leave the room that way in the event of some one entering by the single door. Then he settled down to work. First was the desk, and after a long, minute inspection of the lock he dropped on his knees before it and began trying his skeleton keys. The electric flash, with the light fixed, was on the left leaf of the desk, brightly illuminating the lock and lending a deeper glow of ruby red to his hair. On the right leaf of the desk, within instant reach, was his revolver.

It was nearly half an hour before the lock yielded, and then, with a sigh of relief, Reagan carefully pushed up the roll top. Inside he found a metal box. From a score of pigeonholes he dragged forth papers of all descriptions, ruthlessly scattering them about him after a quick examination of each in turn. Then he went through drawer after drawer, carefully scrutinizing each article before he laid it down.

"Guess it's in the box," he mused at length.

Sitting flat upon the floor, with the box between his knees, he lavished his talents upon it. After a few minutes the lock clicked, and the metal lid lifted. Again Reagan smiled, for here were packages and packages of banknotes. But after a moment they too were spilled out on the floor. It was something else he sought.

"Now, that's funny," he told himself finally. "It isn't here." He paused thoughtfully, while his eyes rested lovingly upon the packages of money. "Of course, if I can't get what I want I'll take what I can get," he went on at last. And he proceeded to stuff the money away in his pockets.

Several times he ran his fingers slowly through his red hair. It was plain that he was deeply puzzled. He was on the point of rising to continue his investigations in other directions, when he heard something. It was a voice—a quiet, soothing, pleasant voice—about fourteen inches behind his right ear.

"Don't try to get your revolver, please!" the voice advised. "If you do, I'll shoot!"

Involuntarily Reagan's hand darted out toward the weapon on the leaf of the desk; but it was drawn back as suddenly when he heard a sharp click behind him. Nonplussed for the moment, he sat down again on the floor, half expecting a shot. It didn't come, and he screwed his head around to see why.

What he saw astounded him. It was a diaphanous, floating, lacy, white something—the figure of a girl. Or was it a girl? The head was sheathed in white, the features covered by a misty, hazy, veily thing, and in the dim reflected light the whole figure seemed ridiculously unsubstantial. It was a girl's voice, though.

"Sit perfectly still, please, and don't make any noise!" the voice advised again. Yes, it was a girl's voice.

Reagan noted the small, gold mounted revolver in her right hand, with the barrel, at just that moment, on a direct line with his head and only a foot or so away; and he noted that it remained steadily where it was without one tremor or quiver.

"Yes'm," he said at last.

The white figure walked around him—or did it float?—and picked up his revolver from the desk.

"This is Mr. Reagan, isn't it?" she inquired.

"Yes'm," responded Reagan. The admission was surprised out of him.

"Did you find it?"

"No'm."

Was this thing real? Reagan rubbed his eyes doubtfully. He was dreaming, of course. He would wake up in a minute. He opened his eyes again. Yes, there she was. But she wasn't real,—she couldn't be real,—she was a ghost. She was certainly not in the room when he entered, and she could not have come in since, because he had bolted the door on the inside.

"I shall trouble you now, Mr. Reagan," the ghost woman went on, "to take all that money from your pocket and put it back in the box."

Reagan stared at the end of the revolver a moment, and the ghost woman wriggled it. That was real enough, anyway. Promptly and without a word he began to disgorge packages of banknotes. Then at last looked up again.

"You put back only eight packages," said the ghost woman calmly. "You took out nine."

"Yes'm," said Reagan.

He fished through his pockets again, in a semi-hypnotic condition, produced more money, and deposited it with the other. He closed the metal lid and snapped the lock.

"That will do very nicely," she said approvingly. "Now I shall trouble you, please, to go on about your business."

Reagan started to rise, awkwardly enough, on hands and knees. The ghost woman stepped back a little; but still she was not far enough away, for when Reagan suddenly came to his feet his outstretched arms struck her violently beneath the wrists and sent the two revolvers flying upward. With another quick movement he swept the electric light from the desk, extinguishing it. There was a sound of scuffling feet in the darkness, as of persons struggling, a little despairing cry, then finally a pistol shot.

Reagan stumbled blindly about the room, seeking the door. He found it at last, still bolted on the inside, and tugged at it frantically. Then came the sound of heavy feet running along the hall outside toward the study, and Reagan stopped. The window! It was the only way now! The shot had aroused the household. He rushed toward the window; but it refused to move.

The clamor was at the door. Desperately Reagan sought for the side grips on the window; but they seemed to have disappeared. The door trembled as some heavy body was hurled against it. The bolt would yield—it was yielding—Reagan heard the woodwork crack. Then deliberately he drove his clenched fist through the glass, took one step on a chair and hurled himself straight through. The door crashed under the onslaught and swung inward.

On the following morning Chester Mills, a wealthy merchant, called on Detective Mallory, chief of the bureau of criminal investigation.

"I own a large country estate forty miles out of town," Mills began abruptly. "Yesterday was the last day of the month. I went to the bank and drew nine hundred dollars, and placed it in a metal box in my desk at home and locked both the box and desk.

"I went to bed at eleven o'clock. About two o'clock this morning I heard a pistol shot in the study. I jumped out of bed and rushed into the hall toward the study, meeting on the way one of my servants, O'Brien. We found the study locked, and started to smash the door in. As we did so we heard a great crash of glass inside.

"Then we did smash the door, and O'Brien turned on the electric lights. One of the two windows was smashed out as if somebody had jumped or been thrown through it; my desk had been ransacked, and my papers scattered all over the floor. The desk was standing open, and I picked up the box. It had a bullet hole in it. The ball went in the top and came out the side. I found it sticking in the desk. It was thirty-two caliber. Here it is."

Mills tossed the misshapen leaden missile on the table, and Detective Mallory examined it.

"Then I found the first real puzzle," Mills went on. "I opened the box and counted the money. Instead of any of it being missing, there was more there than there was when I put the box in the desk. Where there had been only nine hundred dollars, verified by the paying teller and myself, there was now nine hundred and ten dollars—an extra ten-dollar bill."

Detective Mallory chewed his cigar frantically.

"O'Brien found a soft black hat in the room, near the door," continued Mills, "a revolver, thirty-eight caliber, with every chamber loaded, an overcoat, an electric flashlight which had been thrown to the floor and broken, and a very complete kit of burglar's tools. I straightened the women folk all out, had the house searched, and went back to bed. So far as I have been able to find out, nothing was stolen—nothing is missing."

"Well, in that case—" began the detective.

"I haven't started yet," interrupted Mills tersely. "The window was out, as I said; so when we went to bed again we left O'Brien in the study on watch. About half-past three o'clock I was awakened again by a scream—a woman. Again I jumped out and ran along toward the study. The lights were going, but there was no sign of O'Brien. I presumed then that his attention had been attracted by the scream and he had gone to investigate. But—Well, O'Brien has disappeared. No one has seen or heard of him since—there's not a trace."

Detective Mallory sat for a long time silently smoking, and staring into the eyes of his caller.

At this point the problem came under the observation of that eminent logician, Professor Augustus S. F. X. Van Dusen—The Thinking Machine. As Hutchinson Hatch, reporter, related the known facts, the distinguished man of science permitted his eyes to narrow down to mere slits of watery blue, and the tall, dome-like forehead was deeply furrowed.

"Why was any shot fired?" Hatch demanded of the scientist in perplexity. "And who fired it? Were there two burglars? Did they fight? Was one wounded? There were bloodstains on the ground outside the window; but we can see that whoever jumped out might have cut himself on the glass. And why was the hole shot in the tin box? Not to break the lock, obviously; for it could have been taken along. Where does the odd ten-dollar bill in the box figure? Where is O'Brien? Who was the woman who screamed that second time? Why did she scream? Why wasn't something stolen?"

Having relieved himself of this torrent of questions, Hatch dropped back into his chair expectantly and lighted a cigarette. The Thinking Machine permitted two disapproving eyes to settle on the young man for a moment.

"And still you haven't asked the one vital question," he remarked tartly. "That is, What particular object in that study, or supposed to be in that study, is of such great importance to some one unknown that two bold, daring I might say, attempts were made to get it in the same night?"

"It seems to me it would be impossible to learn that, until—"

"Nothing is impossible, Mr. Hatch. It is merely a little sum in arithmetic. Two and two make four; not sometimes but *all* the time. This problem, at the moment, seems remarkably disjointed, particularly when we consider the disappearance of O'Brien. First, then, is Mr. Mills positive nothing was stolen?"

"Absolutely so," replied Hatch. "He has checked off every paper, and accounted for every article."

The furrows in the tall brow deepened perceptibly, and for a long time the crabbed little scientist sat silent. "How much blood was found outside?" he asked suddenly.

"Quite a good deal of it," Hatch responded. "It looks as if some one, whoever jumped or was thrown out, received some nasty cuts. The edges of the glass are stained."

The Thinking Machine nodded. "It is established beyond all question that the woman who screamed that second time was not one of those in the house?" he asked.

"Oh, yes," returned Hatch confidently. "They had all retired after the first fright, and the second didn't even arouse them. They didn't know of O'Brien's disappearance until morning."

"The police have found nothing yet?"

"Not yet. The articles left in the room, of course,—the hat and coat and burglar's tools,—are clues that they are working on. They might establish identity by their aid."

"Well, we'll have to find the man who jumped," remarked the scientist placidly. "When we do that, we can go somewhere with this affair."

"Yes, when we do that," Hatch agreed, with a grin.

"Of course we can do it!" snapped The Thinking Machine. "Here we seek a man with neither hat nor overcoat, who is cut up with glass, possibly badly wounded."

"But he's the sort of man who would scuttle to cover like a scared rabbit," Hatch protested. "Wouldn't matter how badly hurt he was, if he could walk he would hide."

"You seem to think, Mr. Hatch, that leaping through a window, taking all the glass with you, and falling twenty feet to a hard pavement, is a trivial affair," declared the scientist crabbedly. "If this man wasn't badly hurt, it's a miracle; therefore—" He stopped abruptly and squinted at the newspaper man. "I'm going to state a case and ask you a question," he went on suddenly. "Before I do it I'll write the answer you will give on this bit of paper. You are an intelligent man; so I'll demonstrate to you how intelligent minds run in the same channel."

He scribbled a few words hurriedly, folded the paper twice, and handed it to the reporter.

"Now you are the burglar," he resumed, "a man perhaps well known to the police. You jumped from that window and hurt yourself seriously. You need medical attention; yet you can't afford to run the slightest risk of capture. You have no hat or coat. You go to physician, not too near the scene of the affair, and you tell a story to account for your condition. What could you say to do away with all suspicion, and make yourself perfectly safe, at least for the moment?"

Hatch smiled whimsically as he turned and twisted the scrap of paper in his fingers, then lighted a cigarette and got down to the matter in hand seriously.

"I think," he said at last slowly, and feeling unaccountably sheepish about it, "that the safest story to tell the physician would be that I had been thrown from an automobile, lost my hat, say, cut myself going head foremost through the glass front when the car ran away, badly bruised by the violence with which I hit the ground; and all that sort of thing."

The Thinking Machine glared at him aggressively for an instant, then arose and left the room. Hatch drew a long breath, then opened the folded paper reluctantly. He found only these words:

"Runaway automobile—cut by diving through glass front—hat lost—bruises and other lacerations by fall to ground."

When the scientist returned, he wore his hat and overcoat.

"Mr. Hatch, go at once to Mr. Mills, and inquire if he has yet learned of anything being missing from the study—a paper of some sort, in all probability," he instructed. "Then, without mentioning the matter to him, take other steps to learn the nature of any litigation which might be pending in which he is concerned—I imagine something is either now going on or will be going on in a few days. Run by this evening to see me."

"Are you going with me?" inquired the reporter.

"No, no," responded the scientist impatiently. "I'm going to see the man who jumped out of the window."

When Ruby Reagan, expert cracksman, awoke to consciousness he found himself gazing straight into two squinting blue eyes, magnified beyond all proportion by the thick spectacles through which he saw them. The eyes were set far back in a thin, drawn face, and above them was a shock of straw yellow hair.

"Be perfectly quiet," said The Thinking Machine. "You are safe enough, and in a day or so you will be all right."

"Who are you?" demanded Reagan suspiciously.

"I am acting for the gentleman who employed you to get that—that document from Mr. Mills's study," replied the scientist glibly. "You are in my home. The doctor fixed you up, and I brought you here as soon as I found you. He doesn't suspect anything. He thinks you were injured in an automobile accident, as you said."

The cracksman closed his eyes to think about it. Weakly, for he had lost much blood, he gradually pieced together a shattered recollection of events of the last few hours,—the jump, his hurts, that staggering run through deserted streets to get away from that place, the final collapse at the very door of a physician, the muttered story he told to account for his wounds. Then he looked again into the inscrutable face of The Thinking Machine. It all seemed regular enough.

"The cops don't know?" he demanded suddenly.

"No," replied The Thinking Machine emphatically. "Who fired the shot?"

"The ghost lady," replied the cracksman promptly. "Guess she didn't mean to, though, cause she seemed as anxious to be quiet as I was."

"And of course you jumped when you heard someone at the door?"

"Betcher neck!" replied Reagan grimly. "The cops ain't never had me yet, an' I don't intend to break no record."

"And the ghost lady," resumed the scientist. "Tell me about her."

And then the story of the strange happenings in the study that night as Reagan recalled them was told. "And I didn't get the paper at that," he concluded.

"You say the ghost lady was all in white?"

"Sure," was the reply. "I don't know really whether she was a ghost or not; but she started the mix-up." He was silent for a moment. "But le' me tell you she must have been a ghost. She couldn't have got in that room any other way. She slid in through the keyhole or something."

"And she called you by name, you say?"

"Yes. That's another thing that makes me think she's a ghost. How did she know my name. And why did she ask me if I got it?"

Hutchinson Hatch called an hour later. There was something of elation, excitement nearly, in his manner. He found The Thinking Machine stretched out in a huge chair in the laboratory, with unruffled brow, and idly twiddling fingers.

"The litigation, Mr. Hatch," said the latter without turning.

"Well, there are a dozen cases in which he is interested one way or another," Hatch informed him; "but there is one particularly—"

"Something about property rights, I imagine?" interrupted the scientist.

"Yes," said the reporter. "There's a fortune involved, and a vast deal of real estate. A business partner of Mills, Martin Pendexter by name, died three or four years ago and his grandson, now about twenty-two years old, is suing to recover certain money and property from Mills, alleging that Mills assumed it as his own when

Pendexter died. Mills has steadfastly refused to go into the matter, or even discuss it, and finally the boy brought the suit. It has been postponed several times; but it's to come up for hearing soon."

"Mr. Mills, then, holds title to this property?" inquired The Thinking Machine.

"I presume if he hadn't felt safe in his position he would not have permitted the matter to go into court," replied Hatch. "I figure that Mills does hold a release from Pendexter of the property, and intends to produce it in court. He has advised the boy several times not to sue; but would never give a reason."

"Oh!" and for a long time the scientist sat silent. "Of course—of course," he mused, half aloud. "Then the ghost woman was one of the—"

"And there's another thing," Hatch rushed on impatiently. "Detective Downey told me a little while ago the police have established the identity of at least one person who was in the study that night, by the kit of tools left behind. His name is Ruby Reagan."

"Ruby Reagan," repeated the scientist thoughtfully. "Oh, yes. He's asleep in the next room there."

The Thinking Machine was talking; Mills, Detective Mallory, and Hutchinson Hatch were listening.

"There is no puzzle about it at all," declared the scientist. "Briefly what happened was this: A burglar was employed by a man who is suing you, Mr. Mills, to go into your study and find, if indeed such a thing is in existence, the document upon which you must depend to prove your title to the Pendexter property now in dispute.

"Well, this burglar went to that study and looked for that document—vainly, I may say here. While looking for that he found the money in the box. He was tempted then, contrary to orders, perhaps, and put this money in his pocket. Later he was compelled at the point of a revolver to put the money back in the box, and in his hurry to obey orders he put in a ten-dollar bill of his own. The person who compelled him to replace the money was—was—"

He paused, wrote something on a slip of paper, and passed it to Mills.

"What!" exclaimed Mills incredulously.

"No names, please—yet, anyway," broke in the scientist. "Anyway, it was a woman, I may say a woman of great courage, even audacity. She had gained possession of the burglar's revolver, and with two weapons ordered him to go. The burglar precipitated a struggle, a shot was fired by accident, perhaps, and that is the shot which went through the tin box. The burglar jumped through the window and escaped. The woman, who was in the room, perhaps behind the curtain of the door when the burglar entered, had come there to get that particular document he was seeking. At the time he jumped we can imagine how she managed to get out into the hall when the door flew open, and you and your man O'Brien entered.

"The next we know of that woman she was with the others screaming. A little logic shows us that after that first fright, when the house was perfectly still again, the woman, not knowing O'Brien was on watch, returned to that study again to seek that document. He was sitting in the dark, heard her, and flashed on the electric lights. She was surprised, she screamed, was recognized by O'Brien, and then for some consideration that does not appear—probably a bribe—induced O'Brien to disappear. Again she avoided discovery, and if an investigation had been made she would have been found in bed, I dare say.

"Being totally ignorant now, of the incidents leading up to the pistol shot and the burglar's escape, the first point that the logical mind can seize upon is the finding of more money in the tin box than was known to be there. Therefore, we know that that box had been opened, and we know that the burglar was either an honest man or was compelled to be honest. We know too from the fact that a thirty-eight caliber revolver was found, that there was a second revolver—the one from which the shot was fired. Burglars are not honest. Was this one compelled to be honest? What honest person could be in that room—lone with that burglar, remember? You see instantly a thousand possibilities.

"Without pursuing those possibilities at the moment, it came down to a question of finding the burglar—the dishonest one, I may say. That was not difficult, only tedious work on the telephone, seeking a doctor who had treated a man who was probably—*prob-*

ably, you note—injured in an automobile accident. I found your Ruby Reagan, Mr. Mallory, and from him I learned just what happened at first—a woman in white, a ghost woman, obviously some woman in the house. White lacy gowns are not popular for street wear at two o'clock in the morning."

"I wonder if this is absolutely necessary, Mr. Van Dusen?" interrupted Mills. His face was white. "I think I understand, and I assure you the matter has taken a personal turn which may mean a great deal to me and my family."

The Thinking Machine waved his hand as if the matter was dismissed.

"For your benefit, Mr. Mills," continued the scientist, "I will state that the motive for the girl's act was one which reflected her great courage, and her loyalty to you—perhaps at the same time her regard for another man. Do you follow me? In some way—perhaps the man told her—she learned of the plan to engage Reagan for the work, and she could have learned of that only from the man by a relationship which partook of love for him. Her loyalty to you and a natural desire to save this man's name in your eyes, led her to seek in person to recover the document. It merely happened that they both visited the study the same night."

The Thinking Machine stopped as if that was all.

"But here, go on," Detective Mallory insisted. "I want to know the rest."

"Suppose, Mr. Mallory, that you find Reagan for yourself?" suggested The Thinking Machine after a long pause. "I did it. Surely you can."

"Where is he? Where did you see him?"

"I saw him at my house," responded the scientist calmly. "I left him there to come here; but a man who confesses what he confessed to me doesn't stay at a place like that if he can help it. The matter is as I have stated it, Mr. Mills. Your reason for refusing to give the young man any explanation of your holding the property is a good one, I dare say, so I'll not question it."

"I'll tell you," flamed Mills suddenly. "He is not really the grandson of Pendexter. I will be compelled to show that if he sues me—that is why I have advised him not to sue."

"I imagined as much," said The Thinking Machine.

Ruby Reagan left the home of The Thinking Machine in a cab late that night. And a few days later the Pendexter suit was withdrawn by the plaintiff.

The Problem of the Hidden Million

The gray hand of Death had already left its ashen mark upon the wrinkled, venomous face of the old man, who lay huddled up in bed. Save for the feverishly brilliant eyes—cunning, vindictive, hateful—there seemed to be no spark of life in the aged form. The withered lips were mute, and the thin, yellow, claw-like hands lay helplessly outstretched on the white sheets. All physical power was gone; only the brain remained doggedly alive. Two men and two women stood beside the death bed. Upon each in turn the glittering eyes rested with the merciless, unreasoning hatred of age. Crouched on the floor was a huge St. Bernard dog; and on a perch across the room was a parrot which screeched abominably.

The gloom of the wretched little room was suddenly relieved by a ruddy sunbeam which shot athwart the bed and lighted the scene fantastically. The old man noted it, and his lips curled into a hideous smile.

"That's the last sun I'll ever see," he piped feebly. "I'm dying—dying! Do you hear? And you're all glad of it, every one of you. Yes, you are! You are glad of it because you want my money. You came here to make me believe you were paying a last tribute of respect to your old grandfather. But that isn't it. It's the money you want—the money! But I've got a surprise for you. You'll never get the money. It's hidden safely—you'll never get it. You all hate me, you have hated me for years, and after that sun dies you'll all hate me worse. But not more than I hate you. You'll all hate me worse then, because I'll be gone and you'll never know where the money is hidden. It will lie there safely where I put it, rotting and crumbling away; but you shall never warm your fingers with it! It's hidden—hidden—hidden!"

There was rasping in the shrunken throat, a deeply drawn breath, then the figure stiffened and a distorted soul passed out upon the Eternal Way.

Martha held a card within the blinding light of the reflector, and Professor Augustus S. F. X. Van Dusen, with his hands immersed to the elbows in some chemical mess, squinted at it.

"Dr. Walter Ballard," he read. "Show him in."

After a moment Dr. Ballard entered. The scientist was still absorbed in his labors, but paused long enough to jerk his head toward a chair. Dr. Ballard accepted this as an invitation and sat down, staring curiously at the singular, childlike figure of this eminent man of science, at the mop of tangled, straw yellow hair, the enormous brow, and the peering blue eyes.

"Well?" demanded the scientist abruptly.

"I beg your pardon," began Dr. Ballard with a little start. "Your name was mentioned to me sometime ago by a newspaper reporter, Hutchinson Hatch, whom I chanced to meet in his professional capacity. He suggested then that I come and see you, but I thought it useless. Now the affair in which we were both interested at that time seems hopelessly beyond solution, so I come to you for aid.

"We want to find one million dollars in gold and United States bonds, which were hidden by my grandfather, John Walter Ballard, sometime before his death just a month ago. The circumstances are altogether out of the ordinary."

The Thinking Machine abandoned his labors, and dried his hands carefully, after which he took a seat facing Dr. Ballard. "Tell me about it," he commanded.

"Well," began Dr. Ballard reminiscently, as he settled back in his chair, "the old man—my grandfather—died, as I said, a month ago. He was nearly eighty-six, and the last five or six years of his life he spent as a recluse in a little hut twenty miles from the city, a place some distance from any other house. He had a spot of ground there, half an acre or so, and lived like a pauper, despite the fact that he was worth at least a million dollars. Previous to the time he went there to live, there had been an estrangement with my family, his sole heirs. My family consists of myself, wife, son, and daughter.

"My grandfather lived in the house with me for ten years before he went out to this hut; and why he left us then is not clear to any member of my family, unless," and he shrugged his shoulders, "he was mentally unbalanced. Anyway, he went. He would neither come to see us, nor would he permit us to go to see him. As far as we know, he owned no real property of any sort, except this miserable little place, worth altogether—furnishing and all—not more than a thousand or twelve hundred dollars.

"Well, about a month ago someone stopped at the hut for something and found he was ill. I was notified, and with my wife, son and daughter went to see what we could do. He took occasion on his death bed to heap vituperation upon us, and incidentally to state that something like a million dollars was left behind, but hidden.

"For the sake of my son and daughter, I undertook to recover this money. I consulted attorneys, private detectives, and in fact exhausted every possible method. I ascertained beyond question that the money was not in a bank anywhere; and hardly think he would have left it there, because of course, if he had, even with a will disinheriting us, the law would have turned it over to us. He had no safe deposit vault as far as one month's close search revealed, and the money was not hidden in the house or grounds. He stated on his death bed that it was in bonds and gold, and that we should never find it. He was just vindictive enough not to destroy it, but to leave it somewhere, believing we should never find it. Where did he hide it?"

The Thinking Machine sat silent for several minutes, with his enormous yellow head tilted back, and slender fingers pressed together. "The house and grounds were searched?" he asked.

"The house was searched from cellar to garret," was the reply. "Workmen, under my directions, practically wrecked the building. Floors, ceilings, walls, chimney, stairs,—everything,—little cubby holes in the roof, the foundation of the chimney, the pillars, even the flag stones leading from the gate to the door,—everything was examined. The joists were sounded to see if they were solid, and a dozen of them were cut through; the posts on the veranda were cut to pieces; and every stick of furniture was dissected—mattresses, beds, chairs, tables, bureaus—all of it. Outside in the grounds the search was just as thorough. Not one square inch but what was overturned. We dug it all up to a depth of ten feet. Still nothing."

"Of course," said the scientist at last, "the search of the house and grounds was useless. The old man was shrewd enough to know that they would be searched. Also it would appear that the search of banks and safety deposit vaults was equally useless. He was shrewd enough to foresee that too. We shall, for the present, assume that he did not destroy the money or give it away; so it is hidden. If the brain of man is clever enough to conceal a thing, the brain of man is clever enough to find it. It's a little problem in subtraction, Dr. Ballard." He was silent for a moment. "Who was your grandfather's attending physician?"

"I was. I was present at his death. Nothing could be done. It was merely the collapse consequent upon old age. I issued the burial certificate."

"Were any special directions left as to the place or manner of burial?"

"No."

"Have all his papers been examined for a clue as to the possible hiding place?"

"Everything. There were no papers to amount to anything."

"Have you those papers now?"

Dr. Ballard silently produced a packet and handed it to the scientist.

"I shall examine these at my leisure," said The Thinking Machine. "It may be a day or so before I communicate with you."

Dr. Ballard went his way. For a dozen hours The Thinking Machine sat with the papers spread out before him, and the keen, squinting, blue eyes dissected them, every paragraph, every sentence, every word. At the end he arose and bundled up the papers impatiently.

"Dear me! Dear me!" he exclaimed irritably. "There's no cipher—that's certain. Then what?"

Devastating hands had wrought the wreck of the little hut where the old man died. Standing in the midst of its litter, The Thinking Machine regarded it closely and dispassionately for a long time. The work of destruction had been well done.

"Can you suggest anything?" asked Dr. Ballard impatiently.

"One mind may read another mind," said The Thinking Machine, "when there is some external thing upon which there can come concentration as a unit. In other words, when we have a given number the logical brain can construct either backward or forward. There are so many thousands of ways in which your grandfather could have disposed of this money, that the task becomes tremendous in view of the fact that we have no starting point. It is a case for patience, rather than any other quality; therefore, for greater speed, we must proceed psychologically. The question then becomes, not one of where the money is hidden, but one of where that sort of man would hide it.

"Now what sort of man was your grandfather?" the scientist continued. "He was crabbed, eccentric, and possibly not mentally sound. The cunning of a diseased brain is greater than the cunning of a normal one. He boasted to you that the money was in existence, and his last words were intended to arouse your curiosity; to hang over you all the rest of your life and torment you. You can imagine the vindictive, petty brain like that putting a thing safely beyond your reach—but just beyond it—near enough to tantalize, and yet far enough to remain undiscovered. This seems to me to be the mental attitude in this case. Your grandfather knew that you would do just what you have done here; that is, search the house and lot. He knew too that you would search banks and safety deposit vaults, and with a million at stake he knew it would be done thoroughly. Knowing this, naturally he would not put the money in any of those places.

"Then what? He doesn't own any other property, as far as we know, and we shall assume that he did not buy property in the name of some other person; therefore, what have we left? Obviously, if the money is still in existence, it is hidden on somebody's else property. And the minute we say that, we have the whole wide world to search. But again, doesn't the deviltry and maliciousness of the old man narrow that down? Wouldn't he have liked to remember as a dying thought that the money was always just within your reach, and yet safely beyond it? Wouldn't it have been a keener revenge to have you dig over the whole place, while the money was hidden just six feet outside in a spot where you would never dig?

It might be sixty, or six hundred, or six thousand. But then we have the law of probability to narrow those limits; so—"

Professor Van Dusen turned suddenly and strolled across the uneven ground to the property line. Walking slowly and scrutinizing the ground as he went, he circled the lot, returning to the starting point. Dr. Ballard had followed along behind him.

"Are all your grandfather's belongings still in the house?" asked the scientist.

"Yes, everything just as he left it; that is, except his dog and a parrot. They are temporarily in charge of a widow down the road here."

The scientist looked at Dr. Ballard quickly. "What sort of dog is it?" he inquired.

"A St. Bernard, I think," replied Dr. Ballard wonderingly.

"Do you happen to have a glove or something that you know your grandfather wore?"

"I have a glove, yes."

From the debris which littered the floor of the house, a well worn glove was recovered.

"Now, the dog, please," commanded the scientist.

A short walk along the country road brought them to a house, and here they stopped. The St. Bernard, a shaggy, handsome, boisterous old chap, with wise eyes, was led out in leash. The Thinking Machine thrust the glove forward, and the dog sniffed at it. After a moment he sank down on his haunches, and with head thrust forward and upward, whined softly. It was the call of the brute soul to its master.

The Thinking Machine patted the heavy-coated head, and with the glove still in his hand made as if to go away. Again came the whine, but the dog sank down on the floor, with his head between his forepaws, regarding him intently. For ten minutes the scientist sought to coax the animal to follow him, but still he lay motionless.

"I don't mind keepin' that dog here; but that parrot is powerful noisy," said the woman after a moment. She had been standing by watching the scientist curiously. "There ain't no peace in the house."

"Noisy—how?" asked Dr. Ballard.

"He swears, and sings and whistles, and does 'rithmetic all day long," the woman explained. "It nearly drives me distracted."

"Does arithmetic?" inquired The Thinking Machine.

"Yes," replied the woman, "and he swears just terrible. It's almost like havin' a man about the house. There he goes now."

From another room came a sudden, squawking burst of profanity, followed instantly by a whistle, which caused the dog on the floor to prick up his ears.

"Does the parrot talk well?" asked the scientist.

"Just like a human bein'," replied the woman, "an' just about as sensible as some I've seen. I don't mind his whistling, if only he wouldn't swear so, and do all his figgerin' out loud."

For a minute or more the scientist stood staring down at the dog in deep thought. Gradually there came some subtle change in his expression. Dr. Ballard was watching him closely.

"I think perhaps it would be a good idea for me to keep the parrot for a few days," suggested the scientist finally. He turned to the woman. "Just what sort of arithmetic does the bird do?"

"All kinds," she answered promptly. "He does all the multiplication table. But he ain't very good in subtraction."

"I shouldn't be surprised," commented The Thinking Machine. "I'll take the bird for a few days, doctor, if you don't mind."

And so it came to pass that when The Thinking Machine returned to his apartments he was accompanied by as noisy and vociferous a companion as one would care to have.

Martha, the aged servant, viewed him with horror as he entered. "The perfessor do be gettin' old," she muttered. "I suppose there'll be a cat next."

Two days later Dr. Ballard was called to the telephone. The Thinking Machine was at the other end of the wire.

"Take two men whom you can trust and go down to your grandfather's place," instructed the scientist curtly. "Take picks, shovels, a compass, and a long tape line. Stand on the front steps facing east. To your right will be an apple tree some distance off that lot on the adjoining property. Go to that apple tree. A boulder is at its foot. Measure from the edge of that stone twenty-six feet due north by the compass, and from that point fourteen feet due west. You will find your money there. Then please have some one come and take this bird away. If you don't, I'll wring its neck. It's the most blasphemous creature I ever heard. Good bye."

Dr. Ballard slipped the catch on the suit case and turned it upside down on the laboratory table. It was packed—literally packed—with United States bonds. The Thinking Machine fingered them idly.

"And there is this too," said Dr. Ballard.

He lifted a stout sack from the floor, cut the string, and spilled out its contents beside the bonds. It was gold—thousands and thousands of dollars. Dr. Ballard was frankly excited about it; The Thinking Machine accepted it as he accepted all material things.

"How much is there of it?" he asked quietly.

"I don't know," replied Dr. Ballard.

"And how did you find it?"

"As you directed—twenty-six feet north from the boulder, and fourteen feet west from that point."

"I knew that, of course," snapped The Thinking Machine; "but how was it hidden?"

"It's rather peculiar," explained Dr. Ballard. "Fourteen feet brought the man who had measured it to the edge of an old, dried up well, twelve or fifteen feet deep. Not expecting any such thing, he tumbled into it. In his efforts to get out he stepped upon a stone which protruded from one side. That fell out, and revealed the wooden box, which contained all this."

"In other words," said the scientist, "the money was hidden in such a manner that it would in time have come to be buried twelve or fifteen feet below the surface, because the well, being dry, would ultimately, of course, have been filled in."

Dr. Ballard had been listening only hazily. His hands had been plowing in and out of the heap of gold. The Thinking Machine regarded him with something like contempt about his thin-lipped mouth.

"How—how did you ever do it?" asked Dr. Ballard at last.

"I am surprised that you want to know," remarked The Thinking Machine cuttingly. "You know how I reached the conclusion that the money was not hidden either in the house or lot. The plain logic of the thing told me that, even before the search you had made demonstrated it. You saw how logic narrowed down the search, and you saw my experiment with the dog. That was purely an experiment. I wanted to see the instinct of the animal. Would it lead him anywhere?—perhaps to the spot where the money had been hidden? It did not.

"But the parrot? That was another matter. It just happens that once before I had an interesting experience with a bird—a cockatoo which figured in a sleep walking case—and naturally was interested in this bird. Now, what were the circumstances in this case? Here was a bird that talked exceptionally well, yet that bird had been living for five years alone with an old man. It is a fact that, no matter how well a parrot may talk, it will forget in the course of time, unless there is some one around it who talks. This old man was the only person near this bird; therefore, from the fact that the bird talks, we know that the old man talked; from the fact that the bird repeated the multiplication table, we know that the old man repeated it; from the fact that the bird whistles, we know that the old man whistled, perhaps to the dog. And in the course of five years under these circumstances, a bird would have come to that point where it would repeat only the words or sounds that the old man used.

"All this shows too that the old man talked to himself. Most people who live alone a great deal do that. Then came a question as to whether at any time the old man had ever repeated the secret of the hiding place within the hearing of the bird—not once but many times, because it takes a parrot a long time to learn phrases. When we know the vindictiveness which lay behind the old man's actions in hiding the money, when we know how the thing preyed on his mind, coupled with the fact that he talked to himself, and was not wholly sound mentally, we can imagine him doddering about the place alone, repeating the very thing of which he had made so great a secret. Thus, the bird learned it, but learned it disjointedly, not connectedly; so when I brought the parrot here, my idea was to know by personal observation what the bird said that didn't connect—that is, that had no obvious meaning, I hoped to get a clue which would result, just as the clue I did get did result.

"The bird's trick of repeating the multiplication table means nothing except it shows the strange workings of an unbalanced mind. And yet, there is one exception to this. In a disjointed sort of way, the bird knows all the multiplication tables to ten, except one. For instance—listen!"

The Thinking Machine crept stealthily to a door and opened it softly a few inches. From somewhere out there came the screeching of the parrot. For several minutes they listened in silence. There was a flood of profanity, a shrill whistle or two, then the squawking voice ran off into a monotone.

"Six times one are six, six time two are twelve, six times three are eighteen, six times four are twenty-four—and add two."

"That's it," explained the scientist, as he closed the door. "'Six times four are twenty-four—and add two.' That's the one table the bird doesn't know. The thing is incoherent, except as applied to a peculiar method of remembering a number. That number is twenty-six. On one occasion I heard the bird repeat a dozen times, 'Twenty-six feet to the polar star.' That could mean nothing except the direction of the twenty-six feet—due north. One of the first things I noticed the bird saying was something about fourteen feet to the setting sun—or due west. When set down with the twenty-six, I could readily see that I had something to go on.

"But where was the starting point? Again, logic. There was no tree or stone inside the lot, except the apple tree which your workmen cut down, and that was more than twenty-six feet from the boundary of the lot in all directions. There was one tree in the adjoining lot, an apple tree with a boulder at its foot. I knew that by observation. And there was no other tree, I knew also, within several hundred feet; therefore, that tree, or boulder rather, as a starting point—not the tree so much as the boulder, because the tree might be cut down, or would in time decay.

"The chances are the stone would have been allowed to remain there indefinitely. Naturally your grandfather would measure from a prominent point—the boulder. That is all. I gave you the figures. You know the rest."

For a minute or more, Dr. Ballard stared at him blankly. "How was it you knew," he asked, "that the directions should have been first twenty-six feet north, then fourteen feet west, instead of first fourteen west, and then twenty-six feet north?"

"I didn't know," replied The Thinking Machine. "If you had failed to find the money by those directions, I should merely have reversed the order."

Half an hour later Dr. Ballard went away, carrying the money and the parrot in its cage. The bird cursed The Thinking Machine roundly, as Dr. Ballard went down the steps.

The Problem of the Knotted Cord

With the brilliant glare of the noonday sun shining full into his upturned eyes, a venerable man sat beside an open window. The gray-crowned head was a noble one, but strength and rugged manhood was gone; there was only the weakness of years and disaster, illumined and softened by a smile—the appealing, pathetic smile of helplessness. The window framed a vista of green landscape, broken by a dimpled splotch of blue where the sea ran in and lapped the shore, and, far away, a village sprinkled on the hills. But he looked upon it all with sightless eyes—eyes which turned instinctively toward the light as the blind ever seek a ray through their enshrouding gloom. A grateful tang of salt air drifted in, and he breathed deeply of its fragrance.

For a long time he sat thus, silently, then from a distant room came the trill of a song. His smile grew into an expression of infinite tenderness as he listened, and then the closing of a door broke the melody. He sat expectantly for a minute or so, and gradually his mind wandered back into the dreamy thoughtfulness which the voice had interrupted. After awhile he heard a light step in the hall, and then some other sound which he could not interpret. The steps approached the door of the room where he sat, and paused.

"Is that you, deary?" he asked gently.

There was no response, and he turned his sightless eyes expectantly toward the entrance.

"What is it, Mildred?" he inquired.

Again he heard the peculiar sound to which he had been unable to attach a meaning, but still there was no answer.

"Mildred!" he called sharply. He turned quickly in his chair, with a vague uneasiness in his manner, and gripped the arms as if to rise. "Mildred!" he repeated. "Why don't you answer me?"

Suddenly there came an answer—a heart-racking, terrifying answer—shriek after shriek of agony, terror, helplessness. It was here, in this very room in which he stood, but the impenetrable pall of blindness veiled it all. There was a shuffling as of feet for an instant, a gurgling, despairing cry, then the old man tottered forward toward the door.

"Mildred, Mildred, Mildred!" he called despairingly. "What is it, child!"

There was a sound as of a soft body falling, then came utter silence. With straining heart and groping hands the old man kept on blindly seeking. Again he caught the meaningless sound, which he had heard before. One outstretched hand brushed against something which was instantly removed beyond reach. Intuitively he knew that something—somebody—menaced him, that Mildred his granddaughter was now or had been in peril—perhaps it was worse. There was some quick movement to his right, and the old man stretched out his quivering hands straight before him with a pitiful, helpless gesture.

"I am blind!" he said simply.

For a moment he stood there, with hands still outstretched, waiting. For what? He didn't know. At last from the hall outside came a sliding, whispering sound, and the front door closed noiselessly. Instantly he started in that direction. Despite his blindness, he knew his way here in the little house where he had lived for years alone with his granddaughter.

In the hall another thought came to him. Whoever—whatever—it was, had come and gone. And Mildred? He turned and started back toward the room he had just left. One aged hand slipped along the wall to the door frame, and he turned in. For an instant he listened. He heard nothing.

"Mildred?" he called. "My God, child! where are you? What has happened?"

Still silence. He entered and began groping around pitifully. Mildred must be there, somewhere. And finally, as he groped on, he came upon her. One foot struck some yielding obstacle, and he dropped on his knees beside it. A touch of his fingers on the face told him it was Mildred. She was breathing faintly—a gurgle, which as he listened grew fainter.

His brain was instantly awakened to the full possibilities. She had been stabbed, or struck down, perhaps. There had been no shot, and yet, as his hands moved rapidly over the slender form, he found no wound on head, face, or body. The faint gasping breath grew fainter as he listened—she was dying under his hands, and he was helpless, unable to see even what was the matter.

"Mildred, Mildred, Mildred!" he repeated, and he shook the inert body in a frenzy of fear and anxiety.

And then came the end. There was a last faint gurgle, a spasmodic twitching of the body, and it lay rigid. And there crouching on the floor beside his dead, the aged grandfather was found a few minutes later. His sightless eyes were dry and staring, and his lip moved silently in prayer.

One of the first things to come under the observation of the police when they began their investigation of the strange murder of pretty little Mildred Barrett—she was hardly fourteen years old— was the fact that if her grandfather, Wendell Curtis Barrett, had not been blind, he could have saved her life. The girl had been strangled, garroted, with manila twine—a plain cord which is in every day use for the tying of heavy bundles. This twine had been drawn so tight about the child's throat that it sank deep into the white soft flesh and slowly strangled her to death. Had her grandfather been able to see, had he not overlooked the possibility of such a thing, he could probably have saved her by cutting the twine. This, at least, was what the medical examiner said.

Outside attention had been attracted to the tragedy by two men who were driving past the little house overlooking the sea. They heard the child's screams and stopped to investigate, entering by that front door through which, not more than a few seconds before, the slayer of the child had passed. But they had seen no one, nor had they heard anything except the child's screams. They immediately notified the police. The strangler's cord was not found until Detective Mallory arrived with a couple of his men and Hutchinson Hatch, a newspaper reporter.

The detective examined the garroter's twine closely. There was one knot in it just where it pressed down upon the windpipe; and another at the back of the neck where powerful fingers had drawn it tight and fastened it with a knot similar to the running of a lasso.

"It's a good job, all right," commented Detective Mallory heart-lessly enough as he scrutinized the two knots. "It was prepared for just such a purpose, and well prepared at that."

"It isn't unlike the garroting cord that the thugs of India use," remarked Hatch.

"Is that so?" inquired the detective, as he turned quickly on the newspaper man. They had met before many times, and there was a professional friendship between them which amounted almost to enmity. "That may be useful to know."

The reporter remained at the house and in the neighborhood for several hours while the detectives continued their investigations, and then summarized the entire affair, with every established fact, for the benefit of Professor Augustus S. F. X. Van Dusen— The Thinking Machine. They were well acquainted, these two, an acquaintance which had begun with the chess game incident which had given to the noted scientist the soubriquet by which he had since become known beyond the narrow pale of science. On a dozen or more occasions The Thinking Machine had interested himself in every day problems at the request of the newspaper man, and had invariably woven a woof from tangled, disconnected threads which the reporter brought to him.

"It's absolutely astounding," the reporter told the scientist now, "not only the method of the murder—right within reach, almost, of a man who was totally blind—but there is nothing to indicate any motive, so—"

"Begin at the beginning, Mr. Hatch," interrupted The Thinking Machine crustily. "When you do a sum in arithmetic you put down all the figures, don't you? Well, give me all the figures."

"Well, here is every known fact in the case," explained the re-porter. "Mr. Barrett is about seventy-two years old; his grand-daughter Mildred was a little less than fourteen. She was the only relative he had in the world, and had lived with him in the little house, which he owns, since the death of her father, who was killed in the Spanish-American War. They kept no servant, as the child, with a little assistance from the old man, was able to do practically all the simple housework. Occasionally they called in a woman who lived half a mile away to assist in house cleaning and the heavier work. It seems that Barrett has an income of about a thousand a year, and they were able to live comfortably on this.

"Very few persons ever called at the house, and preceding the tragedy there was no caller, at least that Barrett knows of. The child was somewhere in the rear of the house, and he was sitting in his own room. He heard no voices, no sound, nothing except the child singing, until she came along the hall, evidently to his room. The grim horror of the whole thing from that time on has unnerved the old man so that he is almost in a state of collapse.

"To me the mystery of the thing is intensified by the fact that the murdered girl is a mere child. Her extreme youth would indicate at least that there could have been no love affair, certainly from all I have been able to learn there was not. And her youth, too, would make it seem improbable that she could have had an enemy who would have gone to such an extreme. Besides, she seems to have been a sweet-tempered, sunny little girl, intelligent, bright, and lovable. Nothing whatever was stolen. There is positively no clue in the world, not even a vagrant footprint, or any small thing that might have been left to indicate who was there—that is, of course, except the cord with which she was strangled."

"Would the old man have benefited by the child's death?" inquired The Thinking Machine.

"In no way at all," Hatch replied positively, "nor would anyone else. There is no property tied up, as far as anyone can find out, and the miserable little sum which it cost him to keep the child is not so much as he would have had to pay to employ a servant in her absence."

The Thinking Machine sat for a long time with the squint blue eyes turned upward, and his white slender fingers pressed tip to tip. Minute wrinkles in his enormous brow grew momentarily deeper. "It's a remarkable crime, Mr. Hatch," he said at last, "perhaps the most remarkable that I have ever met. As you say, the youth of the child removes all the ordinary motives." He was silent for a moment. "Our greatest criminals are never caught, and rarely ever heard of, Mr. Hatch," he went on musingly. "The greatest crimes are never discovered, as a matter of fact. One might readily conceive of a brain so keen, so accurate, that in, say, a murder, there would be nothing to indicate one. I think perhaps in this case we have a difficult one. It would be best for me to see and talk with Mr. Barrett in person."

They found the aged blind man, and he repeated for them in the minutest detail every fact as he remembered it. The Thinking Machine listened throughout with keen attention, and at the end asked some questions.

"You say, Mr. Barrett, that in addition to your granddaughter's footsteps and voice you heard some other slight sound. Could you describe it?"

"I hardly think so," was the reply. "It was strange—peculiar."

"Was it the sound of a human voice, or of something being moved?" insisted the scientist.

"It could have been made by the human voice, I suppose; but it also could have been made by twanging a rubber band. It sounded guttural, unreal, uncanny."

"And the thing you touched when you started toward your granddaughter, after she screamed?" asked the scientist. "What did that seem to be? Clothing, flesh, wood, some one's hair, or what?"

"I—I—don't know," said Barrett helplessly. "It was a sense of having touched something, rather than actual contact with it. It might have been hair, but I don't know what it was."

The Thinking Machine stared at him curiously for a moment. "How long have you been blind, Mr. Barrett?"

"Only about two years."

The Thinking Machine nodded as if he understood, and then for an hour he sat questioning the old man. Never for a moment did the wrinkles leave his brow, and never for a moment was his tense attention relaxed. At the end he arose, and Hatch looked at him inquiringly. He shook his head.

He spent another hour in an examination of the strangler's cord, the knots, the body, and of the premises. Every nook and corner of the little house was searched with the utmost care, and every foot of the little plot of ground surrounding it was carefully gone over. Gradually his radius of observation widened until he had covered the ground a hundred feet every way from the house in every direction. Then he went inside again. One of the detectives, Cunningham, met him in the hall.

"There is no question whatever of the innocence of the two men who say they heard the girl scream and came in?" he asked.

"There doesn't seem to be," replied Cunningham. "We have taken pains to confirm their stories, and to be certain of their identity. They seem to be all right."

"I imagined so," remarked the scientist. "What about the woman who came here occasionally to assist in the housework?"

"We also looked into that. She had been spending the day with a friend in a village a dozen miles away. We have proof of that."

The Thinking Machine turned and walked into the room where Barrett sat. "Would you be prepared to say," he asked, "that the sounds you heard were made by an animal of any sort? That is, I mean an ape, say, or a baboon?"

"I couldn't say," replied Barrett.

"Or that the hair you touched was bristly like the hair of an animal?"

"I couldn't say," replied Barrett. "I don't even know that it was hair. Whatever it was, it was instantly withdrawn beyond my reach and I had a singular intuitive feeling of being in great peril myself."

For the second time The Thinking Machine picked up and examined the strangler's cord. Again he shook his head.

"What do you make of it?" Hatch ventured at last.

The Thinking Machine squinted at him dully. "I don't make anything of it," he replied frankly. "There is no starting point. I have all unknown quantities. When every conceivable motive is eliminated as seems to be the case here, we must naturally turn to that thing which does things without motive—a brute—say, an ape." He held up the knotted cord. "But those knots were never tied by any but human hands; a directing intelligence fashioned the noose, and human hands applied it. That is indisputable, so we haven't even the ape to start with. This is perhaps the first case I have ever been interested in where all possibilities seem to be removed."

Hatch stared at the scientist a little blankly for a moment. He had never before heard just such an admission from him. "Well," asked the reporter helplessly, "where are we going with it?"

The Thinking Machine didn't say. Instead, he planted his No. 8 hat more firmly on his enormous straw yellow head, and returned to his apartments.

It was ten minutes of one o'clock that night, and Hatch had just finished writing the story of the tragedy for his newspaper, when there came a call for him on the telephone. It was The Thinking Machine.

"Do you know of any crime similar to this any time recently?" asked the scientist. "I mean a crime where the circumstances resembled these in any manner?"

The reporter was thoughtful for a moment. "No," he replied.

"Well, I'm very much afraid that there will be another just like it," volunteered The Thinking Machine enigmatically.

"Why, who—what?" asked Hatch in amazement.

"Of course I don't know who," retorted the scientist crabbedly. "If I did I would prevent it. I may say I know what, but it doesn't do us any good. Good night."

Three days later came another tragedy. Bartow Gillespie and his brother James were found dead in a room together ten miles from the scene of the Barrett affair. Bartow, the eldest, had been strangled to death precisely as Mildred Barrett had been. James Gillespie lay five feet away, with a bullet in his brain. The murderer's revolver had fallen between them. One shot had been fired— the shot which entered James's head at the base of his brain.

The Thinking Machine and Hatch were on the scene of this second crime within a few hours. Again there was a detailed examination to be made, and the scientist made it conscientiously, from the strangler's cord, identical in every way with the one that had slain Mildred Barrett, to the revolver with its one empty chamber. The Thinking Machine weighed the weapon in his hand thoughtfully, and then turned to Detective Mallory.

"Whose is this?" he asked.

"If I knew that we could not only solve this mystery, but also the Barrett affair," retorted the detective grimly.

Then The Thinking Machine did a singular thing. He bent down to within a few inches of the upturned face of James Gillespie, and squinted steadily for a minute or more into the dead, glassy eyes. This done, he ran his slender white fingers through the dead man's hair several times.

"I know whose revolver it is now," he said as he arose. "It belonged to the other dead man there—Bartow Gillespie."

Detective Mallory regarded him in amazement for an instant, and then a slight smile about his lips showed what he thought of it.

"I suppose, professor," he said, "you are going to tell us that Bartow Gillespie killed his brother, and then strangled himself with this cord?"

"No," replied the scientist almost pleasantly.

"Well, then," Mallory ventured, "it's going to be that Bartow Gillespie shot his brother, and then his brother strangled him to death with the cord?"

"No," said the scientist again. "I was going to tell you that James Gillespie attacked his brother Bartow, and attempted to strangle him—did strangle him; that there was a struggle—these two overturned chairs show that; and that Bartow Gillespie, with the strangler's cord about his throat, killed his brother with the revolver. Remember, please, that when James Gillespie murdered Mildred Barrett, he was dealing with a child, but here he was dealing with a man, and a powerful man, who fought fiercely after the knot was fastened.

"We may assume that the revolver was Bartow Gillespie's, and that it was in his possession at the time he was attacked. Why? Because if it had been in James Gillespie's possession he would probably have finished his work by shooting his brother, when his brother began his struggle. Certainly James Gillespie did not kill himself, because the wound is in the back of his head. I am stating these things not as facts but as probabilities. When we know positively that the weapon was Bartow Gillespie's, then the probabilities become facts."

There was still a light, skeptical expression about Detective Mallory's mouth. "And on the other hand," he said, "we have the probability that the strangler came here and killed Bartow Gillespie, that the sound of the struggle attracted James Gillespie's attention, that he came in to investigate, that he was threatened and started to go out, and that the strangler fired the shot which struck him in the back of the head."

"Disproved flatly by two points," said The Thinking Machine curtly. "First, the fact that the strangler deliberately left his revolver, if we accept your hypothesis and second, by the fact that—" He paused and turning stared curiously down into the face of James Gillespie.

Detective Mallory waited impatiently for a moment; then, "And the second is what?" he asked.

"Do you know the motive for the murder of the Barrett child?" asked the scientist irrelevantly.

"No," said Detective Mallory in some surprise.

"And do you know the motive for this double crime, under your hypothesis?"

"No."

"Well, the motive is written here," and the scientist turned and thrust a long finger into the pallid face of James Gillespie. "It is in the eyes, in the mouth, and still again it's written here." He pulled aside the tumbled hair, and disclosed a bare spot. "Here is a scar, left months, perhaps years, ago by some serious injury."

"Why, I don't see—" began the detective protestingly.

"Of course, you don't see!" snapped The Thinking Machine. "What was found in James Gillespie's pockets?"

"I don't know that there has been an examination," said Mallory. "We always leave those things to the medical examiner, where there is no doubt of a man's identity."

With deft fingers the scientist ransacked the slain man's clothes. From a hip pocket he drew a little bundle and threw it on the table before Mallory. "And there is your final proof," he said. "It isn't even necessary now to prove that the revolver was Bartow Gillespie's—we know it—know it as inevitably as that two and two make four, Mr. Mallory, not sometimes but *all* the time."

The little bundle that he had thrown on the table was a roll of plain manila twine—just a couple of yards. At last the detective was beginning to see.

"But what possible motive?" he asked.

"I told Mr. Hatch when I investigated the Barrett affair that when all conceivable human motives were eliminated, as seemed to be the fact in this case, there remained only the thing—the creature, which will act without motive—an ape, for instance," interrupted The Thinking Machine. "I told him afterward that there would probably be a second crime under the same circumstances, and also that we were powerless to prevent it. This is the crime. There is no motive for either.

"The old scar on this man's head, the expression of his face, and his eyes particularly, show conclusively that he was a maniac—just a shade the intellectual superior of an ape, with all the cunning of humanity distorted and diseased into a homicidal mania. An examination of his brain at the autopsy will prove all this even to you, Mr. Mallory. How long he has been a maniac I don't know; your investigations will develop that. That is all, I think. Good day."

The Thinking Machine and Hutchinson Hatch walked down the street together.

"How is it," inquired the reporter, "that James Gillespie didn't kill Barrett at the same time he killed the little girl?"

"I don't know," was the reply. "It is difficult enough, Mr. Hatch, to follow the mental workings of a sane man; when we have a maniac, no one can say what he will do next. We don't look into the matter, but I dare say that Gillespie never knew that child he killed, and could have had no motive."

And subsequently this proved to be true.

The Problem of the Private Compartment

Leaning forward in his seat, the driver lashed his horses into a gallop. The carriage had barely halted at the railroad station, when a woman leaped out. She was closely veiled; but her slender figure revealed the fact that she was little more than a girl. She paused just long enough to hand the driver a bill, then hurried to a train.

When the conductor passed through the cars he found the slender young woman sitting in one of the day coaches. She paid her fare in cash through to Albany, and made inquiry about accommodations in the sleeping car. He volunteered to arrange the matter for her; and so it came to pass that half an hour after she had boarded the train she was ushered into the more exclusive rear car.

"We have only one upper berth," the conductor there apologized.

"Oh, well, it doesn't really matter," she remarked listlessly, and was shown to a seat.

Then for the first time she raised her veil. Her pretty face was still flushed from the excitement of catching the train; but a haunting, furtive fear mingled with a shade of sorrow in the shadowy, dark eyes, and the red lips expressed a sullen defiance. For a long time she sat moodily thoughtful, staring out of the window; then the growing dusk obliterated the flying landscape, and the porter came through to light the lamps.

After awhile the door of the drawing room compartment at one end of the car opened, and a young woman glanced out. It might have been idle curiosity which caused her to scrutinize the lounging passengers; but her eyes paused, with a flash of recognition, on the crisp, brown hair of the slender young woman just half a dozen seats ahead, and she went forward.

"Why, Julia!" she exclaimed. "I hadn't the faintest idea you were on the train!"

First there came an embarrassed surprise into the face of the slender young woman; but it was instantly followed by an expression of relief.

"Oh, Mary! How you startled me!"

There was a little interchange of greetings, which ended by Miss Mary Langham leading Miss Julia Farrar back into the snug little drawing room. They had been classmates at Vassar, these two, and there were a thousand things to talk about; yet in the manner of each was a certain restraint, a vague, indefinable reserve. As a breaking point of a sudden silence which fell between them, Miss Farrar mentioned the upper berth that she had been given.

"Well, don't worry about that a moment, my dear," urged Miss Langham cheerfully. "I have this whole big compartment, and there are two lower berths. You shall take one, and I'll take the other." There was silence for a moment. "But, my dear girl, where are you going?"

"I'm going to Albany—now," was the reply.

"Right on the eve of your—"

"I'm not going to marry Mr. Devore!" interrupted Miss Farrar with quick passion.

Miss Langham lifted her arched brows in astonishment. "Why, Julia, you amaze me!" she exclaimed.

"I'm running away from him now," she went on.

Miss Langham stared at her blankly for an instant. Defiance flamed in Miss Farrar's face; there were tense little lines about the mouth, and the lips were pressed sternly together. But at last some glimmer of comprehension seemed to reach Miss Langham, and with it came an expression which might almost have been of relief. With a quick movement she seized Miss Farrar's hand.

"I think I understand, dear," she said sympathetically at last. "Under all circumstances, I don't know that I can blame you either. Mr. Devore must know that you don't love him."

"Well, if he doesn't, it isn't because I haven't told him so, goodness knows!" replied Miss Farrar.

Miss Langham laughed lightly, and her eyes reflected some strange, new born light, a glimmer of satisfaction.

"Poor fellow!" she mused. "And he is so devoted!"

"I don't want his devotion!" blazed Miss Farrar. "The mere sight of him is intolerable to me. It's all just like—like I was being sold to him. It's perfectly hideous, and I won't—I won't—I won't!"

Defiance melted into tears of anger and mortification, and Miss Farrar lay against Miss Langham's shoulder while her slender figure was shaken by a storm of sobs. Miss Langham stroked the crisp, brown hair back from the white temples, and continued to stare dreamily out of the window.

"Even my father and mother and brother conspired with him against me," Miss Farrar sobbed after a time. "They insisted on the marriage from the first, merely because Mr. Devore happens to be wealthy. I don't know why I ever agreed, unless it was just desperation. I detest the man, and yet the members of my own family, knowing that, could only think of the brilliant match, the money, and social position which marriage would bring."

"To-morrow it was to have been," mused Miss Langham vacantly.

"Yes, to-morrow. For weeks and weeks it has been a nightmare to me, and last night, somehow, I seemed to go all to pieces. The sight of the wedding gown made me perfectly furious. All to-day I thought of it, and thought of it, until my head seemed bursting. Then late this afternoon I could stand it no longer; so I—I ran away. I suppose it's horrid of me, and I know my father and mother will never forgive me for the scandal it will cause; but I don't care. They've made me almost hate them. I'm going to my aunt's in Albany and remain there for a few days. Of course, my father will be furious, and will try to force me to return; but she's a dear loyal soul and won't let them take me away. Then I shall decide about the future."

"I can't imagine a worse fate than marriage with a man whom you don't love," said Miss Langham after a pause. "I don't blame you at all. But remember, my dear, in giving up your family you will have to look out for yourself—perhaps earn your own living?"

"I don't care," continued Miss Farrar passionately. "I have fifty or sixty dollars now, and before that is gone surely I can get a place as teacher, or governess, or something. I will do something."

"And I have no doubt that everything will come right," Miss Langham assured her. She raised the tear stained face between her hands and printed a kiss on each damp cheek. "And now, my dear, you need repose. Lie down and rest for awhile."

With the obedience of a child Miss Farrar lay across the berth, and after awhile, with Miss Langham's hand clasped between her own, closed her red, swollen eyes in sleep.

It was perhaps half an hour later that Miss Langham pressed her call button beside the door. A porter appeared.

"What is the next stop?" she inquired.

"East Newlands," was the reply.

"Can I send a telegram from there?"

"Yes, ma'am."

Miss Langham gently detached her fingers from the clinging clasp of the sleeping girl, and scribbled a telegram on a blank which the porter offered. It was addressed to J. Charles Wingate, in a small city, just beyond Albany, and said:

Have changed my mind. This is irrevocable. M.

When the train pulled into Albany the following morning Miss Julia Farrar was found dead in her berth, fully dressed, except for her hat.

A thirty-two caliber bullet had entered her body just below the left shoulder. Miss Langham herself gave the alarm. When physicians came they agreed that Miss Farrar had been dead for at least two hours.

Professor Augustus S. F. X. Van Dusen—The Thinking Machine—absorbed, digested, and assimilated all the known facts in the problem of the private compartment. Instantly that singular, penetrating brain beneath the mop of tangled, straw yellow hair was alive with questions.

"Who is Miss Langham?" was the first query.

"She is the daughter of Daniel Eustace Langham, president of a national bank in his home city," replied Hutchinson Hatch, reporter. "She and Miss Farrar were classmates in Vassar, and met by accident on the train."

"Do you know they met by accident?"

"It seems to have been by accident," the reporter amended. "As a matter of fact, Miss Langham was on the train first—in fact, had engaged the drawing room compartment a couple of days ahead."

"Does she know—Miss Langham, I mean—know Devore?"

"Very well indeed," responded the reporter. "A couple of years ago he was rather assiduous in his attentions to her. That was before Devore met Miss Farrar."

The Thinking Machine turned suddenly in his chair and squinted into the eyes of the newspaper man. Faint corrugations in the dome-like brow were swept away.

"Oh!" he exclaimed. "An old love affair! How did it come to be broken off?"

"I imagine it was Devore who broke it off," replied Hatch. "When he met Miss Farrar it resulted in a quick transfer of attentions. As a matter of fact, he doesn't seem to be a very pleasant sort of person, anyway—spoiled son and sole heir of a man worth millions. You know what that means."

"And where was Miss Langham going at the time of the tragedy?" inquired the scientist.

"To visit some friends just beyond Albany."

For a long time The Thinking Machine was silent, while Hatch turned over those vague impressions which the scientist's manner and words had created.

"That seems to simplify the matter somewhat," mused The Thinking Machine at last.

"You don't mean," blurted Hatch quickly— "you don't mean that Miss Langham could have had anything to do with Miss Farrar's death?"

"Why not?" demanded The Thinking Machine coldly.

"But her social position, her wealth, everything, would seem to remove her beyond the range of suspicion," Hatch protested.

The Thinking Machine regarded him with frank disapproval. "Two and two always make four, Mr. Hatch," he said shortly. "We have here a motive for the crime—jealousy—and practically exclusive opportunity.

"Social position and wealth do not deter criminals; they only make them more cunning. In this case two and two make four so obviously that I am surprised Miss Langham wasn't arrested immediately. Where is she now, by the way?"

"With her father and mother at the Hotel Bellevoir in town here," Hatch responded. "Immediately after the tragedy was reported she returned here, and her father and mother joined her. She is now suffering from shock, and inaccessible—at least to reporters."

"Any physician?"

"Dr. Barrow and Dr. Curtis are attending her."

"I may call on her in person," remarked The Thinking Machine. "And now about this man Devore? Have you seen him?"

"He was the first man the police wanted to see," explained the reporter. "They have already made him account for his every move on the night of the murder. Of course, a motive in his case would be obvious—anger, revenge, jealousy, anything."

"And where was he between, say, midnight and breakfast that night?"

"He says he was asleep at home."

"He says!" snapped The Thinking Machine abruptly. "Don't you know?"

"Not of my knowledge."

"Well, find out!" was the curt instruction. "That isn't one of the things that we can be at all uncertain about."

Hatch opened his eyes again. Here were two lines of investigation laid out by the scientist, either one of which might, if pursued to a logical conclusion, convict a person of wealth and position of a terrible crime.

"And Miss Farrar's family?" continued The Thinking Machine mercilessly. "Where were her father and brother that night?"

"Surely you can't believe that—"

"I never believe anything, Mr. Hatch, until I know it. I merely wanted to know where they were; for on that side too it is possible to conceive a motive for Miss Farrar's death."

"There has been no inquiry in that direction at all," explained the bewildered reporter. "I'll begin one."

Then for a time The Thinking Machine sat with fingertips pressed idly together, squinting blankly at the ceiling.

"While a motive is never absolutely essential to the solution of any criminal problem," he observed after awhile, "it will frequently indicate a line of investigation. Now, in the usual case when a motive appears the solution is inevitable. But this case differs from the usual case in that we have too many motives—three excellent ones that we know—a jealous woman, a suitor discarded on the eve of his wedding, and perhaps a vengeful father or brother. And beyond those there are other possibilities."

Hatch went about his business with turbulent, troubled thoughts—a vague sense of treading on dangerous ground—while The Thinking Machine turned to the telephone. Five minutes later he picked up his hat and went to the Hotel Bellevoir.

"Did Dr. Curtis telephone you?" he inquired of the clerk.

"Yes. Is this Mr. Van Dusen?"

The Thinking Machine bobbed his head, and was ushered into Miss Langham's apartments.

Pallid as the sheets, resistlessly inert, the girl lay staring upward as if fascinated by the brilliant scintillating point which floated backward and forward rhythmically before her eyes as The Thinking Machine slowly waved his arm. It was like some weird exorcism, some uncanny incantation, but it compelled attention.

"Watch it closely, please!"

The scientist's tone was low, almost a whisper, yet it carried a command. The swing of his arm shortened gradually, almost imperceptibly, and slowly the bright spot passed upward in little erratic circles until it was directly before her eyes. And there it stopped for a moment. After awhile it moved on again, still farther upward, in a straight line, until the girl was aware of a queerly strained feeling in her eyes. It paused again, then very, very slowly began to move round and round.

After awhile the fascination in the girl's eyes gave way to a vacant staring, and the pupils distended, as a mist crept over them. Slowly, slowly, the swing of the bright spot decreased, until at last it hung motionless, suspended in air, between the slim fingers of the scientist. Thus for a time, and the vacant staring became glassy—dead. Then the bright spot was withdrawn, materializing as the lower part of the bowl of a silver spoon which The Thinking Machine laid on the table beside him. One hand passed over the girl's white face once. The long fingers lingered caressingly on the lids, and pressed them together.

The Thinking Machine passed round from the head of the couch where the girl lay and took a seat, with his hand on her wrist. The pulse fluttered a little, but he nodded his head as if satisfied.

"You are on a train—in a private compartment," he said, still in a voice that was almost a whisper.

"Yes," breathed the girl. It was nearly inaudible.

"A young woman is sleeping there."

"Yes," came the sigh again.

"You hate her."

"No."

It was a flat, unequivocal denial, and the dreamy, sighing tone hardened suddenly. Again The Thinking Machine pressed his fingers down on her eyelids, and sat silent for a time.

"You dislike her," he suggested.

"No," the girl denied once more dreamily. "She and I were—" and the phrase drifted off into intangible incoherency.

"You have a revolver in your traveling bag."

"Yes."

The petulant, crabbed face of The Thinking Machine lighted suddenly, exultantly. But when he spoke again it was in the same whispering monotone. "You always carry a revolver when traveling."

"No."

"Your revolver is thirty-two caliber."

"I don't know."

"The sleeping woman loves the man you love."

"Yes."

"She is at your mercy; therefore you will kill her."

"No, no, no!"

There was a sudden horror in the voice, a strange, convulsive working of the face, and the eyelids fluttered. Thrice The Thinking Machine passed his hands over her face, and she became calm again.

"You are back in your own apartments at the Hotel Bellevoir," he continued after a minute.

"Yes," she answered readily.

"Your revolver is in the traveling bag."

"No."

The Thinking Machine glanced quickly round the room, and again his eyes settled on the pallid face.

"It is in the dressing table."

"Yes."

With set, inscrutable face, the scientist arose and went to the table. In the drawer lay a handsomely mounted weapon. He picked it up, examined it closely as he whirled the barrel in his fingers, and then replaced it, after which he returned to the girl.

"You have fainted," he said. "You will return to consciousness in a moment."

He leaned forward and blew gently into the closed eyes, and the girl sighed. Thrice he did this, then a trace of color appeared in the face, and she raised her eyelids. For an instant she stared into the drawn face of the scientist.

"Why, I must have fainted," she said.

Hutchinson Hatch burst into the laboratory, where The Thinking Machine was at work, with an air of excitement which caused the eminent scientist to turn and squint at him in disapproval.

"That man Devore lied about where—" he began.

"Just a moment, Mr. Hatch," interrupted The Thinking Machine curtly. "Did you see the sleeping car in which Miss Farrar was killed?"

"Yes," replied the reporter, and, somewhat abashed, sat down.

"I suppose the windows were all screened, as is usually the case?"

"Why, I suppose so," was the reply.

"Was there any hole of any sort in the screen of the window in the private compartment?"

"Oh, I see what you mean. Shot from the outside. No, there was no hole."

The brow of the scientist had been smooth and unruffled as the summer sea; but now the minute corrugations which Hatch knew so well appeared again, and he sat silent for a time.

"When you came in you started to say—" he remarked at last.

"That Devore lied as to where he was the night Miss Farrar was killed," Hatch hastened to explain. "He said he was at home in bed. I have the word of two servants that he was not, and have learned that he was at Troy that night."

"Well?" inquired the scientist impassively.

"Troy is just a short distance from Albany," the reporter rushed on. "The train had to pass so near there, don't you see, that Devore might have boarded it, and—"

He paused. The Thinking Machine arose suddenly, and paced back and forth across the room twice.

"Why was he in Troy?" he asked.

"It was some sort of dinner—a stag affair, I imagine—the night before the day of the wedding," said Hatch.

"And I dare say young Farrar, Miss Farrar's brother, was with him?"

"Yes, he was. You didn't give me time."

The Thinking Machine passed into the adjoining room, and Hatch heard the telephone bell. Fifteen minutes later he came out.

"Devore and Farrar spent the night—that is from midnight until eight o'clock in the morning of the murder—in adjoining rooms at a hotel in Troy," explained the scientist. "They were asleep there. So that makes the affair perfectly clear."

"Perfectly clear?" exclaimed Hatch. "Perfectly clear? I don't see how you make that out, when—"

The Thinking Machine started out, with Hatch following. They went straight to the Hotel Bellevoir, and sent their cards to Langham. He was staring blankly at a telegram when they entered. He recognized The Thinking Machine by name as a physician who had called on his daughter.

"Your daughter is engaged to be married, isn't she, Mr. Langham?" inquired the scientist.

"Yes, she was," he replied wonderingly. "Why?"

"And she was, I believe, on her way to visit some friends in a small city just beyond Albany when this—this unhappy event occurred?"

"Yes," Langham assented again.

"Perhaps the family of the man to whom she was betrothed?"

Again Langham assented.

"And what is the name of this man, please?"

"J. Charles Wingate," was the reply. "I've just got a telegram from him. Here it is."

The Thinking Machine glanced at the yellow slip of paper. The message was dated at New York city, and said tersely:

Wedding impossible. I cannot explain. Wingate.

"It's an outrage," declared Langham.

"It's a confession," remarked The Thinking Machine.

"When we remove Miss Langham as a possibility," The Thinking Machine told Hatch and Detective Mallory, "we inevitably bring the murder of Miss Farrar down to a man. And I may say that I personally demonstrated Miss Langham's innocence by a little experiment in mechanical hypnotism. She confessed that she had a revolver on the train. But her revolver was a twenty-two caliber, and the bullet that killed Miss Farrar was a thirty-two. So there was no further need to consider her.

"I also removed Devore by establishing an alibi for him even after he had lied to the police as to his whereabouts on the night of the crime. Why he lied doesn't appear, and is of no consequence now. I proved his whereabouts conclusively by telephone, and at the same time proved the whereabouts of Miss Farrar's brother, thus eliminating both at the same time. Then what?

"Everyone had presumed—and I also did at first—that the person who killed Miss Farrar was in the private compartment with her. And yet, if that was true, why didn't the shot awake Miss Langham? When I knew that she was innocent the logic of the thing indicated that the shot came from the outside.

"It was a warm night, and we shall suppose the window was open. Was the screen in it? It did not have a hole in it; so I presumed it was not. Then the possibilities became infinite. The first thing to do was dispose of Devore and Miss Farrar's brother. I did that. Both you gentlemen recall, I dare say, the peculiar circumstances surrounding the murder of the young woman in a box at the opera? Yes. Instantly that came to me—perhaps the wrong woman had been killed. If so, we must look for a motive for the murder of Miss Langham.

"Well, we know that there had once been a love affair between Miss Langham and Devore. Was it possible that, despite her engagement to another man, Miss Langham still loved Devore?—that she learned Miss Farrar's story, and then and there decided to jilt the man to whom she was engaged, because of this love for Devore, who was now, by the act of Miss Farrar, cast aside? If so, would she have telegraphed to him this change of mind? If we suppose that she was expecting to meet him in a few hours—in other words, visit his family—we can imagine her telegraphing from the train, while her intention was to go no further than Albany, where she would turn back.

"That hypothesis made the entire matter perfectly clear. She did telegraph her decision to J. Charles Wingate, and a motive for her murder was instantly created—revenge. Now, he probably knew what train she was on, that she had taken the private compartment in a certain sleeping car on that train, and it is not only possible but probable that he took a train to meet it.

"Sometime between the moment he received the telegram and met the train on which she was a passenger he resolved upon murder. The method? What better than firing through the window while the train was standing at some small station? The shot might not attract attention, particularly as the sleeping car was the last on the train, and it was, say, four o'clock in the morning. He did fire through the window; therefore the shot, being outside, did not disturb Miss Langham, already accustomed to the roar and clatter of the train. Wingate merely looked in, saw a woman asleep, and fired. He did not know that he had killed the wrong woman, perhaps, until the matter got into the newspapers."

There was a long silence. Detective Mallory and Hatch exchanged glances; then the detective turned to The Thinking Machine.

"And where is Wingate?" he inquired.

"Mr. Langham received a telegram from him dated at New York," was the reply. "I imagine it was sent on the eve of his flight, perhaps abroad. I should advise, anyway, that a watch be kept on the steamers as they arrive on the other side."

And eight days later J. Charles Wingate was arrested as he walked down the gangplank of a steamer at Liverpool. He had gone over in the steerage.

The Problem of the Red Rose

Through the open windows of a pleasantly sunny little sitting room a lazy breath of early summer drifted in, and gently stirred the wayward hair of a girl who leaned forward over a small writing desk with her head resting upon one white fore arm, and her face hidden. Her attitude was one of utter collapse, complete abandonment perhaps to grief or perhaps to actual physical suffering; yet there was no movement of the slender, graceful body, nothing to indicate even a passive interest in her surroundings—just this silent, motionless figure, alone.

One arm, the left, swung down listlessly at her side, and in that hand she held a single red rose, a splendid, full blown crimson blossom. The thorny stem touched the floor, and the leaves swayed rhythmically, playthings of the caressing breeze. On the green stem, just below the girl's tightly clenched hand, was a single stain—a drop of blood—as if the thorn had pierced the delicate flesh. On the desk, from which dainty writing trinkets had been pushed back, was a florist's box, open. It was from this box evidently that the red rose had been taken. The wax paper which had been wrapped round the flower was torn.

A Dresden clock on the mantel whirred faintly and chimed the hour of five; but the girl gave not the slightest indication of having heard. And then after a moment a door opened and a maid appeared. She paused as her eyes fell upon the figure of the young woman, made as if to speak, then instead silently withdrew, leaving the door slightly open. She did not seem surprised that no notice was taken of her. A dozen times she had found her young mistress like this, and it was always after the box had come from the florist's with the single red rose. She sighed a little as she went out.

The hands of the clock crept on round the dial slowly, to five minutes past the hour, then to ten, and finally to fifteen. Then there came a scampering of soft feet along the hall, and a white, shaggy little dog thrust his head in at the door inquisitively. Helterskelter he came tumbling in and planted two soiled fore feet in the girl's lap as he awaited the caress which was always ready for him. Now it didn't come. He backed away and regarded her thoughtfully. It must be some new sort of game she was playing. He crouched on the floor and barked playfully; but she didn't look round.

Evidently this was not what was expected of him. He scampered back and forth across the room twice, then returned to the motionless figure and placed his feet in her lap again. She wouldn't look. He barked, whined softly, then off like the wind round the room again. He stopped on her left side this time—the side where the arm swung down, and the hand clutched the rose. His moist tongue caressed the closed hand, and sniffed at it insistently. Suddenly he seemed dazed, and reeled uncertainly as if from an unexpected blow. He whined again as if choking; there was a rattle in his shaggy throat; and then began a violent whirling, twisting, which continued till he fell. After awhile he lay still with all four feet turned upward and glazed, staring eyes. And yet the girl hadn't moved.

The hands of the clock crept on. At five minutes of six o'clock the maid appeared at the door again, paused for a moment, then ventured in. "Will you dress for dinner, ma'am?" she inquired.

The girl didn't answer.

"It's nearly six o'clock, ma'am," said the maid.

Still there was no answer.

The maid approached her young mistress and touched her lightly on the shoulder. "You'll be late, unless—" she began.

And then something about the unresisting, impassive figure frightened her. She shook the girl sharply and called her name many times. Finally with an effort she raised the shapely head. What she saw in the upturned face wrung scream after scream from her lips, now suddenly ashen, and turning she staggered toward the door with unutterable horror in her widely distended eyes. She clutched at the door frame to steady herself, screamed again, and fell forward, fainting. There they found them: Miss Edna Burdock

dead with hideously distorted face,—a face upon which was written some awful agony,—and the rose still clasped so fiercely in her
hand that the thorns had pierced the palm; her little dog Tatters
dead beside her; and the maid, Goodwin, unconscious. For half an
hour two servants worked over the maid; but when at last she
opened her eyes she only screamed and babbled incoherently.
There were no marks on Miss Burdock's body save the prick of
thorns in her left hand—nothing that would indicate the manner
of death; nor was there the slightest thing to explain the death of
the dog.

"The police are not at all certain that Miss Burdock's death was
due to anything more mysterious than heart failure," Hutchinson
Hatch, reporter, was explaining. "In that event, of course—"

"In that event, of course," interrupted Professor Augustus S. F.
X. Van Dusen—The Thinking Machine—crabbedly, "their theory
must be that the pet dog died at the same time of the same disease?"

"That seems to be about the way they look at it, although there
are several curious features," the reporter went on; "for instance,
the expression on her face." He shuddered a little. "I saw her. It
was awful. The dog too. There was not a mark or scratch on the
dog—not even the prick of a thorn like that in the girl's palm, therefore heart failure seems to be the only thing that will cover the
case, unless—"

"Fiddlesticks!" exclaimed the irritable little scientist. "Persons
who die of heart failure don't show suffering in their faces, and
little dogs don't have heart failure. What did the autopsy show?"

"Nothing illuminating," responded the reporter. "There was no
trace of poison in Miss Burdock's system; a blood test showed her
blood to be about normal, and yet she was dead. There was a peculiar constriction of the heart, and the same thing was true of the
dog. The medical examiner's report brought out these facts; but
there was no poison—they were just dead."

"When did this happen, Mr. Hatch?"

"Yesterday afternoon, Monday."

"You tell me the maid found the body. Has she said anything
about noticing any odor when she entered the room?"

"Not a word; but there are curious things—"

"In a minute, Mr. Hatch," interrupted The Thinking Machine impatiently. "Were the windows open?"

"Yes," replied the reporter. "She was sitting at her desk, between two open windows."

The man of science dropped back in his chair, and for a long time sat silent with the perpetually squinting eyes turned upward, and slender white fingers pressed tip to tip. Hatch lighted a cigarette, smoked it, and threw the butt away before he spoke.

"There are peaches in the market, I think, Mr. Hatch," said the scientist at last. "When you go out, buy one, cut the meat off, crush the kernel, take it to the maid, and ask her to smell it. Ask her if she noticed yesterday any odor similar to that when she entered the room and was near the girl's body."

Hatch absorbed the instructions wonderingly, then ventured a remark. "I presume you are thinking of poison. Isn't there a chance that despite the normal condition of her blood some sort of poison was introduced into her system—I mean that the thorns of the rose might have been poisoned, for instance."

"You say there was no scratch or thorn prick on the dog?" asked The Thinking Machine in answer.

"No mark of any sort."

"And the dog is dead. That answers your question, Mr. Hatch." He relapsed into silence.

"Poison on the thorns could not have killed both of them, because only the woman's hand showed the marks?" Hatch asked.

"Precisely," was the reply. "Unless we allow for coincidence, and that has never been reduced to a scientific law, we must say that both the woman and the dog died of the same cause. When we know that, we prove that the thorn prick had nothing to do with the woman's death. Two and two make four, Mr. Hatch, not sometimes but *all* the time. And so what have we left?"

"I don't see that we have anything left," remarked Hatch frankly. "If there is no outward cause, how can we—"

"The mere fact that there is no apparent cause, or outward cause, as you term it, makes the manner of death of both the woman and the dog perfectly plain," declared The Thinking Machine belligerently.

"There is no mystery about that at all—it's obvious. Our problem is not what killed her, but who killed her."

"Yes, that seems quite clear," the reporter admitted.

Minute after minute passed while the scientist sat staring upward. Finally he lowered his eyes to the face of the newspaper man. "Where did this red rose come from?" he demanded.

"I was going to tell you about that," responded Hatch. "It came from Lamperti's, a florist. The police are investigating it now. It seems, according to a statement of the manager of the shop, that on June 16 he received a special delivery letter from Washington with only a typewritten, unsigned slip of paper inclosed. This directed that one dozen red roses be sent to Miss Burdock, one at a time on specified days, Mondays, Wednesdays, and Saturdays. They accepted the order,—there was no way to return the money anyway,—and so—"

He paused to gaze curiously into the eyes of The Thinking Machine. They were drawn down to mere slits of watery blue and some subtle change had altered the straight line of the lips.

"Well, well!" grumbled the scientist. "Go on!"

"As a rule the long box with the one rose was delivered at the house by one of the wagons of the company," the reporter continued; "but some days when the wagon was not going in that direction the box was sent by a messenger boy. This last rose went to her by messenger."

"And have all the roses been sent?"

"So the manager says."

"And where is the red rose—the one she had in her hand when found?"

"Detective Mallory has it in charge, I suppose," explained the reporter. "He has an idea that Miss Burdock was killed by poison on the thorns; so he stripped them off and sent them to a chemist to see if any trace of poison could be found. I presume he kept the flower and the box it came in."

"That's just like Mallory," commented the scientist testily. "Whenever the police want to keep a cat's teeth from falling out they cut off its tail. Now tell me something about Miss Burdock herself. Who was she? What was she? What were her circumstances?" He settled back in his chair for a categorical answer.

"She was the only daughter of Plympton Burdock; a man who is not wealthy, but who is well to do," answered Hatch. "She lived at home with her father, her mother, and a younger brother, a chap about eighteen or nineteen years old. She was something of a social favorite, although not yet quite twenty-one, and went about a great deal; so—"

"So naturally a great many men, some of whom admired her," The Thinking Machine finished for him. "Now who are the men? Tell me about her love affairs?"

"It hasn't appeared yet that there was a love affair, in the sense you mean. At least, if there was no one knew of it."

"Doesn't the maid Goodwin know?" insisted the scientist.

"She says she doesn't."

"But somebody sent the rose. The mere fact that she received the one rose a dozen times indicates that some one was interested in her. Therefore, who was it? Who?"

"That's what the police are trying to find out now."

The Thinking Machine arose suddenly, picked up his hat and planted it aggressively on his enormous yellow head. "I'm going to the florist's," he said. "You get the peach and see the maid Goodwin. Meet me at police headquarters in an hour."

It required ten minutes for The Thinking Machine to reach the florist's shop, and in five minutes more the manager was at liberty.

"All I want to know," the scientist explained, "is the day you sent the first rose of that dozen to Miss Burdock, and I should like to see your records of delivery. That is, when a package is delivered either by your wagon or by messenger you get a receipt for it? Yes. I should like to see those, please."

The manager obligingly consulted his records. "The letter with the inclosure was received on June 16," he explained as he ran his finger down the book. "It came in the morning mail. June 16 was Monday; therefore the first rose of the dozen was sent that afternoon, Monday."

"Are you absolutely certain of that?" demanded The Thinking Machine. "A—a person's life may depend on that record."

The manager stared at him in frank astonishment, then arose. "I can make sure," he said. He went to a cabinet and took out another book—a delivery receipt book, and fluttered the leaves through his fingers. At last he laid it before The Thinking Machine and indicated an entry with his finger. "There it is," he said. "Monday, June 16, at five-thirty in the afternoon. The book was signed by Edna Burdock in person. See."

The Thinking Machine squinted down at the entry for a minute or more in silence. "From that date forward one rose was sent every Monday, Wednesday, and Saturday without a break until the dozen were delivered?" he asked at last.

"Yes; that was the direction. Run through the book on the dates it should have been sent and see, if you like."

The scientist heeded the suggestion, and for ten minutes or so was engrossed in the record. "These slips?" he inquired, as he looked up. "I find three of them."

"Those were the occasions when we didn't happen to have a wagon going in that direction," the manager explained; "so the box was sent by special messenger. Each messenger took a receipt and returned it here. In that way those receipts became a part of our record."

The Thinking Machine scrutinized the slips carefully, made a note of the dates on them, then closed the record book. That seemed to be all. Fifteen minutes later Plympton Burdock, father of the dead girl, received a card from a servant, glanced at it, nodded, and The Thinking Machine was ushered in.

"I should not have disturbed you, believe me, if the necessity for it had not been pressing in the interest of justice," the scientist apologized. "Just one or two questions, please."

Burdock regarded the little man curiously, and motioned to a seat.

"First," began The Thinking Machine, "was your daughter engaged to be married at the time of her—her death?"

"No," replied Burdock.

"She did receive attention, however?"

"Certainly. All girls of her age do. Really, Mr.—Mr.," and he glanced at the card,— "Mr. Van Dusen, this matter is entirely beyond discussion. We believe, my wife and I, that death was due to natural causes, and have so informed the police. I hope it may go no further."

The Thinking Machine looked at him sharply with some strange new expression in his squint eyes. "The investigation won't stop now, Mr. Burdock," he said coldly. "I don't know your object in—in seeking to stop it."

"I don't want to stop it," declared Burdock quickly. "We are convinced that no good can come of an investigation, because there is no ground for suspicion, and certainly it is not pleasant to have one's family affairs constantly pawed over when it is a foregone conclusion that nothing will result except unpleasant notoriety which merely adds to the burden that we now have to bear."

The Thinking Machine understood and nodded. It was almost an apology. "Well, just one more question, please," he said. "What is the name of the man whose attentions to your daughter you in person forbade?"

"How do you know of that?" blazed Burdock quickly.

"What is his name?" repeated The Thinking Machine.

"I will not discuss the matter further with you," was the reply.

"In the interests of justice I demand his name!" The Thinking Machine insisted.

Burdock stared at the slight figure before him with growing horror in his face. "You don't mean to say you suspect—" He stopped. "My God! if I thought that I'd—How was she killed, if she was killed?" he concluded.

"His name, please," urged The Thinking Machine. "If you don't give it to me, you will place me under the necessity of asking the police to compel you to give it. I'd prefer not to."

Burdock seemed not to heed the speech. His face had gone perfectly white, and he stood staring past the scientist, out the window. His hands were clenched tightly and the fingers were working.

"If he did! If he did!" he repeated fiercely. Suddenly he recovered himself and glared down at his visitor. "I beg your pardon," he said simply. His name is—is Paul K. Darrow."

"Of this city," said The Thinking Machine. It was not a question; it was a statement of fact.

"Of this city," repeated Burdock,— "at least formerly of this city. He left here, I am informed, four or five weeks ago."

The Thinking Machine went his way, leaving Burdock sitting with his face in his hands. A few minutes later he appeared in Detective Mallory's office at police headquarters. The officer was sitting with his feet on his desk, smoking furiously, with a dozen deep wrinkles in his brow. He hailed the scientist almost cordially, something unusual for him.

"What do you make of it?" he demanded as he arose.

"Let me see your directory for a moment, please," replied The Thinking Machine. He bent over the book, ran down a page or so of the D's, then finally looked up.

"We don't seem to be able to establish a crime, even," Detective Mallory confessed. "I had the thorns examined, and the chemist reports that there is not a trace of poison about them."

"Silly in the first place," remarked The Thinking Machine ungraciously enough. "Is the rose here?"

The detective produced it from a drawer of his desk, whereupon The Thinking Machine did several things with it which he didn't understand.

First he waved it about in the air at arm's length, then took two steps forward and sniffed. Then he waved it about much closer to him and sniffed. Detective Mallory looked on in mingled curiosity and disgust. Finally the scientist held it close to his nose and sniffed, then examined the petals closely, after which he laid it on the desk again.

"And the box the rose was delivered in?" queried the scientist.

Silently the detective produced that. The Thinking Machine sniffed at it cautiously, then turned it over to examine the handwriting on the address.

"Know who wrote this?" he inquired.

"Some one at the florist's," was the reply.

"Can you lend me a man for half an hour or so?" asked the scientist next.

"Oh, I suppose so," grumbled Detective Mallory. "But what's it all about, anyway?"

"Perhaps I may be able to tell you at the end of the half hour," The Thinking Machine assured him. "Meanwhile lend me the man you said I could have."

Detective Downey was called in, and the diminutive scientist led him into the hall, where he gave him some definite directions. Downey went out the front door at full speed. The Thinking Machine returned to Detective Mallory's private room, to find the officer sulking, like a boy.

"Where'd you send him?" he growled.

"Wait till he comes back and I'll tell you," was the reply. "It isn't necessary to get excited about something that we know nothing of. I'm saving you some excitement."

He dropped back into a chair and sat there idly twiddling his thumbs while Detective Mallory glared at him. After a few minutes the door was thrown open violently and Hutchinson Hatch entered. He was frankly excited.

"Well?" demanded The Thinking Machine without looking round.

"When she smelled that crushed kernel she fainted!" said Hatch explosively.

"Fainted?" repeated the scientist. "Fainted?" The tone was hardly one of surprise, and yet—

"Yes, she took one whiff, and screamed and went right over," the reporter rushed on.

"Dear me! Dear me!" commented The Thinking Machine. He sat still looking up. "Wait a few minutes," he advised. "Let's see what Downey gets."

At the end of fifteen minutes Downey returned. His chief glared at him curiously as he entered and handed a piece of paper to The Thinking Machine. That imperturbable man of science examined the paper closely, then handed it to Detective Mallory.

"Is that the handwriting on the flower box?" he asked.

Mallory, Downey, and Hatch compared it together. The verdict was unanimous: "Yes."

"Then the man who wrote it is the man you want," declared The Thinking Machine flatly. "His name is Paul K. Darrow. Detective Downey knows his address."

Two days passed. Professor Van Dusen stood beside his laboratory table poking idly at the dismembered legs of a frog with a short copper wire. Each time the point touched the flesh there was a spasmodic twitching of the limbs, a simulation of living contraction and extension. There beside the table Hutchinson Hatch found him.

"Watch this a moment, Mr. Hatch," requested the scientist. "It bears, in a way, on our problem in hand."

Then began a rhythmic swinging of his slender hand, not unlike the beat of the musician's baton, the wire touching the frog's legs at each downward swing. Hatch had seen a similar demonstration before.

"Watch the strokes," said the scientist, "and watch the legs after the twentieth."

"Fourteen, fifteen, sixteen," Hatch counted. Each time the wire touched, and each time came the spasmodic motion. "Seventeen, eighteen, nineteen, twenty."

The Thinking Machine, instead of touching the twenty-first time, held the wire aloft. At the instant it would have touched the flesh, according to the beat, there came the same quick, spasmodic twitch, and then the legs were still.

"You see the effect is precisely as if I had touched them the twenty-first time," explained The Thinking Machine, "and that, Mr. Hatch, is one of the things science doesn't attempt to explain. It can be explained some day—it will be explained, but—" He paused. "Darrow hasn't been captured yet?" he said.

"No; no trace of him yet," was the reply. "The police have sent out a general alarm for him all over the country, and to-day Burdock increased the reward he offered from five thousand to ten thousand dollars."

"One of my objections to dealing with the police is that they are prone to jump at conclusions," remarked The Thinking Machine. "I didn't say, of course, that Darrow was a murderer. He may have killed Miss Burdock,—he probably did,—but it isn't conclusive at all. Still he is the next link in the chain, so his presence is necessary."

Hatch gazed at him in amazement, and a hundred questions rushed to his lips. They were stilled by the sudden appearance in the doorway of a young man. A soft hat was pulled down over his eyes, and he was crouching as if about to spring. One hand, the right, was in his coat pocket, clutching something fiercely. His face was perfectly pallid, and roving, glittering eyes blazed with madness.

"Come in," suggested The Thinking Machine calmly.

"I—I must talk to you, quick!" the young man burst out. "It's a matter of the most vital importance, and—"

"I'm at your service, Mr. Darrow," remarked The Thinking Machine pleasantly. "Have a seat."

Darrow! Hatch was startled, made speechless, by the uncanny appearance of this man whom the police of the entire continent were seeking. Darrow was still crouching there in the doorway, staring at them.

"I risked everything to come here," declared the young man—and there was a menace in his tone. "I was on the stoop about to ring the bell when I glanced back and saw Detective Mallory turn the corner. I didn't wait to ring—the door was unfastened and I came on in. Mallory is probably coming here. I must talk to you—and I won't be taken alive. Do you understand what I say?"

"Perfectly," replied The Thinking Machine. "Mr. Mallory won't see you. Come in out of the door."

"No tricks!" warned Darrow fiercely.

"No tricks. Sit down."

With furtive glances to right and left along the hall, the young man entered and dropped into a seat in a corner, facing them. There was a long, tense silence, and finally the door bell rang. Darrow half rose and made as if to take his right hand from his pocket.

"That's Mallory," remarked The Thinking Machine, and he started toward the door.

Darrow took one step forward, blocking his way. "Understand, please," he began in a low, even voice. "I am utterly desperate, and I won't be taken! If you attempt to betray me, I—" He stopped.

The Thinking Machine walked round him to the door leading into the hall. Martha, his aged servant, was just passing.

"Mr. Mallory is at the door, Martha," said the scientist. "Tell him I am not in; but that I shall be at police headquarters within an hour, and Mr. Darrow will come with me."

He stepped back into the laboratory and closed the door, without even a glance at his visitor. They heard Martha open the front door, then they heard Mallory's heavy voice, finally Martha's answer, then the door was closed, and Martha's footsteps passed along the hall. Darrow suddenly rushed to the window and glanced out.

"All right, Mr. Darrow," remarked the little scientist, as he sat down. "I know now you are innocent; I know why you have been hiding out, I know why you came here to see me, and I understand too your deep grief; so we can come immediately to the vital things."

The young man turned and glared at the small, impassive figure. "You said I would be at police headquarters with you in an hour," he said accusingly.

"Certainly," agreed the scientist impatiently. "As an innocent man you will go there of your own free will, with me."

The young man dropped into a chair and sat there for a long time with his face in his hands. After awhile Hatch saw a teardrop trickle through the unsteady fingers, and the shoulders moved convulsively. The Thinking Machine sat with head tilted back, squinting upward and fingers at rest, tip to tip.

"This trouble between you and Mr. Burdock?" suggested the scientist at last.

"You don't know the malignant hatred he has for me," said Darrow suddenly. "He is not a man of great wealth, but he is a man of great power, great influence, and if I should fall into the hands of the police with the circumstantial case against me that now exists he would bring all that power and influence to bear against me, with the result that I should be railroaded to a felon's grave. I don't know just how he would do it; but he would do it. I'm afraid of him—that's why I came here to see you when I wouldn't dare go to the police. I won't be taken by the police until I know I can prove my innocence; then I will surrender."

The Thinking Machine nodded.

"The enmity existing between us is of years' standing, and is not of importance here," Darrow went on. "But I know this man's power,—I have felt it all my life,—he has brought me to the edge of starvation half a dozen times, pursued me in every walk of life, until now—now if I should have to commit murder, he would be the victim. I'm telling you this because—"

"All this is of no consequence," interrupted The Thinking Machine shortly. "Who poisoned the rose?"

"I don't know," replied Darrow helplessly.

"You must have some idea," insisted The Thinking Machine.

"I did have an idea," was the reply. "I went this morning to a place to see a—a person whom I intended to accuse openly of the crime, taking the chance of capture myself, much as I dreaded it; but there was no one there. The door was locked; a servant connected with the apartment house told me that the—the person had not been there for a day or so."

The Thinking Machine turned quickly in his chair and glared at Darrow curiously.

"What's her name?" he demanded sharply.

"I don't know that she could have had anything to do with it," warned Darrow. "It seems awful to suggest such a thing, and yet—" He stopped. "I will go there with you to see her if you wish."

"Mr. Hatch," directed The Thinking Machine, "step into the next room there and telephone for a cab." He turned again to Darrow. "She threatened you, or Miss Burdock, I imagine?"

"Yes," said Darrow reluctantly.

"And now, please, one last question," said the little scientist. "What relation existed between you and Miss Burdock?"

"She was my wife," Darrow replied in a low voice. "We were secretly married four months ago."

"Um-m," mused the scientist. "I imagined as much."

Detective Mallory impatiently strode back and forth across his private office, his brain turbulent with conjecture. The telephone bell rang; The Thinking Machine was at the other end of the wire.

"Come at once and bring the medical examiner to the Craddock apartments!" commanded the irritable voice of the little scientist.

"Another murder?" demanded the detective, aghast.

"No, a suicide," was the reply. "Good by."

Detective Mallory and Medical Examiner Francis found The Thinking Machine, Hutchinson Hatch, and Paul K. Darrow in the sitting room of a small apartment on the fourth floor. Some sinister thing lay outstretched on a couch, covered with a sheet.

"Mr. Mallory, this is Mr. Darrow," the scientist remarked. "And here," he indicated the couch, "is the woman who murdered Miss Burdock, or rather Mrs. Darrow. Her name is Maria di Peculini. Here is a full confession in her own handwriting," he passed an envelope to the detective, "and here are several torn pieces of paper which show how assiduously she practised before she forged Mr. Darrow's handwriting in addressing the box in which the red rose was sent to Miss—I should say Mrs. Darrow. I may add that Signorina di Peculini killed herself by inhaling hydrocyanic acid—perhaps you know it better as Prussic acid—in a bottle from which came the single drop, allowed to settle in the bloom of the rose, which killed Mrs. Darrow."

Detective Mallory remained standing still for a long time to take it all in. At last he opened the confession—only a dozen lines—and read it from end to end. It was a pitiful, disjointed, almost incoherent, revelation of a woman's distorted soul. She too had loved Darrow, and this had changed to hate when he drifted away from her. Then, when by her own hand she had removed the woman he had made his wife, and had sought subtly to place the blame on him by the little forgery,—then had come a revulsion of feeling. She loved again, and overcome by remorse sought relief in death.

"There was no mystery whatever as to the cause of death," The Thinking Machine told Detective Mallory and Hatch a little while later. "Murder by poison was obvious from the fact that both the woman and the dog were dead; and when we knew that there was no mark or scratch on the dog, and the autopsy revealed nothing, we knew by the simplest rule of logic that the poison had been inhaled. The most powerful poison to inhale is hydrocyanic acid,—it kills instantly,—therefore it occurred to me first. It is so powerful that it is never made pure, at least in this country. The strongest you can buy in a drug store, for instance, is about a two per cent solution. One drop of a stronger solution than that, on a rose bloom, would have killed Miss Burdock, and the dog if he sniffed at it, as he must have.

"Therefore, from the very first, we knew the manner of death. When we knew further that hydrocyanic acid is extremely volatile, we see how that single drop on the rose evaporated, was dissipated in the air, as the windows of the room where the young woman was found were open. Still there was a faint odor of it left,—it smells precisely like crushed peach kernels,—and the maid Goodwin was unconsciously affected by it.

"Knowing these things," he continued, "I went to the florist's. Only twelve roses had been bought, paid for, and delivered from there, and the rose that killed Miss Burdock was the thirteenth rose. The roses went from the florist's Mondays, Wednesdays, and Saturdays for four weeks, making twelve roses. They had all been delivered, as the receipt books there showed; but Miss Burdock was killed on Monday; therefore that was the thirteenth rose, and it didn't come direct from the florist's. It was sent by messenger, and the date didn't correspond with any date in the receipt book; therefore it came from another source.

"Incidentally the fact that the roses were sent in that way,—that is one at a time without a card or suggestion of by whom they were sent,—suggested a clandestine arrangement with the girl. In other words, the roses were being sent by some one she knew, in all probability; but no one else must know. It was, I saw, a method of correspondence, I might say a love token of some sort, which would not attract attention at her home as a letter would.

"Thus I established a relationship between Miss Burdock and some one else—unknown. The logic of it all informed me that the reason that unknown didn't communicate with her was because of some objection in her home. Her father! Do you see? I simply asked him about it, and instantly his hatred for a single individual came out, that individual being Mr. Darrow. Thus, things pointed toward Mr. Darrow, who was away. The letter to the florist was from Washington. The joints were fitting nicely.

"At police headquarters I saw the rose, and by cautious experiments detected a faint odor of peach kernels. Then I saw the handwriting on the box. It seemed to be a man's; yet I knew by the receipt book there that it did not come from the florist's, therefore was not addressed by anyone there. Did Mr. Darrow address it? Mr. Downey got for me a sample of Mr. Darrow's writing (I don't know how he got it), and the two were compared. They seemed to be the same. This fact was connecting with all the others. Clandestine communication—poison—Darrow! Do you see? This development made Darrow's presence necessary, and I told you, Mr. Mallory, that he was the man we must find. Yet, from the fact that the handwriting on the box was his I had a first suggestion that he was not guilty of the crime. No intelligent man would address a box like that in his own handwriting.

"The matter rested at this point. Mr. Burdock accepted a murder theory and offered rewards, and then Mr. Darrow in person came to see me. The moment he stepped inside my door, to tell me an improbable story, I knew he was innocent. Mr. Burdock's hatred of him (the cause of the feud between them is not of consequence) told me why he had disappeared; and his mere appearance before me accounted for his not going to the police. So—so that's all. He told me of calling to see Signorina di Peculini, and she was not in. We came here, found the door locked, went in with a pass key, and found the things as I delivered them to you, Mr. Mallory." He stopped and sat silently staring for a little while.

"Briefly," he supplemented, "the woman who killed herself knew of the rose being sent regularly, then determined on revenge, bought one, and sent it herself after dropping a single drop of poison in the bloom. The wax paper which surrounded the flower prevented evaporation, and when it was opened,—We know the rest."

Neither Detective Mallory nor Hatch spoke for a long time. But the reporter had one more question to ask; and at last he put it.

"That peach kernel that you sent me to Goodwin with—" he began.

"Oh, yes," interrupted The Thinking Machine. "That was a little psychological experiment, and the result of it disconcerted me a little. It is one of the many things science doesn't fully understand, Mr. Hatch—like the little experiment with the frog. For instance, nitrite of amyl is a powerful heart stimulant. It smells precisely like banana oil. A person who has used nitrite of amyl, or to whom it has been administered without their knowledge by inhalation, is momentarily affected the same way when they come suddenly upon the odor of banana oil. Prussic acid has an odor like a peach kernel. I sent you to Goodwin, therefore, to prove definitely whether or not prussic acid had been used, and if she had inhaled it unconsciously. The result gave the proof I wanted."

The Problem of the Souvenir Cards

There were three of the post cards. The first one was a vividly colored picture of the Capitol at Washington. It was postmarked, "Philadelphia, November 12, 2:30 p.m." Below the picture, in a small copperplate hand, were these figures and symbols: "I-28-38-4 x 47-30-2 x 21-19-8 x 65-5-3 x 29-32-11 x 40-2-9x."

The second post card was a picture of Park Square, Boston, with the majestic figures of Lincoln and the slave in the foreground. This, too, was postmarked Philadelphia, but the date was November 13. The symbols and figures were unquestionably written by the same hand as those on the first: "II-155-19-9 x 205-2-8 x agree x 228-31-2 x present tense x 235-13-4."

The third card was a colored reproduction of an idyllic bayou near New Orleans. Again the postmark was Philadelphia, but the date was November 14. This card contained only: "III-41-1-9 x 181-15-10 x press."

Professor Augustus S. F. X. Van Dusen—The Thinking Machine—turned and twisted the post cards in his slender fingers while he studied them through squinting, watery, blue eyes. At last he laid them on a table beside him, and sank back into his chair, with long white fingers pressed tip to tip. He was in a receptive mood.

"Well?" he demanded abruptly.

The bearded stranger who had offered the cards for his scrutiny was gazing at the diminutive figure and the drawn, petulant face of the scientist, seemingly in mingled wonder and amusement. It was difficult for him to associate this crabbed little man with those achievements which had placed his name so high in the sciences. After a moment the visitor's gaze wavered a little and dropped.

"My name is William C. Colgate," he began. "Sometime since—four weeks and three days, to be exact—a diamond was stolen from my house in this city, and no trace of it has ever been found. It was one I bought uncut in South Africa five years ago, and its weight is about thirty carats. When cut I imagine it will be eighteen to twenty carats, and it is, as it stands now, worth about forty thousand dollars. You may have read something of the theft in the newspapers?"

"I never read the newspapers," remarked The Thinking Machine.

"Well, in that event," and Colgate smiled, "I can briefly state the facts in the case. I have for several years had in my employment a secretary, Charles Travers. He is about twenty-five years old. Within the last four or five months I have noticed a change in his manner. Where formerly he had been quiet and unassuming, he has, through evil associations I dare say, grown to be a little wild, and, I believe, has lived beyond his income. I took occasion twice to remonstrate with him. The first time he seemed contrite and repentant; the second time he grew angry, and the following day disappeared. The diamond went with him."

"Do you know that?" demanded The Thinking Machine.

"I know it as well as one may know anything," replied Colgate positively. "I doubt if anyone except Travers knew where I kept the jewel. Certainly my servants did not, and certainly my wife and two daughters did not. Besides my wife and daughters have been in Europe for two months. The police seem to be unable to learn anything, so I came to you."

"Just where did you keep the jewel?"

"In a drawer of my desk," was the reply. "Ultimately I had intended to have it cut and present it to my oldest daughter, possibly on the occasion of her marriage. Now—" Colgate waved his hand.

The Thinking Machine sat silent for several minutes. His squint eyes were turned steadily upward and several tiny lines appeared in the domelike brow. "The problem then seems to be merely one of finding your secretary," he stated at last. "The diamond is of course so large that it would be absurd to attempt to dispose of it in its present shape. Travers is an intelligent man; we shall give him credit for realizing this. And yet if it should be cut up into smaller stones its value would dwindle to a tenth part of what it is now. Under those circumstances, would he have it cut up?"

"That is one of the questions which I should like to have answered."

For the second time The Thinking Machine picked up and examined the three post cards. "And what have these to do with it?" he demanded.

"That's another question I should like to have answered," said Colgate. "I can only believe that they in someway bear on the mystery surrounding the disappearance of the gem. Perhaps they give a clue to where it is now."

"This is Travers's handwriting?"

"Yes."

"The cards obviously constitute a cipher of some sort," explained the scientist. "Were you and Travers accustomed to communicating in cipher?"

"Not at all."

"Then why is this in cipher?" demanded The Thinking Machine belligerently. He glared at Colgate much as if he held him to blame.

Colgate shrugged his shoulders.

"Of course," continued the scientist, "I can find out what it means. It is elementary in character, and yet I doubt if, after we know what is in it, it will be particularly illuminating. Still, giving Travers credit for intelligence, I should imagine this to be an offer to return the diamond, probably for a consideration. But why in cipher?"

Colgate did not seem to be able to add to what he had already said, and after a few minutes took his leave, with instructions from The Thinking Machine to return on the following day, after the scientist had had an opportunity to study the post cards. He called at the appointed hour.

"Have you three-volume book of any sort that you read or refer to frequently?"

For some reason Colgate seemed a little startled. It was only momentary, however. "I suppose I have several books of three volumes," he replied.

"No particular one that your secretary would know that you read frequently?" insisted the scientist.

Again some strange impalpable expression flitted across Colgate's face. "No," he said after a moment.

The Thinking Machine arose. "It will be necessary then," he said, "for me to go over your library and see if I can't find the book to which this cipher refers."

"Book?" asked Colgate curiously. "If the cipher has no relation to the diamond, I don't see that—"

"Of course you don't see!" snapped The Thinking Machine. "Come along and let me see."

Colgate seemed a little perturbed by the suggestion. He folded his immaculate gloves over and over as he stared at the inscrutable face before him. "It would be impossible," he said at last, "to find anything in my library just now. As I said, my wife and daughters are abroad, and during their absence I have taken occasion to have my library and one or two other rooms redecorated and refinished. All my books meanwhile are packed away, helter skelter."

The Thinking Machine sat down again and stared at him inquiringly. "Then when your library is in order again you may call," he said tersely. "I can do nothing until I see the books."

"But—but—" stammered Colgate.

"Good day," said The Thinking Machine curtly.

Colgate went away. It was not till three days later that he reappeared. If one might have judged by his manner, he had achieved something in his absence; yet when he spoke it was in the same exquisitely modulated tone of the first visit.

"The work of redecorating has been completed," he told The Thinking Machine. "My library is again in order, and you may examine it at your leisure. If you care to go now, my carriage is at the door."

The Thinking Machine stared at him for a moment, then picked up his hat. At the door of the Colgate mansion Colgate and the scientist were met by a graven-faced footman, who received their hats and coats in silence. Colgate conducted his guest straight into the library. It was a magnificently appointed place, reflecting in its every detail the splendid purchasing power of money. To this sheer luxury, however, The Thinking Machine was oblivious. His undivided attention was on the book shelves.

From one end of the long room to the other he walked time after time, reading the titles of the books as he passed. There were Dickens, Balzac, Kipling, Stevenson, Thackeray, Zola—all of them. Three or four times he paused to draw out a volume and examine it. Each time he replaced it without a word and continued his search. Colgate stood by, watching him curiously.

The Thinking Machine had just paused to draw out one of the Dumas books when the stolid-faced footman appeared in the door with a telegram.

"Is this for you, sir?" he asked of Colgate.

"Yes," replied Colgate.

He drew out the yellow sheet and permitted the envelope to fall to the floor. The Thinking Machine picked it up with something like eagerness in his manner. It was directed to "William C. Colgate." The scientist looked almost astonished as he turned again to the book shelves.

It was ten minutes later that The Thinking Machine took out three volumes together. These comprised the famous old English novel, "Ten Thousand a Year," a rare and valuable first edition. The leaves of volume 1 fluttered through his fingers until he came to page 28. After a moment he said "Ah!" Then he went on to page 47. He studied that for a moment or more, after which he said "Ah!" once again.

"What is it?" inquired Colgate quickly.

The Thinking Machine turned his cold, squint eyes up into the eager face above him. "It is the key to the cipher," he said.

"What is it? Read it!" commanded Colgate. His clear, alert eyes were fastened on the, to him, meaningless page. He sought vainly there something to account for the scientist's exclamation. But he saw only words—a page of words with no apparent meaning beyond the text of the story. "What is it?" he demanded again, and there was a little glitter in his eye. "Does it say where the diamond is?"

"Considering the fact that I have seen only two words of a possible twenty or thirty, I don't know what it says," declared The

Thinking Machine aggressively. "The best I can say now is that with the aid of these books I shall find the diamond."

For half an hour or more the scientist was busy running through the books in an aimless sort of way. Finally he closed the third volume with a snap and stood up.

"Travers says that he will return the gem for ten thousand dollars," he announced.

"Oh, he does, does he?" Colgate's tone was a sneer. Again in his face The Thinking Machine read some subtle quality which brought a slight wrinkle of perplexity to his brow.

"You don't have to pay it, you know," he explained tartly. "I can get it without the ten thousand dollars, of course."

"Well, get it, then!" said Colgate a little impatiently. "I want the diamond, and it is absurd to suppose that I shall pay ten thousand dollars for my own property. Come on! Let's do what is to be done immediately."

"I'll do what is to be done immediately; but I will do it without your assistance," remarked The Thinking Machine. "I shall send for you to-morrow. When you come the diamond will be in my possession. Good day."

Colgate stared after him blankly as he went out.

The Thinking Machine was talking over the telephone with Hutchinson Hatch, reporter.

"Do you know William C. Colgate by sight?" he demanded.

"Very well," Hatch replied.

"Is he red-headed?"

"No."

"Good by."

On the following morning a short advertisement appeared in all the city newspapers. It was simply:

WILL GIVE TEN THOUSAND DOLLARS. MATTER IS NOT IN HANDS OF THE POLICE. TO INSURE YOUR SAFETY, TELEPHONE 1103 BAY AND ARRANGE DETAILS.

It was only a few minutes past nine o'clock that morning when The Thinking Machine was called to the telephone. For some reason he had difficulty in understanding, possibly due to the spluttering of the receiver. Then he did understand, and sat down for some time, apparently to consider what he had heard. Later he telephoned to Hutchinson Hatch.

"It's about this theft of the Colgate diamond," he explained. "The secretary, Travers, who is wanted for the theft, is now somewhere in the North End, either drunk or drugged, and possibly disguised. I imagine his photograph has been in all the newspapers. I have been talking to him over the telephone, and he is to call me again about eleven o'clock. Go down to the North End near the corner of Hanover and Blank Streets, hire a telephone for the morning, and call me. Remain at the phone from half-past ten until I call you. You are to get Travers. When you get him bring him here. Don't notify the police."

"But will I get him?" asked the reporter.

"If you don't you are stupid," retorted The Thinking Machine.

At five minutes of eleven o'clock the scientist's telephone rang. He was sitting staring at it at the moment, but instead of answering stepped to the door and called Martha, his aged servant.

"Answer the telephone," he directed, "and tell whoever is there that I am not here. Tell them I shall return in ten minutes, and to be sure to call me again."

Martha followed the instructions and hung up the receiver. Instantly The Thinking Machine went to the telephone.

"Can you tell me, please, the number of the telephone which just called me?" he asked quickly. "No, I don't want a connection. Number 34710 North, in a café at Hanover and Blank Streets? Thanks."

A minute later he had Hatch on the wire again. "Travers will call me in five minutes from 34710 North, in a café at Hanover and Blank Streets," he said. "Get him and bring him here as quickly as you can. Good by."

So it came about that within less than an hour a cab rushed up to the door, and Hutchinson Hatch, accompanied by a young man, entered. The man was Travers. A week's scrubby beard was on his chin, his face was perfectly pallid; the fever of drink and fear glittered in his eyes. Hatch had to support him to a chair, in which he dropped back limply. The Thinking Machine scowled down into the young man's face, and was met by a fishy, imbecilic stare in return.

"Are you Mr. Travers?" inquired The Thinking Machine.

"That's all right—that's all right," murmured the young man, and overcome by the exertion of speech his head dropped back and in a moment he was sound asleep.

Without apparent compunction The Thinking Machine searched his pockets. After a moment he found what seemed to be a rough rock crystal. He squinted at it closely as he turned and twisted it back and forth in his hand, then passed it to Hatch for inspection.

"That's worth forty thousand dollars," he remarked casually.

"Is this the—"

"It's the Colgate diamond," interrupted The Thinking Machine. "I surmised that he would have it somewhere about him, because he would have no place to hide it. And now for the second man— the brains of the theft. First I shall telephone for Colgate. Look at him when he enters; for I think you will be greatly surprised. And above all, remember to be careful."

Looking deeply into the quiet, squint eyes of the scientist, Hatch read a warning. He understood and nodded. Travers, stupefied, was removed to an adjoining room.

A few minutes later there was a rattle of carriage wheels, the door bell rang, and Colgate entered. Hatch glanced at him, then turned quickly to look out of a window.

"You have the diamond?" burst out Colgate suddenly.

"I said I would have it when you came," retorted The Thinking Machine. "Now for these post cards," and the scientist produced the three cards that had been handed to him at first. "Perhaps you would be interested to know what was really on them?"

"I haven't the slightest curiosity," said Colgate impatiently. "All I want is the diamond. If you will give me that, I think perhaps that will terminate this affair, and there will be no necessity of taking up more of your time."

"Of course you have no desire to prosecute Travers?" asked The Thinking Machine. There was a velvety note in the crabbed voice. Hatch glanced at him.

"I don't think I care to prosecute him," said Colgate steadily.

"I thought perhaps you would not," rejoined The Thinking Machine enigmatically. "But as to these post cards. They constitute what is known as the book cipher. For your information I may state that it is always possible to know a book cipher by the fact that a small number, rarely above twelve or fourteen, always precedes the X; the X merely divides the words. For instance, on the first card we have I-28-38-4; in other words, volume one, page 28, line 38, and the fourth word of that line. Unless one knows or can learn the name of the book which is the basis of the cipher, it is perhaps the most difficult of all. Any ordinary cipher may be solved precisely as Poe solved his great cipher in 'The Gold Bug.'"

"But I am not at all interested—" protested Colgate.

"So really all that was necessary for me to do was to find out what book was the basis of this particular cipher," continued The Thinking Machine to Hatch, without heeding his visitor's remark. "I knew of course it was some book in Mr. Colgate's home. The clue to what book was given, either wittingly or unwittingly, by the single I, the two I's and the three I's on the first, second, and third cards. Did these represent volumes? I found a dozen three volume books in Mr. Colgate's library, but in each instance there was no connection in the first three or four words which I found in accordance with the numbers given; that is, until I came to 'Ten Thousand a Year.' The first word I found in that was 'will'; the second, page 47, line 30, second word, was 'return'; the third was 'diamond.' So I knew that was the book I wanted. Here is the full meaning of the cipher as it appears on the three cards, as I have transcribed it."

He handed Colgate a slip of paper, on which was written:

Will return diamond for ten thousand. If you agree informed [present tense—i.e., inform] me in daily press.

"This all seems very clever and very curious indeed," commented Colgate; "but really I do not think—"

"The book of Mr. Colgate's is a first edition—there is also a first edition in the public library," the scientist went on placidly; "so Travers had no difficulty on that score. We shall admit that the cards were mailed in Philadelphia; perhaps he went there and later returned to this city. The manner in which I got possession of the diamond—by first discovering Travers through an advertisement and then keeping him at the telephone until he was inveigled here by my assistant—is possibly of no interest; it was all very easily done by a prearranged plan with the telephone exchange; so now, Mr.—Mr.—"

"Colgate," his visitor supplied, as if surprised at the hesitancy.

"I mean your real name," said the scientist quietly.

There was a sudden tense silence; Hatch had come a little closer, and was staring at the stranger with keen, inquiring eyes.

"This is not the Mr. William C. Colgate you know, Mr. Hatch?"

"No."

"Do you happen to have an idea who he is?"

"If I am not mistaken," Hatch replied calmly, "this is a gentleman I have met before on an exceedingly interesting occasion— Mr. Bradlee Cunnyngham Leighton."

At the name the erstwhile Colgate turned upon the reporter with a snarl. There was a quick movement of his right hand, and Hatch found himself blinking down the barrel of a revolver, as Leighton slowly moved backward toward the door.

The Thinking Machine moved around behind the aggressor. "Now, Mr. Leighton," he said almost pleasantly, "if you don't lower that revolver I'll blow your brains out."

For one instant Leighton hesitated, then glanced back quickly toward the scientist. That diminutive man stood calmly, with his hands in his pockets. Instantly Hatch leaped. There was a quick, sharp struggle, a few muttered curses, and then the discomfited Leighton, in his turn, was gazing down the revolver barrel.

"Won't you gentlemen sit down?" suggested The Thinking Machine.

They were all sitting down when Detective Mallory rushed up from police headquarters. Leighton was farthest from the door. The Thinking Machine sat staring at him with the revolver held in position for quick use.

"Ah, Mr. Mallory," he said, without turning his head or glancing back. "This is Mr. Bradlee Cunnyngham Leighton. You may have heard of him before?"

"Do you mean the Englishman who brought the Varron necklace to this country?" blurted out the detective.

"The same man of the carrier pigeon case," said Hatch grimly.

"I should like particularly to call your attention to Mr. Leighton," continued The Thinking Machine. "He is a man of accomplishments. We know how he distinguished himself by the simple expedient of using carrier pigeons in the Varron necklace affair. In this case, he has risen to greater heights. First—I am assuming some things—he plotted with young Travers to steal the Colgate diamond. In some manner, which is not essential here, Travers got the diamond and sought to profit by the theft alone by negotiating its return for ten thousand dollars. Travers wrote a cipher to Mr. Colgate making the proposition—it was possible he knew Mr. Colgate would understand his cipher. I shall give Leighton credit for anticipating just this possibility and intercepting the post cards. They meant nothing to him; so—please note this—he came to me as Mr. Colgate, knowing that Mr. Colgate was in Europe with his family, and sought my assistance in recovering the jewel from his fellow conspirator. The sublime audacity of all these conceptions marks Mr. Leighton as little short of a genius in his particular profession.

"Only once was Mr. Leighton embarrassed. That was when I told him I should have to visit his library. But he even rose to this necessity brilliantly. He delayed my visit for a day or so, and in some manner, possibly by forgery, secured an entrance to Mr. Colgate's home, perhaps as a cousin of the same name. There he received me. Two or three things had happened to arouse a doubt in my mind as to whether he was the real Mr. Colgate.

"First was his hesitancy in connection with my visit to the library; then while I was in the house a telegram came for Mr. William C. Colgate. A servant asked Mr. Leighton in my presence if the telegram was for him. That question would never have been asked if he had been the real William C. Colgate. Then finally I asked Mr. Hatch over the phone if William C. Colgate was red-headed. William C. Colgate is not red-headed. This gentleman is, therefore he is not William C. Colgate. I only knew this much. Mr. Hatch recognized him as Leighton. He saw him at the time you were all interested in his escape from a Scotland Yard man—Conway, who wanted him for stealing a necklace. That is all, I think."

"But the diamond and Travers?" asked the detective.

"Here is the diamond," said The Thinking Machine, and he produced it from one of his pockets. "Travers is lying on a bed in the next room in a drunken stupor."

The Three Overcoats

Under the influence of that singular feeling of someone being in the room with him, Carroll Garland opened his eyes suddenly from sound sleep. The intuition was correct; there was someone in the room with him—a man whose back was turned. At that particular moment he was examining the clothing Garland had discarded on retiring. Garland raised himself on one elbow, and the bed creaked a little.

"Don't disturb yourself," said the man, without turning, "I'll be through in a minute."

"Through what?" demanded Garland. "My pockets?"

The stranger straightened up and turned toward him. He was a tall, lithe, clean-cut young man, with crisp, curly hair, and a quizzical expression about his eyes and lips.

He was in evening dress, and Garland could only admire the manner in which it fitted him. He wore an opera hat, and a light weight Inverness coat.

"I didn't mean to wake you, really," the stranger apologized pleasantly. "I'm sure I didn't make any noise."

"No, I dare say you didn't," replied Garland. "What do you want?"

The stranger picked up an overcoat, which lay across a chair, and deftly, with a penknife, slit the lining on each side. He did something then which Garland couldn't see, after which he carefully folded the coat again, and laid it across the chair. "I have taken what you won at bridge at your club this evening," he remarked. "It will save me the trouble of cashing a check."

Garland gazed at this imperturbable, audacious person with a sort of admiration. "I trust you found the amount correct?" he said sarcastically.

"Yes, thirteen hundred and forty-seven dollars. That will do very nicely, thank you. I am leaving two hundred and some odd dollars of your own."

"Oh, take it all," said Garland magnanimously, "because I am going to make you return it, anyway."

The stranger laughed pleasantly. "I am going now," he said; "but before I go I should like to tell you that you play really an excellent game of bridge, except, perhaps, you are a little reckless on no trumps."

"Thank you," said Garland, and started to get out of bed.

"Now, don't get up!" advised the stranger, still pleasantly. "I have something here in my pocket which I should dislike very much to have to use. But I will use it if necessary."

Garland kept right on getting out of bed. "You are not such a fool as to shoot," he said quietly. "You couldn't get out of this hotel to save your life if you did. It is only half-past eleven o'clock, there are people passing in the halls, and always at this time there are a great many people in the lobby. You would have to go that way. So now I'll trouble you for the money."

The stranger drew a glistening, shining object from his pocket, examined it casually, then went over and stood beside the call button.

There was a glitter of determination in his eyes, and the smile had gone from his lips. "I certainly have no intention of returning the money—now," he said. "It would be best for both of us, of course, not to attract anyone's attention."

Garland was coming straight toward him.

"Now, don't do anything foolish," the stranger warned, not unkindly. "You can't reach the call button unless you go over me; you won't shout, because if you do I shall have to use this revolver, and take my chances below. You don't happen to need this money, and I do. It was simply a pick-up for you at the club. If you give an alarm when I go out, it will be disagreeable for me."

Garland stared at him in frank amazement for a moment. The stranger steadily returned the gaze.

"I'll just take one whirl out of you anyhow," declared Garland grimly. "I don't happen to have a gun; but—"

And Garland sent in a vicious right swing, which would have been highly effective had the stranger's head remained stationary. Instead, it ducked suddenly, and a left hand landed jarringly on one of Garland's eyes. Instantly he forgot all about the burglarious intentions of his visitor; it was man to man, and Garland happened to be dexterous in the science of pugilism—Mike Donovan had taught him.

After four blows had been exchanged, Garland became suddenly convinced that the stranger's teacher in the gentle art of bruising was more gifted even than Mike, because, in all the freedom of his pajamas, Garland got in only one blow for two, on a man who was hampered by overcoat and evening dress. A stinging jab to Garland's mouth made him clinch, and in trying to reach the stranger's throat, he forgot all the ethics of the game.

At this close range, the stranger delivered one short arm punch, and as Garland reeled and the world grew dark about him, he recalled the blow as being identical with one which was made famous in Carson City, at the time a world's championship changed hands. Dazzling lights danced before his eyes for a moment, and then all was dark.

The stranger stood looking down at him, planted his opera hat more firmly on his head, drew on his gloves, opened the door, and went out. He sauntered through the lobby carelessly, paused to light a cigar, and disappeared through the revolving doors. At the curb outside, an automobile was waiting. In it sat a veiled woman, and a very much begoggled chauffeur.

"Well?" the woman asked quickly.

The stranger shook his head, climbed in beside her, and the car rushed away.

When Garland recovered consciousness, he had the impression of having experienced a remarkably vivid nightmare. But one look into the mirror at the bulbous black eye, and the absence of thirteen hundred and forty-seven dollars from his pockets, convinced him of the reality of it all. Incidentally he examined the two knife cuts in the overcoat lining, and shook his head in bewilderment.

"What the deuce did he cut those for?" he asked himself.

On the following morning Garland returned the overcoat to its owner, Hal Dickson. There is a freemasonry among roommates at college by which one acknowledges that whatever he owns belongs equally to the other. Garland had exercised certain rights which had accrued to him by reason of this comradeship upon his arrival in the city the day before. He wore then a light weight tan coat, entirely too thin for the extreme cold which set in immediately upon his arrival; so he borrowed a heavier coat, a thick frieze affair, from his old chum, and left his own light coat with him.

"I want to tell you something about this, Hal," he said, and recited in detail the events of the night before. "Now look here where my friend cut your coat," he said in conclusion.

Together they examined the long slits, after which they stared at each other in blank wonderment.

"Send it down to your tailor and have it relined," remarked Garland. "Tell him to send the bill to me."

Dickson continued to stare at the coat lining. "What did he want to cut it for?" he asked.

Garland shook his head. "Give me my own coat," he said; "I've got to go back home at two-thirty, and can manage with this light coat until I get there, and may not have a chance to come here again."

Garland was just about to put on his own coat, when he stopped in fresh amazement. "Well! Look at that!" he exclaimed.

Dickson looked. The lining of the coat was slit wide open on each side, as if with a sharp knife.

Ten minutes later the young men were on their way to police headquarters. Detective Mallory received them. The coats were laid under his official eyes, and he scrutinized them carefully.

Mallory listened, with his feet on his desk, and his cigar clinched in his teeth. "What did the thief look like?" he asked at the end.

"He had every appearance of a gentleman."

"Just like me and you, eh?"

"Well, a little more like me," replied Garland innocently.

"I shall put my men on it at once," said the detective.

Garland caught the two-thirty train for a run of an hour and a half to a small city.

At fifteen minutes before five o'clock Detective Mallory was called to the long distance telephone.

"That Mr. Mallory?" came an excited voice. "Well, this is Carroll Garland. Yes, I am at home. Just as soon as I got here I went straight to my room to get a heavier overcoat. I was putting it on, when I found that the lining had been ripped open just like those other two. Now, what does that mean?"

For the first time in his life a question had been asked to which Mallory would confess that he didn't know the answer. He scratched his head thoughtfully, then stopped doing that to tug violently at his bristly moustache. Finally he hung up the receiver with a bang, and went out personally to look into an affair which had not attracted more than passing interest at the time it was reported.

"I can readily understand," Hutchinson Hatch was saying, "why the burglar took the money; but why did he slit the lining of the overcoat?"

The Thinking Machine didn't say.

"Then why did he go to Dickson's room, and slit the lining of an overcoat which Garland left there?"

Still The Thinking Machine was silent.

"And finally why did he go to Garland's home, in another city forty miles away, and slit the lining of an overcoat there?"

Professor Augustus S. F. X. Van Dusen receded still farther into the depths of a huge chair, and sat for a long time with his squint eyes turned upward, and finger tips pressed together. At last he broke the silence. "You have given me every known fact?"

"Everything," the reporter answered.

"There is really no problem in it at all," The Thinking Machine declared, "unless one of the units remains undiscovered. If all are known, the solution is obvious. When the money is returned to Garland, it will definitely prove the only possible hypothesis that may be advanced."

"When the money is returned?" gasped the reporter.

"That is what I said!" snapped the scientist crustily. "If Garland does not care to lose that thirteen hundred and forty-seven dollars, it would not be wise to press the investigation just now. If you will keep in communication with him, and inform me immediately when he receives the money, I shall undertake to close up the affair. Until then it is really not worth attention."

Nearly a week elapsed before there was another development in the mystery—the return of thirteen hundred and forty-seven dollars, by express from Denver. Accompanying the money was an unsigned note of thanks for the use of it, and a line or two which might have been construed into an apology for the stranger's conduct in Garland's room.

The police were astounded; this was against all the rules of the game. Garland was a little more than astounded, and at the same time delighted at the generosity of the thief. It was not possible to develop any fact as to the identity of the intruder from the express records. Obviously the sender had used a fictitious name in Denver. When Hatch explained this point to The Thinking Machine, it was dismissed with a wave of one slender hand.

"It is really of no consequence," declared the scientist. "Garland knows the name of the man who took the money and cut the overcoat."

"But he says he doesn't," Hatch remonstrated.

"There may be circumstances which make it necessary for him to say that," continued the scientist.

"He is prepared to swear that he never saw the man before."

"That might be quite true," was the curt rejoinder; "but I dare say he does know his name. The next time Garland comes to the city, let me know."

"He is here now," the reporter informed him. "He came in to-day to consult with Detective Mallory about the return of the money."

"That simplifies matters," said the scientist. "We'll see him at once."

Garland was in. Hatch introduced the distinguished man of science, and he came immediately to business.

"Tell me something of your love affairs, Mr. Garland," The Thinking Machine began abruptly.

"My love affairs? I have no love affairs at all."

"Oh, I see; married."

Garland gazed straight into the squinting eyes, with a quizzical expression about his mouth. "I don't see that it is absolutely inconsistent for a man to have a love affair and be married," he said smilingly. "There are men, you know, who are in love with their own wives. I happen to be one of these. When you said love affairs, I presumed you meant—"

"There are men," interrupted The Thinking Machine, "who because of being married dare not admit any other entanglements." The aggressive blue eyes were staring straight into Garland's.

After a moment the young man arose, with something like anger in his manner. "I don't happen to be one of them," he said sharply.

The Thinking Machine shrugged his shoulders. "Now, what is the name of the man who robbed you and cut those coats?" he asked.

"I don't know," retorted Garland.

"I know that is what you told the police," said the scientist; "but believe me, it would be best, and possibly save you trouble, for you to give me the name of that man."

"I don't know it," repeated Garland.

The Thinking Machine seemed satisfied on that point, but with his satisfaction came tiny, sinuous lines in his forehead. Hatch knew what that meant.

"You never saw the man before?" asked the scientist after a moment. The aggressiveness had gone from his voice now.

"No, I never saw him before," Garland replied.

"Nor a photograph of him?"

"No, never."

Almost imperceptibly the lines deepened in the brow of The Thinking Machine. His eyes were narrowed down to mere slits, and his thin lips set into a perfectly straight line. Garland studied the grotesque little figure with a curiosity backed by anger. For a long time there was silence, then:

"Mr. Garland, how long have you been married?"

"Four years."

The Thinking Machine shook his head and arose. "Please pardon me," he continued, "but what is your financial condition?"

"I am a salaried man; but it is a good salary, twelve thousand a year, quite enough for my wife and self."

"Your married life has been happy?"

"Perfectly."

Again The Thinking Machine shook his head.

Ten minutes later he and Hutchinson Hatch were in the street together.

"He has either lied, or else we have overlooked a unit," volunteered the scientist as they walked on. "Now I can't believe that we missed anything—ergo, he lied, and yet I can't believe that."

"Well, that doesn't leave much," the reporter suggested.

"The next step," the scientist went on, "will be to establish beyond all doubt that he told the truth. I leave that to you. Get his record for the last five years, and inquire particularly about his family life, his club life, and always bear in mind the possibility of another woman in the case. There is a woman—some woman—because she was in the automobile. Of course, the case is inconsequential, since the money has been returned; but I happen to be interested in it, because the return of the money bears out my hypothesis, and other things tend to upset it."

Hatch covered the affair thoroughly. Garland had told the truth, as far as investigation could develop. He so informed the scientist.

"It is singular, very singular," remarked The Thinking Machine, in deep abstraction. "By the inexorable rule of logic we reach a point where we must believe that Garland slit the lining of the coats himself, and had the money sent to him from Denver. When we attempt to find a motive for that, we plunge into absurdities. Two and two always make four, Mr. Hatch, not sometimes, but *all* the time. No problem in arithmetic can be correctly solved, if one figure is missing. There is one figure missing. I'll find it. In your investigation of Garland's career you found out something about his father?"

"Yes. He died several years ago. His name, by the way, was also Carroll Garland."

The Thinking Machine turned suddenly and squinted at the reporter. "Here is our missing unit, Mr. Hatch," he said. "Do you happen to know if there were ever any other Carroll Garlands in the family?"

"Years ago, yes. The great-grandfather of the present one was also a Carroll Garland."

The little scientist arose suddenly, paced back and forth half a dozen times, then passed into an adjoining room. Five minutes later he reentered, with his hat and coat. Accompanied by the reporter, he went straight to one of the fashionable clubs, and sent in a card. After a few minutes' wait a young man appeared.

"My name is Van Dusen," began The Thinking Machine. "I came here to see you about a personal matter. Could we go to some place where we should not be disturbed for a minute?"

The young man led the way into a private parlor and closed the door.

"It's about that compromising letter which you carry there," and The Thinking Machine touched the young man on the breast with one long slender finger.

"Did she send you?"

"No."

"Well, what business is it of yours, then?"

"I do not think that a man of honor—a man of your social position—would care to carry about with him a paper which would not only imperil but might wreck the reputation of a woman who is now another man's wife."

That The Thinking Machine had spoken correctly, Hatch could not doubt from the expression on the other's face.

"Another man's wife," repeated the young man in astonishment. "Since when?"

"A week or so ago. She is now in the West with her husband. He knows of the existence of this document, therefore whatever vengeful spirit you may have had in preserving it is wasted. I would advise you to destroy it."

For a minute or more the young man stared straight into the squint eyes. "If the lady in question should have made such a request of me in person, I should have destroyed it," said the young man; "otherwise I—"

"She makes that request now, through me," the scientist lied glibly.

"Did she ask you to come to me?"

"She makes that request now, through me," repeated the scientist.

Again the young man was silent. Finally he slowly removed his overcoat and laid it across the table. Then from a pocket in the lining, the opening of which was concealed in a seam where the sleeve joined the coat, he removed a letter. A strange expression played about his face, reminiscent, thoughtful, even tender, as he offered it to The Thinking Machine. Instead of accepting it, the scientist struck a match and touched it to the corner. In silence the three men watched it burn.

"It is obvious to the dullest intelligence," said The Thinking Machine to Hutchinson Hatch, "that the man who entered Garland's room at the hotel was not a thief. He went there to open the lining of Garland's overcoat. Why? To find something which he had reason to believe was concealed therein. True, he took some money; but we can readily imagine that he happened to need a large sum at the minute, and took it, intending to return it, as he did.

"When we know that he was not a thief, we know that the thing he sought was in the lining of the coat. It just happened that this particular coat was not Garland's. The thief didn't know that when he cut it; but he had been so certain of finding what he sought that he took pains to see if it was Garland's coat. Instead of Garland's name, he found on a tailor's tab inside the pocket the name of Dickson. If we give him credit for intelligence at all, we must give him credit for imagining how another man's coat came into Garland's possession. Therefore, he went to Dickson's room, found Garland's coat, and ripped that as he did the first. Still nothing. Naturally then, he went to Garland's home and ripped open the third coat.

"All this was obvious. Now we come to the less obvious. What was he after? Money? No. He left money behind him. A jewel? Possibly but improbably, because his was not a mercenary pursuit. Then what? The remainder: some document or letter which was of such importance that he practically risked his life for it. Now, was this letter or document of value to himself, or to some one else?

"At this point logic met an obstacle in the veiled woman who waited in the automobile. Would the man permit the woman to take the chance she was taking with him if the document had been of value only to himself? It seems unlikely. On the other hand, if the document was of value to her, might she not insist on accompanying him?

"What paper was he after? A will or a deed? Perhaps; but would not that have gone into a court of law? A letter? More likely. So what did we have? A man risking his life, prison at least, to recover a letter for a woman near and dear to him. She, perhaps, informed him that the letter was concealed in the lining of Carroll Garland's overcoat. How she knew this does not appear. We can even imagine the woman confessing the existence of a letter by which her character was menaced before she consented to become his wife. In that event everything else is accounted for; no other hypothesis would fit all the circumstances, therefore this must be correct. Obviously the stranger knew the name of the man who had the letter; therefore it would seem that there could be no mistake. I failed to see at the moment that there might be another Carroll Garland. When I saw that I telephoned to Garland, and he informed me that he had a cousin of the same name who occasionally visited this city and always stopped at the club where we called. You know what happened when we saw this second Carroll Garland. In searching for a Carroll Garland the stranger came across the wrong man and held him up. That is all, I think."

There was a long silence.

"By the way," Hatch inquired suddenly, "what is the name of the strange man and the woman?"

"Why, I don't know," responded The Thinking Machine in surprise.

The Case of the Scientific Murderer

Certainly no problem that ever came to the attention of The Thinking Machine required in a greater degree subtlety of mind, exquisite analytical sense, and precise knowledge of the marvels of science than did that singular series of events which began with the death of the Honorable Violet Danbury, only daughter and sole heir of the late Sir Duval Danbury, of Leamington, England. In this case The Thinking Machine—more properly, Professor Augustus S. F. X. Van Dusen, Ph. D., M. D., F. R. S., et cetera, et cetera— brought to bear upon an extraordinary mystery of crime that intangible genius of logic which had made him the court of last appeal in his profession. "Logic is inexorable," he has said; and no greater proof of his assertion was possible than in this instance where literally he seemed to pluck a solution of the riddle from the void.

Shortly after eleven o'clock on the morning of Thursday, May 4, Miss Danbury was found dead, sitting in the drawing-room of apartments she was temporarily occupying in a big family hotel on Beacon Street. She was richly gowned, just as she had come from the opera the night before; her marble-white bosom and arms aglitter with jewels. On her face, dark in death as are the faces of those who die of strangulation, was an expression of unspeakable terror. Her parted lips were slightly bruised, as if from a light blow; in her left cheek was an insignificant, bloodless wound. On the floor at her feet was a shattered goblet. There was nothing else unusual, no disorder, no sign of a struggle. Obviously she had been dead for several hours.

All these things considered, the snap judgement of the police— specifically, the snap judgement of Detective Mallory, of the bureau of criminal investigation—was suicide by poison. Miss Danbury had poured some deadly drug into a goblet, sat down, drained it off, and died. Simple and obvious enough. But the darkness in her face? Oh, that! Probably some effect of a poison he didn't happen to be acquainted with. But it looked as if she might have been strangled! Pooh! Pooh! There were no marks on her neck, of fingers or anything else. Suicide, that's what it was—the autopsy would disclose the nature of the poison.

Cursory questions of the usual nature were asked and answered. Had Miss Danbury lived alone? No; she had a companion upon whom, too, devolved the duties of chaperon—a Mrs. Cecelia Montgomery. Where was she? She'd left the city the day before to visit friends in Concord; the manager of the hotel had telegraphed the facts to her. No servants? No. She had availed herself of the service in the hotel. Who had last seem Miss Danbury alive? The elevator attendant the night before, when she had returned from the opera, about half past eleven o'clock. Had she gone alone? No. She had been accompanied by Professor Charles Meredith, of the university. He had returned with her, and left her at the elevator.

"How did she come to know Professor Meredith?" Mallory inquired. "Friend, relative—"

"I don't know," said the hotel manager. "She knew a great many people here. She'd only been in the city two months this time, but once, three years ago, she spent six months here."

"Any particular reason for her coming over? Business, for instance, or merely a visit?"

"Merely a visit, I imagine."

The front door swung open, and there entered at the moment a middle-aged man, sharp-featured, rather spare, brisk in his movements, and distinctly well groomed. He went straight to the inquiry desk.

"Will you please phone to Miss Danbury, and ask her if she will join Mr. Herbert Willing for luncheon at the country club?" he requested. "Tell her I am below with my motor."

At mention of Miss Danbury's name both Mallory and the house manager turned. The boy behind the inquiry desk glanced at the detective blankly. Mr. Willing rapped upon the desk sharply.

"Well, well?" he demanded impatiently. "Are you asleep?"

"Good morning, Mr. Willing," Mallory greeted him.

"Hello, Mallory," and Mr. Willing turned to face him. "What are you doing here?"

"You don't know that Miss Danbury is"—the detective paused a little— "is dead?"

"Dead!" Mr. Willing gasped. "Dead!" he repeated incredulously. "What are you talking about?" He seized Mallory by the arm, and shook him. "Miss Danbury is—"

"Dead," the detective assured him again. "She probably committed suicide. She was found in her apartments two hours ago."

For half a minute Mr. Willing continued to stare at him as if without comprehension, then he dropped weakly into a chair, with his head in his hands. When he glanced up again there was deep grief in his keen face.

"It's my fault," he said simply. "I feel like a murderer. I gave her some bad news yesterday, but I didn't dream she would—" He stopped.

"Bad news?" Mallory urged.

"I've been doing some legal work for her," Mr. Willing explained. "She's been trying to sell a huge estate in England, and just at the moment the deal seemed assured it fell through. I—I suppose it was a mistake to tell her. This morning I received another offer from an unexpected quarter, and I came by to inform her of it." He stared tensely into Mallory's face for a moment without speaking. "I feel like her murderer!" he said again.

"But I don't understand why the failure of the deal—" the detective began; then: "She was rich, wasn't she? What did it matter particularly if the deal did fail?"

"Rich, yes; but land poor," the lawyer elucidated. "The estates to which she held title were frightfully involved. She had jewels and all those things, but see how simply she lived. She was actually in need of money. It would take me an hour to make you understand. How did she die? When? What was the manner of her death?"

Detective Mallory placed before him those facts he had, and finally went away with him in his motor car to see Professor Meredith at the university. Nothing bearing on the case developed as the result of that interview. Mr. Meredith seemed greatly shocked, and explained that his acquaintance with Miss Danbury dated some weeks back, and friendship had grown out of it through a mutual love of music. He had accompanied her to the opera half a dozen times.

"Suicide!" the detective declared, as he came away. "Obviously suicide by poison."

On the following day he discovered for the first time that the obvious is not necessarily true. The autopsy revealed absolutely no trace of poison, either in the body or clinging to the shattered goblet, carefully gathered up and examined. The heart was normal, showing neither constriction nor dilation, as would have been the case had poison been swallowed, or even inhaled.

"It's the small wound in her cheek, then," Mallory asserted. "Maybe she didn't swallow or inhale poison—she injected it directly into her blood through that wound."

"No," one of the examining physicians pointed out. "Even that way the heart would have shown constriction or dilation."

"Oh, maybe not," Mallory argued hopefully.

"Besides," the physician went on, "that wound was made after death. That is proven by the fact that it did not bleed." His brow clouded in perplexity. "There doesn't seem to be the slightest reason for that wound, anyway. It's really a hole, you know. It goes straight through her cheek. It looks as if it might have been made with a large hatpin."

The detective was staring at him. If that wound had been made after death, certainly Miss Danbury didn't make it—she had been murdered! And not murdered for robbery, since her jewels had been undisturbed.

"Straight through her cheek!" he repeated blankly. "By George! Say, if it wasn't poison, what killed her?"

The three examining physicians exchanged glances.

"I don't know that I can make you understand," said one. "She died of absence of air in her lungs, if you follow me."

"Absence of air—well, that's illuminating!" the detective sneered heavily. "You mean she was strangled, or choked to death?"

"I mean precisely what I say," was the reply. "She was not strangled—there is no mark on her throat; or choked—there is no obstruction in her throat. Literally she died of absence of air in her lungs."

Mallory stood silently glowering at them. A fine lot of physicians, these!

"Let's understand one another," he said at last. "Miss Danbury did not die a natural death?"

"No!" emphatically.

"She wasn't poisoned? Or strangled? Or shot? Or stabbed? Or run over by a truck? Or blown up by dynamite? Or kicked by a mule? Nor," he concluded, "did she fall from an aeroplane?"

"No."

"In other words, she just quit living?"

"Something like that," the physician admitted. He seemed to be seeking a means of making himself more explicit. "You know the old nursery theory that a cat will suck a sleeping baby's breath?" he asked. "Well, the death of Miss Danbury was like that, if you understand. It is as if some great animal or—or thing had—" He stopped.

Detective Mallory was an able man, the ablest, perhaps, in the bureau of criminal investigation, but a yellow primrose by the river's brim was to him a yellow primrose, nothing more. He lacked imagination, a common fault of that type of sleuth who combines, more or less happily, a number eleven shoe and a number six hat. The only vital thing he had to go on was the fact that Miss Danbury was dead—murdered, in some mysterious, uncanny way. Vampires were something like that, weren't they? He shuddered a little.

"Regular vampire sort of thing," the youngest of the three physicians remarked, echoing the thought in the detective's mind. "They're supposed to make a slight wound, and—"

Detective Mallory didn't hear the remainder of it. He turned abruptly, and left the room.

On the following Monday morning, one Henry Sumner, a longshoreman in Atlantic Avenue, was found dead sitting in his squalid room. On his face, dark in death, as are the faces of those who die of strangulation, was an expression of unspeakable terror. His parted lips were slightly bruised, as if from a light blow; in his left cheek was an insignificant, bloodless wound. On the floor at his feet was a shattered drinking glass!

'Twas Hutchinson Hatch, newspaper reporter, long, lean, and rather prepossessing in appearance, who brought this double mystery to the attention of The Thinking Machine. Martha, the eminent scientist's one servant, admitted the newspaper man, and he went straight to the laboratory. As he opened the door The Thinking Machine turned testily from his worktable.

"Oh, it's you, Mr. Hatch. Glad to see you. Sit down. What is it?" That was his idea of extreme cordiality.

"If you can spare me five minutes?" the reporter began apologetically.

"What is it?" repeated The Thinking Machine, without raising his eyes.

"I wish I knew," the reporter said ruefully. "Two persons are dead—two persons as widely apart as the poles, at least in social position, have been murdered in precisely the same manner, and it seems impossible that—"

"Nothing is impossible," The Thinking Machine interrupted, in the tone of perpetual irritation which seemed to be a part of him. "You annoy me when you say it."

"It seems highly improbable," Hatch corrected himself, "that there can be the remotest connection between the crimes, yet—"

"You're wasting words," the crabbed little scientist declared impatiently. "Begin at the beginning. Who was murdered? When? How? Why? What was the manner of death?"

"Taking the last question first," the reporter explained, "we have the most singular part of the problem. No one can say the manner of death, not even the physicians."

"Oh!" For the first time The Thinking Machine lifted his petulant, squinting, narrowed eyes, and stared into the face of the newspaper man. "Oh!" he said again. "Go on."

As Hatch talked, the lure of a material problem laid hold of the master mind, and after a little The Thinking Machine dropped into a chair. With his great, grotesque head tilted back, his eyes turned steadily upward, and slender fingers placed precisely tip to tip, he listened in silence to the end.

"We come now," said the newspaper man, "to the inexplicable after developments. We have proven that Mrs. Cecelia Montgomery,

Miss Danbury's companion, did not go to Concord to visit friends; as a matter of fact, she is missing. The police have been able to find no trace of her, and to-day are sending out a general alarm. Naturally, her absence at this particular moment is suspicious. It is possible to conjecture her connection with the death of Miss Danbury, but what about—"

"Never mind conjecture," the scientist broke in curtly. "Facts, facts!"

"Further," and Hatch's bewilderment was evident on his face, "mysterious things have been happening in the rooms where Miss Danbury and this man Henry Sumner were found dead. Miss Danbury was found dead last Thursday. Immediately after the body was removed, Detective Mallory ordered her room locked, his idea being that nothing should be disturbed at least for the present, because of the strange circumstances surrounding her death. When the nature of the Henry Sumner affair became known, and the similarity of the cases recognized, he gave the same order regarding Sumner's room."

Hatch stopped, and stared vainly into the pallid, wizened face of the scientist. A curious little chill ran down his spinal column.

"Some time Tuesday night," he continued, after a moment, "Miss Danbury's room was entered and ransacked; and some time that same night Henry Sumner's room was entered and ransacked. This morning, Wednesday, a clearly defined hand print in blood was found in Miss Danbury's room. It was on the wooden top of a dressing table. It seemed to be a woman's hand. Also, an indistinguishable smudge of blood, which may have been a hand print, was found in Sumner's room!" He paused; The Thinking Machine's countenance was inscrutable. "What possible connection can there be between this young woman of the aristocracy, and this—this longshoreman? Why should—"

"What chair," questioned The Thinking Machine, "does Professor Meredith hold in the university?"

"Greek," was the reply.

"Who is Mr. Willing?"

"One of the leading lawyers of the city."

"Did you see Miss Danbury's body?"

"Yes."

"Did she have a large mouth, or a small mouth?"

The irrelevancy of the questions, to say nothing of their disjointedness, brought a look of astonishment to Hatch's face; and he was a young man who was rarely astonished by the curious methods of The Thinking Machine. Always he had found that the scientist approached a problem from a new angle.

"I should say a small mouth," he ventured. "Her lips were bruised as if—as if something round, say the size of a twenty-five-cent piece, had been crushed against them. There was a queer, drawn, caved-in look to her mouth and cheeks."

"Naturally," commented The Thinking Machine enigmatically. "And Sumner's was the same?"

"Precisely. You say 'naturally.' Do you mean—" There was eagerness in the reporter's question.

It passed unanswered. For half a minute The Thinking Machine continued to stare into nothingness. Finally:

"I dare say Sumner was of the English type? His name is English?"

"Yes; a splendid physical man, a hard drinker, I hear, as well as a hard worker."

Again a pause.

"You don't happen to know if Professor Meredith is now or ever has been particularly interested in physics—that is, in natural philosophy?"

"I do not."

"Please find out immediately," the scientist directed tersely. "Willing has handled some legal business for Miss Danbury. Learn what you can from him to the general end of establishing some connection, a relationship possibly, between Henry Sumner and the Honorable Violet Danbury. That, at the moment, is the most important thing to do. Neither of them may have been aware of the relationship, if relationship it was, yet it may have existed. If it doesn't exist, there's only one answer to the problem."

"And that is?" Hatch asked.

"The murders are the work of a madman," was the tart rejoinder. "There's no mystery, of course, in the manner of the deaths of these two."

"No mystery?" the reporter echoed blankly. "Do you mean you know how they—"

"Certainly I know, and you know. The examining physicians know, only they don't know that they know." Suddenly his tone became didactic. "Knowledge that can't be applied is utterly useless," he said. "The real difference between a great mind and a mediocre mind is only that the great mind applies its knowledge." He was silent a moment. "The only problem remaining here is to find the person who was aware of the many advantages of this method of murder."

"Advantages?" Hatch was puzzled.

"From the viewpoint of the murderer there is always a good way and a bad way to kill a person," the scientist told him. "This particular murderer chose a way that was swift, silent, simple, and sure as the march of time. There was no scream, no struggle, no pistol shot, no poison to be traced, nothing to be seen except—"

"The hole in the left cheek, perhaps?"

"Quite right, and that leaves no clew. As a matter of fact, the only clew we have at all is the certainty that the murderer, man or woman, is well acquainted with physics, or natural philosophy."

"Then you think," the newspaper man's eyes were about to start from his head, "that Professor Meredith—"

"I think nothing," The Thinking Machine declared briefly. "I want to know what he knows of physics, as I said; also I want to know if there is any connection between Miss Danbury and the longshoreman. If you'll attend to—"

Abruptly the laboratory door opened and Martha entered, pallid, frightened, her hands shaking.

"Something most peculiar, sir," she stammered in her excitement.

"Well?" the little scientist questioned.

"I do believe," said Martha, "that I'm a-going to faint!"

And as an evidence of good faith she did, crumpling up in a little heap before their astonished eyes.

"Dear me! Dear me!" exclaimed The Thinking Machine petulantly. "Of all the inconsiderate things! Why couldn't she have told us before she did that?"

It was a labor of fifteen minutes to bring Martha around, and then weakly she explained what had happened. She had answered a ring of the telephone, and some one had asked for Professor Van Dusen. She inquired the name of the person talking.

"Never mind that," came the reply. "Is he there? Can I see him?"

"You'll have to explain what you want, sir," Martha had told him. "He always has to know."

"Tell him I know who murdered Miss Danbury and Henry Sumner," came over the wire. "If he'll receive me I'll be right up."

"And then, sir," Martha explained to The Thinking Machine, "something must have happened at the other end, sir. I heard another man's voice, then a sort of a choking sound, sir, and then they cursed me, sir. I didn't hear any more. They hung up the receiver or something, sir." She paused indignantly. "Think of him, sir, a-swearing at me!"

For a moment the eyes of the two men met; the same thought had come to them both. The Thinking Machine voiced it.

"Another one!" he said. "The third!"

With no other word he turned and went out; Martha followed him grumblingly. Hatch shuddered a little. The hand of the clock went on to half past seven, to eight. At twenty minutes past eight the scientist reentered the laboratory.

"That fifteen minutes Martha was unconscious probably cost a man's life, and certainly lost to us an immediate solution of the riddle," he declared peevishly. "If she had told us before she fainted there is a chance that the operator would have remembered the number. As it is, there have been fifty calls since, and there's no record." He spread his slender hands helplessly. "The manager is trying to find the calling number. Anyway, we'll know to-morrow. Meanwhile, try to see Mr. Willing to-night, and find out about what relationship, if any, exists between Miss Danbury and Sumner; also, see Professor Meredith."

The newspaper man telephoned to Mr. Willing's home in Melrose to see if he was in; he was not. On a chance he telephoned to his office. He hardly expected an answer, and he got none. So it was not until four o'clock in the morning that the third tragedy in the series came to light.

The scrubwomen employed in the great building where Mr. Willing had his law offices entered the suite to clean up. They found Mr. Willing there, gagged, bound hand and foot, and securely lashed to a chair. He was alive, but apparently unconscious from exhaustion. Directly facing him his secretary, Maxwell Pittman, sat dead in his chair. On his face, dark in death, as are the faces of those who die of strangulation, was an expression of unspeakable terror. His parted lips were slightly bruised, as if from a light blow; in his left cheek was an insignificant, bloodless wound!

Within an hour Detective Mallory was on the scene. By that time Mr. Willing, under the influence of stimulants, was able to talk.

"I have no idea what happened," he explained. "It was after six o'clock, and my secretary and I were alone in the offices, finishing up some work. He had stepped into another room for a moment, and I was at my desk. Some one crept up behind me, and held a drugged cloth to my nostrils. I tried to shout, and struggled, but everything grew black, and that's all I know. When I came to myself poor Pittman was there, just as you see him."

Snooping about the offices, Mallory came upon a small lace handkerchief. He seized upon it tensely, and as he raised it to examine it he became conscious of a strong odor of drugs. In one corner of the handkerchief there was a monogram.

"'C. M.,'" he read; his eyes blazed. "Cecelia Montgomery!"

In the grip of an uncontrollable excitement Hutchinson Hatch bulged in upon The Thinking Machine in his laboratory.

"There was another," he announced.

"I know it," said The Thinking Machine, still bent over his worktable. "Who was it?"

"Maxwell Pittman," and Hatch related the story.

"There may be two more," the scientist remarked. "Be good enough to call a cab."

"Two more?" Hatch gasped in horror. "Already dead?"

"There may be, I said. One, Cecelia Montgomery, the other the unknown who called on the telephone last night." He started away, then returned to his worktable. "Here's rather an interesting experiment," he said. "See this tube," and he held aloft a heavy glass vessel, closed at one end, and with a stopcock at the other. "Observe. I'll place this heavy piece of rubber over the mouth of the tube, and then turn the stopcock." He suited the action to the word. "Now take it off."

The reporter tugged at it until the blood rushed to his face, but was unable to move it. He glanced up at the scientist in perplexity.

"What hold it there?"

"Vacuum," was the reply. "You may tear it to pieces, but no human power can pull it away whole." He picked up a steel bodkin, and thrust it through the rubber into the mouth of the tube. As he withdrew it, came a sharp, prolonged, hissing sound. Half a minute later the rubber fell off. "The vacuum is practically perfect—something like one-millionth of an atmosphere. The pin hole permits the air to fill the tube, the tremendous pressure against the rubber is removed, and—" He waved his slender hands.

In that instant a germ of comprehension was born in Hatch's brain; he was remembering some college experiments.

"If I should place that tube to your lips," The Thinking Machine resumed, "and turn the stopcock, you would never speak again, never scream, never struggle. It would jerk every particle of air out of your body, paralyze you; within two minutes you would be dead. To remove the tube I should thrust the bodkin through your cheek, say your left, and withdraw it—"

Hatch gasped as the full horror of the thing burst upon him. "Absence of air in the lungs," the examining physicians had said.

"You see, there was no mystery in the manner of the deaths of these three," The Thinking Machine pointed out. "You knew what I have shown you, the physicians knew it, but neither of you knew you knew it. Genius is the ability to apply the knowledge you may have, not the ability to acquire it." His manner changed abruptly. "Please call a cab," he said again.

Together they were driven straight to the university, and shown into Professor Meredith's study. Professor Meredith showed his astonishment plainly at the visit, and astonishment became indignant amazement at the first question.

"Mr. Meredith, can you account for every moment of your time from mid-afternoon yesterday until four o'clock this morning?" The

Thinking Machine queried flatly. "Don't misunderstand me—I mean every moment covering the time in which it is possible that Maxwell Pittman was murdered?"

"Why, it's a most outrageous—" Professor Meredith exploded.

"I'm trying to save you from arrest," the scientist explained curtly. "If you can account for all that time, and prove your statement, believe me, you had better prepare to do so. Now, if you could give me any information as to—"

"Who the devil are you?" demanded Professor Meredith belligerently. "What do you mean by daring to suggest—"

"My name is Van Dusen," said The Thinking Machine, "Augustus S. F. X. Van Dusen. Long before your time I held the chair of philosophy in this university. I vacated it by request. Later the university honored me with a degree of LL. D."

The result of the self-introduction was astonishing. Professor Meredith, in the presence of the master mind in the sciences, was a different man.

"I beg your pardon," he began.

"I'm curious to know if you are at all acquainted with Miss Danbury's family history," the scientist went on. "Meanwhile, Mr. Hatch, take the cab, and go straight and measure the precise width of the bruise on Pittman's lips; also, see Mr. Willing, if he is able to receive you, and ask him what he can give you as to Miss Danbury's history—I mean her family, her property, her connections, all about everything. Meet me at my house in a couple of hours."

Hatch went out, leaving them together. When he reached the scientist's home The Thinking Machine was just coming out.

"I'm on my way to see Mr. George Parsons, the so-called copper king," he volunteered. "Come along."

From that moment came several developments so curious, and bizarre, and so widely disassociated that Hatch could make nothing of them at all. Nothing seemed to fit into anything else. For instance, The Thinking Machine's visit to Mr. Parsons' office.

"Please ask Mr. Parsons if he will see Mr. Van Dusen?" he requested of an attendant.

"What about?" the query came from Mr. Parsons.

"It is a matter of life and death," the answer went back.

"Whose?" Mr. Parsons wanted to know.

"His!" The scientist's answer was equally short.

Immediately afterward The Thinking Machine disappeared inside. Ten minutes later he came out, and he and Hatch went off together, stopping at a toy shop to buy a small, high-grade, hard-rubber ball; and later at a department store to purchase a vicious-looking hatpin.

"You failed to inform me, Mr. Hatch, of the measurement of the bruise?"

"Precisely one and a quarter inches."

"Thanks! And what did Mr. Willing say?"

"I didn't see him as yet. I have an appointment to see him in an hour from now."

"Very well," and The Thinking Machine nodded his satisfaction. "When you see him, will you be good enough to tell him, please, that I know—*I know, do you understand?*—who killed Miss Danbury, and Sumner, and Pittman. You can't make it too strong. *I know—do you understand?*"

"Do you know?" Hatch demanded quickly.

"No," frankly. "But convince him that I do, and add that to-morrow at noon I shall place the extraordinary facts I have gathered in possession of the police. At noon, understand; and *I know!*" He was thoughtful a moment. "You might add that I have informed you that the guilty person is a person of high position, whose name has been in no way connected with the crimes—that is, unpleasantly. You don't know that name; no one knows it except myself. I shall give it to the police at noon to-morrow."

"Anything else?"

"Drop in on me early to-morrow morning, and bring Mr. Mallory."

Events were cyclonic on that last morning. Mallory and Hatch had hardly arrived when there came a telephone message for the detective from police headquarters. Mrs. Cecelia Montgomery was there. She had come in voluntarily, and asked for Mr. Mallory.

"Don't rush off now," requested The Thinking Machine, who was pottering around among the retorts, and microscopes and what not on his worktable. "Ask them to detain her until you get there. Also, ask her just what relationship existed between Miss Danbury and Henry Sumner." The detective went out; the scientist turned to Hatch. "Here is a hatpin," he said. "Some time this morning we shall have another caller. If, during the presence of that person in this room, I voluntarily put anything to my lips, a bottle, say, or anything is forced upon me, and I do not remove it in just thirty seconds, you will thrust this hatpin through my cheek. Don't hesitate."

"Thrust it through?" the reporter repeated. An uncanny chill ran over him as he realized the scientist's meaning. "Is it absolutely necessary to take such a chance to—"

"I say if I don't remove it!" The Thinking Machine interrupted shortly. "You and Mallory will be watching from another room; I shall demonstrate the exact manner of the murders." There was a troubled look in the reporter's face. "I shall be in no danger," the scientist said simply. "The hatpin is merely a precaution if anything should go wrong."

After a little Mallory entered, with clouded countenance.

"She denies the murders," he announced, "but admits that the hand prints in blood are hers. According to her yarn, she searched Miss Danbury's room and Sumner's room after the murders to find some family papers which were necessary to establish claims to some estate—I don't quite understand. She hurt her hand in Miss Danbury's room, and it bled a lot, hence the hand print. From there she went straight to Sumner's room, and presumably left the smudge there. It seems that Sumner was a distant cousin of Miss Danbury's—the only son of a younger brother who ran away years ago after some wild escapade, and came to this country. George Parsons, the copper king, is the only other relative in this country. She advises us to warn him to be on his guard—seems to think he will be the next victim."

"He's already warned," said The Thinking Machine, "and he has gone West on important business."

Mallory stared.

"You seem to know more about this case than I do," he sneered.

"I do," asserted the scientist, "quite a lot more."

"I think the third degree will change Mrs. Montgomery's story some," the detective declared. "Perhaps she will remember better—"

"She is telling the truth."

"Then why did she run away? How was it we found her handkerchief in Mr. Willing's office after the Pittman affair? How was it—"

The Thinking Machine shrugged his shoulders, and was silent. A moment later the door opened, and Martha appeared, her eyes blazing with indignation.

"That man who swore at me over the telephone," she announced distinctly, "wants to see you, sir."

Mallory's keen eyes swept the faces of the scientist and the reporter, trying to fathom the strange change that came over them.

"You are sure, Martha?" asked The Thinking Machine.

"Indeed I am, sir." She was positive about it. "I'd never forget his voice, sir."

For an instant her master merely stared at her, then dismissed her with a curt, "Show him in," after which he turned to the detective and Hatch.

"You will wait in the next room," he said tersely. "If anything happens, Mr. Hatch, remember."

The Thinking Machine was sitting when the visitor entered—a middle-aged man, sharp-featured, rather spare, brisk in his movements, and distinctly well groomed. It was Herbert Willing, attorney. In one hand he carried a small bag. He paused an instant, and gazed at the diminutive scientist curiously.

"Come in, Mr. Willing," The Thinking Machine greeted. "You want to see me about—" He paused questioningly.

"I understand," said the lawyer suavely, "that you have interested yourself in these recent—er—remarkable murders, and there are some points I should like to discuss with you. I have some papers in my bag here, which"—he opened it— "may be of interest. Some, er—newspaper man informed me that you have certain information indicating the person—"

"I know the name of the murderer," said The Thinking Machine.

"Indeed! May I ask who it is?"

"You may. His name is Herbert Willing."

Watching tensely Hatch saw The Thinking Machine pass his hand slowly across his mouth as if to stifle a yawn; saw Willing leap forward suddenly with what seemed to be a bottle in his hand; saw him force the scientist back into his chair, and thrust the bottle against his lips. Instantly came a sharp click, and some hideous change came over the scientist's wizened face. His eyes opened wide in terror, his cheeks seemed to collapse. Instinctively he grasped the bottle with both hands.

For a scant second Willing stared at him, his countenance grown demoniacal; then he swiftly took something else from the small bag, and smashed it on the floor. It was a drinking glass!

After which the scientist calmly removed the bottle from his lips.

"The broken drinking glass," he said quietly, "completes the evidence."

Hutchinson Hatch was lean and wiry, and hard as nails; Detective Mallory's bulk concealed muscles of steel, but it took both of them to overpower the attorney. Heedless of the struggling trio The Thinking Machine was curiously scrutinizing the black bottle. The mouth was blocked by a small rubber ball, which he had thrust against it with his tongue a fraction of an instant before the dreaded power the bottle held had been released by pressure upon a cunningly concealed spring. When he raised his squinting eyes at last, Willing, manacled, was glaring at him in impotent rage. Fifteen minute later the four were at police headquarters; Mrs. Montgomery was awaiting them.

"Mrs. Montgomery, why,"—and the petulant pale-blue eyes of The Thinking Machine were fixed upon her face— "why didn't you go to Concord, as you had said?"

"I did go there," she replied. "It was simply that when news came of Miss Danbury's terrible death I was frightened, I lost my head; I pleaded with my friends not to let it be known that I was there, and they agreed. If any one had searched their house I would have been found; no one did. At last I could stand it no longer. I came to the city, and straight here to explain everything I knew in connection with the affair."

"And the search you made of Miss Danbury's room? And of Sumner's room?"

"I've explained that," she said. "I knew of the relationship between poor Harry Sumner and Violet Danbury, and I knew each of them had certain papers which were of value as establishing their claims to a great estate in England now in litigation. I was sure those papers would be valuable to the only other claimant, who was—"

"Mr. George Parsons, the copper king," interposed the scientist. "You didn't find the papers you sought because Willing had taken them. That estate was the thing he wanted, and I dare say by some legal jugglery he would have gotten it." Again he turned to face Mrs. Montgomery. "Living with Miss Danbury, as you did, you probably held a key to her apartment? Yes. You had only the difficulty then, of entering the hotel late at night, unseen, and that seemed to be simple. Willing did it the night he killed Miss Danbury, and left it unseen, as you did. Now, how did you enter Sumner's room?"

"It was a terrible place," and she shuddered slightly. "I went in alone, and entered his room through a window from a fire escape. The newspapers, you will remember, described its location precisely, and—"

"I see," The Thinking Machine interrupted. He was silent a moment. "You're a shrewd man, Willing, and your knowledge of natural philosophy is exact if not extensive. Of course, I knew if you thought I knew too much about the murders you would come to me. You did. It was a trap, if that's any consolation to you. You fell into it. And, curiously enough, I wasn't afraid of a knife or a shot; I knew the instrument of death you had been using was too satisfactory and silent for you to change. However, I was prepared for it, and—I think that's all." He arose.

"All?" Hatch and Mallory echoed the word. "We don't understand—"

"Oh!" and The Thinking Machine sat down again. "It's logic. Miss Danbury was dead—neither shot, stabbed, poisoned, nor choked; 'absence of air in her lungs,' the physicians said. Instantly the vacuum bottle suggested itself. That murder, as was the murder of

Sumner, was planned to counterfeit suicide, hence the broken goblet on the floor. Incidentally the murder of Sumner informed me that the crimes were the work of a madman, else there was an underlying purpose which might have arisen through a relationship. Ultimately I established that relationship through Professor Meredith, in whom Miss Danbury had confided to a certain extent; at the same time he convinced me of his innocence in the affair.

"Now," he continued, after a moment, "we come to the murder of Pittman. Pittman learned, and tried to phone me, who the murderer was. Willing heard that message. He killed Pittman, then bound and gagged himself, and waited. It was a clever ruse. His story of being overpowered and drugged is absurd on the face of it, yet he asked us to believe that by leaving a handkerchief of Mrs. Montgomery's on the floor. That was reeking with drugs. Mr. Hatch can give you more of these details." He glanced at his watch. "I'm due at a luncheon, where I am to make an address to the Society of Psychical Research. If you'll excuse me—"

He went out; the others sat staring after him.

The Jackdaw Girl

Monsieur Jean Saint Rocheville lived by his wits, and, being rather witty, he lived rather well. In the beginning he hadn't been Monsieur Jean St. Rocheville at all. Born Jones, christened James Aloysius, nicknamed Jimmie, he had been, first, a pickpocket. Sheer ability lifted him above that; and it came to pass that he graduated from all the cruder professions—second-story work, burglary, and what not—until now, when we meet him, he was a social brigand famous under many names.

For instance, in two cities of the West he was being industriously sought as Wilhelm Van Der Wyde, and was described as of the aesthetic, musical type—young, thick-spectacled, clean-shaven, long-haired, and pale blond, speaking English badly and profusely.

In New York, the police knew him as Hubert Montgomery Wade, card sharp and utterer of worthless checks; and described him as taciturn, past middle age, with fluffy, iron-gray hair, full iron-gray beard, and a singularly pallid face. As we see him, he seemed about thirty, slim, elegant, aristocratic of feature, with close-cut brown hair, carefully waxed mustache, and a suggestion of an imperial. Also, he spoke English with a slight accent.

Monsieur St. Rocheville was smiling as he strode through the spacious estate of Idlewild, whipping his light cane in the early-morning air of a balmy June day. On the whole, he had little to complain of in the way the world was wagging. True, he had failed, at his first attempt, to possess himself of the superb diamond necklace of his hostess, Mrs. Wardlaw Browne; but it had not been a discreditable failure; there had been no unpleasant features connected therewith, no exposure; not even a shadow of suspicion.

Perhaps, after all, he had been hasty. His invitation had several weeks to run; and meanwhile here were all the luxuries of a splendid country place at his command—motors, horses, tennis, golf, to say nothing of a house full of charming women and several execrable players of auction, who insisted on gambling for high stakes. And auction, Monsieur St. Rocheville might have said, was his middle name.

Idly meditating upon all these pleasant things, St. Rocheville dropped down upon a seat in the shade of a hedge overlooking the rose garden, lighted a cigarette, and fell to watching the curious evolutions of three great velvet-black birds swimming in the air above him. Now they rose in a vast spiral, up, up until they were mere specks against the blue void, only to drop sheerly almost to the earth before their wings stayed them; now with motionless pinions, floating away in immense circles; again darting hither and yon swiftly as an arrow flies, weaving strange patterns in the air. Something here for the Wright brothers to learn, Monsieur St. Rocheville thought lazily.

Came finally an odd whistle from the direction of the house behind him. The three birds swooped down with a rush and vanished beyond the hedge. Curiously St. Rocheville peered through the thick-growing screen. On a second-story balcony stood a girl with one of the birds perched upon each shoulder, and the third at rest on her hand.

"Well, by George!" exclaimed St. Rocheville.

As he looked, the girl flipped something into the air. The birds dived for it simultaneously, immediately returning to their perches. Fascinated, he looked on as the trick was repeated. So this was she, to whom he had heard some one refer as the Jackdaw Girl— the young lady he had caught staring at him so oddly the night before, just after her arrival. He had been introduced to her between rubbers—a charming, piquant wisp of a creature, with big, innocent eyes and cameo features, much given to gay little bursts of laughter. Her name? Oh, yes. Fayerwether—Drusila Fayerwether.

St. Rocheville ventured into the open. Miss Fayerwether smiled, and flung a titbit of some sort directly at his feet. The birds came for it like huge black projectiles. Involuntarily he took a step backward. She laughed.

"They won't hurt you, really," she assured him mockingly. "They are quite tame. Let me show you." She held aloft a slice of toast; the powerful black wings quivered expectantly. "No," she commanded. The toast fell at St. Rocheville's feet. Neither of the birds stirred. "Hold it in your left hand," she directed. Mechanically the astonished young man obeyed. "Extend your right and keep it steady." He did so. "Now, Blitz!"

It was a command. The bird from her left shoulder, the largest of the three, came hurtling toward St. Rocheville with a shrill scream. For an instant the giant wings beat about his ears, then the talons closed on his right hand in no gentle grip, and man and bird stared at each other. To the young man there was something evil and cruel in the beady, fixed eyes; in the poise of the head on the glistening, snakelike neck; in the merciless claws. And, gad, what a beak! It was a thing to tear with, to mutilate, destroy.

St. Rocheville shuddered. The whole performance was creepy and uncanny. It chilled his blood. It seemed out of all proportion, this exquisite, dainty, pink-and-white girl, and the sinister, somber, winged things—

He drew a breath of relief when Blitz, having solemnly gobbled up his toast, flew away to his mistress.

"They are my pets," she said affectionately. "Aren't they beautiful? Blitz and Jack and Jill I call them."

"Strange pets they are, mademoiselle," remarked St. Rocheville gravely. "How did you come to choose them?"

"Why, I've known them always," she replied. "Blitz here is old enough, and I dare say wise enough, to be my grandfather. He is nearly sixty, and was in my family thirty-five years before I was born. He used to stalk solemnly around my cradle like a soldier on guard, and swear dreadfully. He talks a little when he will—half a dozen words or so. Jack and Jill are younger. From their conduct, I should say they haven't yet reached the age of discretion."

"Would you mind telling me," he questioned curiously, "how a person would proceed to tame a—a flock of flying machines like that?"

"Sugar," replied Miss Fayerwether tersely. "They will do anything for sugar."

"Sugar!" Blitz screamed harshly, ruffling his silky plumage. "Sugar!"

Monsieur St. Rocheville went away to keep a tennis engagement. Miss Fayerwether disappeared into her room, leaving the three birds perched on the rail of the balcony. On the court, Rex Miller was waiting for St. Rocheville with a question:

"Meet the new girl last night? Miss Fayerwether?"

"Yes."

"They say she's a bird charmer," Rex went on. "She charmed me, all right. Gad, I always knew I was a bird!"

In his own apartments again, St. Rocheville, hot from his exertions on the tennis court, was preparing for a cold plunge, when Blitz fluttered in at the window and perched himself familiarly on the back of a chair.

"Hello!" said St. Rocheville.

"Hello!" Blitz replied promptly.

Astonished, the young man burst out laughing—a laugh which died under the steady glare of the beady eyes. Again, for some unaccountable reason, he was possessed of that singular feeling off horror he had felt at first. He shook it off impatiently and entered the bathroom, leaving Blitz in possession.

He returned just in time to see the big bird darting through the window with something bright dangling from the powerful beak. He knew instantly what it was—his watch! He had left it on a table, and the bird had taken advantage of his absence to steal it. He started toward the window on a run; but, struck by a sudden thought, he stopped, and stood staring into the open, the while he permitted an idea to seep in. Finally he dropped into a chair, his agile mind teeming with possibilities.

Suppose—just suppose—Blitz had been taught to steal? Absurd, of course! Blitz was probably an upright, moral enough bird according to his own lights; but couldn't he be taught to steal? Either Blitz or another bird like him?

He had heard somewhere that magpies would filch any glittering thing and secrete it. Why not jackdaws? Weren't they the same thing, after all? He didn't know.

A tame bird, properly trained, cunning, wary, with an innate faculty of making acquaintances, and powerful on the wing!

St. Rocheville forgot all about his watch in contemplation of a new idea. By George, it was worth an experiment, anyway!

There was a light tapping at his door.

"Monsieur St. Rocheville!" some one called.

"Yes?" he answered.

"It is I, Miss Fayerwether. I think I have your watch here. One of my birds came in my window with it from this direction. Your window was open, so I imagine he—he stole it."

St. Rocheville pulled his bath robe about him and peered out. Miss Fayerwether, with disturbed face, held the watch toward him—the great, solemn-looking bird was perched upon one shoulder.

"Hello!" Blitz greeted him socially.

"It is my watch, yes," said St. Rocheville. "Blitz paid me a visit and took it away with him."

"Naughty, naughty!" and Miss Fayerwether shook one rosy finger under the bird's nose. "He embarrasses me awfully sometimes," she confided. "I can't keep him confined all the time; and he has a trick of picking up any bright thing and bringing it to me."

"Please don't let it disturb you," St. Rocheville begged. "As for you, Monsieur Blitz, I'll keep my eye on you."

Miss Fayerwether vanished down the hall, scolding.

So Blitz had a trick of picking up bright things, eh? Monsieur St. Rocheville was pleased to know it. It was only a question, then, of training the bird to bring the thing he picked up to the right place. Assuredly here was an experiment worth while. In failure or success he was safe. No sane person could blame him for the immoral acts of a bird.

St. Rocheville seemed to have conquered his aversion to Blitz and Jack and Jill, for during the next week he spent hours with them; and hours, too, with their charming mistress. Sometimes he would play games with the birds—curious games—always in the absence of Miss Fayerwether. He would toss bright bits of glass, or even a finger ring, into the grass, or into the open window of his room, and the birds would go hurtling off to search. At length they came to know that there would be a lump of sugar for each on their return, with two pieces for the bird who brought the ring. St. Rocheville found it an absorbing game. He played it for hour after hour, for day after day.

All these things immediately preceded the first public knowledge of that series of robberies within a district of which Idlewild was the center. Miss Fayerwether, it seemed, was the first victim. She had either lost, or mislaid, she said, a diamond and ruby bracelet, and asked Mrs. Wardlaw Browne to have her servants look for it. She pooh-poohed the idea of theft. She had been careless, that was all. Yes, the bracelet was quite valuable; but it would doubtless come to light. She wouldn't have mentioned it at all except for the fact that it was an heirloom.

This politely phrased request opened the floodgates of revelation. Rex Miller had lost a rare scarab stickpin; the elderly Mrs. Scott was minus three valuable rings and an aquamarine hair ornament; Claudia Chanoler had been robbed of a rope of pearls worth thousands—robbed was the word she used; an emerald cameo, the property of Agatha Blalock, was missing. Following closely upon these mysterious happenings came word to Mrs. Wardlaw Browne of similar happening at the near-by estates of friends. A dozen valuable trinkets had vanished from the Willows where the Melville Pages had a house party; and at Sagamore, Mrs. Willets was bewailing the loss of an emerald bracelet which represented a small fortune.

The explosion came the night Mrs. Wardlaw Browne's diamond necklace was stolen. There had been an unpleasant scene of some sort in the card room. Rex Miller seemed to think that there was more than luck in the cards Monsieur St. Rocheville held; and he intimated as much. All things considered, Monsieur St. Rocheville behaved superbly. Being the only winner at the table, he tore the score into bits, and it fluttered to the floor. The other gentlemen understood that he disdained to accept money so long as a doubt remained. So the game ended abruptly, and they joined the ladies in the drawing-room. Ten minutes later Mrs. Wardlaw Browne's necklace vanished utterly.

So ultimately it came to pass that The Thinking Machine—more properly, Professor Augustus S. F. X. Van Dusen, Ph. D., F. R. S., M. D., LL. D., et cetera, et cetera, logician, analyst, and master mind in the sciences—turned his crabbed genius upon the problem. He consented to do so at the request of Hutchinson Hatch, newspaper reporter; and, singularly enough, it was Monsieur Jean St. Rocheville in person who brought the matter to the reporter's attention. Together they went to The Thinking Machine.

"You know," St. Rocheville took the trouble to explain, "every time I read of a robbery of this sort, either in a newspaper or in fiction, some foreign nobleman is always the villain in the piece." He shrugged his shoulders. "It is an honor I do not desire."

"You are a nobleman, then?" queried The Thinking Machine. The narrowed, pale-blue, squinting eyes were fixed tensely upon the young man's face.

"No." St. Rocheville smiled.

"Extraordinary," murmured the little scientist. "And who are you?"

"My father and my father's father are bankers in France." St. Rocheville lied gracefully. "The situation at Idlewild is—"

"Where?" The Thinking Machine interrupted curtly.

"Idlewild."

"I mean, where is your father a banker?"

"Paris."

"In what capacity? What's his position?"

"Managing director."

"What bank?"

"Crédit Lyonnaise."

The Thinking Machine nodded his satisfaction and dropped his enormous head, with its thick, straw-colored thatch, back against the chair comfortably, his slim fingers coming to rest precisely tip to tip. Monsieur St. Rocheville stared at him curiously. Obviously here was a person who was not to be trifled with. However, he felt he had passed his preliminary examination, unexpected as it was, with great credit. Not once had he forgotten his dialect; not for a fraction of a second had he hesitated in answering the abrupt questions. Ability to lie readily is a great convenience.

"Now," The Thinking Machine commanded, his squinting eyes turned upward, "what happened at Idlewild?"

Inadvertently or otherwise, St. Rocheville failed to refer, even remotely, to the three great velvet-black birds—Blitz and Jack and Jill—in his narrative of events at Idlewild. It was rather a chronological statement of the thefts as they had been reported, with no suggestion as to the manner in which they might have been committed.

"Now," and St. Rocheville spoke slowly, as one who wanted to be certain of his words, "I come down to those things which happened immediately before the disappearance of Mrs. Wardlaw Browne's necklace. Frankly my own statement will place me in rather a compromising position—that is, my real motive may not be understood—but it is better that I should tell you in the beginning things that you will surely find out."

"Decidedly better," The Thinking Machine agreed dryly. He didn't alter his position.

"Well, you must know that at Idlewild the men play auction a great deal, and—"

"Auction?" The Thinking Machine repeated. "What is auction, Mr. Hatch?"

"Auction bridge," the reporter told him. "A game of cards—a variation of whist."

Monsieur St., Rocheville stared from the wizened little scientist to the reporter incredulously. He would not have believed a person could have lived in a civilized country and not know what auction was. Perhaps he wouldn't have believed, either, that The Thinking Machine never read a newspaper. So circumscribed is our own viewpoint.

"At Idlewild the men play auction a great deal," The Thinking Machine prompted. "Go on."

"Auction, yes," St. Rocheville resumed. "It happens sometimes that the stakes are rather high. On the night Mrs. Wardlaw Browne's necklace was stolen, four of us were playing in the card room—a Mr. Gordon and myself as partners against a Mr. Miller and Franklin Chanoler, the financier." He hesitated slightly. "Mr. Miller had been losing, and in a burst of temper he intimated that—that I—that I—er—"

"Had been cheating," The Thinking Machine supplied crabbedly. "Go on."

"As a result of that little unpleasantness," St. Rocheville continued, "the game ended, and we joined the ladies. Now, please understand that it is not my wish to retaliate upon Mr. Miller. I have explained my motive—I don't want to be made a scapegoat. I do want the actual facts to come out." Some subtle change passed across his face. "Mr. Miller," he said measuredly, "stole Mrs. Wardlaw Browne's necklace!"

"Miller," Hatch repeated. "Do you mean Rex Miller?"

"That's his name, yes—Rex Miller."

"Rex Miller? The son of John W. Miller, the millionaire?" Hatch came to his feet excitedly.

"Rex Miller is his name, yes," St. Rocheville shrugged his shoulders.

"Oh, that's impossible!" Hatch declared.

"Nothing is impossible, Mr. Hatch," interrupted The Thinking Machine tartly. "Sit down. You annoy me." He shifted his pale-blue eyes, and squinted at Monsieur St. Rocheville through his thick spectacles. "How do you know Mr. Miller stole the necklace?"

"I saw him slip it into the pocket of his dress coat," St. Rocheville declared flatly. "Naturally, I had an idea that, when he drew Mrs. Wardlaw Browne aside immediately after we came out of the card room, it was his intention to—to denounce me as a card sharp. You may imagine that I was watching them both closely, because my honor was at stake. I wanted to see how she took it. It seems that he said nothing whatever to her about the card game; but he did steal the necklace. I saw him hiding it."

Fell a long silence. With inscrutable face The Thinking Machine sat staring at the ceiling.

Twice St. Rocheville shifted his position uneasily. He was wondering if his story had been convincing. Adroit mixture of truth and falsehood that it was, he failed to see a single defect in it. Hatch, too, was staring curiously at the scientist.

"I understand perfectly your hesitation in going into details," said The Thinking Machine at last. "Under all the circumstances your motive might be misconstrued; but I think you have made me understand." He rose suddenly. "That's all," he said. "I'll look into the matter to-morrow."

Monsieur St. Rocheville was about to take his departure, when The Thinking Machine stopped him for a last question.

"You used a phrase just now," he said. "I am anxious to get it exactly—something about your father and your father's father—"

"Oh! I said"—Monsieur St. Rocheville obliged— "that my father and my father's father were bankers in Paris."

"That's it," said the little scientist. "Thanks. Good day."

Monsieur St. Rocheville went out. The Thinking Machine scribbled something on a sheet of paper and handed it to the reporter.

"Attend to that when you get to your office," he directed. Hatch read it, and his eyes opened wide. "Also, do you happen to know a native Frenchman who speaks perfect English?"

"I do; yes."

"Look him up, and ask him to repeat the phrase, 'My father and my father's father.' "

"Why?" inquired the reporter blankly.

"When he says it you'll know why. Immediately this other matter is attended to come back here."

Monsieur St. Rocheville's troubled meditations were disturbed by the appearance of Miss Fayerwether around a bend in the walk. Fluttering about her were her pets, Blitz and Jack and Jill. One after another they would swoop down, gobble up a beakful of sugar from her open hand, then sail off in a circle.

There was something in the sight of Miss Fayerwether to dispel troubled meditations. She was gowned in a filmy white, clinging stuff, with a wide, flapping sun hat, her cheeks glowing with the sun's reflection, her big, innocent eyes repeating the marvelous blue of the sky.

Monsieur St. Rocheville, at sight of her, arose, bowed formally, and made way for her beside him. She sat down, to be instantly submerged in a fluttering cloud of black wings.

"Go away," she ordered. "I have no more sugar. See?" and she extended her empty hands.

The giant birds wandered off seeking what they might find; and for a time the girl and the young man sat silent. Twice Miss Fayerwether's eyes sought St. Rocheville's; twice she caught him staring straight into her face.

"Detectives were here to-day," she remarked at last.

"Yes, I know," said St. Rocheville.

"They had a long talk with Mrs. Wardlaw Browne, and insisted on searching the house—that is, the rooms of the guests—but she would not permit it."

"She made a mistake."

"You mean that some one of the guests—"

"I mean there is a thief here somewhere," said St. Rocheville; "and he should be unmasked." (And this from Jimmie Jones, erstwhile pickpocket, burglar, and what not—Jimmie Jones, alias Wilhelm Van Der Wyde, alias Hubert Montgomery Wade, alias Jean St. Rocheville.) "I am willing for them to search my room; you are willing for them to search your room—the others should be."

The young man's lips were tightly set; there was an uncompromising glint in his eyes. His simulation had been so perfect that even he was feeling the righteous indignation of the hopelessly moral. Whatever else he felt didn't appear at the moment. Miss Fayerwether was gazing dreamily into the void.

"Have you ever been to Chicago?" she queried irrelevantly at last.

"No," said Monsieur St. Rocheville. As a matter of fact, Chicago was one of the cities in which there was being made even then an industrious search for Wilhelm Van Der Wyde.

"Or Denver?" the girl continued dreamily.

That was another city in which Wilhelm Van Der Wyde was badly wanted. Monsieur St. Rocheville turned upon Miss Fayerwether suspiciously.

"No," he declared. "Why?"

"No reason—I was merely curious," she replied carelessly. And then again irrelevantly: "Nothing has been stolen from you?"

For answer, St. Rocheville held out his left hand. A heavy diamond solitaire which he usually wore on his little finger was missing. The print of the ring on the flesh was still visible.

"Oh!" exclaimed Miss Fayerwether; and again: "Oh!" She looked startled. St. Rocheville didn't recall that he had ever seen just such an expression before. "When was your ring stolen? How?"

"I removed it when I got into my bath," St. Rocheville explained. "My window was closed, but my door was unlocked. When I came out of the bath the ring had disappeared—that's all."

"Well"—and there was a flash of indignation in the girl's eyes—"you can't blame that on Blitz, anyway."

"I'm not trying to," said St. Rocheville. "I said my window was closed. My door was closed but unlocked. I don't think Blitz can open a door, can he?"

Miss Fayerwether didn't answer. Once she was almost on the point of saying something further; and, for an instant, there was mute appeal in the innocent eyes as her slim white hand lay on the young man's arm. Then she changed her mind and went on to her room, the birds fluttering along after.

Strange thoughts came to Monsieur St. Rocheville. The light touch on his arm had thrilled him curiously. He found himself staring off moodily in the direction of her window. Also he caught himself remembering the marvelous blue of her eyes! He didn't recall at the moment that he had ever noticed the color of anyone's eyes before.

'Twas an hour after dinner when The Thinking Machine, accompanied by Detective Mallory, the bright light of the Bureau of Criminal Investigation, and one of his satellites, Blanton by name, with Hutchinson Hatch trailing, appeared at Idlewild. It may have been mere accident that St. Rocheville met them as they stepped out of the automobile.

"I neglected to tell you," he remarked to the scientist, "that young Miller has been losing heavily at auction of late; and I hear that he has had some sort of a row with his father about his allowance."

"I understand," The Thinking Machine nodded.

"Also," St. Rocheville ran on, "there has been at least one other theft here since I saw you. A diamond ring of mine was stolen from my room while I was in the bath. I wouldn't venture to say who took it."

"I know," The Thinking Machine assured him curtly. "I will have it in my hand in ten minutes."

Indignant at the intrusion of the police in what she was pleased to term her personal affairs—the detectives who had been there before were from a private agency—Mrs. Wardlaw Browne bustled into the room where The Thinking Machine and his party waited. Monsieur St. Rocheville effaced himself.

"Pray what does this mean?" Mrs. Wardlaw Browne demanded.

"It means, madam, that we have a search warrant, and intend to go through your house, if necessary." The Thinking Machine informed her crustily. Through the half-open door he caught a glimpse of a slender figure—a mere wisp of a girl with big, wonder-stuck eyes. "Mallory, close that door. You, madam,"—this to Mrs. Wardlaw Browne— "can assist us by answering a few questions."

Mrs. Wardlaw Browne was of the tall, gaunt, haughty type; thin to scrawniness, enormously rich, and possessed of all the arrogance that riches bring. She studied the faces of the four men contemptuously; then, with a little resigned expression, sat down.

"Just how did you lose your necklace?" The Thinking Machine began abruptly. "Did you drop it? Was it taken from your neck? Are you sure you had it on?"

"I know I had it on," was the reply. "I did not drop it. It was taken from my neck."

"Did you, by any chance, wear a low-neck gown on the evening it was taken?" The little scientist's squinting eyes were fixed upon her tensely.

"I never wear décolleté," came the frigid response.

With his great head pillowed upon the back of his chair, his thin fingers tip to tip, and his eyes turned upward, The Thinking Machine sat in silence for a minute or more, the while tiny, cobwebby lines appeared in his domelike brow.

"Can you," he inquired finally, "summon a servant without leaving this room?"

"There is a bell, yes." Mrs. Wardlaw Browne was forgetting to be haughty in a certain fascination which grew upon her as she gazed at this little man.

"Will you ring it, please?"

Mrs. Wardlaw Browne arose, touched a button, and sat down again. A moment later a footman entered.

"Tell Mr. Rex Miller," The Thinking Machine directed, "that Mrs. Wardlaw Browne would like to see him immediately in this room."

The footman bowed and withdrew. Followed an interminable wait—interminable, at least, to Detective Mallory, who impatiently clicked his handcuffs together. Mrs. Wardlaw Browne yawned to hide the curiosity that was consuming her.

The door opened, and Rex Miller entered. He stood for a moment staring at the silent party, and finally:

"Did you send for me, Mrs. Browne?"

"I did," said The Thinking Machine. "Sit down, please." Rex sank into a chair mechanically. "Mr. Blanton"—the scientist neither raised his voice nor lowered his eyes— "you will undertake to see that Mr. Miller doesn't leave this room. Mr. Mallory, you will search Mr. Miller's apartments. Somewhere there you will find Mrs. Wardlaw Browne's diamond necklace; also a man's diamond ring."

Rex came to his feet with writhing hands, a thundercloud in his face. Mrs. Wardlaw Browne burst into inarticulate expostulations. Blanton drew a revolver and laid it across his knee. Mallory bustled out. Hatch merely waited. Silence came; a silence so tense, so strained that Mrs. Wardlaw Browne was tempted to scream. At last there were footsteps, the door from the hall was thrown open, and Mallory, triumphant, appeared.

"I have them," he announced grimly. The necklace, a radiant, glittering thing, was dangling from one finger. The ring lay in his open palm. "And now, Mr. Rex Miller"—he fished out his handcuffs and started toward the young man— "if you'll hold out your—"

"Oh, sit down, Mallory!" commanded The Thinking Machine impatiently.

Loitering in a hallway, where he could keep an eye on the stairs leading from the lower part of the house, Monsieur St. Rocheville saw Miss Fayerwether creep stealthily up, silent-footed, chalk-white of face, and come racing toward him across the heavy velvet carpet. For the reason that she would surely see him, he walked toward her, amazed and a little perturbed at something in her manner.

"What's the matter?" inquired St. Rocheville calmly.

"Oh, it's you!" Miss Fayerwether's hand flew to her heart. She was frightened, gasping. "Nothing!"

"But something must be the matter," he insisted. "You are white as a sheet."

With an apparent effort the girl regained control of herself, and stood staring at him mutely. 'Twas in that moment that Monsieur St. Rocheville saw for the first time some strange, new expression in the big, innocent eyes—they seemed to grow hard, worldly, all-wise even as he looked.

"There are detectives in the house," she said.

"I know it. What about it?"

"They have a warrant, and intend to search every room."

"Well?" St. Rocheville refused to get excited about it.

"Including, I imagine, yours and mine."

"I'm willing. I dare say you are."

For an instant the girl's self-possession seemed to desert her completely. Her eyes closed as if in pain, and she swayed a little. St. Rocheville thrust out an arm protectingly.

When she lifted her face again St. Rocheville read terror therein.

"If—if they search my room," she faltered, "I—I am lost!"

"How? Why? What do you mean?"

"I don't know that I could make any one else understand," she went on swiftly. "The birds, you know—Blitz and Jack and Jill. You saw, and I explained to you, a trick they have of—of thieving; stealing bright things."

She stopped. In his impatience St. Rocheville seized her by the arm and shook her soundly.

"Well?" he demanded.

"Nearly every jewel that has been stolen is hidden now in my room," she confessed. "I knew nothing of it until yesterday, when I came across them. Then, after all the excitement about the thefts, I was afraid to return the things, and I could think of no way to proceed. So, you see, if they search my room it will—"

St. Rocheville was possessed of an agile mind; resourceful as it was agile. Suddenly he remembered two questions the girl had asked the day before—questions about Chicago and Denver. His teeth snapped. He thrust out a hand, and, opening the nearest door—he didn't happen to know whose room it was—he dragged her in, and turned on the electric light. Then their eyes met squarely.

"You are the thief, then?" he demanded. "Don't lie to me! You are the thief?"

"The things are in my room." She was sobbing a little. "The birds—"

"You are the thief!" There was a curious note of exultation in his voice. "And you do know something about Chicago and Denver?"

"I know that you are Wilhelm Van Der Wyde," she flashed defiantly. "I recognized you at once. I saw you in old Charles' 'fence' there once when you were not aware of it. I could never be mistaken in your eyes."

Monsieur St. Rocheville laughed blithely; came a faint answering smile, and he gathered her into his arms.

"I've always needed a partner," he said.

"Mr. Miller," The Thinking Machine was saying placidly, "isn't the thief at all." He raised his hand to still a clamor of ejaculation. "Monsieur Rocheville, so called, stole the necklace, at least, and concealed it, with a ring from his own finger, in Mr. Miller's apartment." Again he raised his hand. "Mr. Miller caught Monsieur St. Rocheville cheating at cards, and practically denounced him. Monsieur St. Rocheville took his revenge by undertaking to fasten the jewel thefts upon Mr. Miller. He imagined, shallowly enough, that if the necklace should be found in Mr. Miller's room the police would look no farther. It is barely possible that the police wouldn't have looked farther."

Mrs. Wardlaw Browne's aristocratic mouth had dropped open in sheer astonishment. Detective Mallory looked bewildered, dazed. Rex Miller's face was an animated interrogation mark.

"Then who is the thief?" Mallory found voice to express the burning question.

"I'm sure I don't know," The Thinking Machine confessed frankly. "I think, perhaps, it was Monsieur St. Rocheville, so called; but there's nothing to connect him— Please sit down, Mallory. You annoy me. It would do no good to search his apartment. If he stole anything, it isn't here now; besides—"

The door opened suddenly, and the footman appeared.

"Miss Fayerwether is badly hurt, ma'am," he explained hurriedly. "She seems to have fallen from her window. We found her outside, unconscious."

Mrs. Wardlaw Browne went out hurriedly. Obeying an almost imperceptible nod of The Thinking Machine's head, Detective Mallory followed her. The scientist turned to Detective Blanton.

"Get St. Rocheville," he directed tersely.

Ten minutes later Mallory returned. In one hand he held a small chamois bag. The contents thereof he spilled upon a table. The Thinking Machine glanced around, saw a glittering heap of jewels, then resumed his steady scrutiny of the ceiling.

"The girl had them?"

"Yes," replied the detective. "She tried to escape from her room by sliding down a rope made of sheets. It broke, and she fell."

"Badly hurt?"

"Only a sprained ankle, and shock."

Blanton flung himself in.

"St. Rocheville's gone," he announced hurriedly. "I imagine he cut for it. Went away in one of the automobiles."

When Miss Fayerwether recovered consciousness, and the sharp agony in her ankle had become a mere dull pain, she found herself in some large room, rank with the odor of strange chemical messes. As a matter of fact, it was The Thinking Machine's laboratory; and the three men present were the little scientist in person, Mallory, and Hatch. Blanton had gone on to police headquarters to send out a general alarm for Monsieur St. Rocheville.

"There was no mystery about it," she heard The Thinking Machine saying. "That is, no mystery that the simplest rules of logic wouldn't instantly dissipate. A man, presumably French, but speaking English almost perfectly, comes into this room and betrays himself as an imposter five minutes afterward by using, without a trace of accent, the one phrase in all our language which no Frenchman, unless he is reared from infancy in an English-speaking country, can pronounce as it should be pronounced. This man used the phrase: 'My father and my father's father;' and he pronounced it as either of us would have pronounced it. The French can master our 'th' only with difficulty, and then only at the beginning of a word; otherwise their 'th' becomes almost like our 'z.'

"From the beginning, therefore, I imagined our so-called Monsieur St. Rocheville an imposter. Being an imposter, he was a liar. I proved he was a liar when I made him state who his father was. At my suggestion, Mr. Hatch cabled to Paris, demonstrated that there is not, and never has been a Monsieur St. Rocheville connected with the Crédit Lyonnaise; and, this much established, St. Rocheville's story collapsed utterly. He had been accused of cheating at cards; and in retaliation he tried to shift the thefts upon Mr. Miller. He had seen Mr. Miller, so he said, steal the necklace. His obvious purpose in this was to bring about a search of Mr. Miller's apartment, where he had carefully planted the necklace, also his own ring. The remainder of the story you all know."

Miss Fayerwether had listened breathlessly, with closed eyes. The Thinking Machine arose and came over to her. For an instant his slender, cool hand rested on her brow; and in that instant she fought the fight. She was caught. St. Rocheville, alias Van Der Wyde, was free. He had tried to help her. She was to have gathered the jewels together, escaped through her window to avoid attracting attention, and joined him in the waiting automobile. He was free. She would allow him to remain free. Love, be it said, makes martyrs of us all.

"I stole the jewels," she said quietly. "Monsieur St. Rocheville knew nothing of the thefts. My birds—"

That was all. The door opened and closed. Monsieur St. Rocheville stood before them with a vicious-looking, snub-nosed, automatic pistol in his hand.

"Put up your hands!" he commanded curtly. "You, Mallory, you! Put them up, I say! Put them up!" Mallory put them up. "And you, too! Put them up!" The Thinking Machine and Hutchinson Hatch obeyed unanimously. "Now, Miss Fayerwether, can you walk?"

"I think so." She struggled to her feet.

"Very well." There was a deadly calm in his manner. "Take Mallory's gun, his keys, his handcuffs, and his police whistle. Careful now! Stand on the far side of him. I may have to kill him." The girl obeyed deftly. "Are the handcuffs unlocked? Good! Snap one end around his right wrist. Now, Mallory, lower your right hand!"

"I'll be—" the enraged detective began.

"Lower your right hand." The pistol clicked. "Now, Miss Fayerwether, snap the other end of the handcuff around the leg of his chair, above the rungs." It was done, neatly and quickly. "And I think that will hold you for a few minutes, Mallory. Now, Miss Fayerwether, there's an automobile outside. The motor is running. Get in the car. Take your time. Safely in, honk the horn three times."

The girl hobbled out. Monsieur St. Rocheville took advantage of the pause to sneer a little at the three men—Mallory safely shackled to a heavy chair, which would effectually stop immediate pursuit; Hatch with his hands anxiously stretched into the air, The Thinking Machine placidly meeting his gaze, eye to eye.

"I'll get you yet!" Mallory bellowed in impotent rage.

"Oh, perhaps." Outside, the automobile horn sounded thrice. "Until then, au revoir!" and Monsieur St. Rocheville vanished as silently as he had come.

"There's loyalty for you," observed The Thinking Machine, as if astonished.

"Love, not loyalty," Hatch declared. "He's crazy about her. Nothing on earth would have brought him back but love."

"Love!" mused the little scientist. "A most interesting phenomena. I shall have to look into it some time."

As I have said, Monsieur St. Rocheville was a young man of resource and daring. Later that night he burglariously entered the room Miss Fayerwether had occupied at Idlewild, and took Blitz and Jack and Jill away with him, cage and all.

The Tragedy of the Life Raft

'Twas a shabby picture altogether—old Peter Ordway in his office; the man shriveled, bent, cadaverous, aquiline of feature, with skin like parchment, and cunning, avaricious eyes; the room gaunt and curtainless, with smoke-grimed windows, dusty, cheerless walls, and threadbare carpet, worn through here and there to the rough flooring beneath. Peter Ordway sat in a swivel chair in front of an ancient roll-top desk. Opposite, at a typewriter upon a table of early vintage, was his secretary—one Walpole, almost a replica in middle age of his employer, seedy and servile, with lips curled sneeringly as a dog's.

Familiarly in the financial district, Peter Ordway was "The Usurer," a title which was at once a compliment to his merciless business sagacity and an expression of contempt for his methods. He was the money lender of the Street, holding in cash millions which no one dared to estimate. In the last big panic the richest man in America, the great John Morton in person, had spent hours in the shabby office, begging for the loan of the few millions in currency necessary to check the market. Peter Ordway didn't fail to take full advantage of his pressing need. Mr. Morton got the millions on collateral worth five times the sum borrowed, but Peter Ordway fixed the rate of interest, a staggering load.

Now we have the old man at the beginning of a day's work. After glancing through two or three letters which lay open on his desk, he picked up at last a white card, across the face of which was scribbled in pencil three words only:

One million dollars!

Ordinarily it was a phrase to bring a smile to his withered lips, a morsel to roll under his wicked old tongue; but now he stared at it without comprehension. Finally he turned to his secretary, Walpole.

"What is this?" he demanded querulously, in his thin, rasping voice.

"I don't know, sir," was the reply. "I found it in the morning's mail, sir, addressed to you."

Peter Ordway tore the card across, and dropped it into the battered wastebasket beside him, after which he settled down to the ever-congenial occupation of making money.

On the following morning the card appeared again, with only three words, as before:

One million dollars!

Abruptly the aged millionaire wheeled around to face Walpole, who sat regarding him oddly.

"It came the same way, sir," the seedy little secretary explained hastily, "in a blank envelope. I saved the envelope, sir, if you would like to see it."

"Tear it up!" Peter Ordway directed sharply.

Reduced to fragments, the envelope found its way into the wastebasket. For many minutes Peter Ordway sat with dull, lusterless eyes, gazing through the window into the void of a leaden sky. Slowly, as he looked, the sky became a lashing, mist-covered sea, a titanic chaos of water; and upon its troubled bosom rode a life raft to which three persons were clinging. Now the frail craft was lifted up, up to the dizzy height of a giant wave; now it shot down sickeningly into the hissing trough beyond; again, for minutes it seemed altogether lost in the far-plunging spume. Peter Ordway shuddered and closed his eyes.

On the third morning the card, grown suddenly ominous, appeared again:

One million dollars!

Peter Ordway came to his feet with an exclamation that was almost a snarl, turning, twisting the white slip nervously in his talonlike fingers. Astonished, Walpole half arose, his yellow teeth bared defensively, and his eyes fixed upon the millionaire.

"Telephone Blake's Agency," the old man commanded, "and tell them to send a detective here at once."

Came in answer to the summons a suave, smooth-faced, indolent-appearing young man, Fragson by name, who sat down after having regarded with grave suspicion the rickety chair to which he was invited. He waited inquiringly.

"Find the person—man or woman—who sent me that!"

Peter Ordway flung the card and the envelope in which it had come upon a leaf of his desk. Fragson picked them up and scrutinized them leisurely. Obviously the handwriting was that of a man, an uneducated man, he would have said. The postmark on the envelope was Back Bay; the time of mailing seven p.m. on the night before. Both envelope and card were of a texture which might be purchased in a thousand shops.

"'One million dollars!' " Fragson read. "What does it mean?"

"I don't know," the millionaire answered.

"What do you think it means?"

"Nor do I know that, unless—unless it's some crank, or—or blackmailer. I've received three of them—one each morning for three days."

Fragson placed the card inside the envelope with irritating deliberation, and thrust it into his pocket, after which he lifted his eyes quite casually to those of the secretary, Walpole. Walpole, who had been staring at the two men tensely, averted his shifty gaze, and busied himself at his desk.

"Any idea who sent them?" Fragson was addressing Peter Ordway, but his eyes lingered lazily upon Walpole.

"No." The word came emphatically, after an almost imperceptible instant of hesitation.

"Why"—and the detective turned to the millionaire curiously—"why do you think it might be blackmail? Has any one any knowledge of any act of yours that—"

Some swift change crossed the parchmentlike face of the old man. For an instant he was silent; then his avaricious eyes leaped into flame; his fingers closed convulsively on the arms of his chair.

"Blackmail may be attempted without reason," he stormed suddenly. "Those cards must have some meaning. Find the person who sent them."

Fragson arose thoughtfully, and drew on his gloves.

"And then?" he queried.

"That's all!" curtly. "Find him, and let me know who he is."

"Do I understand that you don't want me to go into his motives? You merely want to locate the man?"

"That understanding is correct—yes."

... a lashing, mist-covered sea; a titanic chaos of water, and upon its troubled bosom rode a life raft to which three persons were clinging. ...

Walpole's crafty eyes followed his millionaire employer's every movement as he entered his office on the morning of the fourth day. There was nervous restlessness in Peter Ordway's manner; the parchment face seemed more withered; the pale lips were tightly shut. For an instant he hesitated, as if vaguely fearing to begin on the morning's mail. But no fourth card had come! Walpole heard and understood the long breath of relief which followed upon realization of this fact.

Just before ten o'clock a telegram was brought in. Peter Ordway opened it:

One million dollars!

Three hours later at his favorite table in the modest restaurant where he always went for luncheon, Peter Ordway picked up his napkin, and a white card fluttered to the floor:

One million dollars!

Shortly after two o'clock a messenger boy entered his office, whistling, and laid an envelope on the desk before him:

One million dollars!

Instinctively he had known what was within.

At eight o'clock that night, in the shabby apartments where he lived with his one servant, he answered an insistent ringing of the telephone bell.

"What do you want?" he demanded abruptly.

"One million dollars!" The words came slowly, distinctly.

"Who are you?"

"One million dollars!" faintly, as an echo.

Again Fragson was summoned, and was ushered into the cheerless room where the old millionaire sat cringing with fear, his face reflecting some deadly terror which seemed to be consuming him. Incoherently he related the events of the day. Fragson listened without comment, and went out.

On the following morning—Sunday—he returned to report. He found his client propped upon a sofa, haggard and worn, with eyes feverishly aglitter.

"Nothing doing," the detective began crisply. "It looked as if we had a clew which would at least give us a description of the man, but—" He shook his head.

"But that telegram—some one filed it?" Peter Ordway questioned huskily. "The message the boy brought—"

"The telegram was inclosed in an envelope with the money necessary to send it, and shoved through the mail slot of a telegraph office in Cambridge," the detective informed him explicitly. "That was Friday night. It was telegraphed to you on Saturday morning. The card brought by the boy was handed in at a messenger agency by some street urchin, paid for, and delivered to you. The telephone call was from an automatic station in Brookline. A thousand persons use it every day."

For the first time in many years, Peter Ordway failed to appear at his office Monday morning. Instead he sent a note to his secretary:

Bring all important mail to my apartment to-night at eight o'clock. On your way uptown buy a good revolver with cartridges to fit.

Twice that day a physician—Doctor Anderson—was hurriedly summoned to Peter Ordway's side. First there had been merely a fainting spell; later in the afternoon came complete collapse. Doctor Anderson diagnosed the case tersely.

"Nerves," he said. "Overwork, and no recreation."

"But, doctor, I have no time for recreation!" the old millionaire whined. "My business—"

"Time!" Doctor Anderson growled indignantly. "You're seventy years old, and you're worth fifty million dollars. The thing you must have if you want to spend any of that money is an ocean trip—a good, long ocean trip—around the world, if you like."

"No, no, no!" It was almost a shriek. Peter Ordway's evil countenance, already pallid, became ashen; abject terror was upon him. ... a lashing, mist-covered sea; a titanic chaos of water, and upon its troubled bosom rode a life raft to which three persons were clinging. ...

"No, no, no!" he mumbled, his talon fingers clutching the physician's hand convulsively. "I'm afraid, afraid!"

The slender thread which held sordid soul to withered body was severed that night by a well-aimed bullet. Promptly at eight o'clock Walpole had arrived, and gone straight to the room where Peter Ordway sat propped up on a sofa. Nearly an hour later the old millionaire's one servant, Mrs. Robinson, answered the door-bell, admitting Mr. Franklin Pingree, a well-known financier. He had barely stepped into the hallway when there came a reverberating crash as of a revolver shot from the room where Peter Ordway and his secretary were.

Together Mr. Pingree and Mrs. Robinson ran to the door. Still propped upon the couch, Peter Ordway sat—dead. A bullet had penetrated his heart. His head was thrown back, his mouth was open, and his right hand dangled at his side. Leaning over the body was his secretary, Walpole. In one hand he held a revolver, still smoking. He didn't turn as they entered, but stood staring down upon the man blankly. Mr. Pingree disarmed him from behind.

Hereto I append a partial transcript of a statement made by Frederick Walpole immediately following his arrest on the charge of murdering his millionaire employer. This statement he repeated in substance at the trial:

> I am forty-eight years old. I had been in Mr. Ordway's employ for twenty-two years. My salary was eight dollars a week. ... I went to his apartments on the night of the murder in answer to a note. (Note produced.) I bought the revolver and gave it to him. He loaded it and thrust it under the covering beside him on the sofa. ... He dictated four letters and was starting on another. I heard the door open behind me. I thought it was Mrs. Robinson, as I had not heard the front-door bell ring.
>
> Mr. Ordway stopped dictating, and I looked at him. He was staring toward the door. He seemed to be frightened. I looked around. A man had come in. He seemed very old. He had a flowing white beard and long white hair. His face was ruddy, like a seaman's.

"Who are you?" Mr. Ordway asked.

"You know me all right," said the man. "We were to-gether long enough on that craft." (Or "raft," prisoner was not positive.)

"I never saw you before," said Mr. Ordway. "I don't know what you mean."

"I have come for the reward," said the man.

"What reward?" Mr. Ordway asked.

"One million dollars!" said the man.

Nothing else was said. Mr. Ordway drew his revolver and fired. The other man must have fired at the same instant, for Mr. Ordway fell back dead. The man disappeared. I ran to Mr. Ordway and picked up the revolver. He had dropped it. Mr. Pingree and Mrs. Robinson came in. ...

Reading of Peter Ordway's will disclosed the fact that he had bequeathed unconditionally the sum of one million dollars to his secretary, Walpole, for "loyal services." Despite Walpole's denial of any knowledge of this bequest, he was immediately placed under arrest. At the trial, the facts appeared as I have related them. The district attorney summed up briefly. The motive was obvious—Walpole's desire to get possession of one million dollars in cash. Mr. Pingree and Mrs. Robinson, entering the room directly after the shot had been fired, had met no one coming out, as they would have had there been another man—there was no other egress. Also, they had heard only one shot—and that shot had found Peter Ordway's heart. Also, the bullet which killed Peter Ordway had been positively identified by experts as of the same make and same caliber as those others in the revolver Walpole had bought. The jury was out twenty minutes. The verdict was guilty. Walpole was sentenced to death.

It was not until then that "The Thinking Machine"—otherwise Professor Augustus S. F. X. Van Dusen, Ph. D., F. R. S., M. D., LL. D., et cetera, et cetera, logician, analyst, master mind in the sciences—turned his crabbed genius upon the problem.

Five days before the date set for Walpole's execution, Hutchinson Hatch, newspaper reporter, introduced himself into

The Thinking Machine's laboratory, bringing with him a small roll of newspapers.

Incongruously enough, they were old friends, these two—on one hand, the man of science, absorbed in that profession of which he was already the master, small, almost grotesque in appearance, and living the life of a recluse; on the other, a young man of the world, worldly, enthusiastic, capable, indefatigable.

So it came about The Thinking Machine curled himself in a great chair, and sat for nearly two hours partially submerged in newspaper accounts of the murder and of the trial. The last paper finished, he dropped his enormous head back against his chair, turned his petulant, squinting eyes upward, and sat for minute after minute staring into nothingness.

"Why," he queried, at last, "do you think he is innocent?"

"I don't know that I do think it," Hatch replied. "It is simply that attention has been attracted to Walpole's story again because of a letter the governor received. Here is a copy of it."

The Thinking Machine read it:

You are about to allow the execution of an innocent man. Walpole's story on the witness stand was true. He didn't kill Peter Ordway. I killed him for a good and sufficient reason.

"Of course," the reporter explained, "the letter wasn't signed. However, three handwriting experts say it was written by the same hand that wrote the 'One million dollar' slips. Incidentally the prosecution made no attempt to connect Walpole's handwriting with those slips. They couldn't have done it, and it would have weakened their case."

"And what," inquired the diminutive scientist, "does the governor purpose doing?"

"Nothing," was the reply. "To him it is merely one of a thousand crank letters."

"He knows the opinions of the experts?"

"He does. I told him."

"The governor," remarked The Thinking Machine gratuitously, "is a fool." Then: "It is sometimes interesting to assume the truth of the improbable. Suppose we assume Walpole's story to be true, assuming at the same time that this letter is true—what have we?"

Tiny, cobwebby lines of thought furrowed the domelike brow as Hatch watched; the slender fingers were brought precisely tip to tip; the pale-blue eyes narrowed still more.

"If," Hatch pointed out, "Walpole's attorney had been able to find a bullet mark anywhere in that room, or a single isolated drop of blood, it would have proven that Peter Ordway did fire as Walpole says he did, and—"

"If Walpole's story is true," The Thinking Machine went on serenely, heedless of the interruption, "we must believe that a man—say, Mr. X—entered a private apartment without ringing. Very well. Either the door was unlocked, he entered by a window, or he had a false key. We must believe that two shots were fired simultaneously, sounding as one. We must believe that Mr. X was either wounded or the bullet mark has been overlooked; we must believe Mr. X went out by the one door at the same instant Mr. Pingree and Mrs. Robinson entered. We must believe they either did not see him, or they lied."

"That's what convicted Walpole," Hatch declared. "Of course, it's impossible—"

"Nothing is impossible, Mr. Hatch," stormed The Thinking Machine suddenly. "Don't say that. It annoys me exceedingly."

Hatch shrugged his shoulders, and was silent. Again minute after minute passed, and the scientist sat motionless, staring now at a plan of Peter Ordway's apartment he had found in a newspaper, the while his keen brain dissected the known facts.

"After all," he announced, at last, "there's only one vital question: Why Peter Ordway's deadly fear of water?"

The reporter shook his head blankly. He was never surprised any more at The Thinking Machine's manner of approaching a problem. Never by any chance did he take hold of it as any one else would have.

"Some personal eccentricity, perhaps," Hatch suggested hopefully. "Some people are afraid of cats, others of—"

"Go to Peter Ordway's place," The Thinking Machine interrupted tartly, "and find if it has been necessary to replace a broken windowpane anywhere in the building since Mr. Ordway's death."

"You mean, perhaps, that Mr. X, as you call him, may have escaped—" the newspaper man began.

"Also find out if there was a curtain hanging over or near the door where Mr. X must have gone out."

"Right!"

"We'll assume that the room where Ordway died has been gone over inch by inch in the search for a stray shot," the scientist continued. "Let's go farther. If Ordway fired, it was probably toward the door where Mr. X entered. If Mr. X left the door open behind him, the shot may have gone into the private hall beyond, and may be buried in the door immediately opposite." He indicated on the plan as he talked. "This second door opens into a rear hall. If both doors chanced to be open—"

Hatch came to his feet with blazing eyes. He understood. It was a possibility no one had considered. Ordway's shot, if he had fired one, might have lodged a hundred feet away.

"Then if we find a bullet mark—" he questioned tensely.

"Walpole will not go to the electric chair."

"And if we don't?"

"We will look farther," said The Thinking Machine. "We will look for a wounded man of perhaps sixty years, who is now, or has been, a sailor; who is either clean-shaven or else has a close-cropped beard, probably dyed—a man who may have a false key to the Ordway apartment—the man who wrote this note to the governor."

"You believe, then," Hatch demanded, "that Walpole is innocent?"

"I believe nothing of the sort," snapped the scientist. "He's probably guilty. If we find no bullet mark, I'm merely saying what sort of man we must look for."

"But—but how do you know so much about him—what he looks like?" asked the reporter, in bewilderment.

"How do I know?" repeated the crabbed little scientist. "How do I know that two and two make four, not sometimes, but *all* the time? By adding the units together. Logic, that's all—logic, logic!"

While Hatch was scrutinizing the shabby walls of the old building where Peter Ordway had lived his miserly life, The Thinking Machine called on Doctor Anderson, who had been Peter Ordway's physician for a score of years. Doctor Anderson couldn't explain the old millionaire's aversion to water, but perhaps if the scientist went farther back in his inquiries there was an old man, John Page, still living who had been Ordway's classmate in school. Doctor Anderson knew of him because he had once treated him at Peter Ordway's request. So The Thinking Machine came to discuss this curious trait of character with John Page. What the scientist learned didn't appear, but whatever it was it sent him to the public library, where he spent several hours pulling over the files of old newspapers.

All his enthusiasm gone, Hatch returned to report.

"Nothing," he said. "No trace of a bullet."

"Any windowpanes changed or broken?"

"Not one."

"There were curtains, of course, over the door through which Mr. X entered Ordway's room." It was not a question.

"There were. They're there yet."

"In that case," and The Thinking Machine raised his squinting eyes to the ceiling, "our sailorman was wounded."

"There is a sailorman, then?" Hatch questioned eagerly.

"I'm sure I don't know," was the astonishing reply. "If there is, he answers generally the description I gave. His name is Ben Holderby. His age is not sixty; it's fifty-eight."

The newspaper man took a long breath of amazement. Surely here was the logical faculty lifted to the nth power! The Thinking Machine was describing, naming, and giving the age of a man whose existence he didn't even venture to assert—a man who never had been in existence so far as the reporter knew! Hatch fanned himself weakly with his hat.

"Odd situation, isn't it?" asked The Thinking Machine. "It only proves that logic is inexorable—that it can only fail when the units fail; and no unit has failed yet. Meantime, I shall leave you to find Holderby. Begin with the sailors' lodging houses, and don't scare him off. I can add nothing to the description except that he is probably using another name."

Followed a feverish two days for Hatch—a hurried, nightmarish effort to find a man who might or might not exist, in order to prevent a legal murder. With half a dozen other clever men from his office, he finally achieved the impossible.

"I've found him!" he announced triumphantly over the telephone to The Thinking Machine. "He's stopping at Werner's, in the North End, under the name of Benjamin Goode. He is clean-shaven, his hair and brows are dyed black, and he is wounded in the left arm."

"Thanks," said The Thinking Machine simply. "Bring Detective Mallory, of the bureau of criminal investigation, and come here to-morrow at noon prepared to spend the day. You might go by and inform the governor, if you like, that Walpole will not be electrocuted Friday."

Detective Mallory came at Hatch's request—came with a mouthful of questions into the laboratory, where The Thinking Machine was at work.

"What's it all about?" he demanded.

"Precisely at five o-clock this afternoon a man will try to murder me," the scientist informed him placidly, without lifting his eyes. "I'd like to have you here to prevent it."

Mallory was much given to outbursts of amazement; he humored himself now:

"Who is the man? What's he going to try to kill you for? Why not arrest him now?"

"His name is Benjamin Holderby," The Thinking Machine answered the questions in order. "He'll try to kill me because I shall accuse him of murder. If he should be arrested now, he wouldn't talk. If I told you whom he murdered, you wouldn't believe it."

Detective Mallory stared without comprehension.

"If he isn't to try to kill you until five o'clock," he asked, "why send for me at noon?"

"Because he may know you, and if he watched and saw you enter he wouldn't come. At half past four you and Mr. Hatch will step into the adjoining room. When Holderby enters, he will face me. Come behind him, but don't lift a finger until he threatens me. If you have to shoot—kill! He'll be dangerous until he's dead."

It was just two minutes of five o'clock when the bell rang, and Martha ushered Benjamin Holderby into the laboratory. He was past middle age, powerful, with deep-bronzed face and the keen eyes of the sea. His hair and brows were dyed—badly dyed; his left arm hung limply. He found The Thinking Machine alone.

"I got your letter, sir," he said respectfully. "If it's a yacht, I'm willing to ship as master; but I'm too old to do much—"

"Sit down, please," the little scientist invited courteously, dropping into a chair as he spoke. "There are one or two questions I should like to ask. First"—the petulant blue eyes were raised toward the ceiling; the slender fingers came together precisely, tip to tip— "first: Why did you kill Peter Ordway?"

Fell an instant's amazed silence. Benjamin Holderby's muscles flexed, the ruddy face was contorted suddenly with hideous anger, the sinewy right hand closed until great knots appeared in the tendons. Possibly The Thinking Machine had never been nearer death than in that moment when the sailorman towered above him—'twas giant and weakling. The tiger was about to spring. Then, suddenly as it had come, anger passed from Holderby's face; came instead curiosity, bewilderment, perplexity.

The silence was broken by the sinister click of a revolver. Holderby turned his head slowly, to face Detective Mallory, stared at him oddly, then drew his own revolver, and passed it over, butt foremost.

No word had been spoken. Not once had The Thinking Machine lowered his eyes.

"I killed Peter Ordway," Holderby explained distinctly, "for good and sufficient reasons."

"So you wrote the governor," the scientist observed. "Your motive was born thirty-two years ago?"

"Yes." The sailor seemed merely astonished.

"On a raft at sea?"

"Yes."

"There was murder done on that raft?"

"Yes."

"Instigated by Peter Ordway, who offered you—"

"One million dollars—yes."

"So Peter Ordway is the second man you have killed?"

"Yes."

With mouth agape, Hutchinson Hatch listened greedily; he had—they had—saved Walpole! Mallory's mind was a chaos. What sort of tommyrot was this? This man confessing to a murder for which Walpole was to be electrocuted! His line of thought was broken by the petulant voice of The Thinking Machine.

"Sit down, Mr. Holderby," he was saying, "and tell us precisely what happened on that raft."

'Twas a dramatic story Benjamin Holderby told—a tragedy tale of the sea—a tale of starvation and thirst torture and madness, and ceaseless battling for life—of crime and greed and the power of money even in that awful moment when death seemed the portion of all. The tale began with the foundering of the steamship *Neptune*, Liverpool to Boston, ninety-one passengers and crew, some thirty-two years ago. In mid-ocean she was smashed to bits by a gale, and went down. Of those aboard only nine persons reached shore alive.

Holderby told the story simply:

"God knows how many of us went through that storm; it raged for days. There were ten of us on our raft when the ship settled, and by dusk of the second day there were only six—one woman, and one child, and four men. The waves would simply smash over us, and when we came to daylight again there was some one missing. There was little enough food and water aboard, anyway, so the people dropping off that way was really what saved—what saved two of us at the end. Peter Ordway was one, and I was the other.

"The first five days were bad enough—short rations, little or no water, no sleep, and all that; but what came after was hell! At the end of that fifth day there were only five of us—Ordway and me, the woman and child, and another man. I don't know whether I went to sleep or was just unconscious; anyway, when I came to there were only the three of us left. I asked Ordway where the woman and child was. He said they were washed off while I was asleep.

"'And a good thing,' he says.

"'Why?' I says.

"'Too many mouths to feed,' he says. 'And still too many.' He meant the other man. 'I've been looking at the rations and the water,' he says. 'There's enough to keep three people alive three days, but if there were only two people—me and you, for instance?' he says.

"'You mean throw him off?' I says.

"'You're a sailor,' says he. 'If you go, we all go. But we may not be picked up for days. We may starve or die of thirst first. If there were only two of us, we'd have a better chance. I'm worth millions of dollars,' he says. 'If you'll get rid of this other fellow, and we ever come out alive, I'll give you one million dollars!' I didn't say anything. 'If there were only two of us,' says he, 'we would increase our chances of being saved one-third. One million dollars!' says he. 'One million dollars!'

"I expect I was mad with hunger and thirst and sleeplessness and exhaustion. Perhaps he was, too. I know that, regardless of the money he offered, his argument appealed to me. Peter Ordway was a coward; he didn't have the nerve; so an hour later I threw the man overboard, with Peter Ordway looking on.

"Days passed somehow—God knows—and when I came to I had been picked up by a sailing vessel. I was in an asylum for months. When I came out, I asked Ordway for money. He threatened to have me arrested for murder. I pestered him a lot, I guess, for a little later I found myself shanghaied, on the high seas. I didn't come back for thirty years or so. I had almost forgotten the thing until I happened to see Peter Ordway's name in a paper. Then I wrote the slips and mailed them to him. He knew what they meant, and set a detective after me. Then I began hating him all over again, worse than ever. Finally I thought I'd go to his house and make a holdup of it—one million dollars! I don't think I intended to kill him; I thought he'd give me money. I didn't know there was any-one with him. I talked to him, and he shot me. I killed him."

Fell a long silence. The Thinking Machine broke it:

"You entered the apartment with a skeleton key?"

"Yes."

"And after the shot was fired, you started out, but dodged be-hind the curtain at the door when you heard Mr. Pingree and Mrs. Robinson coming in?"

"Yes."

Suddenly Hatch understood why The Thinking Machine had asked him to ascertain if there were curtains at that door. It was quite possible that in the excitement Mr. Pingree and Mrs. Robinson would not have noticed that the man who killed Peter Ordway actually passed them in the doorway.

"I think," said The Thinking Machine, "that that is all. You understand, Mr. Mallory, that this confession is to be presented to the governor immediately, in order to save Walpole's life?" He turned to Holderby. "You don't want an innocent man to die for this crime?"

"Certainly not," was the reply. "That's why I wrote to the governor. Walpole's story was true. I was in court, and heard it." He glanced at Mallory curiously. "Now, if necessary, I'm willing to go to the chair."

"It won't be necessary," The Thinking Machine pointed out. "You didn't go to Peter Ordway's place to kill him—you went there for money you thought he owed you—he fired at you—you shot him. It's hardly self-defense, but it was not premeditated murder."

Detective Mallory whistled. It was the only satisfactory vent for the tangled mental condition which had befallen him. Shortly he went off with Holderby to the governor's office; and an hour later Walpole, deeply astonished, walked out of the death cell—a free man.

Meanwhile Hutchinson Hatch had some questions to ask of The Thinking Machine.

"Logic, logic, Mr. Hatch!" the scientist answered, in that perpetual tone of irritation. "As an experiment, we assumed the truth of Walpole's story. Very well. Peter Ordway was afraid of water. Connect that with the one word 'raft' or 'craft' in Walpole's statement of what the intruder had said. Connect that with his description of that man— 'ruddy, like a seaman.' Add them up, as you would a sum in arithmetic. You begin to get a glimmer of cause and effect, don't you? Peter Ordway was afraid of the water because of some tragedy there in which he had played a part. That was a tentative surmise. Walpole's description of the intruder said white hair and flowing white beard. It is a common failing of men who disguise themselves to go to the other extreme. I went to the other extreme in conjecturing Holderby's appearance—clean-shaven or else close-cropped beard and hair—dyed. Since no bullet mark was found in the building—remember, we are assuming Walpole's statement to be true—the man Ordway shot at carried the bullet away with him. Ergo, a seaman with a pistol wound. Seamen, as a rule, stop at the sailors' lodging houses. That's all."

"But—but you knew Holderby's name—his age!" the reporter stammered.

"I learned them in my effort to account for Ordway's fear of water," was the reply. "An old friend, John Page, whom I found through Doctor Anderson, informed me that he had seen some account in a newspaper thirty-two years before, at the time of the wreck of the *Neptune*, of Peter Ordway's rescue from a raft at sea. He and one other man were picked up. The old newspaper files in the libraries gave me Holderby's name as the other survivor, together with his age. You found Holderby. I wrote to him that I was about to put a yacht in commission, and he had been recommended to me—that is, Benjamin Goode had been recommended. He came in answer to the advertisement. You saw everything else that happened."

"And the so-called 'one million dollar' slips?"

"Had no bearing on the case until Holderby wrote to the governor," said The Thinking Machine. "In that note he confessed the killing; ergo I began to see that the 'One million dollar' slips probably indicated some enormous reward Ordway had offered Holderby. Walpole's statement, too, covers this point. What happened on the raft at sea? I didn't know. I followed an instinct, and guessed." The distinguished scientist arose. "And now," he said, "begone about your business. I must go to work."

Hatch started out, but turned at the door. "Why," he asked, "were you so anxious to know if any windowpane in the Ordway house had been replaced or was broken?"

"Because," the scientist didn't lift his head, "because a bullet might have smashed one, if it was not to be found in the woodwork. If it smashed one, our unknown Mr. X was not wounded."

Upon his own statement, Benjamin Holderby was sentenced to ten years in prison; at the end of three months he was transferred to an asylum after an examination by alienists.

The Grinning God

Part I: Wraiths of the Storm
Mrs. Jacques Futrelle

Professor Augustus S. F. X. Van Dusen—The Thinking Machine—readjusted his thick spectacles, dropped back into the depths of the huge chair, manuscript in hand, and read:

"Something less than three months ago I had a photograph taken. As I look upon it now I see a man of about thirty years, clean shaven, full faced, and vigorous with health; eyes which are clear and calm and placid, almost phlegmatic; a brow upon which sits the serenity of perfect physical and mental poise; a pleasant mouth with quizzical lines about the corners; a chin with determination and assurance in every line; hair brown and unmarked with age. I was red blooded then, lusty, buoyant with life and animalism, while now—

"Here is a hand mirror. It reflects back at me the gaunt, haggard face of a man who might be any age; furtive, shifting eyes in which lies perpetual, hideous fear; a brow ruffled over into spidery lines of suffering; a drooping, flabby mouth; a chin weak and utterly devoid of the assurances of manhood; hair dead white over the temples, with strange grey streaks through it. My blood is become water; youth is frozen into senility; all things worth while are gone.

"Fear, Webster says, is apprehension, dread, alarm—and it is more than that. It is a loss of the sense of proportion, an unseating of mental power, a phantasmagoria of perverted imagination; a vampire which saps hope and courage and common sense, and leaves a quivering shell of what was once a man. I know what fear is—no man better. I knew it that night in the forest, and I know it

355

now, when I find myself sitting up in bed staring into nothingness with the echo of screams in my ears; I knew it when that grim, silent old man moved about me, and I know it now when without conscious effort my imagination conjures up those dead, glassy eyes; I knew it when vicious little tongues of flames lapped at me that night, and I know it now when at times I seem to feel their heat.

"I know what fear is! It is typified by a little ivory god which squats upon my mantel as I write, grinning hideously. Perhaps there is some explanation of the event of that night, some single hidden fact which, if revealed, would make it all clear; but seeking that explanation I have grown like this. When it will end, I don't know—I can only wait and listen, always, always!

"Impatient, half famished, and wholly disgusted at a sudden failure of my gasolene supply, I ran my automobile off the main roadway and brought it to a standstill in a small open space before a little country store. I had barely been able to make out the outlines of the building through the utter darkness of the night,—a darkness which was momentarily growing more dense. Black, threatening clouds swooped across the face of the heavens, first obscuring, then obliterating, the brilliant star points.

"I knew where I was perfectly, although I had never been over the road before. Behind me lay Pelham, a quiet little village which had been sound asleep when I rushed through, and somewhere vaguely in front was Millen. I had been due there about seven o'clock; but, thanks to some trouble with a crank, it was now about ten. I was well nigh exhausted from hours at the steering wheel, and nothing to eat since luncheon. I would spend the night in Millen, store up a few hours' sleep, after the insistent demands of my appetite had been appeased, then on the morrow proceed comfortably on my way.

"This was what I had intended to do. The sudden shortage of motive power brought me to a stop in front of the forbidding little store, and a little maneuvering back and forth cleared the road's fairway of the bulk of my machine. No light showed in the house, but as I had not passed another building in two or three miles back, it seemed not improbable that the keeper of the store slept on the premises. I put this hypothesis to a test by a loud halloing, which in the course of time brought a nightcapped head to a window just above the door. I hailed the appearance of the head as a good omen.

"'Got any gasolene?' I asked.

"'I calculate as how I might have a little,' came the answer in a man's voice.

"'Well, will you please let me have enough to get me to Millen?'

"'It's ag'in' the law to draw gasolene at night,' said the man placidly. 'Cal'late as how you'll have to wait till mornin'.'

"'Wait till morning?' I complained. 'Why man, there's a storm coming! I've got to get to Millen.'

"'Can't help that,' was the reply. 'Law's law, you know. I'd be sorter skeered, anyway, to draw gasolene now.'

"Here was another dilemma, unexpected as it was annoying. The tone of the voice left no room for argument, and I knew the obstinacy of this man's type. I was prepared, therefore, to accept the inevitable.

"'Well, if you can't draw any gasolene to-night, can you give me a bite to eat and put me up till morning?' I asked. 'I can't stay out in this storm.'

"'Ain't got no room,' explained the man. 'Jus' enough space up here for me an' the dog, an' he kinder crowds.'

"'Well, something must be done,' I insisted. 'What is the price of your gasolene?' I added by way of suggestion.

"'Twenty-five cents a gallon in day time.'

"'Well, how is fifty cents a gallon at night?' I went on.

"The whitecapped head was withdrawn, and the window banged down suddenly. For a moment I thought I had hopelessly offended some puritanical old man of the woods; but then a light glowed inside the store, and the front door opened. I stepped inside. The light came from a safety lantern in the hands of a shrunken shanked, little old man, who proceeded to draw the gasolene.

"'How far is it to Millen?' I inquired casually.

"'Calculate as how it's about five miles.'

"'Straight roads?'

"'Straight 'cept where it bends,' he replied. 'They ain't no turn-out nor nothin'. You can't go wrong 'less you climb a fence.'

"The gasolene was drawn and paid for, after which the old man accompanied me to the automobile with his safety lantern. He stood looking on curiously as I filled the tank.

"'Pears to be a right smart storm comin' up,' he remarked consolingly.

"I glanced upward. Every star point was lost now behind an impenetrable veil of black; there was a whispering, sighing sound of wind in the trees.

"'I think I can beat it into Millen,' I replied hopefully.

"'I cal'late as how you oughter,' responded the old man. 'Ain't no thunder an' lightnin' yet, an' I cal'late as how they'll be a pile of it before it rains.'

"I handed back the empty gasolene can, cranked up, then climbed aboard my car. There was a whir as I touched the power lever, and the machine trembled beneath me.

"'If I should get caught before I get to Millen, is there any place I might stop,' I inquired.

"'I cal'late as how you might stop anywhere,' the old man chuckled; 'but they ain't no houses nor nothin'. They ain't even a dog kennel 'tween here an' Millen. But they ain't no turnouts, an' you can hit it up as fast as you want to. You'll be all right.'

"A sudden gust of wind brought a whirling cloud of dust upon us, and the thinly clad old man scampered off into the house.

"'Good night,' I called.

"'Good night,' he answered, and the door slammed.

"I backed my car, then straightened out into the road, a wide yellow stretch, as smooth as asphalt, where the swirling, eddying winds awoke little dust devils to play. Then I kicked loose the speed gear, pulled the lever far back, and went plunging off into the night.

"It might have been only my imagination, or it might have been that, as the car swept on, I heard some one calling me; I'll never know which. But the lowering clouds and a quickened rush of wind did not make a stop inviting; so the car sped on.

"I knew a capital little all night restaurant in Millen, and was speculating pleasantly as to whether it should be a chop and a mug of ale, or a more substantial steak and potatoes. I was aroused from this anticipatory mood by the fact that the glittering lamps of my car showed me straight ahead two roads instead of one. Two roads! Here was another unexpected annoyance. I brought the automobile to a stop, in doubt and perplexity.

"To the right the road ran off into the thickening forest, as far as the steady light gleams showed; to the left it seemed a little more marked, as if more traveled, and where the light melted into the enveloping blackness it appeared to widen. I leaped out of the car and went forward, seeking a guide post or something to show my way. There was nothing.

"Then I remembered that I had a road map in my pocket. Of course that would tell me. A grumble of thunder came from far off as I drew near the car to examine the map in the light. Here was Pelham, and here was Millen; here even the little store where I stopped, marked with a star, which meant that gasolene was to be procured there. Now I was somewhere between that store and Millen. The map was a large one. It should show not only the main road, but every little bypath that cut athwart it. Yet from the little store to Millen the road was an unbroken line. There was no branch road on the map; and yet here was one.

"I was perplexed, impatient, and incidentally starving; so hastily made up my mind which road to take: the left and more beaten one. Heaping maledictions upon the head of the man who drew that particular map, I started to climb into the car again, when the veil of night was cleft by a vivid zigzag flash of lightning. It startled me, blinded me almost, and was followed instantly by the crash and roar of thunder.

"Then came another sound,—a curdling, nerve racking scream,—a scream of agony, of pain, of fear,—a hideous, awful thing which seemed to stop my heart for one fearful instant, then was lost in the thunder of the approaching storm. Suddenly all was silent again, save for the wind as it whipped its way through the forest.

"I was not a nervous man; so after the first shock the blood rushed back to my heart, my head cleared, and I was perfectly calm. But I stood waiting with my foot on the step—waiting and listening. I argued calmly. Some one was evidently in distress. But where? In what direction? The singing wind, the whirling dust, left me no guess. And then again came that scream, this time a series of quick, sharp shrieks ending in a wail which made me clench my hands until the nails bit into the flesh, and left me weak and trembling absurdly.

"But now I had the direction. The cries had come apparently from the road, somewhere behind me. I walked to the rear of the car where the tail light shot out a feeble ray, and stood peering off into the blackness in the direction whence I had come. At first I could distinguish nothing, then a white, intangible something slowly grew out of the night,—something hazy, floating, indistinct, yet unmistakably something. Fascinated, I stood still and continued to stare. The floating white figure seemed to grow sensibly larger and clearer. It was coming toward me; it would cross the path of the light in another moment. I caught my breath and waited.

"Suddenly again came the reverberating crash of thunder, nearer and louder, but unaccompanied by lightning. Instantly, as if in echo, came that scream again. Obviously it was some one in distress,—a woman perhaps, lost in the woods and in terror of the approaching storm. If this was true then there was only one thing to do; go to her relief.

"I stopped and tugged at the tail lamp to release it from its fastenings. A ragged edge cut my hand cruelly; but I hardly felt the sting. At last the light was free in my hand, and I started with it back along the road to where I had seen the figure. With the lamp thrust straight out in front of me at arm's length I ran back ten yards, twenty, fifty, and saw—nothing. I screened the light with my hand, and peered about through the gloom, and saw—nothing.

"A panic was growing upon me. I flashed the light to the right, to the left, and it showed only the gaunt, silent trees, straight ahead of me along the yellow road, and behind me toward the panting automobile. There was nothing—absolutely nothing! I rushed back to the car; but no one was there. I called aloud; but the grim forest gave me back only the sound of my own voice, mingled with the swishing of the wind.

"Then I stopped still in silence and awe, and listened. For a long time I stood there, light in hand, until the silence grew more terrifying than the screams had been. I wanted to hear that scream again now, to bring relief to my bursting heart and shaking nerves, to tell me that it was real and not some trick of overwrought fancy. But the silence was unbroken save for the freshening gusts of air which stirred the dry leaves and rained them down in a gentle patter.

"Finally I turned and walked back to where the car stood throbbing like a living, breathing thing. It gave me confidence. I struck the tonneau with my open palm, and laughed suddenly at my unreasoning terror. It was absurd, a school boy running from his shadow, and here I was a man—a sound, healthy, hungry man. I had heard the screams, I knew; I had seen the floating white figure. There was nothing very remarkable about it; it was a thing to be explained, of course.

"So now, deliberately I searched the road again, this time with the light turned toward the ground. I went along, stooping, seeking footprints. I found none; but I could explain even that; the wind gusts had covered them with dust, obliterated them.

"I straightened up suddenly. Something had sounded, something louder than the rustling of the leaves, something louder even than the creaking of the trees. It was a crackling sound—a sound that might have been a foot pressure upon dry twigs. It seemed to be to the left, and I turned the light in that direction. Grotesque shadows danced and swayed as the trees reeled about me. Then high up where the light straggled through the branches I saw something white—dead white!

"I cleared the road at a stride and plunged into the forest with the light turned upward. I stumbled over rocks half buried in the leaves; I slipped once into a ditch which I couldn't see. Finally my foot struck a fallen tree, and I went forward sprawling on my hands and knees. The lamp rolled beyond my reach, and utter blackness swooped down as the light was smothered in the underbrush. As I groped for it I heard again that crackling sound as of breaking twigs. Perhaps it was coming toward me—and I couldn't see!

"At last my frantic fingers closed on the lamp, and I shot the light high above my head, seeking that white something up among the trees. It was gone! I paused to wipe the perspiration from my brow, and tore my collar loose. A sudden shower of leaves came down upon my head; there was another zigzag flash of lightning, a nearby roll of thunder, and the sinister patter of raindrops falling about me like leaden bullets. The storm had burst.

"Heedless of all the intangible horrors of that lonely spot in the forest, maddened by terror at the inexplicable things which had befallen me, I stumbled back to the pulsating automobile, clambered in, and sent it forward headlong on the road to the left,— the well beaten road,—the road which bore evidence of constant travel. The pace was furious; for somewhere behind me I felt was a misty, floating figure of white, and somewhere a woman scream- ing. The rain beat me in the face steadily; the lightning burst forth in livid, flaming tongues; the thunder crashed about me,—and my only haven was Millen.

"Suddenly the road widened where a path cut through the dense wood, and was lost in a perspective of gloom. A single sidelong glance at it as I rushed past told me it was wider than would be naturally worn by persons passing, and yet not wide enough for my car, nor even for a narrow wagon. Here that road map was at fault again. I remembered that grimly, even as the automobile went splashing along through growing pools of water and invisible ruts in the wagonway. I clung grimly to the steering wheel with only one idea in mind: to get to Millen. Already I was wet through from the terrific downpour, and a chilling numbness was seizing upon my limbs.

"Gradually the road turned toward the left, or so it seemed to me. But that too might have been the effect of an overwrought brain. The road did not look so much traveled now, despite the deceptive ruts into which my wheels sank with maddening fre- quency. Yet beneath its sheet of water the steadily gleaming lights showed that there was a road, plainly marked. For a minute or more, I suppose, I went straight on, desperately, recklessly; then an illuminating flash across the sky showed me that I was plung- ing into open country, and that the forest was gradually receding.

"Finally, through the swirling, drenching rain, I saw a faint rosy point in the distance. Whatever it was, a lantern I supposed, it at least indicated the presence of some fellow human being. I drove straight toward it. The gleam did not falter or fade. Another daz- zling burst of lightning answered my question as to the nature of the light. It was in a farm house,—a farm house out here where there weren't any farm houses, squatting in an open field, a ramshackle, two-storied affair. But at least it would serve to shelter me from the fury of the storm. I took in all of it at one glance, even to a small shed in the rear where I might store my machine.

"I didn't pause to call as I drew near, but drove to the shed and ran my car in. Then, guided by the constant lightning flashes, I walked round to the front of the farm house, passing through the stream of light from the window as I went. It cheered me, that light. It offered an unexpected haven, that physical refreshment of which I was so much in need, possible companionship, and above all a refuge.

"I knocked on the front door loudly, the thunder was rolling incessantly now, then shook the water from my dripping garments. I waited—waited patiently enough for half a minute, I suppose. There was no answering sound of any sort, and again I knocked, this time insistently, even clamorously. Still no answer. It was not difficult to imagine that the continuous roar of the elements had drowned the feeble knock, and I repeated the performance with several thumping, banging variations. Still no answer.

"Even in this desperate strait I did not care to enter the house as a thief might, by forcing my way, and run the risk too of being received as a thief, possibly with a bullet. So I stepped down from the veranda, and went to the lighted window, intending to attract attention by rapping on the glass. My first glimpse told me no one was there; but the room gave every evidence of occupancy. A big cheerful log fire was burning, and its flickering light showed books strewn about here and there, inviting chairs, a table, and all the little knickknacks that make a comfortable sitting room. There beside that brightly blazing fire was comfort, and here the penetrating chill of the storm.

"I had no further scruples about it. I was going into that room! I ran up the steps, and was just reaching out my hand to try the knob, when the latch clicked, and slowly, silently, the door swung open. Naturally I expected to meet some one,—some one who had anticipated me in lifting the latch,—but I saw no one. The door had merely opened, revealing a rather long, broad hallway, with a stair in the distance, and unlighted save for the reflection from the sitting room. I took just two steps across the threshold, enough to get out of the swirling rain, then stopped and called. No one answered. I called a second time. For a wonder the thunders were silent just then, and there was no sound save that of my own voice. I ventured along the hall to the sitting room door and looked in. It was cozy, warm, comfortable, more so even than I had imagined when I looked in through the window.

"All at once I was overcome by a guilty sense of intrusion. What right had I to enter a strange house at this time of night in this manner, even to get out of a storm? My personal safety seemed at stake, somehow. I turned and started back for the door by which I had entered, with the intention of remaining there till in someway I could attract the attention of the occupants of the house.

"But I didn't reach the door; for directly in front of me stood a man. He was tall, angular, aged, and a little bent. A straggling gray beard almost covered his face, and thick gray hair hung down limply from beneath the brim of an old slouch hat. He was beside me, almost within reach of my hand, almost treading upon my toes with his great boots, and yet I had not heard one sound, except when the door clicked as I entered. It all came to me at once, and I shivered involuntarily.

"'I must apologize—' I began; but I got no further. He had not heard me, had not even seen me, if I might judge by the manner in which he walked slowly past me with his chin upon his breast, and his hands clasped behind his back. I stepped back to avoid a collision.

"'I beg your pardon—' I began again; but he had disappeared into the sitting room, stalked away noiselessly without even a glance in my direction, leaving me dripping, chilly, and overcome by the indefinable sense of impending danger.

"I paused there in the hall and pondered the situation. Surely the old man had seen me. But I had spoken! Of course, it was possible that he had neither seen nor heard me; yet—yet—

"'I'm going in there, and I am going to stay until the storm moderates!' I told myself. 'Perhaps it is just a peculiar old man's way.'

"I removed my automobile coat, hung it upon a peg, walked along the hallway with a firm tread, and stepped into the sitting room. It was deserted!

"There are moments in every man's life when the weight of a revolver in his hand is tremendously reassuring. This was mine. I drew the weapon from my hip pocket, examined it, and thrust it into my coat within easy reach of my right hand. Then I stood by the table, drumming my fingers upon it idly, and debating with myself as to what I should do. I was looking toward the door by which I had entered. No one came in, and yet— Suddenly the gray bearded old man was throwing a log on the fire. The flames shot up and the sparks flew; but there was not the crackle of fresh burning wood as there should have been—just this silent old man. My heart was in my throat, and I laughed sheepishly.

"'You startled me,' I explained foolishly in apology.

"He did not look at me; but busied himself about the room for a moment, and laid his hat upon a couch. Then he went out by the door into the hallway.

"'Well, upon my soul!' I ejaculated.

"I sat down and deliberately waited for the old man to return. The uncanniness of it all was growing upon me, the silence of his great boots as he walked, the fire which didn't crackle as it burned, the lack of any sign or movement to indicate that he had recognized my presence. Was the old man real? I came to my feet with an exclamation. Or was it—was it some weird continuation of that horrible thing in the forest?

"I put out a cold, clammy hand to the fire. That seemed real— at least a warmth came to me, and gradually my fingers lost their numbness, and looking upon my own hand I fell to remembering the hands of my strange host. They were knotted, toil worn, and the left forefinger was missing. That fact struck sharply upon my memory, and I remembered too a scar over one eye when he removed his hat. That all seemed real too, as did these things upon the mantel here in front of me: an empty spool, an alabaster cat, glaring red and white, a piece of crystal of peculiar shape upon the farthermost corner. And near it, so close that at first it seemed a part of it, was a queer little ivory god sitting upon his haunches, grinning hideously.

"I lifted the ivory image and examined it curiously. It was real enough. I had stepped back from the mantel a pace to let the firelight fall upon it, when suddenly I knew that the old man had returned.

I didn't hear him, I hadn't seen him,—I merely knew he was there. I felt it. I slipped the little image into my pocket involuntarily as I turned; for all my interest was instantly transferred to a tray of food which the old man carried. I remembered I was hungry.

"He placed the things upon the table in the same ghostly silence. There was a jug of milk, some jelly, a little pat of butter, and several biscuits. I went forward and thanked him. He was absolutely impassive, seeing nothing, hearing nothing, and seeming to have no connection with the things around him. He didn't invite me to eat,—I assumed that privilege and gingerly poked a finger into a biscuit. It felt like a biscuit. I bit it; it tasted like a biscuit. In fact, I am convinced to this day that it was a biscuit. And against the reality of that biscuit was the silent old man and his ghostly tread.

"Real, or unreal, the food was refreshing and good, and I fell to with a will. The old man sat down in a rocker by the fire and folded his hands in his lap. I ventured a remark about the storm. He didn't answer. I really had not expected that he would. The modest supper brought a tingle to my blood again. My rioting nerves were calmed, the room cozy, the fire comfortable. I was beginning to enjoy this singular experience; but an occasional glance at the swaying rocker where the old man sat by the fire kept expectation on the *qui vive*. The rocker swayed dismally, but without the slightest sound.

"The warmth, the food, and my utter exhaustion conspired to make me a little drowsy, and I think once I must have closed my eyes. I opened them with a start. From somewhere above me, below me, or outside where the storm still growled, came that awful, heart tearing scream again, ending in a wail that brought me to my feet. The old man did not heed the quick movement by the slightest sign,—he was still comfortably rocking.

"'What is it?' I demanded. 'What is it?'

"Revolver in hand, I rushed toward the door leading into the hallway. The old man was there ahead of me. He didn't touch me, and yet imperceptibly I was forced aside. He crossed the hall and went up the stairs. After a moment I heard a door open and shut.

"Except for the noise of the storm, the scream, and my own voice, it was the only sound I had heard since I entered the house.

"I went up those stairs; why I cannot say, except that some-thing, a vague, undefined curiosity, seemed to impel me. And with this impulse came again, stronger than ever, that sense of personal danger to myself—the feeling that had possessed me ever since I entered the house.

"I groped my way through the darkness to the top of the stairs; then my hand ran along a wall till I came to an open door. I stood there a moment undecided whether to investigate further or to re-trace my steps. I was on the point of going back down the stairs; but the flare of a candle almost in my face stopped me. The old man held the candle, shading it with his left hand, from which the forefinger was missing. The wavering light gave the withered old face a strangely drawn expression.

"He was within three feet of me, gazing straight into my face, and yet I felt, I knew, he didn't see me. It occurred to me even then that it was the first time I had seen his eyes. They were white and glassy. Blind? I do not know. For one moment he stood there star-ing, then passing me entered the room beyond, where he put down the candle. I followed him into the room as a moth follows a flame. It was the light, I think, that lured me in. Here once for all I would make an end of the thing. The old man, still noiselessly, went out the door by which he had entered, off through the darkness—some-where. The door swung to. Like a madman I sprang forward and shot the bolt. I don't know why.

"I felt caged. Whatever was to come, was to come here! It was an intuition more strongly upon me than the sense of danger. I sat down on a clean little bed and stared thoughtfully at the single door,—that only way out save one of two small windows which I imagined overlooked the yard. I examined my revolver carefully. Every chamber was loaded, and the cylinder whirled easily. Well and good. I waited. What for? I don't know.

"The candle burned with a straight, unwavering flame, while I crouched there on the bed for a long time. The grumble of thunder was growing faint and far away; but the rain swished against the windows in sheets. Here was a vigil, it seemed, and a long one; for sleep seemed hopelessly out of the question despite the insistent drowsiness of exhaustion. I wondered if the candle would last throughout the night. It was not yet half burned. I gazed at it with a certain returning sense of assurance; and as I gazed it flickered, flared up suddenly, and went out.

"I don't know what happened then. It might have been ten minutes later, or it might have been half a dozen hours, when strangling, choking fumes of smoke aroused me. My lungs were bursting for air. I struggled up on the bed, and was instantly conscious of the crackling sound of burning wood—of fire. The house was on fire! I rushed toward the bolted door, to find the flames already eating through the thin panels, and little red tongues shot out at me. I was cut off from the stairs.

"From there to one of the little windows! The glow far out through the rain told me instantly that the structure was aflame. I glanced downward. Sinuous forks were below me, on each side of me, above me. There was nothing to do but jump. I had only a moment to decide. I drew in my breath and pulled myself upon the ledge.

"And then again I heard that scream. Far across the open field where the glow from the blaze dimmed off into the shadows, I saw faintly a misty white figure with outstretched arms fleeing toward the forest. A little behind the floating white figure, and nearer to me, well within the range of the firelight, the old man was following. Even at the distance I could see that his chin drooped upon his chest and his hands clasped behind his back. That was all I saw.

"The next instant I had jumped.

"I found myself in my automobile skimming along a smooth, hard road that led through a forest. It was not familiar, and I don't know in what direction I was headed, nor did it matter then so long as I got away from those things behind. My ankle was broken, my clothing torn and burned in spots, and my head was throbbing with pain.

"Then I found myself in what seemed to be a street in a small city. A faint, rosy line was just tinging the eastern sky. Houses to right and left of me were closed forbiddingly; but just ahead was the solitary figure of a man, walking slowly along, swinging a stick.

I ran the automobile alongside him, shouting some senseless question, then fell forward fainting. My last recollection was of shutting off power.

"When I recovered consciousness it was to find myself upon a cot in a strange room, perhaps a hospital. A physician was bandaging my ankle. A thousand questions leaped to my lips; and some of them burst forth in a torrent.

"'Don't talk!' commanded the physician brusquely.

"'But where am I?' I insisted.

"'Millen,' he responded tersely. 'Don't talk!'

"It struck me curiously that I should be here,—that I should have reached the point for which I was bound even after all that had happened to me. It seemed centuries since I had left Pelham somewhere behind. Perhaps it was all a dream. But those screams! That silent old man! This broken ankle! I dropped into agonizing slumber after awhile,—the sleep of sheer exhaustion,—but asleep I lived again those awful moments which had almost driven me mad.

"On the following day I was calmer. The physician asked me some questions, and I answered them to the best of my ability. He did not smile at my fright; only shook his head and gave me something which made me sleep again. And so for a week I lay there, helpless, half asleep, and half awake. But one day I awoke to clear consciousness, comparatively free of the torture of the broken ankle, and myself again. Then the physician and I discussed the matter at length.

"He listened respectfully as I repeated it all, and at the end shook his head.

"'There is no intersecting road between the small store of which you speak and the outskirts of Millen,' he said positively.

"'But, man, I was there!' I protested. 'I turned into the other road, and ran along till I saw the house in the open field. I tell you—'

"But he let me go no further. I knew why. He thought it was some mental vagary; for after awhile he gave me a pill and went away. So I resolved to solve the matter for myself. I would go back along that road by day, and find that silent old man, and, if not the house itself, the charred spot where it had stood. I would know that intersection; I would know even the path which led from the mysterious road off into the wood. When I found these I knew the maze would fade into some simple, plain explanation—perhaps even an absurd one.

"So I bided my time. In the course of another week I was able to leave my cot and hobble about with the aid of crutches. It was then that I took the physician in my car, and we went back along the highway toward Pelham. It was all unfamiliar ground to me; there was no road, and suddenly there ahead of me was the little store where I had bought the gasolene that night. I would question the old man I had seen there; but there was no old man. The little store was unoccupied; it seemed to have been unoccupied for weeks.

"I turned back and traversed the road toward Millen again. I recognized nothing; I couldn't find a trace of a bypath from the highway in any direction. And once more I went over the ground at night. Nothing! After that the physician, a singularly patient man, accompanied me as I hobbled through the forest on each side of the road seeking that house, or its ashes. I never saw anything to lead me, to even suggest, a single incident of that awful night.

"'I know the country, every inch of it,' the physician told me. 'There isn't any such place as you mention.'

"And—well, that's all. I know his opinion was that my story was some sort of delusion—a dream. But how he accounts for the broken ankle I don't know. Then the condition of my clothing! I had been compelled to discard everything I wore for garments sent down from the city. And so in time I came to believe the experience a dream. I was growing content with this story, even knowing it to be wrong, because it brought mental rest, and was beginning to be myself again.

"Then one day I had occasion to search the coat I had worn that night for some papers which had been misplaced. In the course of the search I thrust my hand into an outside pocket, and drew out—a little ivory god, sitting on his haunches, grinning hideously!

"Now I am like this—and the little god sits up laughing at me. He knows!"

When he had finished reading, The Thinking Machine dropped back into the chair, with squint eyes turned steadily upward, and long slender fingers pressed tip to tip. Hutchinson Hatch, reporter, sat staring in silence at the drawn, inscrutable face of the scientist.

"And the writer of this?" demanded The Thinking Machine at last.

"His name is Harold Fairbanks," the reporter explained. "He was removed to an asylum yesterday, hopelessly insane."

Part II: The House That Was
Jacques Futrelle

Editor's Note.—Mrs. Futrelle undertook to set up a problem which The Thinking Machine could not solve. "Wraiths of the Storm," in *The Sunday Magazine* last week, presented what she thought to be a mystery story impossible of solution. Printer's proofs of the story were submitted to Mr. Futrelle, who, after frequent consultations with Professor Van Dusen,—The Thinking Machine,—evolved "The House that Was" as the perfect solution.

The Thinking Machine lowered his squint eyes and favored Hutchinson Hatch with a long, steady stare which for the moment seemed totally to obliterate him as a personality. Gradually, under the continued unseeing but tense gaze, there grew upon the newspaper man a singular sense of utter transparency, a complete invisibility, an uncomfortable feeling of not being present. He laughed a little finally, and lighted a cigarette.

"As I was saying," Hatch began, "this Harold Fairbanks is hopelessly insane, and—"

"I imagine," interrupted the eminent man of science,— "I imagine that this insanity of Fairbanks's is rather a maniacal condition?"

"Yes," Hatch told him. "I was going to say—"

"And that possibly it took a homicidal turn?" The Thinking Machine continued.

"Yes," the reporter assented. "He tried to—"

"Against a woman, perhaps?"

"Precisely. The direct cause of his—"

"Please don't interrupt, Mr. Hatch!" snapped The Thinking Machine. He was silent for a time; Hatch smiled whimsically. "The object of his homicidal mania," the scientist continued slowly, as if feeling his way, "was—was his mother?"

"Yes."

Hatch dropped back into his chair and met the squint blue eyes fairly. He was not surprised at this statement of the case, thus far correct, because he was accustomed to the unerring accuracy of the master mind behind those eyes; but he was curious to know just how far that logical brain would follow a circumstantial thread which it had developed of itself out of an apparent nothingness. Nothing in the manuscript, nothing he had said, had even indicated, to his mind, the more recent developments.

The leaves of the manuscript fluttered through the slender white fingers of The Thinking Machine, and the straight line of the thin lips was drawn down a little as he glanced over a page or so.

"He shot at her?" he queried at last.

"Three times," the reporter informed him. The Thinking Machine raised his eyes quickly, inquiringly, to those of the newspaper man. "She was not wounded," the reporter hastened to say. "The shots went wild."

"That happened in Fairbanks's own room?"

"Yes."

"At night?"

"Yes; about one o'clock."

"Of course!" exclaimed the little scientist crabbedly. "I know that." Again there was a pause. "Mrs. Fairbanks has a room near that of her son—perhaps on the same floor?"

"Just across the hall."

"And she was awakened by some unusual noise in his room?"

"She hadn't been to sleep." The reporter smiled.

"Oh!" and again The Thinking Machine's squint eyes were turned toward the ceiling. "Some unusual noise attracted her attention, then?"

"Yes," the reporter agreed.

"Screams?"

"Yes."

The Thinking Machine nodded. "So she ran to her son's room just as she was—in a white night robe, I imagine?"

"Precisely."

The reporter was leaning forward in his chair now, staring into the impassive face before him. Still he wasn't surprised—he was merely curious and interested in the workings of that mind which laid before him in order these incidents which were not known to it by any tangible method.

"And as she entered her son's room," the scientist resumed, "he shot at her?"

"Three times—yes."

The Thinking Machine was silent for a long time. "That's all?" he remarked inquiringly at last.

"Well, Fairbanks was raving, of course," and Hatch dropped back in his chair. "He was over-powered by two servants, and—"

"Yes, I know," broke in The Thinking Machine. "He is now in a padded cell in a private asylum somewhere." This was not a question; it was a statement. "And this manuscript was found in his room after he had gone?"

"It lay open on his table. That is his handwriting," explained the newspaper reporter.

The Thinking Machine arose and walked the length of the room three times. Finally he stopped before the newspaper man. "And is there really such a thing as this grinning god that he describes?" he demanded.

"Certainly," Hatch responded, and his tone indicated surprise.

"Not necessarily certain," said the scientist sharply. "Do you *know* there is a grinning god?"

"Yes," replied the newspaper man emphatically. "It was taken away from Fairbanks when he was locked up. He fought like a fiend for it."

"Naturally," was the terse comment. "You have seen it, have you?"

"Yes, I saw it. It's about six inches tall, seems to be cut from a solid piece of ivory, and—"

"And has shiny eyes?" interrupted the other.

"Yes. The eyes seem to be of amethyst, highly polished."

Again The Thinking Machine walked the length of the room three times. "Do you know anything about self hypnotism, Mr. Hatch?" he inquired at last.

"Only that there is such a thing," replied the reporter, wondering at the abrupt change in the trend of the conversation. "Why?"

The Thinking Machine didn't say why. "You came to me, of course, to see if it was possible, by throwing light on this affair, to restore Fairbanks's mind?" he inquired instead.

"Well, that was the idea," Hatch agreed. "Fairbanks was evidently driven to his present condition by the haunting mystery of this thing, by brooding over it, and by the tangible existence in his hands of that ivory god which established a definite connection with an experience which might otherwise have been only a nightmare, and it occurred to me that if he could be made to see just what had happened and the underlying causes for its happening, he might be brought back to a normal condition." The reporter was silent for a moment, with eyes set on the drawn, inscrutable face of The Thinking Machine. "Of course," he added, "I am presuming that if it was not a diseased mental condition the things as he set them down did happen, and if they did happen I know you won't believe that they were due to other than natural causes."

"I don't disbelieve in anything, Mr. Hatch," and The Thinking Machine regarded the newspaper man quietly. "I don't even disbelieve in what is broadly termed the supernatural—I merely don't know. It is necessary, in the solution of material problems, to work from a material basis, and then the things which are conjured up by fear and—and failure to understand may be dissipated. That is done by logic, Mr. Hatch. Disregard the supernatural, so called, in our material problems, and logic is as inevitable as that two and two make four, not sometimes, but *all* the time."

"You don't deny the possibility of the so called supernatural, then?" Hatch asked, and again there was a note of surprise in his voice.

"I don't deny anything until I know," was the response. "I don't know that there is a supernatural force; therefore," and he shrugged his slender, stooping shoulders, "I work only from a material basis. If this manuscript states facts, then Fairbanks saw an old man, not a spook; he saw a woman, not a wraith; he jumped to escape a real fire, not a ghost fire. When we disregard the supernatural, we must admit that everything was real, unless it was pure invention, and the broken ankle and burned clothing are against that. If these were real people, we can find them—that's all there is to that. Yet there is a chance that the whole tale is a fiction, or the product of a disordered brain. But even that being true, it interferes in no way with the inevitable logic of the affair. When we know that this manuscript is in existence, and when we know that the man who produced it has since become a raving maniac, the sheer logic of the thing reveals clearly the intermediate steps."

"How, for instance?" Hatch inquired curiously.

"Well, we have this," and The Thinking Machine rattled the sheets of the manuscript impatiently; "and while we'll admit it was written by a sane man, we know that that man has since become a maniac. I stated the incidents which led to his incarceration as logic unfolded them to me. First I knew that insanity from fear and failure to understand nearly always takes the maniacal turn; therefore I saw that instead of being insane, as you stated first, Fairbanks was probably a maniac. There is a difference."

The reporter nodded.

"Next, one of the first manifestations of a maniacal condition is a homicidal tendency. Did Fairbanks attempt homicide? Yes.

"Now the problem grew a little more complex, rather intricately psychological, if I may say it that way," The Thinking Machine explained precisely. "However, it goes back generally to the broad grounds that a woman in a flowing white night robe typifies the popular conception of the ghostly, and when we know that this supposed wraith, or one of them, was a woman in white, we see that in Fairbanks's condition at the moment the appearance of such a figure would have instantly aroused him to the frenzy which led to the subsequent events."

"I understand, so far," Hatch remarked.

"Now the only woman—the most likely woman, I should say—to go to his room in a white night robe was his mother." He paused for a moment. "Therefore, his mother was in all probability the object of his attack. Remember, he was mad with fear, and, appearing suddenly as she did, perhaps in a dim light, she was to his disordered brain the incarnation of that thing he most feared."

Hatch seemed to be perfectly fascinated. His cigarette burned up until the fire touched his fingers; and he barely noticed it.

"In this manuscript," The Thinking Machine resumed after a moment, "Fairbanks tells me that he had a revolver, and shows a distinct weakness for the weapon. Therefore, wouldn't he shoot at this incarnation of the thing which was responsible for his condition. He did shoot. The fact that the incidents happened in Fairbanks's own room at night was an assumption based upon the fact that his mother figured in it, and the further fact that she was dressed for bed when she appeared in his room. Of course, if her room was near, her attention would be attracted by some unusual noise. If these noises were due to a maniac, they were in all probability screams."

"Well, by George!" Hatch remarked fervently. "It's—"

"Now the first thing to do is to see Fairbanks in person," interrupted The Thinking Machine, with a sudden change to a most business like tone. "I think, if he can comprehend at all, that I may be able to do something for him."

The Thinking Machine—Professor Augustus S. F. X. Van Dusen, scientist—was cordially, even deferentially, received by Dr. Pollock, physician in charge of the Westbrook Sanatorium.

"I should like to spend ten minutes in the padded cell with Fairbanks," he announced tersely.

Dr. Pollock regarded him curiously, but without surprise. "It's dangerous," he remarked doubtfully. "I have no objection, of course; but I should advise that a couple of keepers go in with you."

"I'll go alone," announced the diminutive man of science. "It may be that I can quiet him." Dr. Pollock merely stared. "By the way," The Thinking Machine added, "you have that little ivory god here, haven't you? Well, let me see it, please."

It was produced and subjected to a searching scrutiny, after which the scientist set it up on a table, dropped into a seat facing it, leaned forward on his elbows, and sat staring straight into the amethyst eyes for a long time. A curious silence fell upon the watchers as he sat there immovable, minute after minute, staring, staring. Hatch absently glanced at his watch and went over and looked out the window. The thing was getting on his nerves.

At last the scientist arose and thrust the grinning god into his pocket. "Now, please," he directed curtly, "I shall go into the cell with Fairbanks alone. I want the door closed behind me, and I want that door to remain closed for ten minutes. Under no circumstances must there be any interruption." He turned upon Dr. Pollock. "Don't have any fears for me. I'm not a fool."

Dr. Pollock led the way along the corridor, down some stairs, and paused before a door.

"Just ten minutes—no more, no less," directed the scientist.

The key was inserted in the lock, and the door swung on its hinges. Instantly the ears of the three men outside were assailed by a torrent of screams, of blasphemy, hideous imprecations. The maniac rushed for the door, and Hatch for an instant gazed straight into a distorted, pallid face in which there was no trace of intelligence, or even of humanity. He turned away with a shudder. Dr. Pollock thrust his arm forward to stay the swaying figure, and glanced round at The Thinking Machine doubtfully.

"Look at me! Look at me!" commanded the scientist sharply, and the squint blue eyes fearlessly met the glitter of madness in the eyes of Fairbanks. He raised his right hand suddenly in front of his face, and instantly the incoherent ravings stopped, while some strange, sudden change came over the maniacal face. In the scientist's right hand was the grinning god. That was the magic which had stilled the ravings. Slowly, slowly, with his eyes fixed upon those of the maniac, the scientist edged his way into the cell, Fairbanks retreating almost imperceptibly. Never for an instant did the maniacal eyes leave the ivory image; yet he made no attempt to seize it, he seemed merely fascinated.

"Close the door," directed The Thinking Machine quietly, without so much as a glance back. "Ten minutes!"

Dr. Pollock closed the door and turned the key in the lock, after which he looked at the newspaper man with an expression of frank bewilderment on his face. Hatch said nothing, only glanced at his watch and went over to the window, where he stood staring out moodily, with every nerve strained to catch any sound which might by chance penetrate the heavy, padded walls.

One minute, two minutes, three minutes! The second hand of Hatch's watch moved at a snail's pace! Four minutes, five minutes, six minutes! Then through the well nigh impenetrable wall came faintly the sound of hoarse cries, of screams, and finally the crash of something falling. Dr. Pollock's face paled a little and he turned the key in the lock.

"No!" and Hatch sprang forward to seize the physician's hand.

"But he's in danger," declared the doctor emphatically; "maybe even killed!" Again he tugged at the door.

"No!" said Hatch again, and he shoved the physician aside. "He said ten minutes, and—and I know the man!"

Eight minutes! Listening tensely, they knew that the screaming had stopped; there was dead silence. Nine minutes! Still they stood there, Hatch guarding the door, and his eyes unflinchingly fixed on the physician's face. Ten minutes! And Hatch opened the door.

Professor Augustus S. F. X. Van Dusen—The Thinking Machine—was sitting calmly on a padded seat beside Harold Fairbanks, with one slender hand resting on his pulse. Fairbanks himself sat with his ivory image held close up to his eyes, babbling and mumbling at it incoherently. An over-turned table lay in the middle of the cell. So great had been the power used to upset it that an iron bolt which held it fast to the floor had been broken short off. The scientist arose and came toward them; and Hatch drew a deep breath of relief.

"I would advise that this man be placed in another cell," said the little scientist quietly. "There is no further need to keep him in a padded cell. Put him somewhere where he can see out and find something to attract his attention. Meanwhile let him keep that ivory image, and there'll be no more raving."

"What—what did you do to him?" demanded the physician in deep perplexity.

"Nothing—yet," was the enigmatic response. "I'd like for him to stay here a couple of days longer, under constant watch as to

his physical condition,—never mind his mental condition now,—
and then with your permission I'll make a little experiment which
I believe will restore him to a normal condition. Meanwhile he
needs the best of physical care. Let him babble,—he will, anyway,—
that doesn't matter just now."

Harold Fairbanks sat beside The Thinking Machine in the second seat of a huge touring car, with the slender hand of the scientist resting lightly on his wrist. In front of them the chauffeur was
busy with the multiple levers of the great machine; and behind
them sat Hutchinson Hatch and Dr. Pollock. They were scudding
along a smooth road, with the wind beating in their faces, guided
by the ribbons of light which shot out ahead from their forward
lamps. The night was perfectly black, with not a light point visible
save those carried by their own car.

Behind them lay the quiet little village of Pelham, and miles
away in front was the town of Millen. From time to time as the car
rushed on The Thinking Machine peered inquisitively through the
darkness into the face of the man beside him; but he could barely
make out its general shape,—a pallid splotch in the darkness. The
hand lay quietly beside his own, and a senile voice mumbled and
babbled—that was all. The newspaper man and the physician in
the rear seat had nothing to say; they too were peering vainly at
Fairbanks.

At last through the gloom the outlines of a small building
loomed dimly in front of them, just off the road to the left. The
Thinking Machine leaned forward and touched the chauffeur on
the arm.

"We'll stop here for gasolene," he said distinctly.

"Gasolene—stop here for gasolene!" babbled a senseless voice
beside him.

The Thinking Machine felt the hand he held move spasmodically as the huge car ran off the main roadway and maneuvered
back and forth to clear the fairway of its bulk. Finally it stopped,
with its tonneau, end on, within a few feet of the door of the building. The scientist's fingers closed more tightly on the wrist; and
after a moment the incoherent mumbling began again.

Hutchinson Hatch and Dr. Pollock arose and got out. Hatch went straight to the little building and rapped sharply. The sound caused Fairbanks to turn vacant, wavering eyes in that direction. After a moment a nightcapped head appeared at the window above. The Thinking Machine shot an electric flashlight into Fairbanks's face. The eyes, now fixed on the nightcapped head, were wide open, and a glint of childish curiosity lay in them. The babblings were silent for a moment,—somewhere in a recess of the maddened brain a germ of intelligence was struggling. Then, as the scientist regarded him steadily, the expression of the face changed again, the eyes grew vacant, the mouth flabby, the senile mumblings began again.

Hatch began and concluded negotiations for five gallons of gasolene. A shrunken shanked old man brought it out in a can, delivered it, and scuttled back into the house with his safety lantern. Dr. Pollock and Hatch took their seats again, while The Thinking Machine clambered out and went round to the back, where he spoke to the chauffeur, who was busy at the tank. The chauffeur nodded as if he understood, and followed the scientist to his seat.

"Now for Millen," directed the scientist quietly.

"Millen!" Fairbanks repeated meaninglessly.

The chauffeur twisted his wheel, backed a little, caught the forward clutch, whirled his car straight to the road again, and shot out through the darkness.

For two or three minutes there was utter silence, save for the chug and whir of the engine and the clanking rattle of the car; then The Thinking Machine spoke over his shoulder to Hatch and Dr. Pollock.

"Did either of you notice anything peculiar?" he inquired.

"No," was the simultaneous response. "Why?"

"Mr. Hatch, you have that automobile map," the scientist continued without heeding the question. "Take this electric light and examine it once more, to satisfy us that there is no road between the little store and Millen."

"I know there isn't," Hatch told him.

"Do as I say!" directed the other crabbedly. "We can't afford to make mistakes."

Obediently enough Hatch and Dr. Pollock studied the map. There was the road, straight away from the star, to Millen. There was not a bypath or deviation of any kind marked on it.

"Straight as a string," Hatch announced.

"Now look!" directed The Thinking Machine.

The huge car slowed up and came to a standstill. The glittering lamps of the car showed two roads instead of one—two roads, here where there were not two roads! Hatch glared at them for a moment, then fumbled with the automobile map.

"Why, hang it! there can't be two roads!" he declared.

"But there they are," replied The Thinking Machine.

He felt Fairbanks's hand flutter, and then it was raised suddenly. Again he threw the light on the pallid face. A strange expression was there; a set, incredible, vague expression which might have meant anything. The eyes were turned ahead to where the road was split by a small clump of trees.

"Keep on to your left," The Thinking Machine directed the chauffeur, without, however, removing his eyes from the face of the man beside him. "A little more slowly."

The car started up again and swung off to the left, sharply. Every eye, save the squint, blue ones of the scientist, was turned ahead; he was still staring into the face of his patient. His light still showed realization struggling feebly there. Perhaps only the chauffeur realized what a steady turn to the left the car made; but he said nothing, only felt his way along till suddenly the road widened a little where a path cut through the dense forest, and was lost in the perspective of gloom. The car slowed up.

"Don't stop!" commanded the scientist sharply. "Go ahead!"

With a sudden spurt the car rushed forward, skimming along easily for a time, and then the heavy jolting told them all that the road was growing rougher, and here, dimly ahead of them, they saw an open patch of sky. It was evidently the edge of the forest. The car went steadily on and out into the open, clear of the forest; then the chauffeur slowed down.

"There isn't any road here," he remarked.

"Go on!" commanded The Thinking Machine tensely. "Road or no road—straight ahead!"

The chauffeur took a new grip on his wheel and went straight ahead, over plowed ground, apparently, for the bumping and jolting were terrific, and the steering gear tore at the sockets of his arms viciously. For two or three minutes they proceeded this way, while the scientist's light still played on Fairbanks's face and the squint eyes unwaveringly watched every tiny change in it.

"There!" shrieked Fairbanks suddenly, and he came to his feet. "There!"

Hatch and Dr. Pollock saw it at the same instant,—a faint, rosy point in the distance; The Thinking Machine didn't alter the direction of his gaze.

"Straight for the light!" he commanded.

... the room showed every evidence of occupancy ... log fire was burning, and its flickering light showed books strewn about here and there ... directly in front of them stood a man, tall, angular, aged, and a little bent ... hands were knotted, toil worn; and the left forefinger was missing ... eyes white and glassy!

With a choking, gutteral exclamation of some sort, Fairbanks darted forward and placed the grinning god upon the mantel beside a piece of crystal, then turned back to The Thinking Machine and seized him by the arm, as a child might have sought protection. The Thinking Machine nodded at him, and a grin of foolish delight overspread the pallid face.

Meanwhile, the strange old man, who seemed utterly oblivious of their presence, stood beside the fire gazing into it with sightless eyes. The scientist moved toward him slowly, Fairbanks staring as if fascinated. Finally the scientist extended his hand, which held that of Fairbanks, and touched the old man on the shoulder. He started violently and stretched out both hands instinctively.

Then, while Hatch and Dr. Pollock looked on silently, The Thinking Machine stood motionless, while the strange old man's hands ran up his arm, and the fingers touched his face. The right fore-finger paused for an instant at the eyes, then was laid lightly across the thin lips. It remained there.

"You are blind?" asked the scientist.

The strange old man nodded.

"You are deaf?"

Again the old man nodded. His forefinger still rested lightly on The Thinking Machine's lips.

"You are dumb?" the scientist went on.

Again the nod.

"Deafness, dumbness, blindness, result of disease?"

The nod again.

The Thinking Machine turned and lifted Fairbanks's hand till it rested on the old man's shoulder, then slowly down the arm, while his eyes studied the changed expression on the pallid face.

"Real, real!" said The Thinking Machine slowly to Fairbanks. "A man—you understand?"

Fairbanks merely started back; but it was evident that some great struggle was going on in his mind. There was a growing interest in his face, the mouth was no longer flabby, the eyes were fixed.

... then there came another sound ... a curdling, nerve-racking scream ... a scream of agony, of pain, of fear ... a hideous, awful thing ... suddenly all was silent again.

At the first sound Fairbanks straightened up, then slowly he started forward. Three steps, and he fell. Hatch and Dr. Pollock turned him over and found on his face an expression of utter, cringing fear. The eyes were roving, glittering, and he was babbling again. Only his weakness had prevented flight.

"Stay there!" commanded The Thinking Machine hurriedly, and ran out of the room.

Hatch heard him as he went up the steps; then after a moment there came more screams, rather a sharp, intermittent wailing. Fairbanks struggled feebly, then lay still, flat on his back. A minute more, and The Thinking Machine reentered the room, leading a woman by the hand—a woman in a gingham apron and with her hair flying loose about her face. He went straight to the old man, who had stood motionless through it all, and raised the toilworn finger to his lips.

"A woman is here—your wife?" he asked.

The old man shook his head.

"Your sister?"

The old man nodded.

"She is insane?"

Again a nod.

The woman stood for an instant with roving eyes, then rushed toward the mantel with a peculiar sobbing cry. In another instant she had clasped the ugly ivory image to her withered breast, and was crooning to it softly as a mother to her babe. Fairbanks raised himself from the floor, stared at her dully for a moment, then fell back into the arms of Dr. Pollock and Hatch with a sigh. He had fainted.

"I think, gentlemen, this is all," remarked The Thinking Machine.

It was more than a month later that The Thinking Machine called upon Harold Fairbanks at his home. The young man was sitting up in bed, weak but intelligently cognizant of everything about him. There was still an occasional restless roving of his eyes; but that was all.

"You remember me, Mr. Fairbanks?" began the scientist.

"Yes," was the reply.

"You remember the events of the night we were together?"

"Everything, from the time the automobile left the road and the light appeared in the distance," said Fairbanks. "I remember seeing the old man again, and the woman appearing. I know now that he was deaf and dumb and blind, and that she was insane. That seems to clear the situation a great deal." He passed a wasted hand across his brow. "But where is the place. I couldn't find it."

"Listen for just a moment now, please," said The Thinking Machine soothingly. "You don't remember shooting at your mother? No. Don't excite yourself; she was not wounded. Immediately after that you were placed in a sanatorium. I saw you there. The ivory image had been taken away from you. I went into the room where you were confined and gave it back to you. It acted as I thought it would,—quieted you. To make certain that it was this and nothing else that had that effect, I took it away from you again, and you grew violent—as a matter of fact, your condition was such that you overturned a heavy table that was bolted to the floor—broke the bolt. You don't remember that?"

"No."

"I left the image with you. That really was the tangible cause of your condition. If it hadn't been for that, and the brooding over the mystery which it constantly caused, the events of that first night would have passed out of your mind in time. You superinduced self hypnotism with that little image; that is, you must understand that self hypnotism is possible to persons of a certain temperament in a mechanical way, when the object employed is highly polished—shiny, I might say.

"Although that image brought you to the condition you were in, I restored it to you to quiet you physically. That was necessary before I could reproduce for you the events of the first night. You went with us in an automobile, from Pelham to the little store where you had stopped that first night for gasolene. We stopped there for gasolene, and saw the man you saw that first night. As a matter of fact, he had gone away only for a few months, and is now installed in the little store again. This was all done, you understand, to arouse you, if possible, to what was passing around you. In a way it succeeded.

"Well, from the little store we went as you went the night of your first trouble, until we came to the two roads, one leading by sharp turns to the left. Then we went straight to the farm house where the old man and the woman were. There I wanted to convince you that they were real people,—that there was nothing of the ghostly about them. As a matter of fact, that old man and the woman never knew you were in the house that night. The man had no means of knowing it so long as you never touched him nor he you. You say he brought in something to eat. In all probability that was intended for the woman. You assumed it was for yourself. The fire which compelled you to jump and which resulted in the broken ankle for you, did not destroy the house. There were still marks of it there but the heavy rain extinguished it, and carpenters made the necessary repairs. Now all that is clear, isn't it?"

"Perfectly," was the reply; "but the white thing in the road—the screaming I heard there?"

"There is no mystery whatever about that," continued the scientist calmly. "That road that turns to the left turns more sharply than you imagine. After a little distance it goes almost parallel with the main road, so that following it at night you would, without any knowledge of it, pass within a few hundred feet of a point on the main road. Now the house where these people live is say five hundred feet from the road that turns to the left therefore not more than eight hundred feet, we'll say, from the main road. Thus the screaming you heard in the main road was the woman who lived in that house; the figure you saw was that woman. Just why she had left the house and was wandering around through the wood does not appear; it is certain that she was there, and was frightened by the storm. I can only say that she might have known she was pursued by you and taken refuge on an overhanging limb, and thus gave you the impression of her figure rising above the ground and moving about among the trees.

"It followed naturally that by the time you had taken the roundabout way with your automobile and reached the house she had reached it by going straight ahead through the wood—say for eight hundred feet, and again you heard her screams there. Many things happened in that house that night of no consequence in themselves, but which to your excited imagination were mysterious. One of these was the candle going out. It is obvious that a gust of wind did that, or else a single drop of water from a leak in the roof. Do you follow me?"

Fairbanks was silent for several minutes as he lay back with his eyes closed. "But the vital thing, the real thing that bewildered me most of all," he said slowly, "you haven't touched. That is, Why was it that after all my searching for the road to the left and the farm house, I didn't find them, if they were there?"

"Of course you don't remember," explained The Thinking Machine; "but the night our party went over the route I asked Dr. Pollock and Mr. Hatch just after we left the little store whether they had noticed anything peculiar. They replied in the negative. As a matter of fact," and the scientist was speaking very quietly, "our automobile went the same way yours had gone—not toward Millen, as you supposed and they supposed, but back toward

Pelham. You didn't find the road to the left and the farm house when you were searching, for the reason that they were beyond the little store toward Pelham, eight or ten miles away."

A great wave of relief swept over the young man, and he leaned forward eagerly. "But wouldn't I have known when I turned the wrong way?" he demanded.

The Thinking Machine shrugged his shoulders. "You would have known in daylight, yes," was the reply, "but at night, in a hurry and somewhat confused by the flying dust, you turned the wrong way—toward Pelham, not toward Millen. You see that is possible when I tell you that Dr. Pollock and Mr. Hatch didn't notice that we had turned the wrong way, when there was no storm, and when I asked them if they had noticed anything peculiar."

There was a long silence. Fairbanks dropped back in the bed and lay silent.

"In your manuscript," resumed The Thinking Machine at last, "you mentioned that you seemed to hear some one calling you as you started away from the little store. This you attributed vaguely to imagination. As a matter of fact, you did hear some one call—it was the man who sold you the gasolene. He knew you intended going to Millen, saw that you had turned the wrong way, and called to tell you so. You didn't wait to hear."

And that was all of it.

The Chase of the Golden Plate

Part I: The Burglar And The Girl

Chapter I

Cardinal Richelieu and the Mikado stepped out on a narrow balcony overlooking the entrance to Seven Oaks, lighted their cigarettes and stood idly watching the throng as it poured up the wide marble steps. Here was an over-corpulent Dowager Empress of China, there an Indian warrior in full paint and toggery, and mincing along behind him two giggling Geisha girls. Next, in splendid robes of rank, came the Czar of Russia. The Mikado smiled.

"An old enemy of mine," he remarked to the Cardinal.

A Watteau Shepherdess was assisted out of an automobile by Christopher Columbus and they came up the walk arm-in-arm, while a Pierrette ran beside them laughing up into their faces. D'Artagnan, Athos, Aramis, and Porthos swaggered along with insolent, clanking swords.

"Ah!" exclaimed the Cardinal. "There are four gentlemen whom I know well."

Mary Queen of Scots, Pocahontas, the Sultan of Turkey, and Mr. Micawber chatted amicably together in one language. Behind them came a figure which immediately arrested attention. It was a Burglar, with dark lantern in one hand and revolver in the other. A black mask was drawn down to his lips, a slouch hat shaded his eyes, and a kit of the tools of his profession swung from one shoulder.

"By George!" commented the Cardinal. "Now, that's clever."

"Looks like the real thing," the Mikado added.

The Burglar stood aside a moment, allowing a diamond-burdened Queen Elizabeth to pass, then came on up the steps. The Cardinal and the Mikado passed through an open window into the reception-room to witness his arrival.

"Her Royal Highness, Queen Elizabeth!" the graven-faced servant announced.

The Burglar handed a card to the liveried Voice and noted, with obvious amusement, a fleeting expression of astonishment on the stolid face. Perhaps it was there because the card had been offered in that hand which held the revolver. The Voice glanced at the name on the card and took a deep breath of relief.

"Bill, the Burglar!" he announced.

There was a murmur of astonishment and interest in the reception-hall and the ballroom beyond. Thus it was that the Burglar found himself the centre of attention for a moment, while a ripple of laughter ran around. The entrance of a Clown, bounding in behind him, drew all eyes away, however, and the Burglar was absorbed in the crowd.

It was only a few minutes later that Cardinal Richelieu and the Mikado, seeking diversion, isolated the Burglar and dragged him off to the smoking-room. There the Czar of Russia, who was on such terms of intimacy with the Mikado that he called him Mike, joined them, and they smoked together.

"How did you ever come to hit on a costume like that?" asked the Cardinal of the Burglar.

The Burglar laughed, disclosing two rows of strong, white teeth. A cleft in the square-cut, clean-shaven chin, visible below the mask, became more pronounced. A woman would have called it a dimple.

"I wanted something different," he explained. "I couldn't imagine anything more extraordinary than a real burglar here ready to do business, so I came."

"It's lucky the police didn't see you," remarked the Czar.

Again the Burglar laughed. He was evidently a good-natured craftsman, despite his sinister garb.

"That was my one fear—that I would be pinched before I arrived," he replied. "'Pinched,' I may explain, is a technical term in my profession meaning jugged, nabbed, collared, run in. It seemed that my fears had some foundation, too, for when I drove up in my auto and stepped out a couple of plain-clothes men stared at me pretty hard."

He laid aside the dark lantern and revolver to light a fresh cigarette. The Mikado picked up the lantern and flashed the light on
and off several times, while the Czar sighted the revolver at the floor.

"Better not do that," suggested the Burglar casually. "It's
loaded."

"Loaded?" repeated the Czar. He laid down the revolver gingerly.

"Surest thing, you know," and the Burglar laughed quizzically.
"I'm the real thing, you see, so naturally my revolver is loaded. I
think I ought to be able to make quite a good haul, as we say, before unmasking-time."

"If you're as clever as your appearance would indicate," said
the Cardinal admiringly, "I see no reason why it shouldn't be worth
while. You might, for instance, make a collection of Elizabethan
jewels. I have noticed four Elizabeths so far, and it's early yet."

"Oh, I'll make it pay," the Burglar assured him lightly. "I'm
pretty clever; practised a good deal, you know. Just to show you
that I am an expert, here is a watch and pin I took from my friend,
the Czar, five minutes ago."

He extended a well-gloved hand in which lay the watch and diamond pin. The Czar stared at them a moment in frank astonishment; patted, himself all over in sudden trepidation; then laughed
sheepishly. The Mikado tilted his cigar up to a level with the slant
eyes of his mask, and laughed.

"In the language of diplomacy, Nick," he told the Czar, "you
are what is known as 'easy.' I thought I had convinced you of that."

"Gad, you are clever," remarked the Cardinal. "I might have
used you along with D'Artagnan and the others."

The Burglar laughed again and stood up lazily.

"Come on, this is stupid," he suggested. "Let's go out and see
what's doing."

"Say, just between ourselves tell us who you are," urged the
Czar. "Your voice seems familiar, but I can't place you."

"Wait till unmasking-time," retorted the Burglar good-
naturedly. "Then you'll know. Or if you think you could bribe that
stone image who took my card at the door you might try. He'll remember me. I never saw a man so startled in all my life as he was
when I appeared."

The quartet sauntered out into the ballroom just as the signal for the grand march was given. A few minutes later the kaleidoscopic picture began to move. Stuyvesant Randolph, the host, as Sir Walter Raleigh, and his superb wife, as Cleopatra, looked upon the mass of colour, and gleaming shoulders, and jewels, and brilliant uniforms, and found it good—extremely good.

Mr. Randolph smiled behind his mask at the striking incongruities on every hand: Queen Elizabeth and Mr. Micawber; Cardinal Richelieu and a Pierrette; a Clown dancing attendance on Marie Antoinette. The Czar of Russia paid deep and devoted attention to a light-footed Geisha girl, while the Mikado and Folly, a jingling thing in bells and abbreviated skirts, romped together.

The grotesque figure of the march was the Burglar. His revolver was thrust carelessly into a pocket and the dark lantern hung at his belt. He was pouring a stream of pleasing nonsense into the august ear of Lady Macbeth, nimbly seeking at the same time to evade the pompous train of the Dowager Empress. The grand march came to an end and the chattering throng broke up into little groups.

Cardinal Richelieu strolled along with a Pierrette on his arm.

"Business good?" he inquired of the Burglar.

"Expect it to be," was the reply.

The Pierrette came and, standing on her tip-toes—silly, impractical sort of toes they were—made a moue at the Burglar.

"Oooh!" she exclaimed. "You are perfectly horrid."

"Thank you," retorted the Burglar.

He bowed gravely, and the Cardinal, with his companion, passed on. The Burglar stood gazing after them a moment, then glanced around the room, curiously, two or three times. He might have been looking for someone. Finally he wandered away aimlessly through the crowd.

Chapter II

Half an hour later the Burglar stood alone, thoughtfully watching the dancers as they whirled by. A light hand fell on his arm—he started a little—and in his ear sounded a voice soft with the tone of a caress.

"Excellent, Dick, excellent!"

The Burglar turned quickly to face a girl—a Girl of the Golden West, with deliciously rounded chin, slightly parted rose-red lips, and sparkling, eager eyes as blue as—as blue as—well, they were blue eyes. An envious mask hid cheeks and brow, but above a sombrero was perched arrogantly on crisp, ruddy-gold hair, flaunting a tricoloured ribbon. A revolver swung at her hip—the wrong hip—and a Bowie knife, singularly inoffensive in appearance, was thrust through her girdle. The Burglar looked curiously a moment, then smiled.

"How did you know me?" he asked.

"By your chin," she replied. "You can never hide yourself behind a mask that doesn't cover that."

The Burglar touched his chin with one gloved hand.

"I forgot that," he remarked ruefully.

"Hadn't you seen me?"

"No."

The Girl drew nearer and laid one hand lightly on his arm; her voice dropped mysteriously.

"Is everything ready?" she asked.

"Oh, yes," he assured her quickly. His voice, too, was lowered cautiously.

"Did you come in the auto?"

"Yes."

"And the casket?"

For an instant the Burglar hesitated.

392

"The casket?" he repeated.

"Certainly, the casket. Did you get it all right?"

The Burglar looked at her with a new, business-like expression on his lips. The Girl returned his steady gaze for an instant, then her eyes dropped. A faint colour glowed in her white chin. The Burglar suddenly laughed admiringly.

"Yes, I got it," he said.

She took a deep breath quickly, and her white hands fluttered a little.

"We will have to go in a few minutes, won't we?" she asked uneasily.

"I suppose so," he replied.

"Certainly before unmasking-time," she said, "because—because I think there is someone here who knows, or suspects, that—"

"Suspects what?" demanded the Burglar.

"Sh-h-h-h!" warned the Girl, and she laid a finger on her lips. "Not so loud. Someone might hear. Here are some people coming now that I'm afraid of. They know me. Meet me in the conservatory in five minutes. I don't want them to see me talking to you."

She moved away quickly and the Burglar looked after her with admiration and some impalpable quality other than that in his eyes. He was turning away toward the conservatory when he ran into the arms of an oversized man lumpily clad in the dress of a courtier. The lumpy individual stood back and sized him up.

"Say, young fellow, that's a swell rig you got there," he remarked.

The Burglar glanced at him in polite astonishment—perhaps it was the tone of the remark.

"Glad you like it," he said coldly, and passed on.

As he waited in the conservatory the amusement died out of his eyes and his lips were drawn into a straight, sharp line. He had seen the lumpy individual speak to another man, indicating generally the direction of the conservatory as he did so. After a moment the Girl returned in deep agitation.

"We must go now—at once," she whispered hurriedly. "They suspect us. I know it, I know it!"

"I'm afraid so," said the Burglar grimly. "That's why that detective spoke to me."

"Detective?" gasped the Girl.

"Yes, a detective disguised as a gentleman."

"Oh, if they are watching us what shall we do?"

The Burglar glanced out, and seeing the man to whom the lumpy individual had spoken coming toward the conservatory, turned suddenly to the Girl.

"Do you really want to go with me?" he asked.

"Certainly," she replied eagerly.

"You are making no mistake?"

"No, Dick, no!" she said again. "But if we are caught—"

"Do as I say and we won't be caught," declared the Burglar. His tone now was sharp, commanding. "You go on alone toward the front door. Pass out as if to get a breath of fresh air. I'll follow in a minute. Watch for me. This detective is getting too curious for comfort. Outside we'll take the first auto and run for it."

He thoughtfully whirled the barrel of his revolver in his fingers as he stared out into the ballroom. The Girl clung to him helplessly a moment; her hand trembled on his arm.

"I'm frightened," she confessed. "Oh, Dick, if—"

"Don't lose your nerve," he commanded. "If you do we'll both be caught. Go on now, and do as I say. I'll come—but I may come in a hurry. Watch for me."

For just a moment more the Girl clung to his arm.

"Oh, Dick, you darling!" she whispered. Then, turning, she left him there.

From the door of the conservatory the Burglar watched her splendid, lithe figure as she threaded her way through the crowd. Finally she passed beyond his view and he sauntered carelessly toward the door.

Once he glanced back. The lumpy individual was following slowly. Then he saw a liveried servant approach the host and whisper to him excitedly.

"This is my cue to move," the Burglar told himself grimly.

Still watching, he saw the servant point directly at him. The host, with a sudden gesture, tore off his mask and the Burglar accelerated his pace.

"Stop that man!" called the host.

For one brief instant there was the dead silence which follows general astonishment—and the Burglar ran for the door. Several pairs of hands reached out from the crowd toward him.

"There he goes, there!" exclaimed the Burglar excitedly. "That man ahead! I'll catch him!"

The ruse opened the way and he went through. The Girl was waiting at the foot of the steps.

"They're coming!" he panted as he dragged her along. "Climb in that last car on the end there!"

Without a word the Girl ran to the auto and clambered into the front seat. Several men dashed out of the house. Wonderingly her eyes followed the vague figure of the Burglar as he sped along in the shadow of a wall. He paused beneath a window, picked up something and raced for the car.

"Stop him!" came a cry.

The Burglar flung his burden, which fell at the Girl's feet with a clatter, and leaped. The auto swayed as he landed beside her. With a quick twist of the wheel he headed out.

"Hurry, Dick, they're coming!" gasped the Girl.

The motor beneath them whirred and panted and the car began to move.

"Halt, or I'll fire," came another cry.

"Down!" commanded the Burglar.

His hand fell on the Girl's shoulder heavily and he dragged her below the level of the seat. Then, bending low over the wheel, he gave the car half power. It leaped out into the road in the path of its own light, just as there came a pistol-shot from behind, followed instantly by another.

The car sped on.

Chapter III

Stuyvesant Randolph, millionaire, owner of Seven Oaks and host of the masked ball, was able to tell the police only what happened, and not the manner of its happening. Briefly, this was that a thief, cunningly disguised as a Burglar with dark lantern and revolver in hand, had surreptitiously attended the masked ball by entering at the front door and presenting an invitation card. And when Mr. Randolph got this far in his story even he couldn't keep his face straight.

The sum total of everyone's knowledge, therefore, was this:

Soon after the grand march a servant entered the smoking-room and found the Burglar there alone, standing beside an open window, looking out. This smoking-room connected, by a corridor, with a small dining-room where the Randolph gold plate was kept in ostentatious seclusion. As the servant entered the smoking-room the Burglar turned away from the window and went out into the ball-room. He did not carry a bundle; he did not appear to be excited.

Fifteen or twenty minutes later the servant discovered that eleven plates of the gold service, valued roughly at $15,000, were missing. He informed Mr. Randolph. The information, naturally enough, did not elevate the host's enjoyment of the ball, and he did things hastily.

Meanwhile—that is, between the time when the Burglar left the smoking-room and the time when he passed out the front door—the Burglar had talked earnestly with a masked Girl of the West. It was established that, when she left him in the conservatory, she went out the front door. There she was joined by the Burglar, and then came their sensational flight in the automobile—a 40 horse-power car that moved like the wind. The automobile in which the Burglar had gone to Seven Oaks was left behind; thus far it had not been claimed.

The identity of the Burglar and the Girl made the mystery. It was easy to conjecture—that's what the police said—how the Burglar got away with the gold plate. He went into the smoking-room, then into the dining-room, dropped the gold plate into a sack and threw the sack out of a window. It was beautifully simple. Just what the Girl had to do with it wasn't very clear; perhaps a score or more articles of jewelry, which had been reported missing by guests, engaged her attention.

It was also easy to see how the Burglar and the Girl had been able to shake off pursuit by the police in two other automobiles. The car they had chosen was admittedly the fastest of the scores there, the night was pitch-dark, and, besides, a Burglar like that was liable to do anything. Two shots had been fired at him by the lumpy courtier, who was really Detective Cunningham, but they had only spurred him on.

These things were easy to understand. But the identity of the pair was a different and more difficult proposition, and there remained the task of yanking them out of obscurity. This fell to the lot of Detective Mallory, who represented the Supreme Police Intelligence of the Metropolitan District, happily combining a No. 11 shoe and a No. 6 hat.

He was a cautious, suspicious, far-seeing man—as police detectives go. For instance, it was he who explained the method of the theft with a lucidity that was astounding.

Detective Mallory and two or three of his satellites heard Mr. Randolph's story, then the statements of his two men who had attended the ball in costume, and the statements of the servants. After all this Mr. Mallory chewed his cigar and thought violently for several minutes. Mr. Randolph looked on expectantly; he didn't want to miss anything.

"As I understand it, Mr. Randolph," said the Supreme Police Intelligence at last, "each invitation-card presented at the door by your guests bore the name of the person to whom it was issued?"

"Yes," replied Mr. Randolph.

"Ah!" exclaimed the detective shrewdly. "Then we have a clue."

"Where are those cards, Curtis?" asked Mr. Randolph of the servant who had received them at the door.

"I didn't know they were of further value, sir, and they were thrown away—into the furnace."

Mr. Mallory was crestfallen.

"Did you notice if the card presented at the door by the Burglar on the evening of the masked ball at Seven Oaks bore a name?" he asked. He liked to be explicit like that.

"Yes, sir. I noticed it particularly because the gentleman was dressed so queerly."

"Do you remember the name?"

"No, sir."

"Would you remember it if you saw it or heard it again?"

The servant looked at Mr. Randolph helplessly.

"I don't think I would, sir," he answered.

"And the Girl? Did you notice the card she gave you?"

"I don't remember her at all, sir. Many of the ladies wore wraps when they came in, and her costume would not have been noticeable if she had on a wrap."

The Supreme Intelligence was thoughtful for another few minutes. At last he turned to Mr. Randolph again. "You are certain there was only one man at that ball dressed as a Burglar?" he asked.

"Yes, thank Heaven," replied Mr. Randolph fervently. "If there'd been another one they might have taken the piano."

The Supreme Intelligence frowned.

"And this girl was dressed like a Western girl?" he asked.

"Yes. A sort of Spirit-of-the-West costume."

"And no other woman there wore such a dress?"

"No," responded Mr. Randolph.

"No," echoed the two detectives.

"Now, Mr. Randolph, how many invitations were issued for the ball?"

"Three or four hundred. It's a big house," Mr. Randolph apologised, "and we tried to do the thing properly."

"How many persons do you suppose actually attended the ball?"

"Oh, I don't know. Three hundred, perhaps."

Detective Mallory thought again.

"It's unquestionably the work of two bold and clever professional crooks," he said at last judicially, and his satellites hung on his words eagerly. "It has every ear-mark of it. They perhaps planned the thing weeks before, and forged invitation-cards, or perhaps stole them—perhaps stole them."

He turned suddenly and pointed an accusing finger at the servant, Curtis.

"Did you notice the handwriting on the card the Burglar gave you?" he demanded.

"No, sir. Not particularly."

"I mean, do you recall if it was different in any way from the handwriting on the other cards?" insisted the Supreme Intelligence.

"I don't think it was, sir."

"If it had been would you have noticed it?"

"I might have, sir."

"Were the names written on all the invitation-cards by the same hand, Mr. Randolph?"

"Yes: my wife's secretary."

Detective Mallory arose and paced back and forth across the room with wrinkles in his brow.

"Ah!" he said at last, "then we know the cards were not forged, but stolen from someone to whom they had been sent. We know this much, therefore—" he paused a moment.

"Therefore all that must be done," Mr. Randolph finished the sentence, "is to find from whom the card or cards were stolen, who presented them at my door, and who got away with the plate."

The Supreme Intelligence glared at him aggressively. Mr. Randolph's face was perfectly serious. It was his gold plate, you know.

"Yes, that's it," Detective Mallory assented. "Now we'll get after this thing right. Downey, you get that automobile the Burglar left at Seven Oaks and find its owner; also find the car the Burglar and the Girl escaped in. Cunningham, you go to Seven Oaks and look over the premises. See particularly if the Girl left a wrap—she didn't wear one away from there—and follow that up. Blanton, you take a list of invited guests that Mr. Randolph will give you, check off those persons who are known to have been at the ball, and find out all about those who were not, and—follow that up."

"That'll take weeks!" complained Blanton.

The Supreme Intelligence turned on him fiercely.

"Well?" he demanded. He continued to stare for a moment, and Blanton wrinkled up in the baleful glow of his superior's scorn. "And," Detective Mallory added magnanimously, "I will do the rest."

Thus the campaign was planned against the Burglar and the Girl.

Chapter IV

Hutchinson Hatch was a newspaper reporter, a long, lean, hungry-looking young man with an insatiable appetite for facts. This last was, perhaps, an astonishing trait in a reporter; and Hatch was positively finicky on the point. That's why his City Editor believed in him. If Hatch had come in and told his City Editor that he had seen a blue elephant with pink side-whiskers his City Editor would have known that that elephant was blue—mentally, morally, physically, spiritually and everlastingly—not any washed-out green or purple, but blue.

Hatch was remarkable in other ways, too. For instance, he believed in the use of a little human intelligence in his profession. As a matter of fact, on several occasions he had demonstrated that it was really an excellent thing—human intelligence. His mind was well poised, his methods thorough, his style direct.

Along with dozens of others Hatch was at work on the Randolph robbery, and knew what the others knew—no more. He had studied the case so closely that he was beginning to believe, strangely enough, that perhaps the police were right in their theory as to the identity of the Burglar and the Girl—that is, that they were professional crooks. He could do a thing like that sometimes—bring his mind around to admit the possibility of somebody else being right.

It was on Saturday afternoon—two days after the Randolph affair—that Hatch was sitting in Detective Mallory's private office at Police Headquarters laboriously extracting from the Supreme Intelligence the precise things he had not found out about the robbery. The telephone-bell rang. Hatch got one end of the conversation—he couldn't help it. It was something like this:

"Hello! ... Yes, Detective Mallory ... Missing? ... What's her name? ... What? ... Oh, Dorothy! ... Yes? . . . Merritt? ... Oh, Merryman! ... Well, what the deuce is it then? ... SPELL IT! ...

M-e-r-e-d-i-t-h. Why didn't you say that at first? ... How long has she been gone? ... Huh? ... Thursday evening? ... What does she look like? ... Auburn hair. Red, you mean? ... Oh, ruddy! I'd like to know what's the difference."

The detective had drawn up a pad of paper and was jotting down what Hatch imagined to be the description of a missing girl. Then:

"Who is this talking?" asked the detective.

There was a little pause as he got the answer, and, having the answer, he whistled his astonishment, after which he glanced around quickly at the reporter, who was staring dreamily out a window.

"No," said the Supreme Intelligence over the 'phone. "It wouldn't be wise to make it public. It isn't necessary at all. I understand. I'll order a search immediately. No. The newspapers will get nothing of it. Good-by."

"A story?" inquired Hatch carelessly as he detective hung up the receiver.

"Doesn't amount to anything," was the reply.

"Yes, that's obvious," remarked the reporter drily.

"Well, whatever it is, it is not going to be made public," retorted the Supreme Intelligence sharply. He never did like Hatch, anyway. "It's one of those things that don't do any good in the newspapers, so I'll not let this one get there."

Hatch yawned to show that he had no further interest in the matter, and went out. But there was the germ of an idea in his head which would have startled Detective Mallory, and he paced up and down outside to develop it. A girl missing! A red-headed girl missing! A red-headed girl missing since Thursday! Thursday was the night of the Randolph masked hall. The missing Girl of the West was red-headed! Mallory had seemed astonished when he learned the name of the person who reported this last case! Therefore the person who reported it was high up—perhaps! Certainly high enough up to ask and receive the courtesy of police suppression—and the missing girl's name was Dorothy Meredith!

Hatch stood still for a long time on the curb and figured it out. Suddenly he rushed off to a telephone and called up Stuyvesant Randolph at Seven Oaks. He asked the first question with trepidation:

"Mr. Randolph, can you give me the address of Miss Dorothy Meredith?"

"Miss Meredith?" came the answer. "Let's see. I think she is stopping with the Morgan Greytons, at their suburban place."

The reporter gulped down a shout. "Worked, by thunder!" he exclaimed to himself. Then, in a deadly, forced calm:

"She attended the masked ball Thursday evening, didn't she?"

"Well, she was invited."

"You didn't see her there?"

"No. Who is this?"

Then Hatch hung up the receiver. He was nearly choking with excitement, for, in addition to all those virtues which have been enumerated, he possessed, too, the quality of enthusiasm. It was no part of his purpose to tell anybody anything. Mallory didn't know, he was confident, anything of the girl having been a possible guest at the ball. And what Mallory didn't know now wouldn't be found out, all of which was a sad reflection upon the detective.

In this frame of mind Hatch started for the suburban place of the Greytons. He found the house without difficulty. Morgan Greyton was an aged gentleman of wealth and exclusive ideas—wasn't in. Hatch handed a card bearing only his name, to a maid, and after a few minutes Mrs. Greyton appeared. She was a motherly, sweet-faced old lady of seventy, with that grave, exquisite courtesy which makes mere man feel ashamed of himself. Hatch had that feeling when he looked at her and thought of what he was going to ask.

"I came up direct from Police Headquarters," he explained diplomatically, "to learn any details you may be able to give us as to the disappearance of Miss Meredith."

"Oh, yes," replied Mrs. Greyton. "My husband said he was going to ask the police to look into the matter. It is most mysterious—most mysterious! We can't imagine where Dollie is, unless she has eloped. Do you know that idea keeps coming to me and won't go away?"

She spoke as if it were a naughty child.

"If you'll tell me something about Miss Meredith—who she is and all that?" Hatch suggested.

"Oh, yes, to be sure," exclaimed Mrs. Greyton. "Dollie is a distant cousin of my husband's sister's husband," she explained precisely. "She lives in Baltimore, but is visiting us. She has been here for several weeks. She's a dear, sweet girl, but I'm afraid—afraid she has eloped."

The aged voice quivered a little, and Hatch was more ashamed of himself than ever.

"Some time ago she met a man named Herbert—Richard Herbert, I think, and—"

"Dick Herbert?" the reporter exclaimed suddenly.

"Do you know the young gentleman?" inquired the old lady eagerly.

"Yes, it just happens that we were classmates in Harvard," said the reporter.

"And is he a nice young man?"

"A good, clean-cut, straightforward, decent man," replied Hatch. He could speak with a certain enthusiasm about Dick Herbert. "Go on, please," he urged.

"Well, for some reason I don't know, Dollie's father objects to Mr. Herbert's attentions to her—as a matter of fact, Mr. Meredith has absolutely prohibited them—but she's a young, headstrong girl, and I fear that, although she had outwardly yielded to her father's wishes, she had clandestinely kept up a correspondence with Mr. Herbert.

"Last Thursday evening she went out unattended and since then we have not heard from her—not a word. We can only surmise—my husband and I—that they have eloped. I know her father and mother will be heart-broken, but I have always noticed that if a girl sets her heart on a man, she will get him. And perhaps it's just as well that she has eloped now since you assure me he is a nice young man."

Hatch was choking back a question that rose in his throat. He hated to ask it, because he felt this dear, garrulous old woman would have hated him for it, if she could have known its purpose. But at last it came.

"Do you happen to know," he asked, "if Miss Meredith attended the Randolph ball at Seven Oaks on Thursday evening?"

"I dare say she received an invitation," was the reply. "She receives many invitations, but I don't think she went there. It was a costume affair, I suppose?"

The reporter nodded.

"Well, I hardly believe she went there then," Mrs. Greyton replied. "She has had no costume of any sort made. No, I am positive she has eloped with Mr. Herbert, but I should like to hear from her to satisfy myself and explain to her parents. We did not permit Mr. Herbert to come here, and it will be very hard to explain."

Hatch heard the slight rustle of a skirt in the hall and glanced toward the door. No one appeared, and he turned back to Mrs. Greyton.

"I don't suppose it possible that Miss Meredith has returned to Baltimore?" he asked.

"Oh, no!" was the positive reply. "Her father there telegraphed to her to-day—I opened it—saying he would be here, probably to-night, and I—I haven't the heart to tell him the truth when he arrives. Somehow, I have been hoping that we would hear and—and—"

Then Hatch took his shame in his hand and excused himself. The maid attended him to the door.

"How much is it worth to you to know if Miss Meredith went to the masked ball?" asked the maid cautiously.

"Eavesdropping, eh?" asked Hatch in disgust.

The maid shrugged her shoulders.

"How much is it worth?" she repeated.

Hatch extended his hand. She took a ten-dollar bill which lay there and secreted it in some remote recess of her being.

"Miss Meredith did go to the ball," she said. "She went there to meet Mr. Herbert. They had arranged to elope from there and she had made all her plans. I was in her confidence and assisted her."

"What did she wear?" asked Hatch eagerly.

"Her costume was that of a Western Girl," the maid responded. "She wore a sombrero, and carried a Bowie knife and revolver."

Hatch nearly swallowed his palate.

Chapter V

Hatch started back to the city with his brain full of seven-column heads. He thoughtfully lighted a cigar just before he stepped on the car.

"No smoking," said the conductor.

The reporter stared at him with dull eyes and then went in and sat down with the cigar in his mouth.

"No smoking, I told you," bawled the conductor.

"Certainly not," exclaimed Hatch indignantly. He turned and glared at the only other occupant of the car, a little girl. She wasn't smoking. Then he looked at the conductor and awoke suddenly.

"Miss Meredith is the girl," Hatch was thinking. "Mallory doesn't even dream it and never will. He won't send a man out there to do what I did. The Greytons are anxious to keep it quiet, and they won't say anything to anybody else until they know what really happened. I've got it bottled up, and don't know how to pull the cork. Now, the question is: What possible connection can there be between Dorothy Meredith and the Burglar? Was Dick Herbert the Burglar? Why, of course not! Then—what?"

Pondering all these things deeply, Hatch left the car and ran up to see Dick Herbert. He was too self-absorbed to notice that the blinds of the house were drawn. He rang, and after a long time a man-servant answered the bell.

"Mr. Herbert here?" Hatch asked.

"Yes, sir, he's here," replied the servant, "but I don't know if he can see you. He is not very well, sir."

"Not very well?" Hatch repeated.

"No, it's not that he's sick, sir. He was hurt and—"

"Who is it, Blair?" came Herbert's voice from the top of the stair.

"Mr. Hatch, sir."

406

"Come up, Hatch!" Dick called cordially. "Glad to see you. I'm so lonesome here I don't know what to do with myself."

The reporter ran up the steps and into Dick's room.

"Not that one," Dick smiled as Hatch reached for his right hand. "It's out of business. Try this one—" And he offered his left.

"What's the matter?" Hatch inquired.

"Little hurt, that's all," said Dick. "Sit down. I got it knocked out the other night and I've been here in this big house alone with Blair ever since. The doctor told me not to venture out yet. It has been lonesome, too. All the folks are away, up in Nova Scotia, and took the other servants along. How are you, anyhow?"

Hatch sat down and stared at Dick thoughtfully. Herbert was a good-looking, forceful person of twenty-eight or thirty, and a corking right-guard. Now he seemed a little washed out, and there was a sort of pallor beneath the natural tan.

He was a young man of family, unburdened by superlative wealth, but possessing in his own person the primary elements of success. He looked what Hatch had said of him: a "good, clean-cut, straightforward, decent man."

"I came up here to say something to you in my professional capacity," the reporter began at last; "and frankly, I don't know how to say it."

Dick straightened up in his chair with a startled expression on his face. He didn't speak, but there was something in his eyes which interested Hatch immensely.

"Have you been reading the papers?" the reporter asked— "that is, during the last couple of days?"

"Yes."

"Of course, then, you've seen the stories about the Randolph robbery?"

Dick smiled a little.

"Yes," he said. "Clever, wasn't it?"

"It was," Hatch responded enthusiastically. "It was." He was silent for a moment as he accepted and lighted a cigarette. "It doesn't happen," he went on, "that, by any possible chance, you know anything about it, does it?"

"Not beyond what I saw in the papers. Why?"

"I'll be frank and ask you some questions, Dick," Hatch resumed in a tone which betrayed his discomfort. "Remember I am here in my official capacity—that is, not as a friend of yours, but as a reporter. You need not answer the questions if you don't want to."

Dick arose with a little agitation in his manner and went over and stood beside the window.

"What is it all about?" he demanded. "What are the questions?"

"Do you know where Miss Dorothy Meredith is?"

Dick turned suddenly and glared at him with a certain lowering of his eyebrows which Hatch knew from the football days.

"What about her?" he asked.

"Where is she?" Hatch insisted.

"At home, so far as I know. Why?"

"She is not there," the reporter informed him, "and the Greytons believe that you eloped with her."

"Eloped with her?" Dick repeated. "She is not at home?"

"No. She's been missing since Thursday evening—the evening of the Randolph affair. Mr. Greyton has asked the police to look for her, and they are doing so now, but quietly. It is not known to the newspapers—that is, to other newspapers. Your name has not been mentioned to the police. Now, isn't it a fact that you did intend to elope with her on Thursday evening?"

Dick strode feverishly across the room several times, then stopped in front of Hatch's chair.

"This isn't any silly joke?" he asked fiercely.

"Isn't it a fact that you did intend to elope with her on Thursday evening?" the reporter went on steadily.

"I won't answer that question."

"Did you get an invitation to the Randolph ball?"

"Yes."

"Did you go?"

Dick was staring straight down into his eyes.

"I won't answer that, either," he said after a pause.

"Where were you on the evening of the masked ball?"

"Nor will I answer that."

When the newspaper instinct is fully aroused a reporter has no friends. Hatch had forgotten that he ever knew Dick Herbert. To him the young man was now merely a thing from which he might wring certain information for the benefit of the palpitating public.

"Did the injury to your arm," he went on after the approved manner of attorney for the prosecution, "prevent you going to the ball?"

"I won't answer that."

"What is the nature of the injury?"

"Now, see here, Hatch," Dick burst out, and there was a dangerous undertone in his manner, "I shall not answer any more questions—particularly that last one—unless I know what this is all about. Several things happened on the evening of the masked ball that I can't go over with you or anyone else, but as for me having any personal knowledge of events at the masked ball—well, you and I are not talking of the same thing at all."

He paused, started to say something else, then changed his mind and was silent.

"Was it a pistol shot?" Hatch went on calmly.

Dick's lips were compressed to a thin line as he looked at the reporter, and he controlled himself only by an effort.

"Where did you get that idea?" he demanded.

Hatch would have hesitated a long time before he told him where he got that idea; but vaguely it had some connection with the fact that at least two shots were fired at the Burglar and the Girl when they raced away from Seven Oaks.

While the reporter was rummaging through his mind for an answer to the question there came a rap at the door and Blair appeared with a card. He handed it to Dick, who glanced at it, looked a little surprised, then nodded. Blair disappeared. After a moment there were footsteps on the stairs and Stuyvesant Randolph entered.

Chapter VI

Dick arose and offered his left hand to Mr. Randolph, who calmly ignored it, turning his gaze instead upon the reporter.

"I had hoped to find you alone," he said frostily.

Hatch made as if to rise.

"Sit still, Hatch," Dick commanded. "Mr. Hatch is a friend of mine, Mr. Randolph. I don't know what you want to say, but whatever it is, you may say it freely before him."

Hatch knew that humour in Dick. It always preceded the psychological moment when he wanted to climb down someone's throat and open an umbrella. The tone was calm, the words clearly enunciated, and the face was white—whiter than it had been before.

"I shouldn't like to—" Mr. Randolph began.

"You may say what you want to before Mr. Hatch, or not at all, as you please," Dick went on evenly.

Mr. Randolph cleared his throat twice and waved his hands with an expression of resignation.

"Very well," he replied. "I have come to request the return of my gold plate."

Hatch leaned forward in his chair, gripping its arms fiercely. This was a question bearing broadly on a subject that he wanted to mention, but he didn't know how. Mr. Randolph apparently found it easy enough.

"What gold plate?" asked Dick steadily.

"The eleven pieces that you, in the garb of a Burglar, took from my house last Thursday evening," said Mr. Randolph. He was quite calm.

Dick took a sudden step forward, then straightened up with flushed face. His left hand closed with a snap and the nails bit into the flesh; the fingers of the helpless right hand worked nervously.

In a minute now Hatch could see him climbing all over Mr. Randolph.

But again Dick gained control of himself. It was a sort of recognition of the fact that Mr. Randolph was fifty years old; Hatch knew it; Mr. Randolph's knowledge on the subject didn't appear. Suddenly Dick laughed.

"Sit down, Mr. Randolph, and tell me about it," he suggested.

"It isn't necessary to go into details," continued Mr. Randolph, still standing. "I had not wanted to go this far in the presence of a third person, but you forced me to do it. Now, will you or will you not return the plate?"

"Would you mind telling me just what makes you think I got it?" Dick insisted.

"It is as simple as it is conclusive," said Mr. Randolph. "You received an invitation to the masked hall. You went there in your Burglar garb and handed your invitation-card to my servant. He noticed you particularly and read your name on the card. He remembered that name perfectly. I was compelled to tell the story as I knew it to Detective Mallory. I did not mention your name; my servant remembered it, had given it to me in fact, but I forbade him to repeat it to the police. He told them something about having burned the invitation-cards."

"Oh, wouldn't that please Mallory?" Hatch thought.

"I have not even intimated to the police that I have the least idea of your identity," Mr. Randolph went on, still standing. "I had believed that it was some prank of yours and that the plate would be returned in due time. Certainly I could not account for you taking it in any other circumstances. My reticence, it is needless to say, was in consideration of your name and family. But now I want the plate. If it was a prank to carry out the role of the Burglar, it is time for it to end. If the fact that the matter is now in the hands of the police has frightened you into the seeming necessity of keeping the plate for the present to protect yourself, you may dismiss that. When the plate is returned to me I shall see that the police drop the matter."

Dick had listened with absorbed interest. Hatch looked at him from time to time and saw only attention—not anger.

"And the Girl?" asked Dick at last. "Does it happen that you have as cleverly traced her?

"No," Mr. Randolph replied frankly. "I haven't the faintest idea who she is. I suppose no one knows that but you. I have no interest further than to recover the plate. I may say that I called here yesterday, Friday, and asked to see you, but was informed that you had been hurt, so I went away to give you opportunity to recover somewhat."

"Thanks," said Dick drily. "Awfully considerate."

There was a long silence. Hatch was listening with all the multitudinous ears of a good reporter.

"Now the plate," Mr. Randolph suggested again impatiently. "Do you deny that you got it?"

"I do," replied Dick firmly.

"I was afraid you would, and, believe me, Mr. Herbert, such a course is a mistaken one," said Mr. Randolph. "I will give you twenty-four hours to change your mind. If, at the end of that time, you see fit to return the plate, I shall drop the matter and use my influence to have the police do so. If the plate is not returned I shall be compelled to turn over all the facts to the police with your name."

"Is that all?" Dick demanded suddenly.

"Yes, I believe so."

"Then get out of here before I—" Dick started forward, then dropped back into a chair.

Mr. Randolph drew on his gloves and went out, closing the door behind him.

For a long time Dick sat there, seemingly oblivious of Hatch's presence, supporting his head with his left hand, while the right hung down loosely beside him. Hatch was inclined to be sympathetic, for, strange as it may seem, some reporters have even the human quality of sympathy—although there are persons who will not believe it.

"Is there anything I can do?" Hatch asked at last. "Anything you want to say?"

"Nothing," Dick responded wearily. "Nothing. You may think what you like. There are, as I said, several things of which I cannot speak, even if it comes to a question—a question of having to face the charge of theft in open court. I simply can't say anything."

"But—but—" stammered the reporter.

"Absolutely not another word," said Dick firmly.

Chapter VII

Those satellites of the Supreme Police Intelligence of the Metropolitan District who had been taking the Randolph mystery to pieces to see what made it tick, lined up in front of Detective Mallory, in his private office, at police headquarters, early Saturday evening. They did not seem happy. The Supreme Intelligence placed his feet on the desk and glowered; that was a part of the job.

"Well, Downey?" he asked.

"I went out to Seven Oaks and got the automobile the Burglar left, as you instructed," reported Downey. "Then I started out to find its owner, or someone who knew it. It didn't have a number on it, so the job wasn't easy, but I found the owner all right, all right."

Detective Mallory permitted himself to look interested.

"He lives at Merton, four miles from Seven Oaks," Downey resumed. "His name is Blake—William Blake. His auto was in the shed a hundred feet or so from his house on Thursday evening at nine o'clock. It wasn't there Friday morning."

"Umph!" remarked Detective Mallory.

"There is no question but what Blake told me the truth," Downey went on. "To me it seems probable that the Burglar went out from the city to Merton by train, stole the auto and ran it on to Seven Oaks. That's all there seems to be to it. Blake proved ownership of the machine and I left it with him."

The Supreme Intelligence chewed his cigar frantically.

"And the other machine?" he asked.

"I have here a blood-stained cushion, the back of a seat from the car in which the Burglar and the Girl escaped," continued Downey in a walk-right-up-ladies-and-gentlemen sort of voice. "I found the car late this afternoon at a garage in Pleasantville. We knew, of course, that it belonged to Nelson Sharp, a guest at the masked hall. According to the manager of the garage the car was

414

standing in front of his place this morning when he arrived to open up. The number had been removed."

Detective Mallory examined the cushion which Downey handed to him. Several dark brown stains told the story—one of the occupants of the car had been wounded.

"Well, that's something," commented the Supreme Intelligence. "We know now that when Cunningham fired at least one of the persons in the car was hit, and we may make our search accordingly. The Burglar and the Girl probably left the car where it was found during the preceding night."

"It seems so," said Downey. "I shouldn't think they would have dared to keep it long. Autos of that size and power are too easily traced. I asked Mr. Sharp to run down and identify the car and he did so. The stains were new."

The Supreme Intelligence digested that in silence while his satellites studied his face, seeking some inkling of the convolutions of that marvellous mind.

"Very good, Downey," said Detective Mallory at last. "Now Cunningham?"

"Nothing," said Cunningham in shame and sorrow. "Nothing."

"Didn't you find anything at all about the premises?"

"Nothing," repeated Cunningham. "The Girl left no wrap at Seven Oaks. None of the servants remembers having seen her in the room where the wraps were checked. I searched all around the place and found a dent in the ground under the smoking-room window, where the gold plate had been thrown, and there were what seemed to be footprints in the grass, but it was all nothing."

"We can't arrest a dent and footprints," said the Supreme Intelligence cuttingly.

The satellites laughed sadly. It was part of the deference they owed to the Supreme Intelligence.

"And you, Blanton?" asked Mr. Mallory. "What did you do with the list of guests?"

"I haven't got a good start yet," responded Blanton hopelessly. "There are three hundred and sixty names on the list. I have been able to see possibly thirty. It's worse than making a city directory. I won't be through for a month. Randolph and his wife checked off a large number of these whom they knew were there. The others I am looking up as rapidly as I can."

The detectives sat moodily thoughtful for uncounted minutes. Finally Detective Mallory broke the silence:

"There seems to be no question but that any clew that might have come from either of the automobiles is disposed of unless it is the fact that we now know one of the thieves was wounded. I readily see how the theft could have been committed by a man as bold as this fellow. Now we must concentrate all our efforts to running down the invited guests and learning just where they were that evening. All of you will have to get on this job and hustle it. We know that the Burglar did present an invitation-card with a name on it."

The detectives went their respective ways and then Detective Mallory deigned to receive representatives of the press, among them Hutchinson Hatch. Hatch was worried. He knew a whole lot of things, but they didn't do him any good. He felt that he could print nothing as it stood, yet he would not tell the police, because that would give it to everyone else, and he had a picture of how the Supreme Intelligence would tangle it if he got hold of it.

"Well, boys," said Detective Mallory smilingly, when the press filed in, "there's nothing to say. Frankly, I will tell you that we have not been able to learn anything—at least anything that can be given out. You know, of course, about the finding of the two automobiles that figured in the case, and the blood-stained cushion?"

The press nodded collectively.

"Well, that's all there is yet. My men are still at work, but I'm a little afraid the gold plate will never be found. It has probably been melted up. The cleverness of the thieves you can judge for yourself by the manner in which they handled the automobiles."

And yet Hatch was not surprised when, late that night, Police Headquarters made known the latest sensation. This was a bulletin, based on a telephone message from Stuyvesant Randolph to the effect that the gold plate had been returned by express to Seven Oaks. This mystified the police beyond description; but official mystification was as nothing to Hatch's state of mind. He knew of the scene in Dick Herbert's room and remembered Mr. Randolph's threat.

"Then Dick did have the plate," he told himself.

Chapter VIII

Whole flocks of detectives, reporters, and newspaper artists appeared at Seven Oaks early next morning. It had been too late to press an investigation the night before. The newspapers had only time telephonically to confirm the return of the plate. Now the investigators unanimously voiced one sentiment: "Show us!"

Hatch arrived in the party headed by Detective Mallory, with Downey and Cunningham trailing. Blanton was off somewhere with his little list, presumably still at it. Mr. Randolph had not come down to breakfast when the investigators arrived, but had given his servant permission to exhibit the plate, the wrappings in which it had come, and the string wherewith it had been tied.

The plate arrived in a heavy paper-board box, covered twice over with a plain piece of stiff brown paper, which had no markings save the address and the "paid" stamp of the express company. Detective Mallory devoted himself first to the address. It was:

Mr. STUYVESANT RANDOLPH,
"SEVEN OAKS,"
   VIA MERTON.

In the upper left-hand corner were scribbled the words:

FROM JOHN SMITH,
STATE STREET,
   WATERTOWN.

Detectives Mallory, Downey, and Cunningham studied the handwriting on the paper minutely.

"It's a man's," said Detective Downey.

"It's a woman's," said Detective Cunningham.

"It's a child's," said Detective Mallory.

"Whatever it is, it is disguised," said Hatch.

He was inclined to agree with Detective Cunningham that it was a woman's purposely altered, and in that event—Great Caesar! There came that flock of seven-column heads again! And he couldn't open the bottle!

The simple story of the arrival of the gold plate at Seven Oaks was told thrillingly by the servant.

"It was eight o'clock last night," he said. "I was standing in the hall here. Mr. and Mrs. Randolph were still at the dinner table. They dined alone. Suddenly I heard the sound of wagon-wheels on the granolithic road in front of the house. I listened intently. Yes, it was wagon-wheels."

The detectives exchanged significant glances.

"I heard the wagon stop," the servant went on in an awed tone. "Still I listened. Then came the sound of footsteps on the walk and then on the steps. I walked slowly along the hall toward the front door. As I did so the bell rang."

"Yes, ting-a-ling-a-ling, we know. Go on," Hatch interrupted impatiently.

"I opened the door," the servant continued. "A man stood there with a package. He was a burly fellow. 'Mr. Randolph live here?' he asked gruffly. 'Yes,' I said. 'Here's a package for him,' said the man. 'Sign here.' I took the package and signed a book he gave me, and—and—"

"In other words," Hatch interrupted again, "an expressman brought the package here, you signed for it, and he went away?"

The servant stared at him haughtily.

"Yes, that's it," he said coldly.

A few minutes later Mr. Randolph in person appeared. He glanced at Hatch with a little surprise in his manner, nodded curtly, then turned to the detectives. He could not add to the information the servant had given. His plate had been returned, prepaid. The matter was at an end so far as he was concerned. There seemed to be no need of further investigation.

"How about the jewelry that was stolen from your other guests?" demanded Detective Mallory.

"Of course, there's that," said Mr. Randolph. "It had passed out of my mind."

"Instead of being at an end this case has just begun," the detective declared emphatically.

Mr. Randolph seemed to have no further interest in the matter. He started out, then turned back at the door, and made a slight motion to Hatch which the reporter readily understood. As a result Hatch and Mr. Randolph were closeted together in a small room across the hall a few minutes later.

"May I ask your occupation, Mr. Hatch?" inquired Mr. Randolph.

"I'm a reporter," was the reply.

"A reporter?" Mr. Randolph seemed surprised. "Of course, when I saw you in Mr. Herbert's rooms," he went on after a little pause, "I met you only as his friend. You saw what happened there. Now, may I ask you what you intend to publish about this affair?"

Hatch considered the question a moment. There seemed to be no objection to telling.

"I can't publish anything until I know everything, or until the police act," he confessed frankly. "I had been talking to Dick Herbert in a general way about this case when you arrived yesterday. I knew several things, or thought I did, that the police do not even suspect. But, of course, I can print only just what the police know and say."

"I'm glad of that—very glad of it," said Mr. Randolph. "It seems to have been a freak of some sort on Mr. Herbert's part, and, candidly, I can't understand it. Of course he returned the plate, as I knew he would."

"Do you really believe he is the man who came here as the Burglar?" asked Hatch curiously.

"I should not have done what you saw me do if I had not been absolutely certain," Mr. Randolph explained. "One of the things, particularly, that was called to my attention—I don't know that you know of it—is the fact that the Burglar had a cleft in his chin. You know, of course, that Mr. Herbert has such a cleft. Then there is the invitation-card with his name. Everything together makes it conclusive."

Mr. Randolph and the reporter shook hands. Three hours later the press and police had uncovered the Watertown end of the mystery as to how the express package had been sent. It was explained by the driver of an express wagon there and absorbed by greedily listening ears.

"The boss told me to call at No. 410 State Street and get a bundle," the driver explained. "I think somebody telephoned to him to send the wagon. I went up there yesterday morning. It's a small house, back a couple of hundred feet from the street, and has a stone fence around it. I opened the gate, went in, and rang the bell.

"No one answered the first ring, and I rang again. Still nobody answered and I tried the door. It was locked. I walked around the house, thinking there might be somebody in the back, but it was all locked up. I figured as how the folks that had telephoned for me wasn't in, and started out to my wagon, intending to stop by later.

"Just as I got to the gate, going out, I saw a package set down inside, hidden from the street behind the stone fence, with a dollar bill on it. I just naturally looked at it. It was the package directed to Mr. Randolph. I reasoned as how the folks who 'phoned had to go out and left the package, so I took it along. I made out a receipt to John Smith, the name that was in the corner, and pinned it to a post, took the package and the money and went along. That's all."

"You don't know if the package was there when you went in?" he was asked.

"I dunno. I didn't look. I couldn't help but see it when I came out, so I took it."

Then the investigators sought out "the boss."

"Did the person who 'phoned give you a name?" inquired Detective Mallory.

"No, I didn't ask for one."

"Was it a man or a woman talking?"

"A man," was the unhesitating reply. "He had a deep, heavy voice."

The investigators trailed away, dismally despondent, toward No. 410 State Street. It was unoccupied; inquiry showed that it had been unoccupied for months. The Supreme Intelligence picked the lock and the investigators walked in, craning their necks. They expected, at the least, to find a thieves' rendezvous. There was nothing but dirt, and dust, and grime. Then the investigators returned to the city. They had found only that the gold plate had been returned, and they knew that when they started.

Hatch went home and sat down with his head in his hands to add up all he didn't know about the affair. It was surprising how much there was of it.

"Dick Herbert either did or didn't go to the ball," he soliloquised. "Something happened to him that evening. He either did or didn't steal the gold plate, and every circumstance indicates that he did—which, of course, he didn't. Dorothy Meredith either was or was not at the ball. The maid's statement shows that she was, yet no one there recognised her—which indicates that she wasn't. She either did or didn't run away with somebody in an automobile. Anyhow, something happened to her, because she's missing. The gold plate is stolen, and the gold plate is back. I know that, thank Heaven! And now, knowing more about this affair than any other single individual, I don't know anything."

Part II: The Girl and the Plate

Chapter IX

Low-bent over the steering-wheel, the Burglar sent the auto-mobile scuttling breathlessly along the flat road away from Seven Oaks. At the first shot he crouched down in the seat, dragging the Girl with him; at the second, he winced a little and clenched his teeth tightly. The car's headlights cut a dazzling pathway through the shadows, and trees flitted by as a solid wall. The shouts of pur-suers were left behind, and still the Girl clung to his arm.

"Don't do that," he commanded abruptly. "You'll make me smash into something."

"Why, Dick, they shot at us!" she protested indignantly.

The Burglar glanced at her, and, when he turned his eyes to the smooth road again, there was a flicker of a smile about the set lips.

"Yes, I had some such impression myself," he acquiesced grimly.

"Why, they might have killed us!" the Girl went on.

"It is just barely possible that they had some such absurd idea when they shot," replied the Burglar. "Guess you never got caught in a pickle like this before?"

"I certainly never did!" replied the Girl emphatically.

The whir and grind of their car drowned other sounds—sounds from behind—but from time to time the Burglar looked back, and from time to time he let out a new notch in the speed-regulator. Already the pace was terrific, and the Girl bounced up and down beside him at each trivial irregularity in the road, while she clung frantically to the seat.

"Is it necessary to go so awfully fast?" she gasped at last.

The wind was beating on her face, her mask blew this way and that; the beribboned sombrero clung frantically to a fast-failing strand of ruddy hair. She clutched at the hat and saved it, but her hair tumbled down about her shoulders, a mass of gold, and floated out behind.

"Oh," she chattered, "I can't keep my hat on!"

The Burglar took another quick look behind, then his foot went out against the speed-regulator and the car fairly leaped with suddenly increased impetus. The regulator was in the last notch now, and the car was one that had raced at Ormond Beach.

"Oh, dear!" exclaimed the Girl again. "Can't you go a little slower?"

"Look behind," directed the Burglar tersely.

She glanced back and gave a little cry. Two giant eyes stared at her from a few hundred yards away as another car swooped along in pursuit, and behind this ominously glittering pair was still another.

"They're chasing us, aren't they?"

"They are," replied the Burglar grimly, "but if these tires hold, they haven't got a chance. A breakdown would—" He didn't finish the sentence. There was a sinister note in his voice, but the Girl was still looking back and did not heed it. To her excited imagination it seemed that the giant eyes behind were creeping up, and again she clutched the Burglar's arm.

"Don't do that, I say," he commanded again.

"But, Dick, they mustn't catch us—they mustn't!"

"They won't."

"But if they should—"

"They won't," he repeated.

"It would be perfectly awful!"

"Worse than that."

For a time the Girl silently watched him bending over the wheel, and a singular feeling of security came to her. Then the car swept around a bend in the road, careening perilously, and the glaring eyes were lost. She breathed more freely.

"I never knew you handled an auto so well," she said admiringly.

"I do lots of things people don't know I do," he replied. "Are those lights still there?"

"No, thank goodness!"

The Burglar touched a lever with his left hand and the whir of the machine became less pronounced. After a moment it began to slow down. The Girl noticed it and looked at him with new apprehension.

"Oh, we're stopping!" she exclaimed.

"I know it."

They ran on for a few hundred feet; then the Burglar set the brake and, after a deal of jolting, the car stopped. He leaped out and ran around behind. As the Girl watched him uneasily there came a sudden crash and the auto trembled a little.

"What is it?" she asked quickly.

"I smashed that tail lamp," he answered. "They can see it, and it's too easy for them to follow."

He stamped on the shattered fragments in the road, then came around to the side to climb in again, extending his left hand to the Girl.

"Quick, give me your hand," he requested.

She did so wonderingly and he pulled himself into the seat beside her with a perceptible effort. The car shivered, then started on again, slowly at first, but gathering speed each moment. The Girl was staring at her companion curiously, anxiously.

"Are you hurt?" she asked at last.

He did not answer at the moment, not until the car had regained its former speed and was hurtling headlong through the night.

"My right arm's out of business," he explained briefly, then: "I got that second bullet in the shoulder."

"Oh, Dick, Dick," she exclaimed, "and you hadn't said anything about it! You need assistance!"

A sudden rush of sympathy caused her to lay her hands again on his left arm. He shook them off roughly with something like anger in his manner.

"Don't do that!" he commanded for the third time. "You'll make me smash hell out of this car."

Startled by the violence of his tone, she recoiled dumbly, and the car swept on. As before, the Burglar looked back from time to time, but the lights did not reappear. For a long time the Girl was silent and finally he glanced at her.

"I beg your pardon," he said humbly. "I didn't mean to speak so sharply, but—but it's true."

"It's really of no consequence," she replied coldly. "I am sorry—very sorry."

"Thank you," he replied.

"Perhaps it might be as well for you to stop the car and let me out," she went on after a moment.

The Burglar either didn't hear or wouldn't heed. The dim lights of a small village rose up before them, then faded away again; a dog barked lonesomely beside the road. The streaming lights of their car revealed a tangle of crossroads just ahead, offering a definite method of shaking off pursuit. Their car swerved widely, and the Burglar's attention was centred on the road ahead.

"Does your arm pain you?" asked the Girl at last timidly.

"No," he replied shortly. "It's a sort of numbness. I'm afraid I'm losing blood, though."

"Hadn't we better go back to the village and see a doctor?"

"Not this evening," he responded promptly in a tone which she did not understand. "I'll stop somewhere soon and bind it up."

At last, when the village was well behind, the car came to a dark little road which wandered off aimlessly through a wood, and the Burglar slowed down to turn into it. Once in the shelter of the overhanging branches they proceeded slowly for a hundred yards or more, finally coming to a standstill.

"We must do it here," he declared.

He leaped from the car, stumbled and fell. In an instant the Girl was beside him. The reflected light from the auto showed her dimly that he was trying to rise, showed her the pallor of his face where the chin below the mask was visible.

"I'm afraid it's pretty bad," he said weakly. Then he fainted.

The Girl, stooping, raised his head to her lap and pressed her lips to his feverishly, time after time.

"Dick, Dick!" she sobbed, and tears fell upon the Burglar's sinister mask.

Chapter X

When the Burglar awoke to consciousness he was as near heaven as any mere man ever dares expect to be. He was comfortable—quite comfortable— wrapped in a delicious, languorous lassitude which forbade him opening his eyes to realisation. A woman's hand lay on his forehead, caressingly, and dimly he knew that another hand cuddled cosily in one of his own. He lay still, trying to remember, before he opened his eyes. Someone beside him breathed softly, and he listened, as if to music.

Gradually the need of action—just what action and to what purpose did not occur to him—impressed itself on his mind. He raised the disengaged hand to his face and touched the mask, which had been pushed back on his forehead. Then he recalled the ball, the shot, the chase, the hiding in the woods. He opened his eyes with a start. Utter darkness lay about him—for a moment he was not certain whether it was the darkness of blindness or of night.

"Dick, are you awake?" asked the Girl softly. He knew the voice and was content.

"Yes," he answered languidly.

He closed his eyes again and some strange, subtle perfume seemed to envelop him. He waited. Warm lips were pressed to his own, thrilling him strangely, and the Girl rested a soft cheek against his.

"We have been very foolish, Dick," she said, sweetly chiding, after a moment. "It was all my fault for letting you expose yourself to danger, but I didn't dream of such a thing as this happening. I shall never forgive myself, because—"

"But—" he began protestingly.

"Not another word about it now," she hurried on. "We must go very soon. How do you feel?"

"I'm all right, or will be in a minute," he responded, and he made as if to rise. "Where is the car?"

"Right here. I extinguished the lights and managed to stop the engine for fear those horrid people who were after us might notice."

"Good girl!"

"When you jumped out and fainted I jumped out, too. I'm afraid I was not very clever, but I managed to bind your arm. I took my handkerchief and pressed it against the wound after ripping your coat, then I bound it there. It stopped the flow of blood, but, Dick, dear, you must have medical attention just as soon as possible."

The Burglar moved his shoulder a little and winced.

"Just as soon as I did that," the Girl went on, "I made you comfortable here on a cushion from the car."

"Good girl!" he said again.

"Then I sat down to wait until you got better. I had no stimulant or anything, and I didn't dare to leave you, so—so I just waited," she ended with a weary little sigh.

"How long was I knocked out?" he queried.

"I don't know; half an hour, perhaps."

"The bag is all right, I suppose?"

"The bag?"

"The bag with the stuff—the one I threw in the car when we started?"

"Oh, yes, I suppose so! Really, I hadn't thought of it."

"Hadn't thought of it?" repeated the Burglar, and there was a trace of astonishment in his voice. "By George, you're a wonder!" he added.

He started to get on his feet, then dropped back weakly.

"Say, girlie," he requested, "see if you can find the bag in the car there and hand it out. Let's take a look."

"Where is it?"

"Somewhere in front. I felt it at my feet when I jumped out."

There was a rustle of skirts in the darkness, and after a moment a faint muffled clank as of one heavy metal striking dully against another.

"Goodness!" exclaimed the Girl. "It's heavy enough. What's in it?"

"What's in it?" repeated the Burglar, and he chuckled. "A fortune, nearly. It's worth being punctured for. Let me see."

In the darkness he took the bag from her hands and fumbled with it a moment. She heard the metallic sound again and then several heavy objects were poured out on the ground.

"A good fourteen pounds of pure gold," commented the Burglar. "By George, I haven't but one match, but we'll see what it's like."

The match was struck, sputtered for a moment, then flamed up, and the Girl, standing, looked down upon the Burglar on his knees beside a heap of gold plate. She stared at the glittering mass as if fascinated, and her eyes opened wide.

"Why, Dick, what is that?" she asked.

"It's Randolph's plate," responded the Burglar complacently. "I don't know how much it's worth, but it must be several thousands, on dead weight."

"What are you doing with it?"

"What am I doing with it?' repeated the Burglar. He was about to look up when the match burned his finger and he dropped it. "That's a silly question."

"But how came it in your possession?" the Girl insisted.

"I acquired it by the simple act of—of dropping it into a bag and bringing it along. That and you in the same evening—" He stretched out a hand toward her, but she was not there. He chuckled a little as he turned and picked up eleven plates, one by one, and replaced them in the bag.

"Nine—ten—eleven," he counted. "What luck did you have?"

"Dick Herbert, explain to me, please, what you are doing with that gold plate?" There was an imperative command in the voice.

The Burglar paused and rubbed his chin thoughtfully.

"Oh, I'm taking it to have it fixed!" he responded lightly.

"Fixed? Taking it this way at this time of the night?"

"Sure," and he laughed pleasantly.

"You mean you—you—you stole it?" The words came with an effort.

"Well, I'd hardly call it that," remarked the Burglar. "That's a harsh word. Still, it's in my possession; it wasn't given to me, and I didn't buy it. You may draw your own conclusions."

The bag lay beside him and his left hand caressed it idly, lovingly. For a long time there was silence.

"What luck did you have?" he asked again.

There was a startled gasp, a gurgle and accusing indignation in the Girl's low, tense voice.

"You—you stole it!"

"Well, if you prefer it that way—yes."

The Burglar was staring steadily into the darkness toward that point whence came the voice, but the night was so dense that not a trace of the Girl was visible. He laughed again.

"It seems to me it was lucky I decided to take it at just this time and in these circumstances," he went on tauntingly— "lucky for you, I mean. If I hadn't been there you would have been caught."

Again came the startled gasp.

"What's the matter?" demanded the Burglar sharply, after another silence. "Why don't you say something?"

He was still peering unseeingly into the darkness. The bag of gold plate moved slightly under his hand. He opened his fingers to close them more tightly. It was a mistake. The bag was drawn away; his hand grasped—air.

"Stop that game now!" he commanded angrily. "Where are you?"

He struggled to his feet. His answer was the crackling of a twig to his right. He started in that direction and brought up with a bump against the automobile. He turned, still groping blindly, and embraced a tree with undignified fervour. To his left he heard another slight noise and ran that way. Again he struck an obstacle. Then he began to say things, expressive things, burning things from the depths of an impassioned soul. The treasure had gone—disappeared into the shadows. The Girl was gone. He called, there was no answer. He drew his revolver fiercely, as if to fire it; then reconsidered and flung it down angrily.

"And I thought I had nerve!" he declared. It was a compliment.

Chapter XI

Extravagantly brilliant the sun popped up out of the east—not an unusual occurrence—and stared unblinkingly down upon a country road. There were the usual twittering birds and dew-spangled trees and nodding wild-flowers; also a dust that was shoe-top deep. The dawny air stirred lazily and rustling leaves sent long, sinuous shadows scampering back and forth.

Looking upon it all without enthusiasm or poetic exaltation was a Girl—a pretty Girl—a very pretty Girl. She sat on a stone beside the yellow roadway, a picture of weariness. A rough burlap sack, laden heavily, yet economically as to space, wallowed in the dust beside her. Her hair was tawny gold, and rebellious strands drooped listlessly about her face. A beribboned sombrero lay in her lap, supplementing a certain air of dilapidated bravado, due in part to a short skirt, heavy gloves and boots, a belt with a knife and revolver.

A robin, perched impertinently on a stump across the road, examined her at his leisure. She stared back at Signor Redbreast, and for this recognition he warbled a little song.

"I've a good mind to cry!" exclaimed the Girl suddenly.

Shamed and startled, the robin flew away. A mistiness came into the Girl's blue eyes and lingered there a moment, then her white teeth closed tightly and the glimmer of outraged emotion passed.

"Oh," she sighed again, "I'm so tired and hungry and I just know I'll never get anywhere at all!"

But despite the expressed conviction she arose and straightened up as if to resume her journey, turning to stare down at the bag. It was an unsightly symbol of blasted hopes, man's perfidy, crushed aspirations and—Heaven only knows what besides.

"I've a good mind to leave you right there," she remarked to the bag spitefully. "Perhaps I might hide it." She considered the question. "No, that wouldn't do. I must take it with me—and—and—Oh, Dick! Dick! What in the world was the matter with you, anyway?"

Then she sat down again and wept. The robin crept back to look and modestly hid behind a leaf. From this coign of vantage he watched her as she again arose and plodded off through the dust with the bag swinging over one shoulder. At last—there is an at last to everything—a small house appeared from behind a clump of trees. The Girl looked with incredulous eyes. It was really a house. Really! A tiny curl of smoke hovered over the chimney.

"Well, thank goodness, I'm somewhere, anyhow," she declared with her first show of enthusiasm. "I can get a cup of coffee or something."

She covered the next fifty yards with a new spring in her leaden heels and with a new and firmer grip on the precious bag. Then—she stopped.

"Gracious!" and perplexed lines suddenly wrinkled her brow. "If I should go in there with a pistol and a knife they'll think I was a brigand—or—or a thief, and I suppose I am," she added as she stopped and rested the bag on the ground. "At least I have stolen goods in my possession. Now, what shall I say if they ask questions? What am I? They wouldn't believe me if I told them really. Short skirt, boots and gloves: I know! I'm a bicyclist. My wheel broke down, and—"

Whereupon she gingerly removed the revolver from her belt and flung it into the underbrush—not at all in the direction she had intended—and the knife followed to keep it company. Having relieved herself of these sinister things, she straightened her hat, pushed back the rebellious hair, yanked at her skirt, and walked bravely up to the little house.

An Angel lived there—an Angel in a dizzily beflowered wrapper and a crabbed exterior. She listened to a rapidly constructed and wholly inconsistent story of a bicycle accident, which ended with a plea for a cup of coffee. Silently she proceeded to prepare it. After the pot was bubbling cheerfully and eggs had been put on and biscuits thrust into a stove to be warmed over, the Angel sat down at the table opposite the Girl.

"Book agent?" she asked.

"Oh, no!" replied the Girl.

"Sewing-machines?"

"No."

There was a pause as the Angel settled and poured a cup of coffee.

"Make to order, I s'pose?"

"No," the Girl replied uncertainly.

"What do you sell?"

"Nothing, I—I—" She stopped.

"What you got in the bag?" the Angel persisted.

"Some—some—just some—stuff," stammered the Girl, and her face suddenly flushed crimson.

"What kind of stuff?"

The Girl looked into the frankly inquisitive eyes and was overwhelmed by a sense of her own helplessness. Tears started, and one pearly drop ran down her perfect nose and splashed in the coffee. That was the last straw. She leaned forward suddenly with her head on her arms and wept.

"Please, please don't ask questions!" she pleaded. "I'm a poor, foolish, helpless, misguided, disillusioned woman!"

"Yes'm," said the Angel. She took up the eggs, then came over and put a kindly arm about the Girl's shoulders. "There, there!" she said soothingly. "Don't take on like that! Drink some coffee, and eat a bite, and you'll feel better!"

"I have had no sleep at all and no food since yesterday, and I've walked miles and miles and miles," the Girl rushed on feverishly. "It's all because—because—" She stopped suddenly.

"Eat something," commanded the Angel.

The Girl obeyed. The coffee was weak and muddy and delightful; the biscuits were yellow and lumpy and delicious; the eggs were eggs. The Angel sat opposite and watched the Girl as she ate.

"Husband beat you?" she demanded suddenly.

The Girl blushed and nearly choked on a biscuit.

"No," she hastened to say. "I have no husband."

"Well, there ain't no serious trouble in this world till you marry a man that beats you," said the Angel judicially. It was the final word.

The Girl didn't answer, and, in view of the fact that she had sufficient data at hand to argue the point, this repression required heroism. Perhaps she will never get credit for it. She finished the breakfast in silence and leaned back with some measure of returning content in her soul.

"In a hurry?" asked the Angel.

"No. I have no place to go. What is the nearest village or town?"

"Watertown, but you'd better stay and rest a while. You look all tuckered out."

"Oh, thank you so much," said the Girl gratefully. "But it would be so much trouble for—"

The Angel picked up the burlap bag, shook it inquiringly, then started toward the short stairs leading up.

"Please, please!" exclaimed the Girl suddenly. "I—I—let me have that, please!"

The Angel relinquished the bag without a word. The Girl took it, tremblingly, then, suddenly dropping it, clasped the Angel in her arms and placed upon her unresponsive lips a kiss for which a mere man would have endangered his immortal soul. The Angel wiped her mouth with the back of her hand and went on up the stairs with the Girl following.

For a time the Girl lay, with wet eyes, on a clean little bed, thinking. Humiliation, exhaustion, man's perfidy, disillusionment, and the kindess of an utter stranger all occupied her until she fell asleep. Then she was chased by a policeman with automobile lights for eyes, and there was a parade of hard-boiled eggs and yellow, lumpy biscuits.

When she awoke the room was quite dark. She sat up a little bewildered at first; then she remembered. After a moment she heard the voice of the Angel, below. It rippled on querulously; then she heard the gruff voice of a man.

"Diamond rings?"

The Girl sat up in bed and listened intently. Involuntarily her hands were clasped together. Her rings were still safe. The Angel's voice went on for a moment again.

"Something in a bag?" inquired the man.

Again the Angel spoke.

Terror seized upon the Girl; imagination ran riot, and she rose from the bed, trembling. She groped about the dark room noiselessly. Every shadow lent her new fears. Then from below came the sound of heavy footsteps. She listened fearfully. They came on toward the stairs, then paused. A match was struck and the step sounded on the stairs.

After a moment there was a knock at the door, a pause, then another knock. Finally the door was pushed open and a huge figure—the figure of a man—appeared, sheltering a candle with one hand. He peered about the room as if perplexed.

"Ain't nobody up here," he called gruffly down the stairs.

There was a sound of hurrying feet and the Angel entered, her face distorted by the flickering candlelight.

"For the land's sakes!" she exclaimed.

"Went away without even saying thank you," grumbled the man. He crossed the room and closed a window. "You ain't got no better sense than a chicken," he told the Angel. "Take in anybody that comes."

Chapter XII

If Willie's little brother hadn't had a pain in his tummy this story might have gone by other and devious ways to a different conclusion. But fortunately he did have, so it happened that at precisely 8.47 o'clock of a warm evening Willie was racing madly along a side street of Watertown, drug-store-bound, when he came face to face with a Girl—a pretty Girl—a very pretty Girl. She was carrying a bag that clanked a little at each step.

"Oh, little boy!" she called.

"Hunh?" and Willie stopped so suddenly that he endangered his equilibrium, although that isn't how he would have said it.

"Nice little boy," said the Girl soothingly, and she patted his tousled head while he gnawed a thumb in pained embarrassment. "I'm very tired. I have been walking a great distance. Could you tell me, please, where a lady, unattended, might get a night's lodging somewhere near here?"

"Hunh?" gurgled Willie through the thumb.

Wearily the Girl repeated it all and at its end Willie giggled. It was the most exasperating incident of a long series of exasperating incidents, and the Girl's grip on the bag tightened a little. Willie never knew how nearly he came to being hammered to death with fourteen pounds of solid gold. "Well?" inquired the Girl at last.

"Dunno," said Willie. "Jimmy's got the stomach-ache," he added irrelevantly.

"Can't you think of a hotel or boarding-house near by?" the Girl insisted.

"Dunno," replied Willie. "I'm going to the drug store for a pair o' gorrick."

The Girl bit her lip, and that act probably saved Willie from the dire consequences of his unconscious levity, for after a moment the Girl laughed aloud.

"Where is the drug store?" she asked.

"'Round the corner. I'm going."

"I'll go along, too, if you don't mind," the Girl said, and she turned and walked beside him. Perhaps the drug clerk would be able to illuminate the situation.

"I swallyed a penny oncst," Willie confided suddenly.

"Too bad!" commented the Girl.

"Unh unnh," Willie denied emphatically. "'Cause when I cried, Paw gimme a quarter." He was silent a moment, then: "If I'd 'a' swallyed that, I reckin he'd a gimme a dollar. Gee!"

This is the optimism that makes the world go round. The philosophy took possession of the Girl and cheered her. When she entered the drug store she walked with a lighter step and there was a trace of a smile about her pretty mouth. A clerk, the only attendant, came forward.

"I want a pair o' gorrick," Willie announced.

The Girl smiled, and the clerk, paying no attention to the boy, went toward her.

"Better attend to him first," she suggested. "It seems urgent."

The clerk turned to Willie.

"Paregoric?" he inquired. "How much?"

"About a quart, I reckin," replied the boy. "Is that enough?"

"Quite enough," commented the clerk. He disappeared behind the prescription screen and returned after a moment with a small phial. The boy took it, handed over a coin, and went out, whistling. The Girl looked after him with a little longing in her eyes.

"Now, madam?" inquired the clerk suavely.

"I only want some information," she replied. "I was out on my bicycle"—she gulped a little— "when it broke down, and I'll have to remain here in town over night, I'm afraid. Can you direct me to a quiet hotel or boarding-house where I might stay?"

"Certainly," replied the clerk briskly. "The Stratford, just a block up this street. Explain the circumstances, and it will be all right, I'm sure."

The Girl smiled at him again and cheerfully went her way. That small boy had been a leaven to her drooping spirits. She found the Stratford without difficulty and told the usual bicycle lie, with a natural growth of detail and a burning sense of shame. She registered as Elizabeth Carlton and was shown to a modest little room.

Her first act was to hide the gold plate in the closet; her second was to take it out and hide it under the bed. Then she sat down on a couch to think. For an hour or more she considered the situation in all its hideous details, planning her desolate future—women like to plan desolate futures—then her eye chanced to fall upon an afternoon paper, which, with glaring headlines, announced the theft of the Randolph gold plate. She read it. It told, with startling detail, things that had and had not happened in connection therewith.

This comprehended in all its horror, she promptly arose and hid the bag between the mattress and the springs. Soon after she extinguished the light and retired with little shivers running up and down all over her. She snuggled her head down under the cover. She didn't sleep much—she was still thinking—but when she arose next morning her mind was made up.

First she placed the eleven gold plates in a heavy card-board box, then she bound it securely with brown paper and twine and addressed it: "Stuyvesant Randolph, Seven Oaks, via Merton." She had sent express packages before and knew how to proceed, therefore when the necessity of writing a name in the upper left-hand corner appeared—the sender—she wrote in a bold, desperate hand: "John Smith, Watertown."

When this was all done to her satisfaction, she tucked the package under one arm, tried to look as if it weren't heavy, and sauntered downstairs with outward self-possession and inward apprehension. She faced the clerk cordially, while a singularly distracting smile curled her lips.

"My bill, please?" she asked.

"Two dollars, madam," he responded gallantly.

"I don't happen to have any money with me," she explained charmingly. "Of course, I had expected to go back on my wheel, but, since it is broken, perhaps you would be willing to take this until I return to the city and can mail a check?"

She drew a diamond ring from an aristocratic finger and offered it to the clerk. He blushed furiously, and she reproved him for it with a cold stare.

"It's quite irregular," he explained, "but, of course, in the circumstances, it will be all right. It is not necessary for us to keep the ring at all, if you will give us your city address."

"I prefer that you keep it," she insisted firmly, "for, besides, I shall have to ask you to let me have fare back to the city—a couple of dollars? Of course it will be all right?"

It was half an hour before the clerk fully awoke. He had given the Girl two real dollars and held her ring clasped firmly in one hand. She was gone. She might just as well have taken the hotel along with her so far as any objection from that clerk would have been concerned.

Once out of the hotel the Girl hurried on.

"Thank goodness, that's over," she exclaimed.

For several blocks she walked on. Finally her eye was attracted by a "To Let" sign on a small house—it was No. 410 State Street. She walked in through a gate cut in the solid wall of stone and strolled up to the house. Here she wandered about for a time, incidentally tearing off the "To Let" sign. Then she came down the path toward the street again. Just inside the stone fence she left her express package, after scribbling the name of the street on it with a pencil. A dollar bill lay on top. She hurried out and along a block or more to a small grocery.

"Will you please 'phone to the express company and have them send a wagon to No. 410 State Street for a package?" she asked sweetly of a heavy-voiced grocer.

"Certainly, ma'am," he responded with alacrity.

She paused until he had done as she requested, then dropped into a restaurant for a cup of coffee. She lingered there for a long time, and then went out to spend a greater part of the day wandering up and down State Street. At last an express wagon drove up, the driver went in and returned after a little while with the package.

"And, thank goodness, that's off my hands!" sighed the Girl. "Now I'm going home."

Late that evening, Saturday, Miss Dollie Meredith returned to the home of the Greytons and was clasped to the motherly bosom of Mrs. Greyton, where she wept unreservedly.

Chapter XIII

It was late Sunday afternoon. Hutchinson Hatch did not run lightly up the steps of the Greyton home and toss his cigar away as he rang the bell. He did go up the steps, but it was reluctantly, dragging one foot after the other, this being an indication rather of his mental condition than of physical weariness. He did not throw away his cigar as he rang the bell because he wasn't smoking—but he did ring the bell. The maid whom he had seen on his previous visit opened the door.

"Is Mrs. Greyton in?" he asked with a nod of recognition.

"No, sir."

"Mr. Greyton?"

"No, sir."

"Did Mr. Meredith arrive from Baltimore?"

"Yes, sir. Last midnight."

"Ah! Is he in?"

"No, sir."

The reporter's disappointment showed clearly in his face.

"I don't suppose you've heard anything further from Miss Meredith?" he ventured hopelessly.

"She's upstairs, sir."

Anyone who has ever stepped on a tack knows just how Hatch felt. He didn't stand on the order of being invited in—he went in. Being in, he extracted a plain calling-card from his pocketbook with twitching fingers and handed it to the waiting maid.

"When did she return?" he asked.

"Last night, about nine, sir."

"Where has she been?"

"I don't know, sir."

"Kindly hand her my card and explain to her that it is imperative that I see her for a few minutes," the reporter went on. "Impress upon her the absolute necessity of this. By the way, I suppose you know where I came from, eh?"

"Police headquarters, yes, sir."

Hatch tried to look like a detective, but a gleam of intelligence in his face almost betrayed him.

"You might intimate as much to Miss Meredith," he instructed the maid calmly.

The maid disappeared. Hatch went in and sat down in the reception-room, and said "Whew!" several times.

"The gold plate returned to Randolph last night by express," he mused, "and she returned also, last night. Now what does that mean?"

After a minute or so the maid reappeared to state that Miss Meredith would see him. Hatch received the message gravely and beckoned mysteriously as he sought for a bill in his pocketbook.

"Do you have any idea where Miss Meredith was?"

"No, sir. She didn't even tell Mrs. Greyton or her father."

"What was her appearance?"

"She seemed very tired, sir, and hungry. She still wore the masked ball costume."

The bill changed hands and Hatch was left alone again. There was a long wait, then a rustle of skirts, a light step, and Miss Dollie Meredith entered. She was nervous, it is true, and pallid, but there was a suggestion of defiance as well as determination on her pretty mouth. Hatch stared at her in frank admiration for a moment, then, with an effort, proceeded to business.

"I presume, Miss Meredith," he said solemnly, "that the maid informed you of my identity?"

"Yes," replied Dollie weakly. "She said you were a detective."

"Ah!" exclaimed the reporter meaningly, "then we understand each other. Now, Miss Meredith, will you tell me, please, just where you have been?"

"No."

The answer was so prompt and so emphatic that Hatch was a little disconcerted. He cleared his throat and started over again.

"Will you inform me, then, in the interest of justice, where you were on the evening of the Randolph ball?" An ominous threat lay behind the words, Hatch hoped she believed.

"I will not."

"Why did you disappear?"

"I will not tell you."

Hatch paused to readjust himself. He was going at things back-ward. When next he spoke his tone had lost the official tang—he talked like a human being.

"May I ask if you happen to know Richard Herbert?"

The pallor of the girl's face was relieved by a delicious sweep of colour.

"I will not tell you," she answered.

"And if I say that Mr. Herbert happens to be a friend of mine?"

"Well, you ought to be ashamed of yourself!"

Two distracting blue eyes were staring him out of countenance; two scarlet lips were drawn tightly together in reproof of a man who boasted such a friendship; two cheeks flamed with indigna-tion that he should have mentioned the name. Hatch floundered for a moment, then cleared his throat and took a fresh start.

"Will you deny that you saw Richard Herbert on the evening of the masked ball?"

"I will not."

"Will you admit that you saw him?"

"I will not."

"Do you know that he was wounded?"

"Certainly."

Now, Hatch had always held a vague theory that the easiest way to make a secret known was to intrust it to a woman. At this point he revised his draw, threw his hand in the pack, and asked for a new deal.

"Miss Meredith," he said soothingly after a pause, "will you admit or deny that you ever heard of the Randolph robbery?"

"I will not," she began, then: "Certainly I know of it."

"You know that a man and a woman are accused of and sought for the theft?"

"Yes, I know that."

"You will admit that you know the man was in Burglar's garb, and that the woman was dressed in a Western costume?"

"The newspapers say that, yes," she replied sweetly.

"You know, too, that Richard Herbert went to that ball in Burglar's garb and that you went there dressed as a Western girl?" The reporter's tone was strictly professional now.

Dollie stared into the stern face of her interrogator and her courage oozed away. The colour left her face and she wept violently.

"I beg your pardon," Hatch expostulated. "I beg your pardon. I didn't mean it just that way, but—"

He stopped helplessly and stared at this wonderful woman with the red hair. Of all things in the world tears were quite the most disconcerting.

"I beg your pardon," he repeated awkwardly.

Dollie looked up with tear-stained, pleading eyes, then arose and placed both her hands on Hatch's arm. It was a pitiful, help-less sort of a gesture; Hatch shuddered with sheer delight.

"I don't know how you found out about it," she said tremulously, "but, if you've come to arrest me, I'm ready to go with you."

"Arrest you?" gasped the reporter.

"Certainly. I'll go and be locked up. That's what they do, isn't it?" she questioned innocently.

The reporter stared.

"I wouldn't arrest you for a million dollars!" he stammered in dire confusion. "It wasn't quite that. It was—"

And five minutes later Hutchinson Hatch found himself wan-dering aimlessly up and down the sidewalk.

Chapter XIV

Dick Herbert lay stretched lazily on a couch in his room with hands pressed to his eyes. He had just read the Sunday newspapers announcing the mysterious return of the Randolph plate, and naturally he had a headache.

Somewhere in a remote recess of his brain mental pyrotechnics were at play; a sort of intellectual pinwheel spouted senseless ideas and suggestions of senseless ideas. The late afternoon shaded off into twilight, twilight into dusk, dusk into darkness, and still he lay motionless.

After a while, from below, he heard the tinkle of a bell and Blair entered with light tread:

"Beg pardon, sir, are you asleep?"

"Who is it, Blair?"

"Mr. Hatch, sir."

"Let him come up."

Dick arose, snapped on the electric lights, and stood blinkingly in the sudden glare. When Hatch entered they faced each other silently for a moment. There was that in the reporter's eyes that interested Dick immeasurably; there was that in Dick's eyes that Hatch was trying vainly to fathom.

Dick relieved a certain vague tension by extending his left hand. Hatch shook it cordially.

"Well?" Dick inquired.

Hatch dropped into a chair and twirled his hat.

"Heard the news?" he asked.

"The return of the gold plate, yes," and Dick passed a hand across his fevered brow. "It makes me dizzy."

"Heard anything from Miss Meredith?"

"No. Why?"

"She returned to the Greytons last night."

443

"Returned to the—" and Dick started up suddenly. "Well, there's no reason why she shouldn't have," he added. "Do you happen to know where she was?"

The reporter shook his head.

"I don't know anything," he said wearily, "except—" He paused.

Dick paced back and forth across the room several times with one hand pressed to his forehead. Suddenly he turned on his visitor.

"Except what?" he demanded.

"Except that Miss Meredith, by action and word, has convinced me that she either had a hand in the disappearance of the Randolph plate or else knows who was the cause of its disappearance."

Dick glared at him savagely.

"You know she didn't take the plate?" he demanded.

"Certainly," replied the reporter. "That's what makes it all the more astonishing. I talked to her this afternoon, and when I finished she seemed to think I had come to arrest her, and she wanted to go to jail. I nearly fainted."

Dick glared incredulously, then resumed his nervous pacing. Suddenly he stopped.

"Did she mention my name?"

"I mentioned it. She wouldn't admit even that she knew you."

There was a pause.

"I don't blame her," Dick remarked enigmatically. "She must think me a cad."

Another pause.

"Well, what about it all, anyhow?" Dick went on finally. "The plate has been returned, therefore the matter is at an end."

"Now look here, Dick," said Hatch. "I want to say something, and don't go crazy, please, until I finish. I know an awful lot about this affair—things the police never will know. I haven't printed anything much for obvious reasons."

Dick looked at him apprehensively.

"Go on," he urged.

"I could print things I know," the reporter resumed; "swear out a warrant for you in connection with the gold plate affair and have you arrested and convicted on your own statements, supplemented by those of Miss Meredith. Yet, remember, please, neither your name nor hers has been mentioned as yet."

Dick took it calmly; he only stared.

"Do you believe that I stole the plate?" he asked.

"Certainly I do not," replied Hatch, "but I can prove that you did; prove it to the satisfaction of any jury in the world, and no denial of yours would have any effect."

"Well?" asked Dick, after a moment.

"Further, I can, on information in my possession, swear out a warrant for Miss Meredith, prove she was in the automobile, and convict her as your accomplice. Now that's a silly state of affairs, isn't it?"

"But, man, you can't believe that she had anything to do with it! She's—she's not that kind."

"I could take oath that she didn't have anything to do with it, but all the same I can prove that she did," replied Hatch. "Now what I am getting at is this: if the police should happen to find out what I know they would send you up—both of you."

"Well, you are decent about it, old man, and I appreciate it," said Dick warmly. "But what can we do?"

"It behoves us—Miss Meredith and you and myself—to get the true facts in the case all together before you get pinched," said the reporter judicially. "Suppose now, just suppose, that we three get together and tell each other the truth for a change, the whole truth, and see what will happen?"

"If I should tell you the truth," said Dick dispassionately, "it would bring everlasting disgrace on Miss Meredith, and I'd be a beast for doing it; if she told you the truth she would unquestionably send me to prison for theft."

"But here—" Hatch expostulated.

"Just a minute!" Dick disappeared into another room, leaving the reporter to chew on what he had, then returned in a little while, dressed for the street. "Now, Hatch," he said, "I'm going to try to get to Miss Meredith, but I don't believe she'll see me. If she will, I may be able to explain several things that will clear up this affair in your mind, at any rate. If I don't see her— By the way, did her father arrive from Baltimore?"

"Yes."

"Good!" exclaimed Dick. "I'll see him, too—make a show-down of it, and when it's all over I'll let you know what happened."

Hatch went back to his shop and threatened to kick the office-boy into the waste-basket.

At just about that moment Mr. Meredith, in the Greyton home, was reading a card on which appeared the name, "Mr. Richard Hamilton Herbert." Having read it, he snorted his indignation and went into the reception-room. Dick arose to greet him and offered a hand, which was promptly declined.

"I'd like to ask you, Mr. Meredith," Dick began with a certain steely coldness in his manner, "just why you object to my attention to your daughter, Dorothy?"

"You know well enough!" raged the old man.

"It is because of the trouble I had in Harvard with your son, Harry. Well and good, but is that all? Is that to stand forever?"

"You proved then that you were not a gentleman," declared the old man savagely. "You're a puppy, sir."

"If you didn't happen to be the father of the girl I'm in love with I'd poke you in the nose," Dick replied, almost cheerfully. "Where is your son now? Is there no way I can place myself right in your eyes?"

"No!" Mr. Meredith thundered. "An apology would only be a confession of your dishonour!"

Dick was nearly choking, but managed to keep his voice down.

"Does your daughter know anything of that affair?"

"Certainly not."

"Where is your son?"

"None of your business, sir!"

"I don't suppose there's any doubt in your mind of my affection for your daughter?"

"I suppose you do admire her," snapped the old man. "You can't help that, I suppose. No one can," he added naively.

"And I suppose you know that she loves me, in spite of your objections?" went on the young man.

"Bah! Bah!"

"And that you are breaking her heart by your mutton-headed objection to me?"

"You—you—" sputtered Mr. Meredith.

Dick was still calm.

"May I see Miss Meredith for a few minutes?" he went on.

"She won't see you, sir," stormed the irate parent. "She told me last night that she would never consent to see you again."

"Will you give me your permission to see her here and now, if she will consent?" Dick insisted steadily.

"She won't see you, I say."

"May I send a card to her?"

"She won't see you, sir," repeated Mr. Meredith doggedly.

Dick stepped out into the hall and beckoned to the maid.

"Please take my card to Miss Meredith," he directed.

The maid accepted the white square, with a little uplifting of her brows, and went up the stairs. Miss Meredith received it languidly, read it, then sat up indignantly.

"Dick Herbert!" she exclaimed incredulously. "How dare he come here? It's the most audacious thing I ever heard of! Certainly I will not see him again in any circumstances." She arose and glared defiantly at the demure maid. "Tell Mr. Herbert," she said emphatically, "tell him—that I'll be right down."

Chapter XV

Mr. Meredith had stamped out of the room angrily, and Dick Herbert was alone when Dollie, in regal indignation, swept in. The general slant of her ruddy head radiated defiance, and a most depressing chilliness lay in her blue eyes. Her lips formed a scarlet line, and there was a how-dare-you-sir tilt to nose and chin. Dick started up quickly at her appearance.

"Dollie!" he exclaimed eagerly.

"Mr. Herbert," she responded coldly. She sat down primly on the extreme edge of a chair which yawned to embrace her. "What is it, please?"

Dick was a singularly audacious sort of person, but her manner froze him into sudden austerity. He regarded her steadily for a moment. "I have come to explain why—"

Miss Dollie Meredith sniffed.

"I have come to explain," he went on, "why I did not meet you at the Randolph masked hall, as we had planned."

"Why you did not meet me?" inquired Dollie coldly, with a little surprised movement of her arched brows. "Why you did not meet me?" she repeated.

"I shall have to ask you to believe that, in the circumstances, it was absolutely impossible," Dick continued, preferring not to notice the singular emphasis of her words. "Something occurred early that evening which—which left me no choice in the matter. I can readily understand your indignation and humiliation at my failure to appear, and I had no way of reaching you that evening or since. News of your return last night only reached me an hour ago. I knew you had disappeared."

Dollie's blue eyes were opened to the widest and her lips parted a little in astonishment. For a moment she sat thus, staring at the young man, then she sank back into her chair with a little gasp.

"May I inquire," she asked, after she recovered her breath, "the cause of this—this levity?"

"Dollie, dear, I am perfectly serious," Dick assured her earnestly. "I am trying to make it plain to you, that's all."

"Why you did not meet me?" Dollie repeated again. "Why you did meet me! And that's—*that's* what's the matter with everything!"

Whatever surprise or other emotion Dick might have felt was admirably repressed.

"I thought perhaps there was some mistake somewhere," he said at last. "Now, Dollie, listen to me. No, wait a minute, please! I did not go to the Randolph ball. You did. You eloped from that ball, as you and I had planned, in an automobile, but not with me. You went with some other man—the man who really stole the gold plate."

Dollie opened her mouth to exclaim, then shut it suddenly.

"Now just a moment, please," pleaded Dick. "You spoke to some other man under the impression that you were speaking to me. For a reason which does not appear now, he fell in with your plans. Therefore, you ran away with him—in the automobile which carried the gold plate. What happened after that I cannot even surmise. I only know that you are the mysterious woman who disappeared with the Burglar."

Dollie gasped and nearly choked with her emotions. A flame of scarlet leaped into her face and the glare of the blue eyes was pitiless.

"Mr. Herbert," she said deliberately at last, "I don't know whether you think I am a fool or only a child. I know that no rational human being can accept that as true. I know I left Seven Oaks with you in the auto; I know you are the man who stole the gold plate; I know how you received the shot in your right shoulder; I know how you afterward fainted from loss of blood. I know how I bound up your wound and—and—I know a lot of things else!"

The sudden rush of words left her breathless for an instant. Dick listened quietly. He started to say something—to expostulate—but she got a fresh start and hurried on:

"I recognised you in that silly disguise by the cleft in your chin. I called you Dick and you answered me. I asked if you had received the little casket and you answered yes. I left the ballroom as you directed and climbed into the automobile. I know that horrid ride we had, and how I took the gold plate in the bag and walked— walked through the night until I was exhausted. I know it all—how I lied and connived, and told silly stories—but I did it all to save you from yourself, and now you dare face me with a denial!"

Dollie suddenly burst into tears. Dick now attempted no further denial. There was no anger in his face—only a deeply troubled expression. He arose and walked over to the window, where he stood staring out.

"I know it all," Dollie repeated gurglingly— "all, except what possible idea you had in stealing the miserable, wretched old plate, anyway!" There was a pause and Dollie peered through teary fingers. "How—how long," she asked, "have you been a—a—a—kleptomaniac?"

Dick shrugged his sturdy shoulders a little impatiently.

"Did your father ever happen to tell you why he objects to my attentions to you?" he asked.

"No, but I know now." And there was a new burst of tears. "It's because—because you are a—a—you take things."

"You will not believe what I tell you?"

"How can I when I helped you run away with the horrid stuff?"

"If I pledge you my word of honour that I told you the truth?"

"I can't believe it, I can't!" wailed Dollie desolately. "No one could believe it. I never suspected—never dreamed—of the possibility of such a thing even when you lay wounded out there in the dark woods. If I had, I should certainly have never—have never— kissed you."

Dick wheeled suddenly.

"Kissed me?" he exclaimed.

"Yes, you horrid thing!" sobbed Dollie. "If there had previously been the slightest doubt in my mind as to your identity, that would have convinced me that it was you, because—because—just because! And besides, if it wasn't you I kissed, you ought to have told me!"

Dollie leaned forward suddenly on the arm of the chair with her face hidden in her hands. Dick crossed the room softly toward her and laid a hand caressingly about her shoulders. She shook it off angrily.

"How dare you, sir?" she blazed.

"Dollie, don't you love me?" he pleaded.

"No!" was the prompt reply.

"But you did love me—once?"

"Why—yes, but I—I—"

"And couldn't you ever love me again?"

"I—I don't ever want to again."

"But couldn't you?"

"If you had only told me the truth, instead of making such a silly denial," she blubbered. "I don't know why you took the plate unless—unless it is because you—you couldn't help it. But you didn't tell me the truth."

Dick stared down at the ruddy head moodily for a moment. Then his manner changed and he dropped on his knees beside her.

"Suppose," he whispered, "suppose I should confess that I did take it?"

Dollie looked up suddenly with a new horror in her face.

"Oh, you did do it then?" she demanded. This was worse than ever!

"Suppose I should confess that I did?"

"Oh, Dick!" she sobbed. And her arms went suddenly around his neck. "You are breaking my heart. Why? Why?"

"Would you be satisfied?" he insisted.

"What could have caused you to do such a thing?"

The love-light glimmered again in her blue eyes; the red lips trembled.

"Suppose it had been just a freak of mine, and I had intended to—to return the stuff, as has been done?" he went on.

Dollie stared deeply into the eyes upturned to hers.

"Silly boy," she said. Then she kissed him. "But you must never, never do it again."

"I never will," he promised solemnly.

Five minutes later Dick was leaving the house, when he met Mr. Meredith in the hall.

"I'm going to marry your daughter," he said quite calmly.

Mr. Meredith raved at him as he went down the steps.

Chapter XVI

Alone in her room, with the key turned in the lock, Miss Dollie Meredith had a perfectly delightful time. She wept and laughed and sobbed and shuddered; she was pensive and doleful and happy and melancholy; she dreamed dreams of the future, past and present; she sang foolish little ecstatic songs—just a few words of each—and cried again copiously. Her father had sent her to her room with a stern reprimand, and she giggled joyously as she remembered it.

"After all, it wasn't anything," she assured herself. "It was silly for him to—to take the stuff, of course, but it's back now, and he told me the truth, and he intended to return it, anyway." In her present mood she would have justified anything. "And he's not a thief or anything. I don't suppose father will ever give his consent, so, after all, we'll have to elope, and that will be—perfectly delightful. Papa will go on dreadfully and then he'll be all right."

After a while Dollie snuggled down in the sheets and lay quite still in the dark until sleep overtook her. Silence reigned in the house. It was about two o'clock in the morning when she sat up suddenly in bed with startled eyes. She had heard something—or rather in her sleep she had received the impression of hearing something. She listened intently as she peered about.

Finally she did hear something—something tap sharply on the window once. Then came silence again. A frightened chill ran all the way down to Dollie's curling pink toes. There was a pause, and then again came the sharp click on the window, whereupon Dollie pattered out of bed in her bare feet and ran to the window, which was open a few inches.

With the greatest caution she peered out. Vaguely skulking in the shadows below she made out the figure of a man. As she looked it seemed to draw up into a knot, then straighten out quickly. Involuntarily she dodged. There came another sharp click at the window. The man below was tossing pebbles against the pane with the obvious purpose of attracting her attention.

"Dick, is that you?" she called cautiously.

"Sh—h—h—h!" came the answer. "Here's a note for you. Open the window so I may throw it in."

"Is it really and truly you?" Dollie insisted.

"Yes," came the hurried, whispered answer. "Quick, someone is coming!"

Dollie threw the sash up and stepped back. A whirling, white object came through and fell noiselessly on the carpet. Dollie seized upon it eagerly and ran to the window again. Below she saw the retreating figure of a man. Other footsteps materialised in a bulky policeman, who strolled by seeking, perhaps, a quiet spot for a nap.

Shivering with excitement, Dollie closed the window and pulled down the shade, after which she lighted the gas. She opened the note eagerly and sat down upon the floor to read it. Now a large part of this note was extraneous verbiage of a superlative emotional nature—its vital importance was an outline of a new plan of elopement, to take place on Wednesday in time for them to catch a European-bound steamer at half-past two in the afternoon.

Dollie read and reread the crumpled sheet many times, and when finally its wording had been indelibly fixed in her mind she wasted an unbelievable number of kisses on it. Of course this was sheer extravagance, but—girls are wonderful creatures.

"He's the dearest thing in the world!" she declared at last.

She burned the note reluctantly and carefully disposed of the ashes by throwing them out of the window, after which she returned to her bed. On the following morning, Monday, father glared at daughter sternly as she demurely entered the breakfast-room. He was seeking to read that which no man has ever been able to read— a woman's face. Dollie smiled upon him charmingly.

After breakfast father and daughter had a little talk in a sunny corner of the library.

"I have planned for us to return to Baltimore on next Thursday," he informed her.

"Oh, isn't that delightful?" beamed Dollie.

"In view of everything and your broken promise to me—the promise not to see Herbert again—I think it wisest," he continued.

"Perhaps it is," she mused.

"Why did you see him?" he demanded.

"I consented to see him, only to bid him good-by," replied Dollie demurely, "and to make perfectly clear to him my position in this matter."

Oh, woman! Perfidious, insincere, loyal, charming woman! All the tangled skeins of life are the work of your dainty fingers. All the sins and sorrows are your doing!

Mr. Meredith rubbed his chin thoughtfully.

"You may take it as my wish—my order even," he said as he cleared his throat—for giving orders to Dollie was a dangerous experiment, "that you must not attempt to communicate in any way with Mr. Herbert again—by letter or otherwise."

"Yes, papa."

Mr. Meredith was somewhat surprised at the ease with which he got away with this. Had he been blessed with a little more wisdom in the ways of women he would have been suspicious.

"You really do not love him, anyway," he ventured at last. "It was only a girlish infatuation."

"I told him yesterday just what I thought of him," she replied truthfully enough.

And thus the interview ended.

It was about noon that day when Hutchinson Hatch called on Dick Herbert.

"Well, what did you find out?" he inquired.

"Really, old man," said Dick kindly, "I have decided that there is nothing I can say to you about the matter. It's a private affair, after all."

"Yes, I know that you know about that, but the police don't know it," commented the reporter grimly.

"The police!" Dick smiled.

"Did you see her?" Hatch asked.

"Yes, I saw her—and her father, too."

Hatch saw the one door by which he had hoped to solve the riddle closing on him.

"Was Miss Meredith the girl in the automobile?" he asked bluntly.

"Really, I won't answer that."

"Are you the man who stole the gold plate?"

"I won't answer that, either," replied Dick smilingly. "Now, look here, Hatch, you're a good fellow. I like you. It is your business to find out things, but, in this particular affair, I'm going to make it my business to keep you from finding out things. I'll risk the police end of it." He went over and shook hands with the reporter cordially. "Believe me, if I told you the absolute truth—all of it— you couldn't print it unless—unless I was arrested, and I don't intend that that shall happen."

Hatch went away.

That night the Randolph gold plate was stolen for the second time. Thirty-six hours later Detective Mallory arrested Richard Herbert with the stolen plate in his possession. Dick burst out laughing when the detective walked in on him.

Part III: The Thinking Machine

Chapter XVII

Professor Augustus S. F. X. Van Dusen, Ph. D., LL. D., F. R. S., M. D., etc., etc., was the Court of Last Appeal in the sciences. He was five feet two inches tall, weighed 107 pounds, that being slightly above normal, and wore a number eight hat. Bushy, yellow hair straggled down about his ears and partially framed a clean-shaven, wizened face in which were combined the paradoxical qualities of extreme aggressiveness and childish petulance. The mouth drooped a little at the corners, being otherwise a straight line; the eyes were mere slits of blue, squinting eternally through thick spectacles. His brow rose straight up, domelike, majestic even, and added a whimsical grotesqueness to his appearance.

The Professor's idea of light literature, for rare moments of recreation, was page after page of encyclopaedic discussion on "ologies" and "isms" with lots of figures in 'em. Sometimes he wrote these discussions himself, and frequently held them up to annihilation. His usual speaking tone was one of deep annoyance, and he had an unwavering glare that went straight through one. He was the son of the son of the son of an eminent German scientist, the logical production of a house that had borne a distinguished name in the sciences for generations.

Thirty-five of his fifty years had been devoted to logic, study, analysis of cause and effect, mental, material, and psychological. By his personal efforts he had mercilessly flattened out and read-justed at least two of the exact sciences and had added immeasurably to the world's sum of knowledge in others. Once he had held the chair of philosophy in a great university, but casually one day he promulgated a thesis that knocked the faculty's eye out, and he was invited to vacate. It was a dozen years later that that university had openly resorted to influence and diplomacy to induce him to accept its LL. D.

For years foreign and American institutions, educational, scientific, and otherwise, crowded degrees upon him. He didn't care. He started fires with the elaborately formal notifications of these unsought honours and turned again to his work in the small laboratory which was a part of his modest home. There he lived, practically a recluse, his simple wants being attended to by one aged servant, Martha.

This, then, was The Thinking Machine. This last title, The Thinking Machine, perhaps more expressive of the real man than a yard of honorary initials, was coined by Hutchinson Hatch at the time of the scientist's defeat of a chess champion after a single morning's instruction in the game. The Thinking Machine had asserted that logic was inevitable, and that game had proven his assertion. Afterward there had grown up a strange sort of friendship between the crabbed scientist and the reporter. Hatch, to the scientist, represented the great, whirling outside world; to the reporter the scientist was merely a brain—a marvellously keen, penetrating, infallible guide through material muddles far removed from the delicately precise labours of the laboratory.

Now The Thinking Machine sat in a huge chair in his reception-room with long, slender fingers pressed tip to tip and squint eyes turned upward. Hatch was talking, had been talking for more than an hour with infrequent interruptions. In that time he had laid bare the facts as he and the police knew them from the incidents of the masked ball at Seven Oaks to the return of Dollie Meredith.

"Now, Mr. Hatch," asked The Thinking Machine, "just what is known of this second theft of the gold plate?"

"It's simple enough," explained the reporter. "It was plain burglary. Some person entered the Randolph house on Monday night by cutting out a pane of glass and unfastening a window-latch. Whoever it was took the plate and escaped. That's all anyone knows of it."

"Left no clew, of course?"

"No, so far as has been found."

"I presume that, on its return by express, Mr. Randolph ordered the plate placed in the small room as before?"

"Yes."

"He's a fool."

"Yes."

"Please go on."

"Now the police absolutely decline to say as yet just what evidence they have against Herbert beyond the finding of the plate in his possession," the reporter resumed, "though, of course, that's enough and to spare. They will not say, either, how they first came to connect him with the affair. Detective Mallory doesn't—"

"When and where was Mr. Herbert arrested?"

"Yesterday, Tuesday, afternoon in his rooms. Fourteen pieces of the gold plate were on the table."

The Thinking Machine dropped his eyes a moment to squint at the reporter.

"Only eleven pieces of the plate were first stolen, you said?"

"Only eleven, yes."

"And I think you said two shots were fired at the thief?"

"Yes."

"Who fired them, please?"

"One of the detectives—Cunningham, I think."

"It was a detective—you know that?"

"Yes, I know that."

"Yes, yes. Please go on."

"The plate was all spread out—there was no attempt to conceal it," Hatch resumed. "There was a box on the floor and Herbert was about to pack the stuff in it when Detective Mallory and two of his men entered. Herbert's servant, Blair, was away from the house at the time. His people are up in Nova Scotia, so he was alone."

"Nothing but the gold plate was found?"

"Oh, yes!" exclaimed the reporter. "There was a lot of jewelry in a case and fifteen or twenty odd pieces—fifty thousand dollars' worth of stuff, at least. The police took it to find the owners."

"Dear me! Dear me!" exclaimed The Thinking Machine. "Why didn't you mention the jewelry at first? Wait a minute." Hatch was silent while the scientist continued to squint at the ceiling. He wriggled in his chair uncomfortably and smoked a couple of cigarettes before The Thinking Machine turned to him and nodded.

"That's all I know," said Hatch.

"Did Mr. Herbert say anything when arrested?"

"No, he only laughed. I don't know why. I don't imagine it would have been at all funny to me."

"Has he said anything since?"

"No, nothing to me or anybody else. He was arraigned at a preliminary hearing, pleaded not guilty, and was released on twenty thousand dollars bail. Some of his rich friends furnished it."

"Did he give any reason for his refusal to say anything?" insisted The Thinking Machine testily.

"He remarked to me that he wouldn't say anything, because, even if he told the truth, no one would believe him."

"If it should have been a protestation of innocence I'm afraid nobody would have believed him," commented the scientist enigmatically. He was silent for several minutes. "It could have been a brother, of course," he mused.

"A brother?" asked Hatch quickly. "Whose brother? What brother?"

"As I understand it," the scientist went on, not heeding the question, "you did not believe Herbert guilty of the first theft?"

"Why, I couldn't," Hatch protested. "I couldn't," he repeated.

"Why?"

"Well, because—because he's not that sort of man," explained the reporter. "I've known him for years, personally and by reputation."

"Was he a particular friend of yours in college?"

"No, not an intimate, but he was in my class—and he's a whacking, jam-up, ace-high football player." That squared everything.

"Do you now believe him guilty?" insisted the scientist.

"I can't believe anything else—and yet I'd stake my life on his honesty."

"And Miss Meredith?"

The reporter was reaching the explosive point. He had seen and talked to Miss Meredith, you know.

"It's perfectly asinine to suppose that she had anything to do with either theft, don't you think?"

The Thinking Machine was silent on that point.

"Well, Mr. Hatch," he said finally, "the problem comes down to this: Did a man, and perhaps a woman, who are circumstantially proven guilty of stealing the gold plate, actually steal it? We have the stained cushion of the automobile in which the thieves escaped to indicate that one of them was wounded; we have Mr. Herbert with an injured right shoulder—a hurt received that night on his own statement, though he won't say how. We have, then, the second theft and the finding of the stolen property in his possession along with another lot of stolen stuff—jewels. It is apparently a settled case now without going further."

"But—" Hatch started to protest.

"But suppose we do go a little further," The Thinking Machine went on. "I can prove definitely, conclusively, and finally by settling only two points whether or not Mr. Herbert was wounded while in the automobile. If he was wounded while in that automobile, he was the first thief; if not, he wasn't. If he was the first thief, he was probably the second, but even if he were not the first thief, there is, of course, a possibility that he was the second."

Hatch was listening with mouth open.

"Suppose we begin now," continued The Thinking Machine, "by finding out the name of the physician who treated Mr. Herbert's wound last Thursday night. Mr. Herbert may have a reason for keeping the identity of this physician secret, but, perhaps—wait a minute," and the scientist disappeared into the next room. He was gone for five minutes. "See if the physician who treated the wound wasn't Dr. Clarence Walpole."

The reporter blinked a little. "Right," he said. "What next?"

"Ask him something about the nature of the wound and all the usual questions."

Hatch nodded.

"Then," resumed The Thinking Machine casually, "bring me some of Mr. Herbert's blood."

The reporter blinked a good deal, and gulped twice.

"How much?" he inquired briskly.

"A single drop on a small piece of glass will do very nicely," replied the scientist.

Chapter XVIII

The Supreme Police Intelligence of the Metropolitan District was doing some heavy thinking, which, modestly enough, bore generally on his own dazzling perspicacity. Just at the moment he couldn't recall any detector of crime whose lustre in any way dimmed his own, or whose mere shadow, even, had a right to fall on the same earth as his; and this lapse of memory so stimulated his admiration for the subject of his thoughts that he lighted a fresh cigar and put his feet in the middle of the desk.

He sat thus when The Thinking Machine called. The Supreme Intelligence—Mr. Mallory—knew Professor Van Dusen well, and, though he received his visitor graciously, he showed no difficulty in restraining any undue outburst of enthusiasm. Instead, the same admirable self-control which prevented him from outwardly evidencing his pleasure prompted him to square back in his chair with a touch of patronising aggressiveness in his manner.

"Ah, Professor," was his noncommittal greeting.

"Good-evening, Mr. Mallory," responded the scientist in the thin, irritated voice which always set Mr. Mallory's nerves a-jangle. "I don't suppose you would tell me by what steps you were led to arrest Mr. Herbert?"

"I would not," declared Mr. Mallory promptly.

"No, nor would you inform me of the nature of the evidence against him in addition to the jewels and plate found in his possession?"

"I would not," replied Mr. Mallory again.

"No, I thought perhaps you would not," remarked The Thinking Machine. "I understand, by the way, that one of your men took a leather cushion from the automobile in which the thieves escaped on the night of the ball?"

"Well, what of it?" demanded the detective.

461

"I merely wanted to inquire if it would be permissible for me to see that cushion?"

Detective Mallory glared at him suspiciously, then slowly his heavy face relaxed, and he laughed as he arose and produced the cushion.

"If you're trying to make any mystery of this cushion, you're in bad," he informed the scientist. "We know the owner of the automobile in which Herbert and the Girl escaped. The cushion means nothing."

The Thinking Machine examined the heavy leather carefully and paid a great deal of attention to the crusted stains which it bore. He picked at one of the brown spots with his penknife and it flaked off in his hand.

"Herbert was caught with the goods on," declared the detective, and he thumped the desk with his lusty fist. "We've got the right man."

"Yes," admitted The Thinking Machine, "it begins to look very much as if you did have the right man—for once."

Detective Mallory snorted.

"Would you mind telling me if any of the jewelry you found in Mr. Herbert's possession has been identified?"

"Sure thing," replied the detective. "That's where I've got Herbert good. Four people who lost jewelry at the masked ball have appeared and claimed pieces of the stuff."

For an instant a slightly perplexed wrinkle appeared in the brow of The Thinking Machine, and as quickly it passed.

"Of course, of course," he mused.

"It's the biggest haul of stolen goods the police of this city have made for many years," the detective volunteered complacently. "And, if I'm not wrong, there's more of it coming—no man knows how much more. Why, Herbert must have been operating for years, and he got away with it, of course, by the gentlemanly exterior, the polish, and all that. I consider his capture the most important that has happened since I have been connected with the police."

"Indeed?" inquired the scientist thoughtfully. He was still gazing at the cushion.

"And the most important development of all is to come," Detective Mallory rattled on. "That will be the real sensation, and make the arrest of Herbert seem purely incidental. It now looks as if there would be another arrest of a—of a person who is so high socially, and all that—"

"Yes," interrupted The Thinking Machine, "but do you think it would be wise to arrest her now?"

"Her?" demanded Detective Mallory. "What do you know of any woman?"

"You were speaking of Miss Dorothy Meredith, weren't you?" inquired The Thinking Machine blandly. "Well, I merely asked if you thought it would be wise for your men to go so far as to arrest her."

The detective bit his cigar in two in obvious perturbation.

"How—how—did you happen to know her name?" he demanded.

"Oh, Mr. Hatch mentioned it to me," replied the scientist. "He has known of her connection with the case for several days, as well as Herbert's, and has talked to them both, I think."

The Supreme Intelligence was nearly apoplectic.

"If Hatch knew it why didn't he tell me?" he thundered.

"Really, I don't know," responded the scientist. "Perhaps," he added curtly, "he may have had some absurd notion that you would find it out for yourself. He has strange ideas like that sometimes."

And when Detective Mallory had fully recovered The Thinking Machine was gone.

Meanwhile Hatch had seen and questioned Dr. Clarence Walpole in the latter's office, only a stone's throw from Dick Herbert's home. Had Doctor Walpole recently dressed a wound for Mr. Herbert? Doctor Walpole had. A wound caused by a pistol-bullet? Yes.

"When was it, please?" asked Hatch.

"Only a few nights ago."

"Thursday night, perhaps?"

Doctor Walpole consulted a desk-dairy.

"Yes, Thursday night, or rather Friday morning," he replied. "It was between two and three o'clock. He came here and I fixed him up."

"Where was the wound, please?"

"In the right shoulder," replied the physician, "just here," and he touched the reporter with one finger. "It wasn't dangerous, but he had lost considerable blood."

464 | THE THINKING MACHINE

Hatch was silent for a moment, dazed. Every new point piled up the evidence against Herbert. The location of the wound—a pistol-wound—the very hour of the dressing of it! Dick would have had plenty of time between the moment of the robbery, which was comparatively early, and the hour of his call on Doctor Walpole to do all those things which he was suspected of doing.

"I don't suppose Mr. Herbert explained how he got the wound?" Hatch asked apprehensively. He was afraid he had.

"No. I asked, but he evaded the question. It was, of course, none of my business, after I had extracted the bullet and dressed the hurt."

"You have the bullet?"

"Yes. It's the usual size—thirty-two calibre."

That was all. The prosecution was in, the case proven, the verdict rendered. Ten minutes later Hatch's name was announced to Dick Herbert. Dick received him gloomily, shook hands with him, then resumed his interrupted pacing.

"I had declined to see men from other papers," he said wearily.

"Now, look here, Dick," expostulated Hatch, "don't you want to make some statement of your connection with this affair? I honestly believe that if you did it would help you."

"No, I cannot make any statement—that's all." Dick's hand closed fiercely. "I can't," he added, "and there's no need to talk of it." He continued his pacing for a moment or so; then turned on the reporter. "Do you believe me guilty?" he demanded abruptly.

"I can't believe anything else," Hatch replied falteringly. "But at that I don't want to believe it." There was an embarrassed pause. "I have just seen Dr. Clarence Walpole."

"Well?" Dick wheeled on him angrily.

"What he said alone would convict you, even if the stuff had not been found here," Hatch replied.

"Are you trying to convict me?" Dick demanded.

"I'm trying to get the truth," remarked Hatch.

"There is just one man in the world whom I must see before the truth can ever be told," declared Dick vehemently. "And I can't find him now. I don't know where he is!"

"Let me find him. Who is he? What's his name?"

"If I told you that I might as well tell you everything," Dick went on. "It was to prevent any mention of that name that I have allowed myself to be placed in this position. It is purely a personal matter between us—at least I will make it so—and if I ever meet him—" his hands closed and unclosed spasmodically, "the truth will be known unless I—I kill him first."

More bewildered, more befuddled, and more generally betangled than ever, Hatch put his hands to his head to keep it from flying off. Finally he glanced around at Dick, who stood with clenched fists and closed teeth. A blaze of madness lay in Dick's eyes.

"Have you seen Miss Meredith again?" inquired the reporter.

Dick burst out laughing.

Half an hour later Hatch left him. On the glass top of an inkstand he carried three precious drops of Herbert's blood.

Chapter XIX

Faithfully, phonographically even, Hatch repeated to The Thinking Machine the conversation he had had with Doctor Walpole, indicating on the person of the eminent scientist the exact spot of the wound as Doctor Walpole had indicated it to him. The scientist listened without comment to the recital, casually studying meanwhile the three crimson drops on the glass.

"Every step I take forward is a step backward," the reporter declared in conclusion with a helpless grin. "Instead of showing that Dick Herbert might not have stolen the plate I am proving conclusively that he was the thief—nailing it to him so hard that he can't possibly get out of it."

He was silent a moment. "If I keep on long enough," he added glumly, "I'll hang him."

The Thinking Machine squinted at him aggressively.

"You still don't believe him guilty?" he asked.

"Why, I—I—I—" Hatch burst out savagely. "Damn it, I don't know what I believe," he tapered off. "It's absolutely impossible!"

"Nothing is impossible, Mr. Hatch," snapped The Thinking Machine irritably. "The worst a problem can be is difficult, but all problems can be solved as inevitably as that two and two make four—not sometimes, but *all* the time. Please don't say things are impossible. It annoys me exceedingly."

Hatch stared at his distinguished friend and smiled whimsically. He was also annoyed exceedingly on his own private, individual account—the annoyance that comes from irresistibly butting into immovable facts.

"Doctor Walpole's statement," The Thinking Machine went on after a moment, "makes this particular problem ludicrously simple. Two points alone show conclusively that Mr. Herbert was not the man in the automobile. I shall reach the third myself."

Hatch didn't say anything. The English language is singularly inadequate at times, and if he had spoken he would have had to invent a phraseology to convey even a faint glimmer of what he really thought.

"Now, Mr. Hatch," resumed the scientist, quite casually, "I understand you graduated from Harvard in ninety-eight. Yes? Well, Herbert was a classmate of yours there. Please obtain for me one of the printed lists of students who were in Harvard that year—a complete list."

"I have one at home," said the reporter.

"Get it, please, immediately, and return here," instructed the scientist.

Hatch went out and The Thinking Machine disappeared into his laboratory. He remained there for one hour and forty-seven minutes by the clock. When he came out he found the reporter sitting in the reception-room again, holding his head. The scientist's face was as blankly inscrutable as ever.

"Here is the list," said Hatch as he handed it over.

The Thinking Machine took it in his long, slender fingers and turned two or three leaves. Finally he stopped and ran a finger down one page.

"Ah," he exclaimed at last. "I thought so."

"Thought what?" asked Hatch curiously.

"I'm going out to see Mr. Meredith now," remarked The Thinking Machine irrelevantly. "Come along. Have you met him?"

"No."

Mr. Meredith had read the newspaper accounts of the arrest of Dick Herbert and the seizure of the gold plate and jewels; he had even taunted his charming daughter with it in a fatherly sort of a way. She was weeping, weeping her heart out over this latest proof of the perfidy and loathsomeness of the man she loved.

Incidentally, it may be mentioned here that the astute Mr. Meredith was not aware of any elopement plot—either the first or second.

When a card bearing the name of Mr. Augustus S. F. X. Van Dusen was handed to Mr. Meredith he went wonderingly into the reception-room. There was a pause as the scientist and Mr.

Meredith mentally sized each other up; then introductions—and The Thinking Machine came down to business abruptly, as always.

"May I ask, Mr. Meredith," he began, "how many sons you have?"

"One," replied Mr. Meredith, puzzled.

"May I ask his present address?" went on the scientist.

Mr. Meredith studied the belligerent eyes of his caller and wondered what business it was of his, for Mr. Meredith was a belligerent sort of a person himself.

"May I ask," he inquired with pronounced emphasis on the personal pronoun, "why you want to know?"

Hatch rubbed his chin thoughtfully. He was wondering what would happen to him when the cyclone struck.

"It may save him and you a great deal of annoyance if you will give me his address," said The Thinking Machine. "I desire to communicate with him immediately on a matter of the utmost importance—a purely personal matter."

"Personal matter?" repeated Mr. Meredith. "Your abruptness and manner, sir, were not calculated to invite confidence."

The Thinking Machine bowed gravely.

"May I ask your son's address?" he repeated.

Mr. Meredith considered the matter at some length and finally arrived at the conclusion that he might ask.

"He is in South America at present—Buenos Ayres," he replied.

"What?" exclaimed The Thinking Machine so suddenly that both Hatch and Mr. Meredith started a little. "What?" he repeated, and wrinkles suddenly appeared in the domelike brow.

"I said he was in South America—Buenos Ayres," repeated Mr. Meredith stiffly, but a little awed. "A letter or cable to him in care of the American Consul at Buenos Ayres will reach him promptly."

The Thinking Machine's narrow eyes were screwed down to the disappearing point, the slender white fingers were twiddled jerkily, the corrugations remained in his brow.

"How long has Mr. Meredith been there?" he asked at last.

"Three months."

"Do you know he is there?"

Mr. Meredith started to say something then swallowed it with an effort.

"I know it positively, yes," he replied. "I received this letter dated the second from him three days ago, and to-day I received a cable-dispatch forwarded to me here from Baltimore."

"Are you positive the letter is in your son's handwriting?"

Mr. Meredith almost choked in mingled bewilderment and resentment at the question and the manner of its asking.

"I am positive, yes," he replied at last, preserving his tone of dignity with a perceptible effort. He noted the inscrutable face of his caller and saw the corrugations in the brow suddenly swept away. "What business of yours is it, anyway?" blazed Mr. Meredith suddenly.

"May I ask where you were last Thursday night?" went on the even, steady voice.

"It's no business of yours," Mr. Meredith blurted. "I was in Baltimore."

"Can you prove it in a court of law?"

"Prove it? Of course I can prove it!" Mr. Meredith was fairly bellowing at his impassive interrogator. "But it's nobody's business."

"If you can prove it, Mr. Meredith," remarked The Thinking Machine quietly, coldly, "you had best make your arrangements to do so, because, believe me, it may be necessary to save you from a charge of having stolen the Randolph gold plate on last Thursday night at the masked ball. Good-day, sir."

Chapter XX

"But Mr. Herbert won't see anyone, sir," protested Blair.

"Tell Mr. Herbert, please, that unless I can see him immediately his bail-bond will be withdrawn," directed The Thinking Machine.

He stood waiting in the hall while Blair went up the stairs. Dick Herbert took the card impatiently and glanced at it.

"Van Dusen," he mused. "Who the deuce is Van Dusen?"

Blair repeated the message he had received below.

"What does he look like?" inquired Dick.

"He's a shrivelled little man with a big yellow head, sir," replied Blair.

"Let him come up," instructed Dick.

Thus, within an hour after he had talked to Mr. Meredith, The Thinking Machine met Dick Herbert.

"What's this about the bail-bond?" Dick inquired.

"I wanted to talk to you," was the scientist's calm reply. "That seemed to be the easiest way to make you believe it was important, so—"

Dick's face flushed crimson at the trick.

"Well, you see me!" he broke out angrily. "I ought to throw you down the stairs, but—what is it?"

Not having been invited to a seat, The Thinking Machine took one anyway and settled himself comfortably.

"If you will listen to me for a moment without interruption," he began testily, "I think the subject of my remarks will be of deep personal concern to you. I am interested in solving this Randolph plate affair and have perhaps gone further in my investigation than anyone else. At least, I know more about it. There are some things I don't happen to know, however, that are of the greatest importance."

"I tell you—" stormed Dick.

"For instance," calmly resumed the scientist, "it is very important for me to know whether or not Harry Meredith was masked when he came into this room last Thursday night."

Dick gazed at him in surprise which approached awe. His eyes were widely distended, the lower part of his face lax, for the instant; then his white teeth closed with a snap and he sat down opposite The Thinking Machine. Anger had gone from his manner; instead there was a pallor of apprehension in the clean-cut face.

"Who are you, Mr. Van Dusen?" he asked at last. His tone was mild, even deferential.

"Was he masked?" insisted the scientist.

For a long while Dick was silent. Finally he arose and paced nervously back and forth across the room, glancing at the diminutive figure of The Thinking Machine each time as he turned.

"I won't say anything," he decided.

"Will you name the cause of the trouble you and Meredith had at Harvard?" asked the scientist.

Again there was a long pause.

"No," Dick said finally.

"Did it have anything to do with theft?"

"I don't know who you are or why you are prying into an affair that, at least on its face, does not concern you," replied Dick. "I'll say nothing at all—unless—unless you produce the one man who can and shall explain this affair. Produce him here in this room where I can get my hands on him!"

The Thinking Machine squinted at the sturdy shoulders with admiration in his face.

"Did it ever happen to occur to you, Mr. Herbert, that Harry Meredith and his father are precisely of the same build?"

Some nameless, impalpable expression crept into Dick's face despite an apparent fight to restrain it, and again he stared at the small man in the chair.

"And that you and Mr. Meredith are practically of the same build?"

Tormented by unasked questions and by those emotions which had compelled him to silence all along, Dick still paced back and forth. His head was whirling. The structure which he had so care-fully guarded was tumbling about his ears. Suddenly he stopped and turned upon The Thinking Machine.

"Just what do you know of this affair?" he asked.

"I know for one thing," replied the scientist positively, "that you were not the man in the automobile."

"How do you know that?"

"That's beside the question just now."

"Do you know who was in the automobile?" Dick insisted.

"I can only answer that question when you have answered mine," the scientist went on. "Was Harry Meredith masked when he entered this room last Thursday night?"

Dick sat staring down at his hands, which were working ner-vously. Finally he nodded.

The Thinking Machine understood.

"You recognised him, then, by something he said or wore?"

Again Dick nodded reluctantly.

"Both," he added.

The Thinking Machine leaned back in his chair and sat there for a long time. At last he arose as if the interview were at an end. There seemed to be no other questions that he desired to ask at the moment.

"You need not be unnecessarily alarmed, Mr. Herbert," he as-sured Dick as he picked up his hat. "I shall act with discretion in this matter. I am not representing anyone who would care to make it unpleasant for you. I may tell you that you made two serious mistakes: the first when you saw or communicated with Mr. Ran-dolph immediately after the plate was stolen the second time, and again when you undertook something which properly belonged within the province of the police."

Herbert still sat with his head in his hands as The Thinking Machine went out.

It was very late that night—after twelve, in fact—when Hutch-inson Hatch called on The Thinking Machine with excitement evi-dent in tone, manner, and act. He was accustomed to calling at any hour; now he found the scientist at work as if it were midday.

"The worst has happened," the reporter told him.

The Thinking Machine didn't look around.

"Detective Mallory and two of his men saw Miss Meredith this evening about nine o'clock," Hatch hurried on, "and bully-ragged her into a confession."

"What sort of a confession?"

"She admitted that she was in the automobile on the night of the ball and that—"

"Mr. Herbert was with her," the scientist supplied.

"Yes."

"And—what else?"

"That her own jewels, valued at twenty thousand dollars, were among those found in Herbert's possession when he was arrested."

The Thinking Machine turned and looked at the reporter, just casually, and raised his hand to his mouth to cover a yawn.

"Well, she couldn't do anything else," he said calmly.

Chapter XXI

Hutchinson Hatch remained with The Thinking Machine for more than an hour, and when he left his head was spinning with the multitude of instructions which had been heaped upon him.

"Meet me at noon in Detective Mallory's office at police headquarters," The Thinking Machine had said in conclusion. "Mr. Randolph and Miss Meredith will be there."

"Miss Meredith?" Hatch repeated. "She hasn't been arrested, you know, and I doubt if she will come."

"She will come," the scientist had replied, as if that settled it.

Next day the Supreme Intelligence was sitting in his private office. He had eaten the canary; mingled triumph and gratification beamed upon his countenance. The smile remained, but to it was added the quality of curiosity when the door opened and The Thinking Machine, accompanied by Dollie Meredith and Stuyvesant Randolph, entered. "Mr. Hatch called yet?" inquired the scientist.

"No," responded the detective.

"Dear me!" grumbled the other. "It's one minute after twelve o'clock now. What could have delayed him?"

His answer was the clattering rush of a cab and the appearance of Hatch in person a moment later. He came into the room headlong, glanced around, then paused.

"Did you get it?" inquired The Thinking Machine.

"Yes, I got it, but—" began the reporter.

"Nothing else now," commanded the other.

There was a little pause as The Thinking Machine selected a chair. The others also sat down.

"Well?" inquired the Supreme Intelligence at last.

"I would like to ask, Mr. Mallory," the scientist said, "if it would be possible for me to convince you of Mr. Herbert's innocence of the charges against him?"

"It would not," replied the detective promptly. "It would not while the facts are before me, supplemented by the statement of Miss Meredith here—her confession."

Dollie coloured exquisitely and her lips trembled slightly.

"Would it be possible, Miss Meredith," the even voice went on, "to convince you of Mr. Herbert's innocence?"

"I—I don't think so," she faltered. "I—I know."

Tears which had been restrained with difficulty gushed forth suddenly, and The Thinking Machine squinted at her in pained surprise.

"Don't do that," he commanded. "It's—it's exceedingly irritating." He paused a moment, then turned suddenly to Mr. Randolph. "And you?" he asked.

Mr. Randolph shrugged his shoulders.

The Thinking Machine receded still further into his chair and stared dreamily upward with his long, slender fingers pressed tip to tip. Hatch knew the attitude; something was going to happen. He waited anxiously. Detective Mallory knew it, too, and wriggled uncomfortably.

"Suppose," the scientist began, "just suppose that we turn a little human intelligence on this problem for a change and see if we can't get the truth out of the blundering muddle that the police have helped to bring about. Let's use logic, inevitable logic, to show, simply enough, that instead of being guilty, Mr. Herbert is innocent."

Dolly Meredith suddenly leaned forward in her chair with flushed face, eyes widely opened and lips slightly parted. Detective Mallory also leaned forward in his chair, but there was a different expression on his face—oh, so different.

"Miss Meredith, we know you were in the automobile with the Burglar who stole the plate," The Thinking Machine went on. "You probably knew that he was wounded and possibly either aided in dressing the wound—as any woman would—or else saw him dress it himself?"

"I bound my handkerchief on it," replied the Girl. Her voice was low, almost a whisper.

"Where was the wound?"

"In the right shoulder," she replied.

"Back or front?" insisted the scientist.

"Back," she replied. "Very near the arm, an inch or so below the level of the shoulder."

Except for The Thinking Machine himself Hatch was the only person in the room to whom this statement meant anything, and he restrained a shout with difficulty.

"Now, Mr. Mallory," the scientist went on calmly, "do you happen to know Dr. Clarence Walpole?"

"I know of him, yes," replied the detective. "He is a man of considerable reputation."

"Would you believe him under oath?"

"Why, certainly, of course."

The Supreme Intelligence tugged at his bristly moustache.

"If Doctor Walpole should dress a wound and should later, under oath, point out its exact location, you would believe him?"

"Why, I'd have to, of course."

"Very well," commented The Thinking Machine tersely. "Now I will state an incontrovertible scientific fact for your further enlightenment. You may verify it any way you choose. This is, briefly, that the blood corpuscles in man average one-thirty-three hundredths of an inch in diameter. Remember that, please: one-thirty-three hundredths of an inch. The system of measurement has reached a state of perfection almost incomprehensible to the man who does not understand."

He paused for so long that Detective Mallory began to wriggle again. The others were leaning forward, listening with widely varied expressions on their faces.

"Now, Mr. Mallory," continued The Thinking Machine at last, "one of your men shot twice at the Burglar in the automobile, as I understand it?"

"Yes—two shots."

"Mr. Cunningham?"

"Yes, Detective Cunningham."

"Is he here now?"

The detective pressed a button on his desk and a uniformed man appeared. Instructions were given, and a moment later Detective Cunningham stood before them wonderingly.

"I suppose you can prove beyond any shadow of a doubt," resumed the scientist, still addressing Mr. Mallory, "that two shots—and only two—were fired?"

"I can prove it by twenty witnesses," was the reply.

"Good, very good," exclaimed the scientist, and he turned to Cunningham. "You know that only two shots were fired?"

"I know it, yes," replied Cunningham. "I fired 'em."

"May I see your revolver?"

Cunningham produced the weapon and handed it over. The Thinking Machine merely glanced at it.

"This is the revolver you used?"

"Yes."

"Very well, then," remarked the scientist quietly, "on that statement alone Mr. Herbert is proven innocent of the charge against him."

There was an astonished gasp all around. Hatch was beginning to see what The Thinking Machine meant, and curiously watched the bewitchingly sorrowful face of Dollie Meredith. He saw all sorts of strange things there.

"Proven innocent?" snorted Detective Mallory. "Why, you've convicted him out of hand so far as I can see."

"Corpuscles in human blood average, as I said, one-thirty-three hundredths of an inch in diameter," resumed the scientist. "They vary slightly each way, of course. Now, the corpuscles of the Burglar in the automobile measured just one-thirty-one-forty-seven hundredths of an inch. Mr. Herbert's corpuscles, tested the same way, with the same instruments, measure precisely one-thirty-five-sixty hundredths." He stopped as if that were all.

"By George!" exclaimed Mr. Randolph. "By George!"

"That's all tommy-rot," Detective Mallory burst out. "That's nothing to a jury or to any other man with common sense."

"That difference in measurement proves beyond question that Mr. Herbert was not wounded while in the automobile," went on The Thinking Machine as if there had been no interruption. "Now, Mr. Cunningham, may I ask if the Burglar's back was toward you when you fired?"

"Yes, I suppose so. He was going away from me."

"Well, that statement agrees with the statement of Miss Meredith to show that the Burglar was wounded in the back. Doctor Walpole dressed Mr. Herbert's wound between two and three o'clock Friday morning following the masked ball. Mr. Herbert had been shot, but the wound was in the front of his right shoulder."

Delighted amazement radiated from Dollie Meredith's face; she clapped her hands involuntarily as she would have applauded a stage incident. Detective Mallory started to say something, then thought better of it and glared at Cunningham instead.

"Now, Mr. Cunningham says that he shot the Burglar with this revolver." The Thinking Machine waved the weapon under Detective Mallory's nose. "This is the usual police weapon. Its calibre is thirty-eight. Mr. Herbert was shot with a thirty-two calibre. Here is the bullet." And he tossed it on the desk.

Chapter XXII

Strange emotions all tangled up with turbulent, night-marish impressions scrambled through Dollie Meredith's pretty head in garish disorder. She didn't know whether to laugh or cry. Finally she compromised by blushing radiantly at the memory of certain lingering kisses she had bestowed upon—upon—Dick Herbert? No, it wasn't Dick Herbert. Oh, dear!

Detective Mallory pounced upon the bullet as a hound upon a hare, and turned and twisted it in his hands. Cunningham leaned over his shoulder, then drew a cartridge from the revolver and compared it, as to size, with the bullet. Hatch and Mr. Randolph, looking on, saw him shake his head. The ball was too small for the revolver.

The Supreme Intelligence turned suddenly, fiercely, upon Dollie and thrust an accusing finger into her startled face.

"Mr. Herbert confessed to you that he was with you in the automobile, didn't he?"

"Y-yes," she faltered.

"You know he was with you?"

"I thought I knew it."

"You wouldn't have gone with any other man?"

"Certainly not!" A blaze of indignation suffused her cheeks.

"Your casket of jewels was found among the stolen goods in his possession?"

"Yes, but—"

With a wave of his hand the Supreme Intelligence stopped explanations and turned to glare at The Thinking Machine. That imperturbable gentleman did not alter his position in the slightest, nor did he change the steady, upward squint of his eyes.

"If you have quite finished, Mr. Mallory," he said after a moment, "I will explain how and in what circumstances the stolen plate and jewels came into Mr. Herbert's possession."

479

"Go on," urged Mr. Randolph and Hatch in a breath.

"Explain all you please; I've got him with the goods on," declared the Supreme Intelligence doggedly.

"When the simplest rules of logic establish a fact it becomes incontrovertible," resumed the scientist. "I have shown that Mr. Herbert was not the man in the automobile—the Burglar. Now, what did happen to Mr. Herbert? Twice since his arrest he has stated that it would be useless for him to explain because no one would believe it, and no one would have believed it unsupported, least of all you, Mr. Mallory.

"It's an admitted fact that Miss Meredith and Mr. Herbert had planned to elope from Seven Oaks the night of the ball. I daresay that Mr. Herbert did not deem it wise for Miss Meredith to know his costume, although he must, of necessity, have known hers. Therefore, the plan was for him to recognise her, but as it developed she recognised him—or thought she did—and that was the real cause of this remarkable muddle." He glanced at Dollie. "Is that correct?"

Dollie nodded blushingly.

"Now, Mr. Herbert did not go to the ball—why not I will explain later. Therefore, Miss Meredith recognised the real Burglar as Mr. Herbert, and we know how they ran away together after the Burglar had stolen the plate and various articles of jewelry. We must credit the Burglar with remarkable intelligence, so that when a young and attractive woman—I may say a beautiful woman—spoke to him as someone else he immediately saw an advantage in it. For instance, when there came discovery of the theft the girl might unwittingly throw the police off the track by revealing to them what she believed to be the identity of the thief. Further, he was a daring, audacious sort of person; the pure love of such an adventure might have appealed to him. Still, again, it is possible that he believed Miss Meredith a thief who was in peril of discovery or capture, and a natural gallantry for one of his own craft prompted him to act as he did. There is always, too, the possibility that he knew he was mistaken for Mr. Herbert."

Dollie was beginning to see, too.

"We know the method of escape, the pursuit, and all that," continued the Professor, "therefore we jump to the return of the gold plate. Logic makes it instantly apparent that that was the work of Miss Meredith here. Not having the plate, Mr. Herbert did not send it back, of course; and the Burglar would not have sent it back. Realising, too late, that the man she was with was really a thief— and still believing him, perhaps, to be Mr. Herbert—she must have taken the plate and escaped under cover of darkness?"

The tone carried a question and The Thinking Machine turned squintingly upon Dollie. Again she nodded. She was enthralled, fascinated, by the recital.

"It was a simple matter for her to return the gold plate by express, taking advantage of an unoccupied house and the willingness of a stranger to telephone for an express wagon. Thus, we have the plate again at Seven Oaks, and we have it there by the only method it could have been returned there when we account for, and consider, every known fact."

The Thinking Machine paused and sat silently staring upward. His listeners readjusted themselves in their chairs and waited impatiently.

"Now, why did Mr. Herbert confess to Miss Meredith that he stole the plate?" asked the scientist, as if of himself. "Perhaps she forced him to it. Mr. Herbert is a young man of strong loyalty and a grim sense of humour, this latter being a quality the police are not acquainted with. However, Mr. Herbert did confess to Miss Meredith that he was the Burglar, but he made this confession, obviously, because she would believe nothing else, and when a seeming necessity of protecting the real Burglar was still uppermost in his mind. What he wanted was the Girl. If the facts never came out he was all right; if they did come out they would implicate one whom he was protecting, but through no fault of his— therefore, he was still all right."

"Bah!" exclaimed the Supreme Intelligence. "My experience has shown that a man doesn't confess to a theft unless—"

"So we may safely assume," The Thinking Machine continued almost pleasantly, "that Mr. Herbert, by confessing the theft as a prank, perhaps, won back Miss Meredith's confidence; that they planned an elopement for the second time. A conversation Mr. Hatch had with Mr. Herbert immediately after Mr. Herbert saw

Miss Meredith practically confirms it. Then, with matters in this shape, the real Burglar, to whom I have accredited unusual powers, stole the plate the second time—we know how."

"Herbert stole it, you mean!" blazed Detective Mallory.

"This theft came immediately on top of the reconciliation of Miss Meredith and Mr. Herbert," The Thinking Machine went on steadily, without heeding the remark by the slightest sign. "Therefore, it was only natural that he should be the person most vitally interested in seeing that the plate was again returned. He undertook to do this himself. The result was that, where the police had failed, he found the plate and a lot of jewels, took them from the Burglar, and was about to return Mr. Randolph's property when the detectives walked in on him. That is why he laughed."

Detective Mallory arose from his seat and started to say something impolite. The presence of Dollie Meredith choked the words back and he swallowed hard.

"Who then," he demanded after a couple of gulps— "who do you say is the thief if Herbert is not?"

The Thinking Machine glanced up into his face, then turned to Hatch.

"Mr. Hatch, what is that name I asked you to get?"

"George Francis Hayden," was the stammering reply, "but—but—"

"Then George Francis Hayden is the thief," declared The Thinking Machine emphatically.

"But I—I started to say," Hatch blurted— "I started to say that George Francis Hayden has been dead for two years."

The Thinking Machine rose suddenly and glared at the reporter. There was a tense silence, broken at last by a chuckle from Detective Mallory.

"Dead?" repeated the scientist incredulously. "Do you know that?"

"Yes, I—I know it."

The Thinking Machine stood for another moment squinting at him, then, turning, left the room.

Chapter XXIII

Half an hour later The Thinking Machine walked in, unannounced, upon Dick Herbert. The front door had not been locked; Blair was somewhere in the rear. Herbert, in some surprise, glanced up at his visitor just in time to see him plank himself down solidly into a chair.

"Mr. Herbert," the scientist began, "I have gone out of my way to prove to the police that you were not in the automobile with Miss Meredith, and that you did not steal the gold plate found in your possession. Now, I happen to know the name of the thief, and—"

"And if you mention it to one living soul," Dick added suddenly, hotly, "I shall forget myself and—and—"

"His name is George Francis Hayden," the scientist continued.

Dick started a little and straightened up; the menace dropped from him and he paused to gaze curiously into the wizened face before him. After a moment he drew a sigh of deep relief.

"Oh!" he exclaimed. "Oh!"

"I know that that isn't who you thought it was," resumed the other, "but the fact remains that Hayden is the man with whom Miss Meredith unwittingly eloped, and that Hayden is the man who actually stole the plate and jewels. Further, the fact remains that Hayden—"

"Is dead," Dick supplemented grimly. "You are talking through your—" He coughed a little. "You are talking without any knowledge of what you are saying."

"He can't be dead," remarked the scientist calmly.

"But he is dead!" Dick insisted.

"He can't be dead," snapped the other abruptly. "It's perfectly silly to suppose such a thing. Why, I have proven absolutely, by the simplest rules of logic, that he stole the gold plate, therefore he cannot be dead. It's silly to say so."

Dick wasn't quite certain whether to be angry or amused. He decided to hold the matter in abeyance for the moment and see what other strange thing would develop.

"How long has he been dead?" continued the scientist.

"About two years."

"You know it?"

"Yes, I know it."

"How do you know it?"

"Because I attended his funeral," was the prompt reply. Dick saw a shadow of impatience flash into his visitor's face and instantly pass.

"How did he die?" queried the scientist.

"He was lost from his catboat," Dick answered. "He had gone out sailing, alone, while in a bathing-suit. Several hours after the boat drifted in on the tide without him. Two or three weeks later the body was recovered."

"Ah!" exclaimed The Thinking Machine.

Then, for half an hour or so, he talked, and—as he went on, incisively, pointedly, dramatically, even, at times—Dick Herbert's eyes opened wider and wider. At the end he rose and gripped the scientist's slender white fingers heartily in his own with something approaching awe in his manner. Finally he put on his hat and they went out together.

That evening at eight o'clock Detective Mallory, Hutchinson Hatch, Mr. Randolph, Mr. Meredith, Mr. Greyton, and Dollie Meredith gathered in a parlour of the Greyton home by request of The Thinking Machine. They were waiting for something—no one knew exactly what.

Finally there came a tinkle at the bell and The Thinking Machine entered. Behind him came Dick Herbert, Dr. Clarence Walpole, and a stranger. Mr. Meredith glanced up quickly at Herbert, and Dollie lifted her chin haughtily with a stony stare which admitted of no compromise. Dick pleaded for recognition with his eyes, but it was no use, so he sat down where he could watch her unobserved.

Singular expressions flitted over the countenance of the Supreme Intelligence. Right here, now, he knew the earth was to be jerked out from under him and he was not at all certain that there would be anything left for him to cling to. This first impression was strengthened when The Thinking Machine introduced Doctor Walpole with an ostentatious squint at Mr. Mallory. The detective set his teeth hard.

The Thinking Machine sat down, stretched out his slender legs, turned his eyes upward, and adjusted his fingers precisely, tip to tip. The others watched him anxiously.

"We will have to go back a few years to get the real beginning of the events which have culminated so strangely within the past week," he said. "This was a close friendship of three young men in college. They were Mr. Herbert here, a freshman, and Harry Meredith and George Francis Hayden, juniors. This friendship, not an unusual one in college, was made somewhat romantic by the young men styling themselves The Triangle. They occupied the same apartments and were exclusive to a degree. Of necessity Mr. Herbert was drawn from that exclusiveness, to a certain extent by his participation in football."

A germ of memory was working in Hatch's mind.

"At someone's suggestion three triangular watch charms were made, identical in every way save for initials on the back. They bore a symbol which was meaningless except to The Triangle. They were made to order and are, therefore, the only three of the kind in the world. Mr. Herbert has one now on his watch chain, with his own initials; there is another with the initials 'G. F. H.' in the lot of jewelry Mr. Mallory recovered from Mr. Herbert. The third is worn by Harry Meredith, who is now in Buenos Ayres. The American Consul there has confirmed, by cable, that fact.

"In the senior year the three young men of The Triangle were concerned in the mysterious disappearance of a valuable diamond ring. It was hushed up in college after it seemed established that Mr. Herbert was a thief. Knowing his own innocence and seeing what seemed to be an exclusive opportunity for Harry Meredith to have done what was charged, Mr. Herbert laid the matter to him, having at that time an interview with Harry's father. The result of that interview was more than ever to convince Mr. Meredith of Mr. Herbert's guilt. As a matter of fact, the thief in that case was George Francis Hayden."

There were little murmurs of astonishment, and Mr. Meredith turned and stared at Dick Herbert. Dollie gave him a little glance out of a corner of her eye, smiled, then sat up primly.

"This ended The Triangle," resumed the scientist. "A year or so later Mr. Herbert met Miss Meredith. About two years ago George Francis Hayden was reported drowned from his catboat. This was confirmed, apparently, by the finding of his body, and an insurance company paid over a large sum—I think it was $25,000—to a woman who said she was his wife. But George Francis Hayden was not drowned; he is alive now. It was a carefully planned fraud against the insurance company, and it succeeded.

"This, then, was the situation on last Thursday—the night of the masked ball at Seven Oaks—except that there had grown up a love affair between Miss Meredith and Mr. Herbert. Naturally, the father opposed this because of the incident in college. Both Miss Meredith and Mr. Herbert had invitations to that ball. It was an opportunity for an elopement and they accepted it. Mr. Herbert sent word to her what costume to wear; she did not know the nature of his.

"On Thursday afternoon Miss Meredith sent her jewel-casket, with practically all her jewels, to Mr. Herbert. She wanted them, naturally; they probably planned a trip abroad. The maid in this house took the casket and gave it into Mr. Herbert's own hands. Am I right?" He turned squarely and squinted at Dollie.

"Yes," she gasped quickly. She smiled distractingly upon her father and he made some violent remarks to himself.

"At this point, Fate, in the guise of a masked Burglar, saw fit to step into the affair," the scientist went on after a moment. "About nine-thirty, Thursday evening, while Mr. Herbert was alone, the masked Burglar, George Francis Hayden, entered Mr. Herbert's house, possibly thinking everyone was away. There, still masked, he met Mr. Herbert, who—by something the Burglar said and by the triangular charm he wore—recognised him as Harry Meredith. Remember, he thought he knew George Francis Hayden was dead.

"There were some words and a personal encounter between the two men. George Francis Hayden fired a shot which struck Mr. Herbert in the right shoulder—in front—took the jewel-casket in which Mr. Herbert had placed his card of invitation to the ball, and went away, leaving Mr. Herbert senseless on the floor."

Dollie's face blanched suddenly and she gasped. When she glanced involuntarily at Dick she read the love-light in his eyes, and her colour returned with a rush.

"Several hours later, when Mr. Herbert recovered consciousness," the unruffled voice went on, "he went to Doctor Walpole, the nearest physician, and there the bullet was extracted and the wound dressed. The ball was thirty-two calibre?"

Doctor Walpole nodded.

"And Mr. Cunningham's revolver carried a thirty-eight," added the scientist. "Now we go back to the Burglar. He found the invitation in the casket, and the bold scheme, which later he carried out so perfectly, came to him as an inspiration. He went to the ball just as he was. Nerve, self-possession, and humour took him through. We know the rest of that.

"Naturally, in the circumstances, Mr. Herbert, believing that Harry Meredith was the thief, would say nothing to bring disgrace upon the name of the girl he loved. Instead, he saw Miss Meredith, who would not accept his denial then, and in order to get her first— explanations might come later—he confessed to the theft, whereupon they planned the second elopement.

"When Miss Meredith returned the plate by express there was no anticipation of a second theft. Here is where we get a better understanding of the mettle of the real Burglar—George Francis Hayden. He went back and got the plate from Seven Oaks. Instantly that upset the second elopement plan. Then Mr. Herbert undertook the search, got a clew, followed it, and recovered not only the plate, but a great lot of jewels."

There was a pause. A skyrocket ascended in Hatch's mind and burst, illuminating the whole tangled story. Detective Mallory sat dumbly, thinking harsh words. Mr. Meredith arose, went over to Dick Herbert, and solemnly shook his hand, after which he sat down again. Dollie smiled charmingly.

Chapter XXIV

"Now that is what actually happened," said The Thinking Machine, after a little while. "How do I know it? Logic, logic, logic! The logical mind can start from any given point and go backward or forward, with equal facility, to a natural conclusion. This is as certain as that two and two make four—not sometimes, but all the time.

"First in this case I had Mr. Hatch's detailed examination of each circumstance. By an inspiration he connected Mr. Herbert and Miss Meredith with the affair and talked to both before the police had any knowledge at all of them. In other words, he reached at a bound what they took days to accomplish. After the second theft he came to me and related the story."

The reporter blushed modestly.

"Mr. Hatch's belief that the things that had happened to Mr. Herbert and Miss Meredith bore on the theft," resumed the scientist, "was susceptible of confirmation or refutation in only one way, this being so because of Mr. Herbert's silence—due to his loyalty. I saw that. But, before I went further, I saw clearly what had actually happened if I presupposed that there had been some connection. Thus came to me, I may say here, the almost certain knowledge that Miss Meredith had a brother, although I had never heard of him or her."

He paused a little and twiddled his thumbs thoughtfully.

"Suppose you give us just your line of reasoning," ventured Hatch.

"Well, I began with the blood-stains in the automobile to either bring Mr. Herbert into this affair or shut him out," replied the scientist. "You know how I made the blood tests. They showed conclusively that the blood on the cushion was not Mr. Herbert's. Remember, please, that, although I knew Miss Meredith had been in the automobile, I also knew she was not wounded; therefore the blood was that of someone else—the man.

"Now, I knew Mr. Herbert had been wounded—he wouldn't say how. If at home, would he not go to the nearest physician? Probably. I got Doctor Walpole's name from the telephone-book—he being nearest the Herbert home—and sent Mr. Hatch there, where he learned of the wound in front, and of the thirty-two calibre ball. I already knew the police revolvers were thirty-eight calibre; therefore Mr. Herbert was not wounded while in the automobile.

"That removed Mr. Herbert as a possibility in the first theft, despite the fact that his invitation-card was presented at the door. It was reasonable to suppose that invitation had been stolen. Immediately after the plate was returned by express, Mr. Herbert effected a reconciliation with Miss Meredith. Because of this and for other reasons I could not bring myself to see that he was a party to the second theft, as I knew him to be innocent of the first. Yet, what happened to him? Why wouldn't he say something?

"All things must be imagined before they can be achieved; therefore imagination is one of the most vital parts of the scientific brain. In this instance I could only imagine why Mr. Herbert was silent. Remember, he was shot and wouldn't say who did it. Why? If it had been an ordinary thief—and I got the idea of a thief from the invitation-card being in other hands than his—he would not have hesitated to talk. Therefore, it was an extraordinary thief in that it connected with something near and dear to him. No one was nearer and dearer to him than Miss Meredith. Did she shoot him? No. Did her father shoot him? Probably not, but possibly. A brother? That began to look more reasonable. Mr. Herbert would probably not have gone so far to protect one less near to her than brother or father.

"For the moment I assumed a brother, not knowing. How did Mr. Herbert know this brother? Was it in his college days? Mr. Hatch brought me a list of the students of three years before his graduating year and there I found the name, Harry Meredith. You see, step by step, pure logic was leading me to something tangible, definite. My next act was to see Mr. Meredith and ask for the address of his son—an only son—whom at that time I frankly believed was the real thief. But this son was in South America. That startled me a little and brought me up against the father as a possible thief. He was in Baltimore on that night.

"I accepted that as true at the moment after some—er—some pleasant words with Mr. Meredith. Then the question: Was the man who stole from Mr. Herbert, probably entering his place and shooting him, masked? Mr. Herbert said he was. I framed the question so as to bring Harry Meredith's name into it, much to Mr. Herbert's alarm. How had he recognised him as Harry Meredith? By something he said or wore? Mr. Herbert replied in the affirmative—both. Therefore I had a masked Burglar who could not have been either Harry Meredith or Harry Meredith's father. Who was he?

"I decided to let Mr. Hatch look into that point for me, and went to see Doctor Walpole. He gave me the bullet he had extracted from Mr. Herbert's shoulder. Mr. Hatch, shortly after, rushed in on me with the statement that Miss Meredith had admitted that Mr. Herbert had confessed to her. I could see instantly why he had confessed to her. Then Mr. Hatch undertook for me the investigation of Herbert's and Harry Meredith's careers in college. He remembered part of it and unearthed the affair of The Triangle and the theft of a diamond ring.

"I had asked Mr. Hatch to find for me if Harry Meredith and Mr. Herbert had had a mutual intimate in college. They had: George Francis Hayden, the third member of the Triangle. Then the question seemed to be solved, but Mr. Hatch upset everything when he said that Mr. Hayden was dead. I went immediately to see Mr. Herbert. From him I learned that, although Mr. Hayden was supposed to be dead and buried, there was no positive proof of it; the body recovered had been in the water three weeks and was consequently almost unrecognisable. Therefore, the theft came inevitably to Mr. Hayden. Why? Because the Burglar had been recognised by something he said and wore. It would have been difficult for Mr. Herbert to recognise a masked man so positively unless the masked man wore something he absolutely knew, or said something he absolutely knew. Mr. Herbert thought with reason that the masked man was Harry Meredith, but, with Harry Meredith in South America, the thief was incontrovertibly George Francis Hayden. There was no going behind that.

"After a short interview as to Hayden, during which Mr. Herbert told me more of The Triangle and the three watch charms, he and I went out investigating. He took me to the room where he had found the plate and jewels—a place in an apartment-house which this gentleman manages." The scientist turned to the stranger, who had been a silent listener. "He identified an old photograph of George Francis Hayden as an occupant of an apartment.

"Mr. Herbert and I searched the place. My growing idea, based on the established knavery of George Francis Hayden, that he was the real thief in the college incident, was proven when I found this ring there—the ring that was stolen at that time—with the initials of the owner in it."

The Thinking Machine produced the ring and offered it to Detective Mallory, who had allowed the earth to slip away from him slowly but surely, and he examined it with a new and absorbed interest.

"Mr. Herbert and I learned of the insurance fraud in another manner—that is, when we knew that George Francis Hayden was not dead, we knew there had been a fraud. Mr. Hayden has been known lately as Chester Goodrich. He has been missing since Mr. Herbert, in his absence, recovered the plate and the jewels in his apartments. I may add that, up to the day of the masked ball, he was protected from casual recognition by a full beard. He is now clean-shaven."

The Thinking Machine glanced at Mr. Mallory.

"Your man—Downey, I think it was—did excellent work," he said, "in tracing Miss Meredith from the time she left the automobile until she returned home, and later leading you to Mr. Herbert. It was not strange that you should have been convinced of his guilt when we consider the goods found in his possession and also the wound in his shoulder. The only trouble is he didn't get to the real insides of it."

That was all. For a long time there was silence. Dollie Meredith's pretty face was radiant and her eyes were fastened on her father. Mr. Meredith glanced at her, cleared his throat several times, then arose and offered his hand to Dick Herbert.

"I have done you an injustice, sir," he said gravely. "Permit me to apologise. I think perhaps my daughter—"

That was superfluous. Dollie was already beside Dick, and a rousing, smacking, resounding kiss echoed her father's words. Dick liked it some and was ready for more, but Dollie impetuously flung her arms around the neck of The Thinking Machine, and he—passed to his reward.

"You dear old thing!" she gurgled. "You're just too sweet and cute for anything."

"Dear me! Dear me!" fussed The Thinking Machine. "Don't do that. It annoys me exceedingly."

Some three months later, when the search for George Francis Hayden had become only lukewarm, this being three days before Miss Meredith's wedding to Dick Herbert, she received a small box containing a solitaire ring and a note. It was brief:

> In memory of one night in the woods and of what hap-
> pened there, permit me to give this—you can't return it. It
> is one of the few things honest money from me ever paid
> for.
>
> Bill, the Burglar.

While Dollie examined the ring with mingled emotions Dick stared at the postmark on the package.

"It's a corking good clew," he said enthusiastically.

Dollie turned to him, recognising a menace in the words, and took the paper which bore the postmark from his hands.

"Let's pretend," she said gently— "let's pretend we don't know where it came from!"

Dick stared a little and kissed her.

Coachwhip Publications

CoachwhipBooks.com

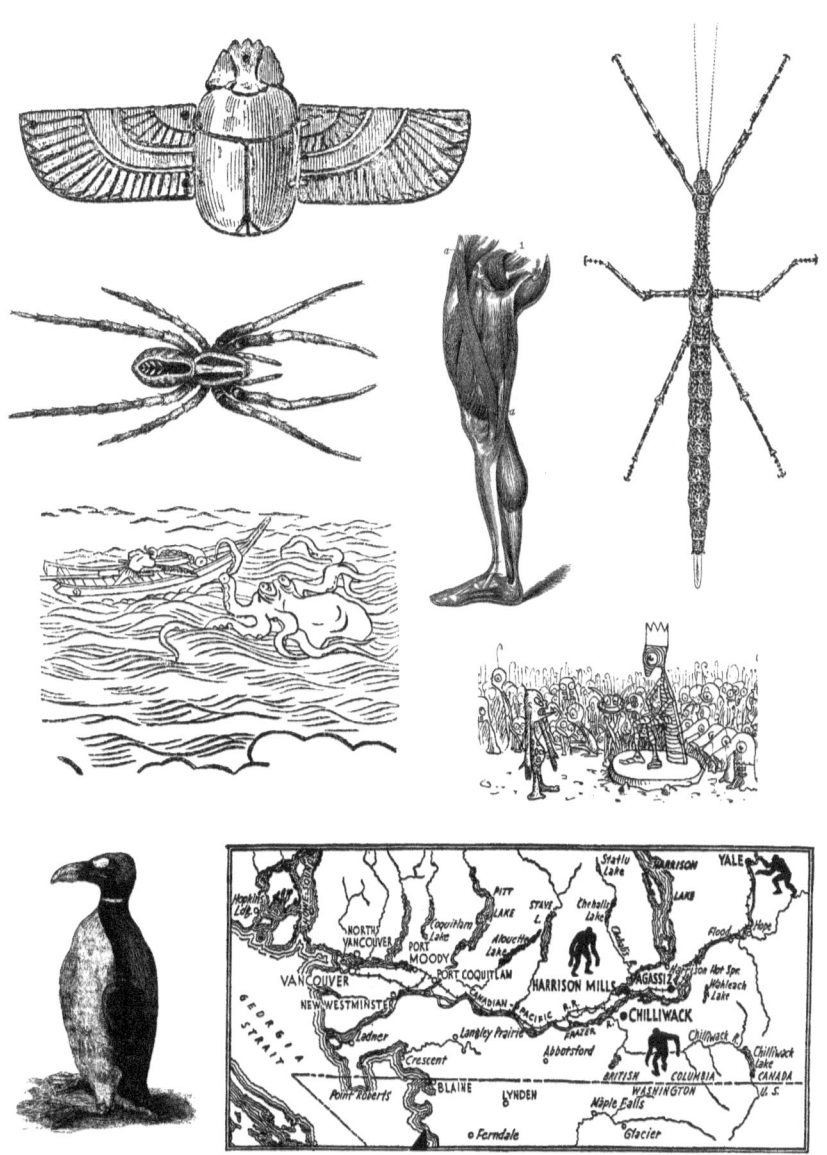

ALSO AVAILABLE

Mystery and Detection with
THE THINKING MACHINE

Volume
I

JACQUES FUTRELLE

Mystery and Detection with The Thinking Machine
Volume 1

ISBN 1-930585-70-5

ALSO AVAILABLE

Crime and Adventure
with A. J. Raffles,
Gentleman Thief

ISBN 1-930585-68-3

The Dupin Mysteries
and Other Tales of
Ratiocination

ISBN 1-930585-69-1

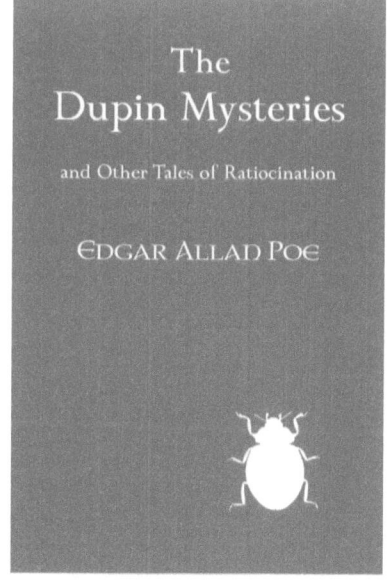

www.ingramcontent.com/pod-product-compliance
Lightning Source LLC
Chambersburg PA
CBHW020459020726
47493CB00001B/95